Royally Yours

THE WEXTONE ROYALS BOOK 1

JULES KYLE

ISBN: 979-8-9997788-0-2 (Paperback)

ISBN: 979-8-9997788-1-9 (e-Book)

Book cover art by Rebekah Hamersley

Book cover design by Jessica Clickener

First edition 2025

www.juleskyle.com

To the original Jules, who shaped this story long before it even began. I miss you with every heartbeat.

-S

To BDD, thanks for always believing in me. To NG, this is for your future.

-K

A NOTE FROM THE AUTHOR

Dearest reader,

Thank you for choosing to travel to Wexstone with us. It is our sincerest hope that you enjoy the journey and the time you spend with Birdie, Knox, Oliver, and their friends. To that end, please keep in mind that this book contains depictions of or references to:

- Grief
- Death of a parent (off page, remembered)
- Cancer (off page, remembered)
- Bullying
- Anxiety, depression, and panic attacks/disorders
- Sexual content
- Reconciliation with a parent

With that, we encourage you to sit back, relax, and enjoy your visit to Wexstone!

-Jules Kyle

ROYALLY YOURS PLAYLIST

Get the playlist on Spotify

Get the playlist on Apple Music

1. 9 to 5 | Dolly Parton
2. Close To You | Gracie Abrams
3. Pony | Ginuwine
4. Movement | Hozier
5. Shivers | Ed Sheeran
6. "Slut!" (Taylor's Version) (From The Vault) | Taylor Swift
7. Awake My Soul | Mumford & Sons
8. Do I Wanna Know? (Live At the BBC) | Hozier
9. Bad Habits | Vitamin String Quartet
10. Kids | Midnite String Quartet
11. You Belong with Me | Midnite String Quartet
12. Love Me Like You Do (Acoustic) | Jada Facer
13. Cosmic Love | Florence + The Machine
14. Guilty as Sin? | Taylor Swift
15. Fall For Me | Sleep Token
16. Silver Lining | Laufey
17. Let It Snow | Canyon City
18. Stubborn Love | The Lumineers
19. Wild Love | James Bay
20. Say Don't Go (Taylor's Version) (From The Vault) | Taylor Swift
21. Winter Song | Sara Bareilles, Ingrid Michaelson
22. Christmas Lights | Coldplay
23. The Christmas Waltz | She & Him
24. Electric Love | BØRNS
25. I'll Be Home For Christmas | Max McNown

CHAPTER 1
BIRDIE

A loud knock at the door made me jump. I set my things down on my minuscule kitchen counter, crossing the few steps it took to get from one side of the apartment to the other as another knock echoed through the small space.

"I'm coming!" I yelled. Not that there was any need to raise my voice; you could clearly hear someone having a conversation in the apartment next door, even with the TV or radio on. It certainly made it awkward to bring guys home, not that that had been an issue in quite some time.

I opened the door to an unfamiliar older bald man with permanent wrinkle lines running from his scalp down to his forehead. It was as if he had spent his entire life mad.

"Bernadette Hamilton?" he gruffed out.

"That's me."

"You're being evicted. Have a nice day." He handed me a white envelope, turned his back, and made his way to Mrs. Slater's apartment next door.

"I'm sorry, what?" The room spun as I tried to wrap my

mind around his words. I had lived in my East Village apartment since moving to New York six years ago and was, by my estimation, a model resident. I had never thrown a party, certainly wasn't loud, and had actually fixed up the small studio, repairing the plumbing, fixtures, and cabinets when the super refused to stop by. The rent check was always on time, never a day late. And now I was being evicted?

"Reason's in the letter. If you have comments or questions, take it up with my lawyer."

I slammed the door shut, ripped open the envelope, and read aloud from the first page:

Dear Resident,

    Your rental agreement is hereby terminated. This building has been purchased by Burlington Corporation. You have two weeks to evacuate. Should you choose to stay, you will be under prosecution from the law offices of Kline, Burke, and Bridges.

    Best of luck in your future home endeavors.

I dropped the paper with its five short sentences on the counter. "What the fuck?!" A whirlwind of thoughts flooded my mind.

They can't do this. This can't be legal.

Where the hell am I going to live?

What am I going to do?

This is bullshit.

I took a deep breath, trying to keep myself from bursting into tears. I headed to the bathroom, hoping a shower would help clear my head and ebb my emotions.

It didn't work. In an angry rush, I grabbed my coat, shoes,

and work bag and decided to head to the bar early in hopes that I could pick up a couple of extra hours. We always needed extra hands on Fridays, and apparently I would need the money if I was going to be moving in two weeks.

But first, a latte was in order if I had any hope of avoiding a complete mental breakdown.

———

I opened the door to the Greenwich Village coffee shop, letting the smell of ground coffee beans and fresh bagels wash over me. This was one of my favorite spots in the city: It was long and narrow and gave the feel of a renovated warehouse, with exposed pipes and HVAC in the ceiling and spots of bare brick along the walls. The areas where the brick was plastered over were painted in an array of colors ranging from neon green to deep purple, with local artists' works displayed for sale. As a bonus, it was conveniently located on my way to work.

You could find people from every walk of life here. On the weekends the shop hosted live music, spoken poetry, and even a drag brunch on the first Sunday of every month. But that afternoon, Tucker's was unusually busy as I met a line that stretched to the door. What else could I expect though? A bullshit eviction letter and now a line that felt half like a block long? Yeah, that seemed about right.

As I waited in line, I scrolled through my social media feeds. I double-tapped photos of kids in their Halloween costumes and scrolled past a few gossip site posts about what celebrities were doing and with whom. I had no idea who most of them were, to be honest. I liked a post about a college acquaintance's new job and hearted a video of a friend's baby taking his first steps. Everyone else's life seemed to be moving on to better and greater things.

Feelings of envy rose in my throat, but I tamped them down and kept scrolling. I refused to think about my own dead-end job or the announcement of baby number two that was sure to be coming soon from my brother and his wife. And you could forget about pondering the upcoming holidays. I had more pressing problems if I was going to be apartment hunting.

"Hey, Birdie!" The cashier greeted me with a cheerful smile. I looked forward to seeing Chuck on Fridays. They were always adorned in an eclectic assortment of jewelry from their ears, across their face, and down to a ring on nearly every finger. This week their hair was neon pink, and they sported a tiny rainbow jewel in their nose and a matching pin on their apron that read, "My pronouns are they/them."

"Hey, Chuck. I love that hair color on you."

"Thank you! I just did it last night," they said, running a hand over their hair. "Your usual? Vanilla latte with oat milk?"

"Please. I desperately need it today. And you know what, let's do a bacon, egg, and cheese on an everything bagel while we're at it." I knew I'd regret my choices midway through my shift later if I didn't get some protein in my body now, and I didn't need to be in an even fouler mood.

"Rough day, huh?"

"The worst."

"Hang in there, Birdie." They handed me my receipt. "You're order number 35. We'll get that up for you in just a bit."

As I took a seat at a hand-painted table by the window, I pulled out my phone and sent off a text to my best friend, Sam.

> Can you stop by the bar after work tonight?

Sam was a lawyer; surely she would know what to do. In the meantime, I opened a search tab, figuring I better start looking at apartment listings. It had taken me ages to find my little studio, and I knew the current economy wasn't going to make it any easier to find a new place in my price range.

"Order 35!"

I distractedly dodged the other customers, grabbed my order from the counter, and headed back to my seat. I took a bite from my sandwich, the yolk of the over-easy egg bursting just the way I liked it, before I took a sip from the cardboard cup.

Oh, hell no, that is not mine.

Instead of the sweet, mellow flavor of vanilla and frothed oat milk, I was met with...oh, that was an americano. Absolutely not.

I sighed and made my way back up to the counter, where Chuck had just finished taking a customer's order. "Hey, I think there was some mix up back there, this definitely isn't my drink."

A brusque voice just behind me spoke. "You have my drink, I believe."

I turned toward the voice and was struck speechless.

I was never the type to be lost for words, especially by a guy. I had always been confident and easily brushed off intimidation or embarrassment. But this man. *Damn.*

He was tall—surely a foot taller than my five-foot-four—and breathtakingly handsome. This was the type of guy you would find on the cover of a romance novel or holding a puppy in a firefighter calendar. His eyes, circled in wire-rimmed glasses, were a shade of bright blue I'd once seen on the Aegean Sea. His dark beard was grown in just enough to be full without being out of control, the skin above it golden in the morning's sunshine. He was standing close enough for me to notice that he smelled like pine and mint.

I tore my eyes from Tall and Handsome's face to look at the

drink he was holding, the name *Birdie* clearly written across the cup.

"Well, yeah. Unless your name is also Birdie, which I somehow doubt," I snarked, glancing over his perfectly muscular form, "that would be mine. So why, exactly, did you take a drink that had someone else's name on it?"

Tall and Handsome raised an eyebrow. "Oh, I don't know, maybe because I was nearly bowled over by a distracted crazy woman who grabbed what was apparently *not* her order either. Honestly, this is why I visit New York as infrequently as possible."

My face flushed. I had been so in my head about the eviction that I hadn't even noticed this guy, much less realized that I had nearly run into him.

On a normal day, I would have apologized for my rudeness. But today? Today was not that day.

"Well, how unfortunate for wherever you live to have you as a resident." My voice dripped with disdain. Regardless of how handsome this man was, he was about to learn that hell hath no fury like a pissed-off woman.

Tall and Handsome snorted. "Could say the same about you for New York City."

Chuck cleared their throat, glancing back and forth between me and the unbearable man beside me.

I snatched my drink from Tall and Handsome and handed both cups to Chuck, shaking my head. "Sorry, Chuck. Can you have them remake my latte?"

"Of course, Birdie," they replied, taking the cup. "Another vanilla latte with oat milk coming right up. Is your sandwich okay? Is the egg runny enough for you?"

"Yes, the sandwich is great."

"Runny yolks, huh? Figures," Tall and Handsome muttered as Chuck disappeared behind the counter.

"Excuse me?" I hissed, turning on him. "Now you have opinions on my sandwich?"

He shrugged. "Bagels are meant to be sweet. Just like coffee is meant to be black. And eggs should definitely never be runny."

I blinked. *This man is unhinged.* "I don't even know where to start with that."

He shrugged again. "You just seem like you're a little worked up, I thought maybe goading you into a debate might help you blow off some steam."

The absolute fucking nerve of this guy! "I'm perfectly fine. I don't need to debate you about bagels—which, for the record, can absolutely be savory and make the best breakfast sandwiches. With runny eggs. And you know what? The vanilla lattes here are a work of fucking art. So go ride off on your high horse back to wherever you came from, okay?"

The corner of Tall and Handsome's mouth tugged upward slightly as though he was trying to suppress a grin. I was about to comment on that, too, when Chuck returned.

"Fresh latte for you, Birdie, and a fresh americano for you," they said, handing us each our drinks.

I took a sip and was finally greeted with the sweet richness I had been craving. "Thanks, Chuck. See you next week." I tossed a dollar in the tip jar and grabbed the rest of my sandwich as I headed out the door. "And good riddance," I grumbled under my breath as I left Tall and Handsome behind me.

———

I tossed my empty coffee cup and sandwich wrapper into a trash can as I ducked into Americana, the hole-in-the-wall bar I had worked at since moving to the city. My boss was a jerk, but I made good money waiting tables and occasionally bartending.

I walked through the dim bar and straight to the back office where I knew Chad, my boss, would be doing inventory.

"Knock, knock," I announced as I gently tapped on the door. "Hey, Chad?"

"What."

Oh goody, he's happy.

"Do you mind if I clock in a couple of hours early?"

"Why? You don't even like being here when you're scheduled," he ground out as he made a mark on the list.

"Well, that's not entirely true." I gave him my most charming smile. It actually was true, but I wasn't beyond sucking up and flirting a little to get the extra hours. "I need the extra cash. I have to move and could use the hours."

Chad grunted. "If you're going to clock in early, make it worth my money. Go out back and sort through the trash. Pull out the bottles to recycle. The city is cracking down on recycling. I expect they'll be sending someone out in a few days, and it needs to look like we've been doing it all along."

My smile faltered. "You...want me to dig through the trash?"

"Do you want the extra money?"

I don't really have any other option, do I?

I entered my PIN into the point-of-sale system behind the bar, grabbed a pair of gloves from the kitchen, and headed out back to start rummaging through the trash bags sitting on the loading dock. As degrading as it felt, it wasn't as bad as I had expected. And it was kind of peaceful in the alley. I let myself get lost in my thoughts as I worked, my bad mood starting to ebb.

If anything, sorting through the trash was a metaphor for what was ahead of me. When I first moved to the city, I looked at seventeen apartments before I stumbled upon my studio. Most of them were either too expensive, too run down, or in New Jersey. The thing that really bothered me was the suspicion that they wouldn't be remodeling the apartments, either. They were almost certainly going to turn the building into some kind of shopping center or slimy bank. I didn't want to go through the apartment hunt again.

I jolted as I felt a tap on my shoulder. I spun around, swinging with all of my might. My heart slowed as I realized it wasn't a mugger, just my coworker Jake, who was now rubbing his upper arm where I had laid into him.

"Holy shit, Jake! You scared the life out of me."

"Sorry, I thought you heard me open the door," he apologized as he kept rubbing his arm. "You've been out here for a while. We're kind of in the weeds and could use some hands on the floor."

I glanced at my watch. Sure enough, it was time for the Friday rush. "Damn. Hopefully the bar smell will cover the trash smell."

Jake sniffed. "You don't stink that bad."

I shook my head and walked through the back door as Jake held it open. Thankfully I kept an extra shirt and a bottle of perfume in my locker. I had learned that the hard way one unfortunate St. Patrick's Day after a patron vomited all over his table and me.

After swapping out my shirt for one with the bar's logo spread across my chest, redoing my ponytail, tying on my black half-apron, and spritzing myself with a few sprays of perfume for good measure, I waded into the packed bar. I knew some servers hated working weekends, but I loved nights like this. It meant great money, the night went by fast, and I actually enjoyed being around all of the people.

Jake hadn't been kidding: the bar was buzzing. There

wasn't a seat available. The bass of the pop song that played throughout the building made the floor vibrate and it pulsated throughout my body.

My feet ached as I ran beer, appetizers, burgers, and the occasional water to my tables. As orders came in left and right, I wasn't sure there was an end in sight.

The door opened, letting in a welcome cool breeze and five extremely handsome men looking as if they had stepped out of GQ. They were well dressed and, quite frankly, out of place for a bar like Americana. One of them in particular caught my eye.

He was tall, dark, and handsome. While the others were dressed to the nines in preppy high-fashion looks, he wore jeans that fit him in all the right places and a thick red-and-black flannel that accentuated his built chest. The sleeves were rolled up to his elbows, showcasing a sleeve of tattoos that ended just above his right wrist. The wire-rimmed glasses were missing, but his eyes were unmistakably blue. My stomach fell into my ass.

I couldn't believe what I was seeing. Tall and Handsome was standing in my bar.

CHAPTER 2
BIRDIE

I blinked, shaking myself out of my shock to focus. *Do your job, Birdie!*

The man standing beside Tall and Handsome looked around for an empty table. When none could be found, he whispered to another of their friends, a very handsome Black man with an impeccable fade, who looked like he might be in charge.

Tall and Handsome caught my eye as I spotted a newly empty booth in the back corner of the bar. I sighed. *You better be a good tipper,* I thought. If his friends' clothes were any indication, they weren't short on money.

I approached the group. "Hey, guys, there's a booth available in the back corner."

Tall and Handsome inclined his head toward me, raising an eyebrow. "Imagine seeing you here."

"Don't worry, I'm a much better server than I am a debater," I quipped as I led them to the table.

"Let's hope so," he replied, his friends exchanging glances behind him as we walked.

"I'll be back in a sec to take your order," I said as the guys shuffled into the booth. I wondered what Tall and Handsome was doing with a group of GQ models. His scruffy, casual look certainly didn't seem to fit in with the impeccably tailored trousers, Chelsea boots and loafers, and fitted sweaters of his friends.

As I turned to the bar, I heard a familiar voice.

"Damn, it's busy in here tonight!" Sam exclaimed as she hugged me.

"Hey!" I returned her hug. "I know! We expected it last weekend with Halloween, but didn't think tonight would be quite this bad. I'm not going to have time to talk for a while. I'm sorry you came all this way."

"Oh, don't worry. It was a good excuse to leave early from a bad date." Sam laughed. "I'll grab some food and wait. Maybe I'll find someone less irritating to buy me a drink." She winked, fluffing her dark curls at the roots as she glanced around the bar, her tawny skin glowing even in the terrible lighting.

I laughed. "That bad?" Sam had started the year with a resolution to date more and, true to her personality, had fully embraced the challenge.

"She was a total narcissist. Although possibly better than the guy last week who said he didn't believe in showering."

I shuddered. "All right, well I'm gonna take this order and then I'll come back and grab yours."

"Um, no need. I'll have a tall glass of one of those guys," Sam said, nodding to Tall and Handsome's table.

"I mean, you're not wrong. How is it that they are all that perfect looking? I need to go take their orders. I'll be right back —you will not believe me when I tell you about my day."

I grabbed my rarely used notepad out of my apron and the

pen I kept tucked into the base of my ponytail and made my way back to the corner booth.

"All right, gentlemen, welcome to Americana. I'm Birdie and I'll be taking care of you tonight. What can I get started for ya?"

Tall and Handsome and three of his companions looked to the man sitting in the back corner of the booth. He had thick blond hair, a chiseled jaw, and silvery-gray eyes. He looked to Tall and Handsome and in a European accent I couldn't place, asked, "What do I get?"

Tall and Handsome looked at me. "He'll have a Budweiser in a bottle. A dozen wings, mild sauce, and a side of blue cheese dressing." He glanced back at the blond man. "That's about the most American thing you could order here."

"Actually, the most American thing you could order would probably be our bacon cheeseburger with smothered fries and a can of Natty Light," I shot back. Tall and Handsome looked like he clearly disagreed. *What else is new?* I thought.

The blond man laughed. "Yes, I want that!"

"You got it. What else can I get y'all?"

Three replies of "same" in the same European accent as the blond man's echoed through the booth. I looked at Tall and Handsome, wondering where this man with his standard American accent had collected four European companions.

"And for you, sir?"

"I'll have what I ordered earlier for my friend."

I refrained from snorting as I nodded. Tucking my pen back into my ponytail, I ducked behind the bar to grab their beers, dropping them at the table before heading to the POS to put in their orders. A scan of the room told me it had emptied out a bit, so I slipped over to talk to Sam before I had to run my next orders out.

"What do you need to talk about?" Sam asked as Jake slid her a basket with a cheeseburger and fries.

"I'm being evicted."

"What?" Sam nearly choked on the bite of burger she had just taken. "How is that possible? You're like, the perfect tenant."

"Apparently the building has been bought by some corporation and we all have two weeks to find somewhere else to live."

"That is ludicrous."

"It is. My landlord has a lawyer and said to contact them with any questions or comments." I rolled my eyes and handed Sam the letter that the man had so nicely delivered that morning.

Sam skimmed the letter and the two accompanying pages while I grabbed another round of drinks for one of my tables and delivered the burgers and wings to the corner booth.

"So? What do you think? Am I screwed and really need to move out in two weeks?" I asked as I returned.

"Fuck," she huffed. "Those bastards over there at Kline, Burke, and Bridges are the absolute worst. And I say that coming from a firm of equally shitty bastards." She handed back the pages, which I folded and tucked into my apron pocket. "Yeah, babe, a bunch of real estate lawyers have recently found this stupid loophole of a law to force you to move out. They've been evicting people left and right lately. I'm so sorry."

"Great. Just great. And I've put so much work into that place, too! It was finally feeling like home." I leaned my elbows on the bar and rubbed the spot between my eyes.

"Well, you know you can crash at my place until you find somewhere more permanent," Sam offered.

"Excuse me, miss?" The man from the corner booth with

the perfect fade tapped me on the shoulder. His eyes, so dark they appeared black in the bar's lighting, rolled over Sam, clearly checking her out. He realized that I had caught him, and the side of his mouth tipped up in a sly grin. "May we get some more napkins for our table?"

"Of course, I'll be right over." I glanced at Sam. "We can finish talking about this later."

I grabbed a handful of napkins from the server station. When I got to the table, I realized that the man was still talking to Sam at the bar.

"Here you go, guys. How are those burgers?" I asked, taking it as a good sign when the responses were satisfied nods and mumbles as they chewed.

"I'm going to go out on a limb and guess that y'all aren't from around here," I said.

"We're visiting from Wexstone," one of the men responded, swallowing his bite and wiping ketchup off his umber-colored cheek. His biceps were the size of tree trunks, and he had pulled his dreadlocks back while he ate.

I quickly sifted through my sparse geography knowledge, silently cursing my terrible high school geography teacher. I couldn't place Wexstone anywhere.

The blond man must have read my mind. "It's in Northern Europe, in the mountains. We're a small country, about 500,000 people. We're best known for our pine trees and cranberry production."

"Wow, impressive," I admired. "What brings you to New York City?"

"I think in America you call it a bachelor party," the last of the men—wiry, with salt-and-pepper hair—answered.

"Okay! Which one of you good-looking men is getting hitched?"

"That would be Prince Oliver," said the guy who had been

talking to Sam. He scooted back into the booth, pointing to the blond man.

"Prince?" I laughed. "Right, and I'm the pope."

The table went silent as the guys glanced at each other awkwardly. Mr. Blond cleared his throat, his pale cheeks betraying the pink flush that instantly appeared.

I looked around the table, then glanced throughout the bar. As I did, I realized there were three additional men, all dressed in black, stationed strategically by the exits and near the restrooms. I spotted headsets tucked behind their ears. *Holy shit, they aren't kidding.*

"How do you do?" the blond man—Prince Oliver—said, holding out his hand as I turned back to the group. It was my turn to blush furiously. Was there a protocol I was supposed to follow after making a complete idiot of myself?

"Um, it's nice to meet you, Your Highness, sir..." I stammered, taking his hand and shaking it. "I'm so sorry, I uh...I don't know what the proper protocol is here..."

"You can just shake his hand." Tall and Handsome smirked. He seemed to be enjoying this. I shook Prince Oliver's hand for what felt like too long and then awkwardly let my hand go limp.

"Birdie," Sam said from behind me, "Vince here invited us to join them once your shift is over." She slid into the booth next to her new friend.

"Did he now?" Tall and Handsome asked, staring daggers at the man who was apparently named Vince.

"Come on, Knox. I thought it would be fun to have some locals show us around the city."

"So, I'm not good enough? I'm American, after all," Knox forged an offense. "Besides, it's Oliver's weekend, I think he should get a say here."

"I wouldn't mind at all," Prince Oliver chimed in.

"There we have it! What the prince wants, the prince gets!" Vince clapped his hands together before popping a fry into his mouth, a satisfied grin on his face.

———

Three hours later, the seven of us were gathered around that same table, Sam squeezed in between Vince and the dread-locked Chauncey while I perched between Prince Oliver and Tej, who appeared to be in his mid-twenties despite his prematurely gray hair. Knox had pulled a chair up to the open end of the table, seeming to prefer his personal space unimpeded. Vince and Chauncey had spent much of the last hour silently vying for who got to drape his arm around Sam's shoulders, with Vince currently winning. The three men dressed in black —the prince's security for the weekend—now occupied their own booth with a clear view of our table, thanks to the late hour and the nearly empty bar. Most of the earlier patrons had moved along to one of the city's many nightclubs. I had cleared our table of beer cans and bottles several times but could easily fill another tray with the empties that had accumulated again.

"I feel like we kind of crashed your party," I said, looking at Prince Oliver. "What did you have planned?"

"Nothing appropriate for two women to tag along to," Knox interjected.

"Ah." I smirked. If he was under the assumption that Sam and I had never been to a strip club, he could think again. Our early twenties had been a wild time. Plus, there was the time Sam's brothers had busted up my twenty-fifth birthday pretending to be strippers.

"This morning when you said you were visiting the city, you didn't mention being friends with a prince," I said, looking at Knox pointedly as I took a sip of my beer.

"It's not something I typically lead with. You never know if people are just looking for an in," Knox replied as he looked straight into my eyes. My stomach flipped.

I raised my eyebrow, offended. I certainly wasn't "looking for an in"—whatever that meant. I had never even heard of Wexstone *or* Prince Oliver and wasn't sure how the group had ended up at Americana, of all places.

"Wait." Prince Oliver interrupted my thoughts. "Do you two know each other?"

"Yeah," I answered, as Knox replied, "No."

We side-eyed each other. The rest of the group had quieted, the alcohol making it impossible for them to hide their curiosity.

"Sort of," I amended. "We met this afternoon at a coffee shop and Knox here belittled my opinion on bagels and how I like my eggs cooked."

"I think 'belittle' is an exaggeration," Knox cut in. "I simply stated that runny eggs are a product of the devil."

"Ah, so you were treated to a classic Knox argument," Prince Oliver said, laughing. His face had become more and more flushed the more he drank.

"I don't know if you can call it an argument. It was more like a proclamation," I replied.

The prince gave me a warm smile that made me believe he too had been on the receiving end of those proclamations a time or two.

"Do you know how to play darts?" Sam asked, glancing to the men flanking her.

Chauncey nodded. "Knox taught us how to play years ago."

"Perfect. Let's go!" Sam grabbed both Vince and Chauncey's hands and dragged them from the booth to the opposite corner of the bar, where we kept two dart boards and a few high-top tables.

Prince Oliver, Tej, and Knox followed, watching as Sam, Vince, and Chauncey started throwing the darts, while I grabbed us another bucket of cold beers. As I walked back over, the entire group let out a roar of laughter.

"What did I miss?" I asked.

"Your friend is quite cheeky!" Prince Oliver laughed.

"Oh no." I chuckled. "What did she do this time?"

Sam grabbed a beer. "I didn't do anything. I just told Vince and Chauncey that if they want any of this"—she waved her hand over her toned body—"they're going to have to work for it."

"You're making them play against each other and you're going to go home with the winner, aren't you?" I rolled my eyes. I had seen her do this once or twice.

"Yeah, that's what I said." She giggled.

I saddled up to the nearby high top as Chauncey and Vince played their little hearts out. They were like teenage boys, talking shit and interfering with the other's throws.

Prince Oliver, Tej, and I talked as the others played darts for about an hour. I couldn't brush off the feeling that Knox didn't want me there, though. Other than looking completely disinterested, he didn't participate in any of our conversations. He just focused on his beer bottle and tearing off the label. *What a buzzkill.* Not that I really cared—I was in a bar with my best friend and a prince; I wasn't going to let Mr. Moody ruin our fun.

"I'm going to find the loo," Knox said to Prince Oliver as he stood up.

"He wasn't always like this," Prince Oliver murmured, leaning close to me and inclining his head toward Knox. "This brooding, I mean."

"Oh?" I said, trying to pretend that the prince hadn't just read my mind. "Have you been friends for a long time?"

"For over twenty years now," Prince Oliver answered as Tej stepped away to moderate the darts competition. "Knox's family moved to Wexstone when we were children; his father was a professor of literature at the university. We became friends at prep school and were inseparable. When his parents passed away when we were teenagers, we found out that my parents had been listed as his legal guardians, and he's been a part of our family ever since."

Hearing about Knox's parents hit a tender spot in my heart. I knew that sort of loss and what it could do to someone. "Is he a prince too, then?"

"No. My parents offered to legally adopt him, but he didn't want that. Yet it never changed the way they treated him. They have set the expectation that he be treated and respected as a member of the royal family, regardless of title."

"A tie?!"

"How the hell do you tie at darts?"

A commotion in the corner interrupted Prince Oliver's story. The darts game was over, but it looked like Sam wouldn't be going home with anyone just yet.

"Okay, we need a tie breaker. Rock, paper, scissors!" Chauncey said.

"Boys, boys, it's okay. I guess this just means that you'll both have to come with me." She winked at me.

The guys looked at each other like they were considering it before Chauncey spoke up again.

"Rock, paper, scissors or you concede, Vincent."

"Don't call me Vincent—and saddle up, mate," Vince said, shoving Chauncey's shoulder.

They brought their hands up, slapped their fists three times, and threw their choices out. Paper for Chauncey and scissors for Vince.

"Fuck! Best out of three?" Chauncey shot Sam a charming smile.

Vince laughed loudly and Sam grinned at them both. My minx of a friend was loving this. She had spent so much of the past few years wrapped up at the law firm, but her dating resolution had brought back a side of her I had missed. Seeing her flirt with these men was a welcome change.

The guys played two more rounds and Vince came out victorious.

"Better luck next time, mate." Tej patted Chauncey on the shoulder.

"Fuck off," Chauncey shrugged him off. "Let's go, I'm tired."

"And a sore loser," Tej muttered under his breath, rolling his eyes. Chauncey punched Vince in the arm before pulling him into a hug as he said goodbye, showing that maybe he wasn't such a sore loser after all.

I was loving the dynamics of this group. They reminded me a lot of Sam's older brothers and even a little bit of my younger brother Connor and his friends. I had never been a part of a big friend group like that, typically sticking to one or two girlfriends at a time. But watching these guys interact and joke around with each other made me feel like maybe I was missing out on something.

"Hey, Bee!" Sam called out to me as she and Vince meandered to my table.

"Yeah?"

"Vince invited us to meet up with them again tomorrow, you in?"

Another evening with our new friends? *Twist my arm,* I thought. "Yeah, I work the lunch shift tomorrow, but I'll be done by four or five. I'm in."

"Great! Are you okay getting home tonight?"

"Of course. I do it all the time. Plus, I have my trusty taser in my bag thanks to Connor." I patted my purse.

Years ago, after a rather wild shift at the bar, I was walking home, and a mugger stole my bag right off my shoulder. Once my brother caught wind of it, he sent me five different cans of pepper spray and a rechargeable taser to keep in my pocket.

"I'll walk her home," I heard Knox's deep voice say over my shoulder.

CHAPTER 3
BIRDIE

I looked at Knox and then back to Sam. "I'm more than capable of walking myself home." I rolled my eyes.

"It's almost 2:00 a.m. in New York City; I can't let you just walk home in the dark by yourself."

"Good thing this is the city of lights and I do this almost every night," I quipped back. "You should worry more about the prince and make sure he gets back to the hotel safely."

"He has security from one of the most highly reputable firms with him. He will be fine. My dad taught me to always walk a lady home." His eyes flashed with sadness before reverting to their impassive stare.

"Then it's settled. Knox will walk Birdie home. Text me when you get there." Sam smiled a bit too cheerily. "Make good choices, love you!" She wiggled her fingers at me as she said our customary goodbye.

"Make good choices. Love you," I replied dryly.

While Knox said his goodbyes to Prince Oliver, Tej, and Chauncey, I cleared the table of the beer bottles and trash and took it to the back. I grabbed my stuff out of my locker and made sure my taser was in my pocket. When I came out, everyone was gone, and Knox was sitting at the table by himself.

"I'm just going to wipe these tables down and then we can get going."

He gave me the solemn nod I was coming to think of as his signature response. *What a grump*, I thought.

We left Americana and headed east toward my apartment. The winter air was crisp, and, despite the late hour, there were plenty of people out and about. It was true what they said: This city never slept. At this time of night, it was people heading home from the bars and clubs. There were two girls walking arm in arm in front of us with their five-inch heels in their hands. One of them darted into an alley and I heard her friend yell at her to not pee in the middle of the alleyway—she at least needed to squat down behind the dumpster.

"God, I do not miss being twenty-one and peeing in the street," I laughed to myself.

"You've peed in the street?" Knox asked from beside me, giving me an incredulous look.

It shook me to hear him talk. I had almost forgotten he was walking next to me—almost. His towering height was pretty hard to ignore.

"Sure have." I smiled at him. I honestly didn't care what he thought about me anymore. I had tried my damnedest all night to include him in our conversations and connect with him, but he was a tough nut to crack.

We walked in silence for a few more blocks, passing the party goers that littered the sidewalks. I tossed a ten-dollar bill into the hat of a homeless man who sat on the corner as we crossed the street.

"Do you like shawarma?" I asked, realizing I hadn't had

more than a few bites of fries since finishing my shift. I needed something to soak up the beer flowing through my system. One of my favorite things about New York: it didn't matter what time it was, you could always find something to eat and had a full array of food choices at your disposal.

He looked me over and said, "Sure. But if I had to pick, I'd go with a gyro."

Jesus, take the wheel, here we go again.

"Okay. Well, there is this amazing shawarma place on the corner of my street. For walking me home, I'll buy you one."

"You don't have to do that. I'm good."

"Oh, come on. Are you one of those guys who doesn't eat after a certain hour to keep your body in tip-top shape?"

He rolled his beautiful blue eyes at me.

"Come on, let me buy you food."

We walked a few more blocks until we got to Khallas, my favorite corner shop that always had beautiful Arabic music blaring from the speakers and people shuffling in and out regardless of the hour. As soon as we walked through the door, the smell of cardamom, cumin, turmeric, and roasting meats filled my nose. I ordered us two shawarma pitas to go and said goodbye to my favorite late-night clerk, Hamza, before continuing the walk to my apartment.

"How do you like it?" I asked Knox.

"Not bad. But I prefer tzatziki sauce over this tahini."

"Sir, we are not doing this again." I chuckled. Prince Oliver wasn't wrong; this man loved to have any type of debate.

"I'm just saying, it's so refreshing. It's the superior sauce."

"I don't know, you could have fooled me about not liking it since you have it running down your shirt." I pointed to the sauce dripping down the red-and-black flannel. He looked to where I gestured and swore under his breath.

"Lucky for you, this is my apartment right here. You can come up and clean it off."

"Thanks," he said in that smooth monotone.

I entered my code to unlock the lobby door and we walked to the elevator. As we stood there waiting for the ancient elevator to make its way to us, I noticed Knox looking around.

"I know it's not much, but when I first moved here, it was all that I could afford. It's a miracle I found something with an elevator at all, really."

"I wasn't thinking that," he said, shaking his head slightly.

The elevator dinged and we stepped inside. I had obviously noticed how tall Knox was when we met, but it wasn't until we were in the small enclosure of the elevator that I noticed how built he was. His shoulders were broad, his thighs were the size of both of mine put together and—*dear God*—he smelled great, even with shawarma covering his shirt.

I unlocked my door and walked inside, hanging my bag and keys on a hook as I flipped on the lights. Knox took a look around my apartment. I loved this place, but watching him analyze everything shook my usual confidence.

"Here, let me get you some paper towels and we can wipe that stuff off your shirt."

I dampened a paper towel and started to work on the stain. Damn, this guy was nothing but hard muscle. I didn't know if it was the fact that I hadn't slept with anyone in months or the alcohol still coursing its way through my bloodstream, but this had me sensing things I hadn't felt in a while. My pulse quickened and I was having a hard time just focusing on wiping at the spot. His muscles tensed under every touch.

"Um..." I cleared my throat. "Maybe you should take your shirt off and just rinse it in the sink?" I needed to stop touching this guy.

He stared at me like he was digesting what I had just said before it clicked for me.

"Oh gosh! I don't want you to take your shirt off just so you get naked. Sorry. I just thought maybe rinsing it off would help it not look like you had dried cum on your shirt." *Did I just say that?* "Oh my gosh, that's not what I mean. I mean, it is what I mean but not in a bad way...." *Boy, I am digging myself a very large hole here.* "I'm going to go see if I have another shirt for you."

I turned to my dresser and started digging through the drawers. Surely I had an old shirt from an ex-boyfriend. Although even if I did, I wasn't sure the shirt would fit Knox. I had never dated anyone his size and build.

I kept searching and heard the sink running. I found an old shirt of my brother's and hoped it would fit. It would probably hug him like glue, but it would do the job. I turned around to see Knox shirtless in my kitchen, tattoos of mountains and pine trees trailing up his right arm before morphing into an enormous dragon and scrolls that spanned from his shoulder blade across to his chest.

Holy shit. The muscles on his back were tense as he rubbed the shirt in the sink. *Is back porn a thing? Because I think a new kink has been unlocked for me.*

Get a grip, Birdie! He's a human being, not a piece of meat for you to ogle at. But if he was a piece of meat, he'd be wagyu beef, because damn.

Knox turned around and caught me staring. *Abort dirty thoughts, he knows! Play it cool.*

"I have this shirt!" I yelled. *Yep, you're so cool.*

The next thing I knew, water was spraying all over my tiny kitchenette and Knox was fumbling to turn the knob on the sink.

"Oh shit!" I sprinted across the small space to discover that the faucet had fallen into the sink, spraying water all over the counter and walls—and Knox.

"The knob isn't working," Knox said, his usual cool demeanor wavering.

I dropped to my knees and reached under the sink to cut off the water.

When I pulled myself out from under the sink, I was face to face with a wet crotch. Just like everything else on Knox's body, it was large and well-built, his wet jeans doing absolutely nothing to hide the outline of his thick cock.

Knox cleared his throat.

Oh shit. I was just staring at his dick!

I jumped up, slipped on a puddle, and fell straight into Knox's chest.

"I am so sorry. I did a lot of the improvements myself, but this faucet has been acting finicky lately. Typically, I'm really good with my hands and working tools. I mean," I choked on my words, cursing the alcohol fogging my brain and making me unable to form coherent sentences, "not like that. Well, I mean I'm not bad in bed, I just mean—" I stopped myself and took a breath. "You know what? I'm just going to stop talking."

"Where's your toolbox? I'll fix this and then I'll leave."

"No! It's freezing outside. You can't walk back to the hotel with wet clothes. That's just asking for a cold or pneumonia. There's a dryer down the hall, it'll take maybe ten minutes. You take your clothes off and I'll go get some towels."

I went to the bathroom and grabbed a few towels from under my sink. This night was not going how I had thought or even planned. Never in my wildest dreams could I have thought I would meet a prince, drink with him and his friends, and then have his right-hand man covered in water in my kitchen. *What a night.*

I stepped out of the bathroom and locked eyes with a

boxer-briefed Knox. I stood there for a good few moments just looking at him.

Towels! The man needed a towel.

"Here!" I basically screamed. I needed to get a grip on myself. I had seen a naked man before. Several, if we're being honest, but none of them ever looked like the Adonis standing by my sink. I handed him the towels, swiped a few coins from the quarter jar on the counter, and ran down the hall to throw his clothes in the dryer, hoping that it wouldn't take long, because the tension in the apartment was thick and I needed him to leave soon. The alcohol in my system was making me think crazy thoughts and act like a complete idiot. I was not an idiot. I had a master's degree, for God's sakes. I was a confident woman who didn't fumble her words and get caught staring like a freaking weirdo.

I returned to the apartment, grabbed the toolbox from my storage closet, and handed it to Knox.

"There's not much in there but I'm sure it's got what you need. Are you sure you know how to do this?"

He huffed out a small laugh. "Yeah, I know how to do this."

My phone dinged with a text message as he opened the toolbox and shuffled a few things around. I pulled the phone from my pocket to find a text from Sam.

SAM

You make it home ok?

Yes! Sry I didn't text, got home and things got wild

Wild?! Did you hook up w/ the lumberjack?

No…but he is standing in my kitchen in nothing but his boxer briefs

WHAT?!

I'll have to tell you tomorrow. Good night, love u. Make good choices

Love you, make good choices…by sleeping w/ the lumberjack!

I laughed and threw the phone onto my bed. Knox looked over at me and I gave him a smile in return.

"Do you need any help?"

"No," was all he answered.

I plopped onto the bench at the foot of my bed and watched as he worked on the sink, enthralled by the way his shoulders tightened and relaxed as he worked the wrench. The veins in his forearms bulged as he gripped the faucet and screwed it back into place. This man was unlocking new kinks for me left and right. I tried not to look at him, but it was so hard given that the behemoth of a man who stood half-naked in my kitchen really was an elephant in the room. My mind wandered to the last time I'd had a man in my apartment.

Through the alcohol fog, I recalled that it had been some hipster guy that I met at an art gallery opening I attended with my friends Stefan and Clark a few months prior. The free champagne had snatched away my good judgment. In hindsight, the fact that he was couch surfing with friends should have raised a red flag, but once he started talking about Jackson Pollock, I was done for. My panties drop for art, I can't help it.

That guy didn't hold a candle to Knox, though. Where he had been skinny and all limbs, Knox was thick and muscular with an ass that didn't quit, and his boxer briefs didn't help by leaving nothing to the imagination. They clung to his cock so tightly that I could clearly see the head of his dick. It looked thick and long enough to both satisfy and leave you wanting more.

Well, hello, Knox Junior...

"I think I'm done," his deep voice echoed as he pulled himself away from the counter.

I shook my head, bringing myself out of the satisfying but objectifying thoughts I was having about this man who was just being nice and fixing my sink.

The timer on my phone went off to check on his clothes. I dashed down the hall to make sure they were dry before bringing them back to him.

"Here you go." I blushed, trying not to think about his penis as he pulled on his pants and buttoned the shirt over the deep V of his hips.

"Thank you. I'll get going." He walked to the front door, and I followed. He opened it, taking two steps into the hallway before he paused, then turned around.

"Hey, make sure you lock this," he deadpanned, motioning to the door.

"Will do." I smiled. "See you tomorrow."

He looked me once over and I swore I saw a small smile run across his face.

CHAPTER 4
KNOX

Light shone through the curtains in my room. It took me a minute to realize where I was and why there wasn't a wet nose in my face like every other morning when I woke up to my dog, Eugene, licking me and wanting breakfast. I sat up, putting on my glasses and blinking as the hotel room, with its jewel tones, rich fabrics, and art-deco-inspired art and light fixtures, came into focus. I got up and headed into the bathroom to brush my teeth and use the toilet.

There was a lot on the agenda for the day. We had meetings at the embassy and some stupid lunch with the mayor. I knew that this trip was part business and part pleasure, but I hated going to this stuff with Oliver. Even though he would never force me to accompany him, I would never leave him high and dry to do it by himself. While it wasn't my role in the family, people saw me as a working royal in some capacities.

When I wasn't managing the palace's grounds team in Wexstone, I often accompanied the royal family on philanthropic outings such as visiting the children's wards at the public hospitals. I never minded those excursions, but that particular morning I had no desire to play nice with politicians; I had only gotten about three hours of sleep and could feel the exhaustion deep in my bones.

I got ready for the day and padded into the kitchen. It was easy to forget that we were even staying in a hotel. The penthouse suite was more like an apartment, with the metallic art deco accents and plush furnishings of the bedrooms echoed throughout the communal living spaces. Not too bad for a home away from home. Breakfast had already been delivered, and I grabbed a mug from the cupboard and poured some coffee.

"Good morning," I heard from behind me. I turned around to find a freshly showered Oliver.

"Morning. How'd you sleep?" I sank into one of the cream curve-backed dining room chairs.

"Great." He grabbed the coffee cup out of my hand. *That little shit.*

"Dick." I laughed and popped a blueberry into my mouth.

Oliver settled into the chair across from mine. "I didn't hear you come in last night. What time did you get in?"

"Fuck." I scratched my head, rising to grab another cup. "Like four? Four thirty?"

He raised his eyebrows, giving me a "please, go on" look.

"Nothing happened," I assured him as I poured myself another cup of coffee.

"Then why did you get back so late?"

"I walked her to her apartment, we stopped and got food. I walked her upstairs and her sink started going crazy, so I fixed it. Then I came home. Nothing happened."

He gave me the once-over and nodded. "I wouldn't blame

you if anything did happen, though. Birdie is hot. And she's quite funny."

He wasn't wrong. She was incredibly attractive. She wasn't willowy or a size zero like a lot of the women from the old-money families in Wexstone strove to be but instead had strong thighs and an ass that wouldn't quit. Somehow, she had even managed to make her work jeans, unisex T-shirt, and nonslip sneakers seem alluring. And she had an air of confidence about her. I loved that in a woman—someone who could stand up for themselves and be self-assured was so sexy.

Not to mention her full lips. Last night I noticed that when she was in her head, she would bite on her bottom lip. It made me want to go over to her and suck it into my mouth just to see if it was as good as she made it look.

"Who else is coming with us this morning?" I asked, redirecting my focus back to the present.

"Just us and Vince. That is, if he ever gets back. I texted him but he hasn't responded."

I laughed. I couldn't help it. Never in my wildest dreams did I think this trip would go like this. I knew that, between Vince and Chauncey, there would be girls. But when I thought there would be girls, I thought strippers—not local women. And certainly not one whom I was actually attracted to.

"Are you having fun?" This was meant to be Oliver's last hurrah, after all.

Oliver laughed. "Yeah, I had a great time last night, and I'll have fun again tonight once we get this bullshit out of the way."

We headed out the door and Vince texted us to let us know that he would meet us at the embassy. Neither of us worried about him looking disheveled after a night out; somehow the man always managed to turn up on time and looking sharp as a tack, regardless of the previous night's activities.

The morning dragged on with meeting after meeting. Luckily, I didn't have to talk much—that was Oliver's job—and I let myself fall into my typical bodyguard persona. We always had top-of-the-line security trailing us, but in situations like this, I always kept an extra eye on our surroundings. I would never let anything happen to Oliver. He was more than my best friend; he was my brother.

———

"I'm going back to the hotel and taking the best nap after this," Vince said as we got into the blacked-out SUV to take us to lunch with the mayor.

"Same," I agreed.

It had taken me a while to get to sleep when I got back to the hotel from Birdie's apartment. I couldn't stop thinking about the way her hands felt on my chest while she was rubbing the stain out of my shirt. Or the way she looked up at me when she was on her knees in front of me. I shifted in my seat and adjusted my pants at that thought.

Lunch was blessedly short, and we headed back to the hotel to find Tej and Chauncey watching a movie in the living room. I took the spot next to Tej and settled into the deep cushions of the brown leather couch, deciding I would just rest my eyes for a few minutes. The next thing I knew, the sun had set, and I heard a knock on the door.

"I'll get it!" Vince yelled, barreling out of his room to answer the door. I was still a little out of it until I heard the soft soprano of Birdie's voice. I turned my head from where I had been laying and saw Birdie and Sam hanging their coats on the rack by the door. Sam looked lovely in a black leather skirt and gold silk camisole top, her black curls loose, but it was Birdie who took my breath away. She was wearing a short white dress that shimmered almost silvery-blue in the light and hugged her curves like it had been made just for her. Her rich brown hair was pulled halfway back, leaving a few pieces framing her face. Her makeup was simple, but she didn't need any; she was simply stunning.

The ladies took in the sizable suite with awe in their eyes. Birdie's gaze landed on me as I sat up, a small smirk skating across her face.

"Well, good morning," she mocked, her voice saccharine.

I huffed a small laugh and tipped my hand in greeting as the women made their way into the kitchen with Vince.

I ducked around the corner into my bathroom and turned the shower on. I needed the warm water to wake me up and wash the sleep from my eyes. After I got out and dressed in dark jeans and a black Henley shirt, I strolled into the kitchen where everyone was sitting around the marble island, laughing and shouting.

"What are you guys doing?" I asked Oliver.

"We were talking about what it was like for the girls to go to high school in America and Tej said he had never played spin the bottle or seven minutes in heaven—he's just seen them in the American teen movies. They suggested truth or dare as a drinking game before we go out. If you don't want to answer the question, you drink."

Oh God, I thought. I fucking hated childish games, especially truth or dare. I never felt like I could play the game honestly because I would become a major buzzkill. And I didn't like being told what to do or making an idiot of myself in front of people, so dares annoyed me. Looked like I was going to be drunk off my ass before we even left the hotel.

"Okay! Sam's turn to ask a question!" Birdie chimed in enthusiastically.

"Chauncey, truth: Was there a song playing when you lost your virginity? And if so, what was it?"

A roar of laughter echoed through the kitchen. I knew for a fact that Chauncey lost his virginity to Ginny Wu-Murphy at university. And everyone knew the story because we never let him live it down.

Chauncey started laughing along with us and answered, "We were in my dorm at uni and she came over to hang out. We were watching a movie—"

"What movie was it again, Chaunce?" Tej interrupted.

"I was getting there!" Chauncey shot back. "We were watching *Spice World* and the song 'Spice Up Your Life' was playing."

The girls laughed so hard that Birdie buckled over, holding her stomach, and Sam had tears running down her cheek by the time she was done laughing. I couldn't blame them because we had never let Chauncey forget it. Sometimes we would add the song to random playlists just to fuck with him.

"I feel like I was set up! Did Vince tell you to ask me that?"

"No!" Sam exclaimed in our friend's defense. "I swear he didn't, but man, am I glad I thought of that question. That was amazing."

"Next!" Birdie said. "Chauncey, your turn."

The game went on for a few rounds, including daring Tej to get on the bar and do a strip tease for us. Thank God the girls stopped him before his black briefs came off. I mercifully kept getting skipped over, but I knew my luck was out as soon as Birdie locked eyes with me.

"Knox, truth: What features do you find most attractive in a woman?"

I met her gaze and looked over her body. Could I tell her that she was my type to a T? Should I tell her that her full lips and even fuller breasts made my cock hard just thinking of them? Could I tell her that her quick wit and carefree attitude were the most attractive things about her? I thought about being completely honest since I'd never see her again after this weekend. But instead, I just picked up the cold beer in front of me and took a large swig. A resounding "boo" filled the room.

Oliver elbowed me in the side and laughed. "Come on, Knox! Play the game with us."

"Yeah!" Sam added. "It's your turn to ask."

I thought over my question and took another drink of my beer.

"Birdie." I pointed the top of my bottle to her. "Truth: Do you think size really matters?"

Her cheeks turned bright red as a flush washed over her face. I wasn't a cocky person, but I knew for a fact that I had caught her looking at my package several times the previous night while I was standing in her kitchen in my boxers. And from the look on her face, I knew she liked what she saw and was thinking about it at that moment.

She cleared her throat and looked between Oliver and me like she was trying to come up with a smart-ass answer. "I mean, we both know that you're not lacking in that department so why does it matter what I answer?"

"Damn!" Tej yelled.

"Oh shit!" Chauncey howled.

"Girl! You didn't tell me you saw his dick!" Sam screamed.

Birdie simply stared at me and cocked her eyebrow. I knew she would have a quippy comeback to my question. I had to smile because she got me.

After a few more rounds of truth or dare, it was Sam's turn. "Birdie: I dare you and Knox to spend seven minutes in heaven."

Birdie's eyebrows flew up her forehead. My stomach fell to my ass. A chorus of "ooooooh" filled the room as Tej said,

"There's a walk-in closet in Oliver's room." He nodded down the hall to the penthouse's master bedroom.

Birdie paused, her hand lingering on the rim of her rum and cola. I thought she might drink, but at the last second, she jumped up, grabbed my hand, and marched down the hall. I turned back to see Oliver tipping his glass to me before taking a swig.

I followed Birdie into Oliver's room, where she paused for the briefest moment as she located the closet before pulling me in with her and closing the door. I blinked as my eyes adjusted to the dark. She dropped my hand, leaning against the door frame.

"Sorry," she said. "I never turn down a dare from Sam. But we don't have to do anything, we can just stand here for seven minutes."

I looked her way, her dress catching the light that spilled in from under the door. Magnetized, I took a step in her direction. "If that's what you want."

"I mean, it's not...that's not...I just didn't want to make you uncomfortable," she stammered. Her body was tense in the small space.

"I'm not uncomfortable," I replied, my voice low.

Birdie laughed. "Well, then I guess we should at least be able to tell them that we did something, right? Or they'll never let us live it down." She stepped forward, closing the gap between us. I felt her rise onto her tiptoes as she pulled my face down toward hers and brushed a kiss onto my cheek.

Instinctively, I wrapped my arm around her waist before she could pull away, lifting her off the ground. We both paused; in the darkness, we could barely make out each other's features, but I could feel her gaze, our faces a hair's breadth away from each other.

"Is that all you want?" I asked.

I felt her head move ever so slightly side to side. "No," she answered, her voice barely audible.

I swept my free arm under her ass, tucking her legs around my waist as I hoisted her higher. Her face caught the light, and I could see her studying me, her eyes bright.

"I have a rule," I murmured.

"What's that?" she breathed.

"I need an enthusiastic yes before I go any further. Not just a soft whisper of a yes." My eyes had finally adjusted to the darkness, and I could see the side of her mouth quirk up.

"Kiss me," she said, her voice louder than before. She grabbed the back of my head and brought her mouth over mine, linking our lips together. The lingering sweetness and spice of her rum and cola rolled over my tongue as I explored her mouth with mine. Her nipples hardened against my chest, and it took everything in me not to reach up and set them free from that skin-tight dress.

Her fingers scratched across the back of my scalp and a soft moan escaped my mouth before I could swallow it down.

Jesus.

This woman knew exactly what I liked and what set me off. After she scratched down my back, she brought her fingers back up to my head, laced them through my short hair, and tugged.

I ground my hips up and started to suck my way down her neck. She let a not-so-quiet moan slip from her lips. Our mouths met again as I adjusted my grip on her ass. Her cheeks were firm yet so pliable in my hands as I squeezed my fingers into them. I ran my hand along the hem of her dress and was just about to slide it up to her waist when there was a banging on the door. We quickly pulled apart and looked at each other, both a bit shell-shocked.

"Hey kids, the cars are here!" Vince's voice was muffled through the closet door.

I set Birdie down and she fixed her dress. I adjusted myself, making sure my zipper was in the right place so it didn't bruise my bulging cock.

"So..." I cleared my throat.

"Good game." She smiled, eyes twinkling. "You did great for someone who has never played seven minutes in heaven."

CHAPTER 5
KNOX

I opened the door and let Birdie exit first. She headed straight to the kitchen and started whispering with Sam while I grabbed my wallet and phone from the bedroom and trailed the group to the elevator. Trying to fit seven people inside was a fun game of Tetris. I ended up in the left corner with Birdie's ass tucked into my crotch, still semi-hard from our closet make-out. She smelled of lavender and vanilla—refreshing and warm all at the same time. It took everything in me not to get fully hard.

Her scent lingered in my nose all the way to the club until all I could smell was the fog machine and smoke that seeped out of the loud, modern building. Vince talked to a formidable man standing just to the side of the door. He waved over Oliver's security team, and they went ahead inside of us. A few minutes passed before a petite woman dressed in all black arrived to lead us up a small flight of stairs to a sectioned-off VIP area.

The VIP area was in the corner of the posh club, opposite

the DJ booth. It held two L-shaped black leather couches with a glass coffee table between them. On the table was a metal bucket full of ice-cold beers next to an array of hard liquor and glassware.

I took a seat in the corner of a couch so I could have a clear view of the club, the coolness of the leather seeping through my shirt. I liked to sit in the corner so I could have a full view of the room and assess the crowd. The place was packed, and the dance floor was full. Even though we had security with us at all times, I still hated being in crowded places like this, especially with Oliver.

"Should we take some shots?" Tej asked.

Chauncey grabbed a bottle of tequila from the table and popped the top off. Everyone grabbed a shot glass, letting Chauncey pour. After the glasses were full to the brim, we raised them together.

The guys all looked to Oliver, our resident toast maker.

"I'll keep this one clean for the ladies." He winked at the girls. "To those who wish us well, and the rest can go to hell!"

We all downed the silky liquor, and I settled back into my corner.

Ginuwine's "Pony" started playing, the bass bumping throughout the building. Sam let out a squeal.

"Let's go dance!" she yelled at Vince as she grabbed his arm and pulled him to a small sliver of the dance floor.

Birdie and Oliver sat across from me on the other couch and Tej sat next to me, eyeing a shirtless bartender across the room.

"Go talk to him," I encouraged, nudging Tej with my elbow.

"What? He's working."

"So? You could still get his number and invite him back to the hotel."

Tej mulled it over for a bit and then stood, fixed his shirt, and strolled across the room to the bar, striking up a conversation with the bartender.

Oliver and Birdie's conversation grabbed my attention from watching Tej trying to score.

"So, if someone posts a picture of you sitting next to me, will your fiancée freak out? I don't want to cause any trouble." Birdie laughed, mostly to herself. "I think I'd be super jealous if the future king was hanging out with some random girls while away from home." She took a drink of the beer she had just opened. "I bet being a prince, girls throw themselves at you all the time hoping to score with the future king."

"No, that sounds more like my brother," Oliver laughed.

"Oh, you have a brother?" she said with her head cocked to the side like she was trying to remember something. "He must be younger?"

"No, he's four years older. He was supposed to take the crown, but he abdicated a few months ago."

"Wow! Why did he give it up?" She started to bring her beer to her full lips but stopped midway. "Oh God, I'm so sorry. You don't have to answer that; it's none of my business. I apologize."

Oliver chuckled. "No, it's fine. Honestly, you could pull up any European gossip magazine and find Xavier's face plastered all over the pages." He looked annoyed, rather than mad or embarrassed. I knew he was still processing his feelings about Xavier and his abdication. Oliver sighed. "We have a rule that you must be engaged to marry before your coronation. Xavier refused. He doesn't want to marry. Even at thirty-four, he would rather continue partying and"—he smiled wryly—"hooking up than put down roots."

"Oh, wow," Birdie said, her beer drifting back down to her lap.

"Anyway, it was get married and give up his 'friends with

benefits' lifestyle or abdicate. He chose the latter. So here I am, a few months away from my own coronation."

"And what about your fiancée, what does she think of all of this?"

"Well…I don't have a fiancée just yet."

Birdie's brow furrowed. "I'm sorry, I must be confused. I thought you said this was a bachelor party? Does that mean something different in Wexstone?"

Oliver looked over at me with a sly smile. "No. My friends and I are here to celebrate before the contest begins." He looked down at the ice in his glass.

Birdie looked between Oliver and me. "Contest?"

"It's all so ridiculous," Oliver sighed.

"Well, you've sparked my interest, Prince Oliver. What contest?"

"You see, I was thrown into all of this so fast. I was casually dating a woman I had grown up with but broke it off about a month before Xavier decided to abdicate. And now…"

Vince walked back to us, grabbed a bottle of water, and downed half of it in one go. I saw something fly through the air and land in Oliver's lap. Oliver reached down and brought up a long-stemmed rose. I looked around to see where Vince had even gotten it, then spotted a woman in the center of the dance floor with two huge bouquets, throwing them at people and screaming, "Fuck all men, and especially fuck men who try to make up with you by sending flowers from his wife's floral shop! Fuck you, Jeremy!"

"What's going on?" Birdie asked, taking the rose as Oliver handed it to her and watching with trepidation as Vince walked away, Sam grinning mischievously behind him.

"Well, you know that TV show *The Bachelor*?"

"I'm an American millennial, of course I know about *The*

Bachelor," she replied, the suspicion in her voice growing by the moment.

"It's a little bit like that. Several noble families are each sponsoring a woman. I date them through a series of events over the course of a couple of months and...pick the one whom I think would be the best fit for my country and myself."

"Wow. I uh...I'm actually speechless."

Honestly, I didn't blame her; the contest was one of the most bizarre ideas I had ever heard when the guys had brought it up. I had watched more seasons of *The Bachelor* than I was ready to admit, and it seemed to work out every once in a while, but in this setting? It seemed just shy of an arranged marriage. I still wasn't sure how Oliver could get to know someone while courting multiple women at the same time.

"I can see the wheels turning in your head," Oliver said over the loud club music. "I can tell you it's probably not as bad as you're thinking. My intention isn't to lead anyone on, I do not condone drama, and I'm not in it to make out with a bunch of beautiful women. This was never how I imagined finding my wife, but the law is the law and if this is what I have to do to find a partner to help run my country, then it's what I'll do."

I looked over at him. There was a resignation, almost sadness, backed by determination in his eyes. I admired his dedication to his country. He took his future role as king seriously and he would be a great ruler. I kept my mouth shut, not wanting my own opinions on this to tarnish the night. After all, Oliver was a grown man and could make his own decisions, and I would always support him in any way possible.

"Bee!" Sam yelled as she walked up the few steps it took to get from the dance floor to our small corner of the club. "Come dance with me!"

Birdie took another drink of her beer and linked hands with Sam, following her to the dark dance floor.

Birdie's white dress glowed under the blacklights of the club. Her heels made her calves look toned and delicious as she moved in time to the music. The girls danced on each other like they had been doing this for ages. Birdie had her back to Sam; she rolled her body and then dipped down and twisted her way back up. She turned around to face Sam as they danced in tandem.

The girls didn't notice the two guys talking right behind them. But I did. I kept my eyes on them as they made their way closer and then split up and took positions behind Birdie and Sam. The girls tried to move to the side and dance by themselves but every move they made, the two dipshits followed. They couldn't seem to take the hint that the girls didn't want to dance with them. The short weaselly looking man behind Birdie moved to grab her ass, and she turned around just in time for him to fumble her breast. Her eyes flared and her shoulders tightened just before she wound back and punched him square in the nose.

Good girl, I thought as I jumped up to get over there but was cut off by Oliver. I put my hand across his chest and pushed my way in front of him, not wanting him to get in the middle of this. He didn't need a headline about punching out some asshat Americans in a club. The two of us charged onto the packed dance floor and I pushed my way in between Birdie and the guy with the now-bloody nose.

I loomed over the man, who was several inches shorter than me. "You need to keep your fucking hands to yourself," I growled.

"Who do you think you are?" the guy spat out, words slurring together.

"Turn around and walk away or I'll remove you myself," I

said firmly, crossing my arms across my chest and flexing slightly.

"Hey!" He poked his finger in the middle of my chest. "I'd like to see you fry…I mean try!"

The guy could barely make eye contact through his hooded eyes. I grabbed him under the arm and turned around to find his partner in crime, but he was already gone. I started walking the bloody-nosed guy toward the door.

One of Oliver's security guards approached and looked at the guy I had by the arm.

"Everything good?"

"Get this guy out here. His evening is over."

"Got it." The guard took him by the collar and escorted him out of the building.

I turned back to the dance floor to find Birdie, wanting to make sure she was okay, and spotted her dancing with Oliver to a remix of "Shivers" by Ed Sheeran.

Of course, I thought. Now that she knew he wasn't engaged or had a girlfriend, of course she would want to go for him. That's how it always went. And I couldn't blame her. Oliver was an amazing guy—he was funny, charismatic, and handsome. Women always flocked to him, and he was smooth with them. Our few minutes in the closet back at the hotel had been a game, nothing more.

I went back to my seat in our corner of the club and grabbed a bottle of Maker's from the table, opened it, and downed two huge swigs, letting the burn coat my throat. I knew in a ritzy club like this I could order just about any top-shelf bourbon, but in that moment, I merely needed something stronger than beer to take the edge off. I faced the dance floor and took in Birdie dancing with—and on—Oliver. I couldn't look away. I thought watching her wind and grind her body up and down my best friend's would take the sting out of this blow, but it just made the jealousy roll through every limb of my body.

"Oi! They look like they're getting on pretty well." Vince hit my knee and pointed to Oliver and Birdie on the dance floor.

I didn't answer. I just took another taste of the liquor, hoping it would start to numb my envy. Vince nestled into a conversation with Sam, and I looked back to see Oliver skim his hands up Birdie's legs and run one hand along the hem of her short dress. She rubbed her ass against his front and then shimmied down and popped back up. I couldn't help but think of earlier that evening and how her eyes glistened when she looked up at me before I kissed her. And the sounds that she made when I sucked her bottom lip and ran my hands over her plump ass.

Thankfully, the song ended, and I was put out of the misery of watching them dance as Oliver guided her back toward our group.

"I'll be back in a moment, I need to locate the loo," Oliver excused himself.

"Sorry to interrupt, but I need to sit down for a minute," Birdie said, settling in next to Sam and Vince.

"Not a problem. Are you having fun? You and Prince Oliver looked like you were having a good chat earlier," Sam said as she nudged Birdie's shoulder with hers.

"Yeah, he was just explaining the contest he's headed back to."

"Vince was telling me the same thing."

"Yeah, I thought so. What the hell are you two up to?" she asked, eyeing them suspiciously.

"We have a proposition for you." Vince smiled. "Let me start by saying that I've never seen Ollie look at someone the way he looks at you."

What the fuck? I hadn't noticed Oliver looking at Birdie at all, but then again, I'd been wrapped up in making sure *I* wasn't getting caught up with her and making sure everything went according to plan while we were here.

Vince continued. "Come to Wexstone with us. Let my family sponsor you."

I nearly dropped the liquor bottle.

Birdie choked. "You're kidding me, right? No way."

"We actually think this would be perfect for you," Sam interjected.

"We? Wait, was this your idea? Samantha Grace Rickett, you have lost your damn mind."

"It was a joint idea," Vince laughed, throwing his arm casually around Sam's shoulder. My blood boiled and I wanted to punch him for how laid back he seemed about this.

Sam put her hand on Birdie's knee. "Look, you know you haven't been very open to love lately. And you do need a place to live for a bit. Go to Wexstone, do the contest, give love a chance."

"I can't just pick up and move to another country for a few months. I have a job!"

Sam looked at her pointedly. "I'm pretty sure the bar will still be here in a few months." Her voice was firm.

"Well, what about my stuff? And Connor would freak out if I missed Thanksgiving and Christmas. You know how he is about the holidays. I can't just jump on a plane and leave."

"You wouldn't need to fly out until next week. You could take the week to get your affairs in order," Vince said.

"I barely know Prince Oliver. I don't know anything about your country. I definitely don't know the first thing about being noble or royalty or a socialite. I'm just a girl from the Midwest who swears like a sailor and would rather wear jeans than dresses. There's no way the prince would want me, he's way out of my league." He wasn't; if anything, she was out of all of our leagues.

"I think you're just what he's looking for." Vince smiled reassuringly, winking at me. A dimple appeared in his left cheek. "My family has been waiting to announce who we are sponsoring until we found just the right woman, and Birdie, it's you." Damn him, he always knew how to turn on the charm. For once, I hated him for it.

"What are you guys talking about?" Oliver asked as he walked up and took a seat next to me.

"I want to sponsor Birdie for the contest!" Vince said with so much excitement he could barely contain it.

Oliver looked between Vince and Birdie and then over to me like he was considering it.

"Does Ms. Birdie want to come?"

Her face flushed as she grabbed her beer and took a large gulp from it. I felt my focus narrow, my heart racing as I waited to hear what she'd say.

"I *am* homeless in two weeks," she laughed nervously. "And it would be fun to hang out with you guys some more." I could tell she was more than a little tipsy by her slightly too-loud voice.

I stood up fast and strode to the bathrooms, passing a smiling Tej on the way. I needed to remove myself from the conversation so I could process my thoughts.

———

I had too many emotions and too much alcohol flooding my system. Oliver needed to find a wife so he could take the throne; I wanted that for him. But I didn't want it to be Birdie.

I didn't have a good reason for my jealousy—I had met her

less than thirty-six hours ago and had no claim on her whatsoever.

But what if you want *to claim her?* a voice whispered in the back of my head. I would certainly like to claim her mouth again and again like I had a few hours before, or even her whole body—the way it felt against mine was heavenly.

I shook my head, trying to dispel the mental image of our entwined bodies. *Get it together, Knox.*

When I stepped out of the bathroom, Oliver was leaning against the wall waiting for me.

"Hey," he said nonchalantly.

"Hey."

"Are you good if Birdie comes to Wexstone?"

Not really.

"Yeah, why wouldn't I be?" I avoided making eye contact with him. I didn't want to have this conversation. Birdie could do whatever she wanted. What I wanted didn't matter here.

"Well, it looked like you guys were hitting it off."

Yeah, I thought we were, too.

"So did you guys," I quipped back. "There's nothing going on between us; I don't care if she comes. Do you like her?" His answer was important; if he genuinely liked her, I would tamp down my own feelings and let him have his chance at happiness with her.

"I wouldn't mind getting to know her a little better. It would be fun to have someone else who we don't know. Maybe it would be a good idea to have someone from America in the contest. Maybe that's what the country needs?"

I thought she might be what I needed.

"Great. Then it sounds like she's coming to Wexstone," I said coolly. I turned and stalked back to the group, eyeing Birdie and Sam, their heads together as they whispered to each other excitedly. I reminded myself to push my feelings down. Protecting and supporting my future king was more important; it was what I would always do.

CHAPTER 6
BIRDIE

I stared out the window at the white, puffy clouds that floated by as the jet speared through them on its way to Wexstone. I couldn't believe that a week ago I was living a normal—perhaps even mundane, but pleasant—life in the city, and now I was on my way to participate in a royal love contest fashioned after one of TV's most ridiculous reality shows.

I couldn't make this shit up if I tried.

I was still unsure how I felt about the contest at all. It seemed like a disservice to the country, but somehow I had found myself packing my things, using the ticket Vince had bought, and boarding the plane anyway. All while catching myself thinking back to the kiss I'd had with Knox in the closet and wondering if this is what I should really be doing.

Sam and I had packed my belongings into a storage pod earlier in the week and she had hugged me goodbye, promising to visit before the contest ended in December.

I sighed, settling back into my seat. My mind floated back

over the hardest part of the previous week: Telling my brother about this little adventure.

Connor was eighteen months younger than me, but he may as well have been a decade older, given how together his life was. He and his wife Colleen were college sweethearts who got married almost immediately after graduating and wasted no time starting a family. They already owned their own home out in Oregon where they lived with my three-year-old niece Eleanor and their golden retriever Scout. They belonged on a fucking postcard.

As much as I loved teasing Connor about his Norman Rockwell life, he was a great dad and loved the holidays, so telling him that I would be missing Thanksgiving *and* Christmas had given me a knot in my stomach. While we didn't get to see each other as often as we'd like, we video chatted at least once a month and always spent the holidays together. I knew he wasn't going to take this lightly.

"You're doing *what?!*" he had exclaimed when I got him on a video call two days after meeting Prince Oliver. "You know how insane this sounds, right? No fucking way."

"Connor," I heard Colleen gently chide from off screen. I said a silent word of thanks for my sister-in-law. She was the only one who could successfully diffuse our sibling arguments. She appeared just behind Connor. "Birdie is a grown woman and can make her own decisions."

"Yeah, but she doesn't usually make *absolutely insane decisions.*"

"Hey, you're the one who keeps pressuring me to find a guy and settle down and live the American dream. Maybe the prince will be my love match and you can get after me about something else." I wasn't sure I believed it even as I said it, but I loved nothing more than getting the last word with my brother.

Prince Oliver was great; there was no refuting that. He was handsome and polite and a great conversationalist. And I couldn't deny that I'd had a great time dancing with him at the club. I was sure he would be a wonderful husband and partner —but the jury was still out on whether he would be the right husband and partner for *me*. At least I could enjoy the adventure in the meantime.

Connor drew a breath to speak, but Colleen set her hand on his shoulder and gave him a sharp look. He sighed. "Fine. But this is the first year that Ellie understands what's happening with the holidays, so you have to promise me that we'll celebrate over a video call."

A knife of guilt twisted my gut. I loved that little girl more than anything and would never want to disappoint her. "Of course. Tell her I promise we'll still make our handprint turkeys for Thanksgiving, even if it's from a distance."

The flight attendant worked her way down the aisle, bringing me back to the present. My eyes felt heavy, so I popped in my earbuds, started up my favorite plane album by Mumford & Sons, reclined my comfy first-class seat, and promptly fell asleep.

The next thing I knew, the attendant was waking me up, asking me to put my seat forward in preparation for landing.

I hadn't realized just how nervous I was until I looked out the tiny window at the snow-covered mountains of Wexstone.

Why are you nervous? I asked myself. *You're here to have fun on a once-in-a-lifetime experience and get a stamp on your passport. It doesn't have to be anything more than that. Chill out.*

But the butterflies in my stomach refused to settle as the plane touched down and made its way to the gate.

As exited the plane, I couldn't shake the feeling that eyes were on me. Even though I couldn't spot anyone outright watching me, I was reminded that I was sure to be under scrutiny as this country dissected every last inch of me. The thought did nothing to settle my nerves.

Carry-on and passport in hand, I cleared immigration, grabbed my two checked bags, and headed to customs. I was still lost in my thoughts as I sent my suitcases through the scanner when I heard a customs officer say, "Miss? Miss, can you step this way, please?"

I looked up, startled to realize he was speaking to me. What in the hell could have flagged their attention? I had breezed through TSA PreCheck at JFK.

A jolt of panic swept through me as I remembered my friend Maggie's bachelorette party in Las Vegas three months earlier and the small container of weed gummies I had tossed into one of my suitcase pockets and promptly forgotten. Where they still in there? They must have spotted them, and I was about to kick off my time here in Wexstone with a visit to jail. *Fuck.*

I breathed in deeply through my nose, willing myself to stay calm.

"Miss, we need to take a look in your suitcase. We spotted something unusual on our scanners." My vision narrowed as gloved hands unzipped the suitcase from the Vegas weekend. This was it. I was glad I had committed Sam's phone number to memory for my one phone call from jail.

The customs officer rifled through the suitcase. Through my panic, I heard him say, "Ah." He straightened, awkwardly holding up a black silicone vibrator.

My panic immediately turned to embarrassment. In addition to forgetting about the edibles, which I was now wishing they had found instead, I had also forgotten about the "prize" I had won at Maggie's party by getting the most phone numbers over the course of the weekend.

"Our apologies, miss. We saw a, uh...a dark mass on the

scanners and needed to check it out," the officer said, quickly setting the vibrator back in the suitcase and zipping it up. "You are cleared and can head on your way."

My face was still beet red as I took the suitcase. I was vaguely aware of whispers around me. I glanced over my shoulder to see several college-aged girls snapping photos on their phones before being reprimanded by an officer for using the devices.

Shit, shit, shit.

I quickly wheeled my bags down the short hallway and out a set of automatic doors and spotted Vince waiting for me, his hands in his coat pockets.

"Birdie! Welcome to Wexstone. How was your flight?" he asked as he kissed my cheek in greeting.

"Uh. Fine?" I responded, still flustered.

Vince grabbed my two suitcases, giving me a quizzical look as he led me to a sleek black SUV.

"Care to expand?" he asked.

I blushed again. I wasn't eager to recount the experience to anyone besides Sam—I could already hear her howling with laughter—but Vince was my sponsor for the contest, and I knew that any bad press would reflect on him. He had been too kind to hide this from him, especially if those photos made it online.

I buckled myself into the front seat as Vince settled in behind the wheel—I noticed that they drove on the right side of the road here—and I sheepishly told him what had happened.

Vince threw back his head, his deep laughter filling the car. He reached up and wiped his eyes as he continued howling.

"Are you *crying* right now?!" I whacked his upper arm in a sisterly manner. He nodded, tears of mirth streaming down his face. My embarrassment ebbed and I started chuckling in spite of myself. Soon we were both doubled over, gasping for breath as our laughter subsided.

"Okay, so I guess you aren't mad," I said, relieved.

"No," he answered as he started the car. "First of all, cannabis has been legal here since the beginning of the year. Second, don't worry about the girls with the photos. Chances are good that the customs officers confiscated their phones after they saw them taking pictures. But no one knows who you are and why you are here yet, and if they do end up online, we'll handle it. Besides, it might do this country some good to remember that royals are humans with needs, too," he said with one of his charming winks.

I hit him in the arm again. "Great, thanks. So reassuring."

"You're welcome. Now, I hope you don't mind a busy time." His grin widened as he drove.

"I'm ready," I said. I had to be.

"We'll head to my family manor. Tonight we'll get you settled in and cleaned up, make sure you're up to speed on what you need to know about Wexstone, maybe a bit of media training, and tomorrow night will kick off the introduction gala." He reached into his jacket and handed me a piece of paper. I unfolded it to find an itinerary of the next several weeks.

"You weren't lying when you implied we'd hit the ground running, huh?"

"At a full sprint. Love can't wait!" He smiled from ear to ear.

An amiable silence settled over us as we drove through the capital city of Altborn. Colorful old buildings lined the cobblestone streets, standing out against the bright white of the snow covering the ground. On each street corner, street signs were hung above winter wreaths on antique-looking lampposts. The Hallmark Channel had nothing on this place.

After winding through the quaint city, I was captivated by the beauty of the quiet countryside. Fresh powdery snow covered the rolling hills, and in the distance, I could make out picturesque mountain peaks covered with lush pine trees. I cracked my window, and the smell of pine and snow flooded the SUV. It was breathtaking.

As we turned into a long drive, Vince buzzed through an ornate wrought-iron gate leading to an immaculate manor. I could tell that in the spring the gray stone walls would be covered in ivy and imagined that the sizable fountain out front must be magnificent when the weather was warm.

"Here we are," Vince announced.

"*This* is your house?" It was a far cry from the split-level I had grown up in in Michigan.

"Well, it's my family's home. I live here with my brother, Bronson."

"It's beautiful." I stared at the three-story house growing bigger as we rounded the long cobblestone drive. I couldn't wrap my head around the fact that this would be my own home for the next several weeks.

Vince parked the car. I paused.

"Vince, you seem like a really nice guy. And I really appreciate you sponsoring me. But I have to ask, in your honest opinion, do you actually think I have a chance? Because I can't picture Prince Oliver wanting to marry some American waitress when he has the opportunity to marry someone...like him."

Vince stopped from where he had been about to open the driver's-side door and turned to me. He took my hands in his own.

"You want my honest opinion? I believe you are exactly what he needs. Someone who doesn't have an ulterior agenda. Someone who can remind him what it is like to be human, not just sovereign. It has been a long time since I have seen him as relaxed as he was in New York—thanks in large part, I believe, to you. He was just a man, not a man with the weight of a country on his shoulders."

I didn't know what to make of that. Vince was being genuine, that I could tell. But I needed time to digest what he'd said.

I turned to see an older man in a tailored suit walking toward us from the manor's arched entrance. He opened my door as Vince stepped out of the driver's side.

"Mr. Alexander. It's a pleasure to see you, sir." The man nodded to Vince.

"Levin, it's always good to see you as well. I'd like to introduce you to our guest." Vince rounded the SUV and held his hand out to assist me. "This is Bernadette Hamilton."

"Oh, please call me Birdie," I said, reaching out to shake Levin's hand.

Levin politely took my hand. I made a mental note to ask Vince how I was supposed to greet people, as it felt like a handshake wasn't it. "It's a pleasure to meet you, Ms. Hamilton. If you'd like to follow me inside, we can get you to your room."

"Sounds great."

I followed Vince and Levin through the magnificent French doors and was greeted by a large, curving staircase. On the second step stood a man who had to be Vince's brother, and while the family resemblance was clear, his face lacked the warmth of Vince's. He appeared to be several years older than Vince's late twenties; his black hair was speckled with gray and starting to thin. He wore a pinstriped suit with a purple pocket square peeking out from the chest pocket, and his immaculately polished black shoes reflected the light from the crystal chandelier and the white marble floor. He was exactly what I had pictured when I thought of someone from a noble house.

"Birdie, this is my brother, Lord Bronson Alexander. Bronson, this is Birdie Hamilton," Vince introduced.

"Birdie?" Bronson asked, raising his eyebrows. He said my name as if it tasted sour on his tongue.

I held back my handshake this time. "It's short for Bernadette." I wasn't sure why I was so quick to correct him, but Bronson had a presence about him that demanded order and manners.

"Mmm," he responded, lips pursed. "Welcome to Lexington Manor. I will show you to your room. Vincent will spend some time preparing you for tomorrow's gala. We clearly have our work cut out for us." His muddy brown eyes narrowed as he glanced me up and down.

"Bronson, don't be rude." Vince's voice was clipped, a tone I had yet to hear from him.

Bronson turned sharply to his brother. "I would never be rude. I am simply stating the obvious. We must prepare the American if she is going to contend for a royal heart."

I bristled at his use of "the American" as though I was not standing right in front of him.

As Bronson turned and we climbed the stairs, I took notice of the family portraits lining the wall. Generation after generation of Alexanders stood frozen in time, posed in their frames with dour expressions on their faces, the family sigil featuring a silver wolf with its teeth bared marked in the corner. The clear legacy here in this house and this country was jarring to me. No doubt there was a book somewhere here detailing every birth, death, and marriage in this family going back hundreds of years. Meanwhile, I could barely remember the names of all my great-grandparents.

And they are just a noble family, not even a royal one, I thought. *Prince Oliver must be able to recite his family tree going back to Adam and Eve.* Yet again, feelings of inferiority swept over me. I was an outsider; no matter how hard I tried or how much Vince tried to prepare me, I was sure to make an idiot of myself. And the prince didn't deserve that.

But you're here now. You can't exactly turn back at this point without looking like a total ass, I reminded myself as we came to a spacious landing, with wide hallways stretching out on either side. *Make the best of it. Someday you can tell your kids and grandkids about this.*

Bronson stopped in front of a set of double doors, opening them to a large, high-ceilinged room. A carved four-poster bed stood against the wall to our left. A white duvet was laid over it like a cloud, with fur-lined throw pillows and a delicate blanket arranged perfectly. Across the room, a large mirror stood in the corner next to a velvet loveseat and armchair. A writing desk sat between two of the large windows. An open door led into what looked to be a spacious ensuite bathroom.

"I hope this will suffice for your stay," said Vince.

"This is my room?" I asked. *It's bigger than my entire apartment back home!*

"Yes. This is where you will be staying while you are here," Bronson quipped. "Now, if you don't mind, I will let Clarence know that we are ready to begin."

I tore my eyes from the beautiful room and turned to Bronson. "Start what? Who is Clarence?"

"You need to be fitted for your formal dresses. Clarence will be assisting with this. And you will certainly need a lesson on our customs and etiquette."

I knew I was about to piss him off, but I couldn't help myself. I turned on my best New Yorker accent. "What, are you sayin' there's something wrong with the way I dress?"

"That's exactly what I'm saying," Bronson replied, not bothering to hide the disdain in his voice. He turned sharply on his heel and strode out of the room.

"Don't mind him, Birdie." Vince sounded tired.

"He doesn't respond well to humor, does he?"

"That he does not." Vince smiled. "Given how well I know Oliver, Bronson entrusted me to choose the woman we would sponsor. But now that I have chosen an American, he is feeling the pressure and, per usual, questioning everything I do."

"The pressure?"

"To have you be chosen. You may have picked up on this, but Bronson is hyper fixated on image and status. He feels that the positive press and accolades that would come from assisting in finding our queen would be a boon to our family legacy."

I flushed, realizing that there was more riding on my being there than I had previously thought. I hadn't considered the ways in which my participation in this nonsense could affect Vince and his family, even if I personally might not understand them.

Our conversation was cut short as Bronson reentered the room, followed by a short, squat man in a green velvet jacket and four lithe assistants. The man in the velvet jacket introduced himself with a flourish as Clarence. "I will be helping you to stun the prince."

Before I knew it, the assistants were unfolding a screen and rolling in racks of gowns. One by one, dresses were shoved into my hands as I was shuffled behind the screen to change. Some dresses elicited a furrowed brow and a shake of the head from Clarence, while others prompted a quick snap of his fingers, leading the assistants to adjust hemlines, mark where the bodices needed to be taken in or let out, and, at more than one point, adjust my cleavage to their apparent liking.

When I had tried on what felt like a hundred dresses, Clarence approached, pulling my chestnut hair out of its ponytail. It fell just past my shoulders. He inspected the ends, then peered closely at my face.

"Well. At least we don't have any split ends to contend with, although those eyebrows need some cleaning up." He snapped his fingers again, and I was rushed into a chair, where I received an eyebrow wax and had some kind of mud mask applied to my face.

Now I know how Mia Thermopolis felt, I thought.

Bronson and Vince, who had disappeared while I was poked and prodded and pinned, returned as one of the assistants finished wiping the mask from my face.

"Bernadette. Are you familiar with any of the royal customs? Have you ever met royalty before?" Bronson asked.

"I once spotted Beyoncé at a Starbucks in Brooklyn, does that count?"

Bronson rolled his eyes. Vince let a half-grin slide across his face, his dimple appearing.

"Your quick remarks and less-than-serious attitude will not get you far in this courtship. You should take this seriously. This isn't an American beauty pageant; this is the prince's hand in marriage," Bronson lectured.

I sobered. "I apologize, Bronson. I assure you I am taking this seriously," I promised. As much as I already enjoyed getting under Bronson's skin, I reminded myself that he was going out on a limb for me. My talent for quick comebacks and laughing things off may have helped me when I was being teased by the popular kids in junior high for my second-hand jeans and braces, but I would need to rein it in when I met the rest of the royal family.

"When you enter the royal palace, you will be led to the grand ballroom. At dinner, you are not allowed to sit until the royal family sits," Bronson continued. "As you are not a citizen of Wexstone, you are not required to curtsy when meeting the royal family, but it is a sign of respect should you wish to do so." His eyes narrowed. "People will be watching you extra carefully, so it would do you well to go above and beyond in niceties."

"Ok. Not sitting until they sit, curtsy when I shake their hands."

"No shaking!" Bronson exclaimed, panic in his voice. "You will *place* your hand in theirs if offered. Do *not* shake."

"No shaking," I repeated. "Got it. How do I address them? That's what I'm most nervous about. Is it Your Highness? King? Queen? Majesty?"

"When you meet the king and queen for the first time, address them as Your Majesty. For other members of the royal family, address them as Your Highness or Your Royal Highness. After the first time you speak to them, it is acceptable to address them as sir or ma'am." Bronson glanced at his watch. "If you'll excuse me, I have other duties to attend to. Clarence, I will see you and your team out. Bernadette, they will be back tomorrow to help you prepare for the gala. Vincent, please continue educating our guest."

Bronson led Clarence and his assistants out of the room. The door clicked closed behind them.

I collapsed onto the velvet loveseat, thoroughly exhausted. My mind was swimming. Vince lowered himself into the adjacent armchair. He crossed his legs and tilted his head, looking at me with amusement.

"I take it you are tired?" he asked.

I laughed. "Between jet lag and"—I gestured vaguely at spot where my makeover had just taken place—"all of that... yeah, you could say that. Your brother is a lot. Has he always been so...strung up?"

"Bronson is intense. Our mother passed away shortly after I was born, and it changed him. He only knows how to thrive through control and order. I think that has only worsened since our father died last year."

I felt a pang in my chest. Maybe I should give Bronson a break.

"Dinner will be ready soon," Vince continued. "How about I ask them to bring it up here. We can talk while we eat and then you can get a good night's rest before tomorrow?"

"That sounds great," I said, relieved I wouldn't need to move from where I was any time soon.

Twenty minutes later, a gangly young man in a chef coat, whom Vince introduced as Thomas, set plates of succulent roast beef, potatoes, carrots, and rich au jus in front of each of us. I sighed happily, only just realizing how hungry I really was.

Vince had spent the time while we waited debriefing me on the press that was expected to cover each event, as well as how to best answer questions directed at me. His greatest word of caution, however, was reserved for the tabloids.

"Our tabloids are not anywhere as vicious as those in the UK," he explained, "but I do not doubt that the paparazzi will be on the hunt for anything they think can fetch them a good price related to this contest. Be yourself, always smile, but do not be afraid to answer their questions with, 'No comment.'"

No comment. Smile. Don't shake hands. Your Majesty.

Now, as we dug into our dinner, Vince looked up at me. "Before we finish up, is there anything else you would like to know?"

"Actually, yes," I said, setting my fork down and wiping my mouth with my napkin. "What the hell is the deal with this marriage rule? And if the king is still alive, why is Prince Oliver about to be crowned? I thought that didn't happen until the king died? And how much power does the royal family really have?"

"Ah, wonderful questions." Vince settled back in his chair. "You are no doubt familiar with the British royal family, and while we share some similarities with them, a number of our laws and customs differ quite a bit.

"I'll answer your last question first: We are a constitutional monarchy. Most of the governmental power is held by the Council of Lords, which at one point did consist solely of titled nobility, though the seats are now elected positions. The monarch is primarily a symbolic role, although do not be mistaken—they hold quite a bit of sway over the Council's decisions."

"Is it only men who can rule?"

"No, the line of succession goes in birth order, regardless of sex. Although it has been many generations since the royal family has had a first-born daughter.

"The answers to your other questions stem from the same place. King Leroy's grandfather—Oliver's great-grandfather— King Alfred II, inherited the throne from his uncle, who had never married and ruled for almost sixty years. By the time he passed away, he was extremely out of touch with where the country was, and without a partner by his side to help him rule, he didn't have anyone to balance him out. He nearly led Wexstone to ruin. So, when King Alfred took the throne, he established two laws in an attempt to prevent that from happening again. The first was that each sovereign can only rule for thirty years, or until their death—whichever comes first. The second was that the ruler must be married; King Alfred believed that a ruling partnership would keep balance on the throne, while only allowing a sovereign to rule for a maximum of thirty years would prevent them from becoming out of touch with younger generations and new technologies.

"This year marks King Leroy's thirtieth year on the throne. I believe Oliver already told you about Xavier's abdication, which means that Oliver will be crowned just after the new year."

I blinked. What I had assumed was a rule rooted in patriarchal ideals had been established to provide stability to a country on the brink of ruin. While I wasn't convinced that it was the right answer, it was a reminder to me not to judge a book too harshly by its cover.

"Is there anything else you'd like to know?" Vince inquired as he returned his attention to his plate.

For a split second I considered asking for more information about Knox and his place within the family but thought better of it. I was here to court Prince Oliver, after all. Knox was...well, I wasn't sure what he was, but he wasn't supposed to be my priority. Instead, I simply shook my head.

We finished our meal, and Vince placed our empty plates on a tray. "All right. I think that's enough for today. I'm going to take this back down to the kitchen. You get some sleep; we'll hit the ground running again tomorrow."

I stood and walked him to the door.

"Hey, Vince?" He turned to me, brows raised. "Thanks for everything. I hope I don't let you down."

"Birdie, I have a feeling you could never let me down."

I closed the door, grateful for the reassurance. I grabbed a pair of pajamas from my suitcase, washed my face, and a few minutes later was sound asleep under the fluffy white duvet.

CHAPTER 7
BIRDIE

There was a knock on the door. I flipped over to look at the alarm clock on my nightstand to see what time it was and why someone was knocking at my apartment. When I opened my eyes, I didn't recognize anything. I shot straight up, heart racing, and looked to my right as a short, stout woman walked through the white double doors.

Oh, right. I'm in Wexstone. I flew here yesterday. I took a deep breath as my heart rate slowed.

"Good morning, Ms. Hamilton," the woman greeted as she pulled back the floor-to-ceiling drapes that ran the length of the room.

"Good morning," I greeted as I rubbed sleep out of my eyes, still trying to get my bearings.

"Breakfast will be served downstairs in the dining room in an hour. Would you like me to have any tea sent up while we get you ready?"

"Um, we?" I questioned.

"Yes, miss. I'm Sonya, your maid, and I can start the shower or run you a bath if you'd like. Or if you'd rather wait, I can go ahead and lay out the clothes you'll wear for breakfast. Whatever your morning routine is, let me know and I can help get you started."

My maid? Many of my friends growing up had cleaning ladies that came to their house once a week, something my own family could never afford. And now the idea of having my own personal attendant made my head spin. *It's too early for this. I need coffee.*

Sonya looked at me with big, round eyes, waiting for me to respond to her.

"I would love a cup of coffee if you have any, thank you."

"Right away, love," she answered as she hurried out the door.

I made my way to the ensuite and stopped in my tracks after taking a step in. I had been so exhausted the night before that I had failed to properly take in the room when I washed my face before bed. This wasn't a bathroom, it was a hotel. I was sure that they ran a high-end spa out of here on the weekends or something.

To my right, a marble vanity ran along what had to be a fifteen-foot wall, and to my left was the largest shower I had ever seen. I counted four shower heads pointing in every possible direction, and the bathtub that sat next to it looked like you could swim in it. What caught my eye next was the fireplace on the far back wall. *A fireplace?! In a* bathroom?! A girl could really get used to this.

After seeing to my needs, I washed my hands and heard a knock on the bathroom door.

"Come in," I called.

Sonya entered, carrying a tray filled with an assortment of

tiny serving bowls and pitchers with sugar cubes, cream, honey, milk, and a French press full of dark liquid gold.

"Here you go, miss."

"Thank you, Sonya. And please, call me Birdie." I took the delicate coffee cup and the saucer it sat on and filled it to the top with coffee and cream.

"I can't do that, miss," she replied, looking nervous.

"No, seriously. Please just call me Birdie. You don't have to be formal with me."

"Thank you for the offer, but I don't think Lord Alexander would be very happy if he caught on that I was being informal with you."

I cocked my head. I was already out of my comfort zone being waited on by household staff. I was used to being the one serving. But the fact that Sonya didn't feel like she would be allowed to call me by my name?

"Is Lord Alexander nice to you? Is he good to the staff?" The questions tumbled out of my mouth before I could stop myself, but I didn't think I could stomach staying here if the staff was afraid of Bronson. Vince was a nice guy; Sam's bullshit meter was never wrong, so I knew that she would have told me if something felt off with him. But Bronson was so uptight and close-lipped that I had to ask.

"Oh dear, yes! The Alexanders are wonderful employers and a lovely family. I couldn't have asked for a better house to serve, other than perhaps the royal family."

Well, that was something, at least. Sonya glanced at me, spotting the lingering questions in my eyes. After a beat, she continued.

"King Leroy's father, Francis, set into place a number of laws protecting household staff and domestic workers. They say it was because his childhood love was a maid in the palace, but no one can confirm if that's true or not. Either way, he made sure we would be given the protections that many of us had lacked before then, things like a proper wage and time off. In that way, I believe, we are quite a bit ahead of the United States, yes?"

"By about a mile," I answered ruefully.

"I have worked for the Alexanders for most of my adult life—in fact, I was even there when each of the boys was born. My own sons were raised on these grounds and are now attending university themselves. I expect I will retire soon; Lord and Mr. Alexander have both assured me that I have a home here for as long as I would like one. Perhaps I will take them up on that offer, perhaps I will use my savings to buy a small flat in the city. Only time will tell."

"I think that's beautiful, Sonya. Thank you for your service to the house and to me," I said as I lightly squeezed her forearm. "How much time do I have to get ready for breakfast?"

She glanced at her watch. "About fifteen minutes. Lord Alexander is already waiting."

Oh geez. I'll never hear the end of it if I'm late.

I quickly brushed my teeth, threw my hair into a knot on the top of my head, changed out of my comfy pajamas into a pair of black leggings and a loose cable-knit sweater, and dashed down the stairs. I realized once I got to the bottom of the staircase that I had no idea where I was going.

"Good morning." Vince was walking toward me from the hall to my right.

"Good morning. I'm glad to see you. I have no idea how to get to the dining room."

"I figured so. That's why I was coming to wait by the staircase for you. It's this way."

We walked down the corridor lined with paintings of landscapes and military battles. I could only assume they had some meaning to the family and the events that led this house to greatness. Vince opened the dark wood door to the dining room, where Bronson sat at the head of the table.

"Lord Alexander," I greeted, inclining my head toward him. I decided I would play Bronson's game and display all the lessons he had instructed me in yesterday. What better way to practice than at the breakfast table with Lord Stick-Up-His-Butt.

After sitting at the beautiful mahogany table, I placed an ironed linen napkin into my lap and scanned the trays of sweet breakfast pastries, bowls of fruit, scrambled eggs, roasted potatoes, and thick slices of bacon. I knew I would have to pace myself here if this was going to be the normal at every meal.

"Good morning, Ms. Hamilton. How was your stay last night?" Bronson inquired, sipping a cup of tea.

"Wonderful. Thank you," I smiled. "Is there an agenda today?"

"Yes, there is. Tonight is the welcoming gala, so Clarence and his staff will be here precisely at five and twenty past three p.m."

Of course he'd even be formal when telling me the time. I swallowed back a laugh. "Sounds delightful."

"Are you ready for tonight?" Vince asked as he scooped a few spoonfuls of eggs onto the porcelain plate in front of him.

"I'm nervous, but I'm ready. It'll be nice to see Oliver again."

"*Prince* Oliver," said Bronson.

"Shit. You're right. I'm sorry."

Bronson closed his eyes and then set his thumb and forefinger on the bridge of his nose. "And please do not curse in front of His Royal Highness or any other member of the royal family."

Vince let out a small chuckle.

Good grief. I've got to make sure that I'm on my game tonight. Prince Oliver. Your Royal Highness. No handshaking. Curtsy. For the love of God, don't swear. I guessed showing Bronson everything I learned yesterday was a bust.

"I think it would be best if you and Vincent took the rest of the morning to review and practice your curtsy. I will have Sonya fetch you once Clarence arrives." Bronson took a final sip of his tea, stood, and walked out the door without another word. He hadn't touched any food.

The air returned to the room once Bronson was gone, allowing Vince and I to make comfortable small talk as we ate our breakfast.

"Once you're done eating, we can meet in the sunroom at the back of the manor. I think you'll love it. Sonya will be waiting outside the door and can show you where to go. Please, take your time." Vince stood and left out the same door as Bronson had.

With both of them gone, any attempt to be ladylike was out the window. I finished scarfing down a cherry Danish, two slices of bacon, half a grapefruit, and eggs drenched in syrup— a habit I had picked up as a child that thoroughly grossed Sam out. After flying yesterday and all of the nerves, my appetite had come back with vengeance.

Once I was done eating, I wiped my mouth and stepped out into the hall. True to Vince's word, Sonya was there waiting.

"Right this way, dear."

"Thank you, Sonya." I smiled and followed her down the long hall to the back of the manor. We passed several doors that led to God-knew-where, as well as more paintings and sculptures. As we reached the back of the house, I was met with the most breathtaking view.

Like everything else in the manor, the sunroom was enormous and immediately became my favorite spot in the house. The three outer walls were made of glass and overlooked a frozen river snaking through a snow-covered valley, a towering mountain visible in the distance. It was like stepping into a postcard.

At the back wall, a fire roared in the brick fireplace, which was flanked by two plush armchairs. There was already a tray of tea on the pedestal end table between the chairs.

Behind me, Vince asked, "What do you think?"

"I think I'm actually speechless."

"That does seem unusual for you."

I gave him a playful shove and rolled my eyes. He just chuckled and walked over to an armchair.

"Okay, let's do this," he said as he clapped his hands together.

After hours of being quizzed by Vince and practicing my curtsy, my thighs and calves were on fire. I would have thought that after years of ice skating and countless mornings in the barre studio that I would have the perfect curtsy and my legs could endure an hour of practice. *Forget Jane Fonda, nobility should have their own workout DVD.* I could barely walk up the stairs to my room to shower before the entire glam squad made their appearance.

After a late lunch and the best shower of my life—*How will I ever go back to one measly shower head?*—all hopes for a nap to stave off the jet lag were dashed by Clarence's minions as they bobby pinned my hair into a low chignon at the base of my neck.

Another assistant painstakingly applied feathery false lashes and a deep mauve lipstick as the last one filed and painted my nails. Once they were done, I stepped into a floor-length cobalt-blue gown. I loved this dress. The satin hugged my curves in all the right places and the sweetheart neckline accentuated my breasts without making them the star of the show. It was classy, yet sexy. It felt just like me.

"How do I look?" I asked, turning to Vince and Bronson as they entered the room.

"Breathtaking," Vince said as Bronson responded with, "Acceptable."

"Thank you for all of your hard work today," I said to the team who had spent hours measuring, fixing, and sewing me into the gorgeous dress.

As I looked at myself in the floor-length mirror, an emotion that I hadn't felt in a long time came washing over me: I was beautiful. I had avoided prom and other formal dances growing up because my family never had the money. I preferred to pretend that school dances were too cliché to attend, turning down any boys who asked me. I never imagined that this would be my first time wearing a formal gown.

The thought that I could see myself this way and be dressed in couture for the rest of my life if I married Prince Oliver was fleeting, but it still made me feel...well, that wasn't worth pondering on right then. *Soak this in. Enjoy this experience.*

———

The 1950s Rolls-Royce Silver Cloud was warm but a little cramped as Carter, the Alexander family's driver, drove Vince, Bronson, and me to the palace. Wexstone's countryside continued to awe me. I hoped the wonder of this country would never wear off.

We took one last turn around a snow-covered mountain and onto a straight stretch of road as the palace came into view.

Large, black wrought-iron gates opened to an expansive

drive leading to the four-story building. Countless windows lined the stone walls. Pristine snow covered the lawn, not marred by even a single footprint. Crystal-clear water bubbled out of an alabaster fountain, which had to be heated. It was exactly what little girls and boys dreamed of when thinking of far-off kingdoms and Prince Charming.

My stomach flipped at the thought of seeing Prince Oliver and Knox again. I needed to see some familiar faces to remind myself that this was real and not some fantasy I had stumbled upon.

I wondered what it was like for the prince to grow up in the palace. Did he run the halls and play hide and seek? Did he have a favorite corner to read in? What was dinner like? Did they sit at a large table that could hold dozens of guests or did they dine as a family in a private dining room?

And Knox. Did he live here as well? Did he ever feel half as nervous as I was when he approached the palace? *The man is so cocky, he probably never feels nervous about anything.*

Bronson interrupted my thoughts. "Vincent told me he reviewed the members of the royal family with you. I trust he discussed your fellow contestants as well?" I didn't miss the doubt in his voice that belied his use of the word "trust."

"Yes, he did," I assured. "Let's see. There's Mellie Schneider —she's a journalist. Sabine Thorne is an environmentalist, right?" Vince nodded encouragingly. I continued. "Adelaide Levy is a primary-school teacher. Cora Maximo is a baker. Three of the women are from titled families: Gemma Rousseau-Wu, Ginny Wu-Murphy, and Renata..." I trailed off, unable to remember her last name.

"Raines. Yes. That will do." Bronson's voice was clipped as he dismissed the conversation.

The car came to a stop, and I took one final deep breath. This was happening. It was go time.

Vince reached over and gave my hand a light squeeze. "You're going to do amazingly," he said reassuringly.

"I hope so. I'm a little nervous."

"What's there to be nervous about? It's just your entire reputation and our entire house name at stake," Bronson quipped dryly.

I turned to look at him over my shoulder. "Exactly, what's there to lose, right?" I replied in a sugary voice.

Bronson scowled and shook his head as he ran his hands over his face. I resisted the urge to say, "Watch out, your face might get stuck like that."

"I'm sorry, but you walked right into that," I said instead. "I promise that's my last sarcastic comment of the night." *Out loud. To you.* I smiled.

Our car crept forward as those in front of us let out their passengers and turned back down the drive. A red carpet lined the walkway to the palace's front doors. What looked like a hundred reporters and paparazzi swarmed each side of the carpet, snapping photos and calling out questions. Vince and Bronson had prepared me for their presence, but seeing them made me swallow hard.

"Just remember," Vince said softly, "if you don't want to answer a question..."

"No comment," I finished.

"Exactly. Here we go."

Cameras flashed and snapped as the car door opened. I pulled my faux-fur shawl around my shoulders and stepped onto the carpet.

A breeze hit as I smoothed my dress out. It was ungodly cold in Wexstone—the type of cold I was used to from Michigan winters, but still often made me wish I lived on a beach instead. I drew the shawl tighter as I looked up at the palace.

I didn't have much time to take in its beauty before I was hit by a torrent of questions.

"Who are you wearing?"

"Is this your first time in Wexstone?"

"How did you meet His Royal Highness?"

"Have you been sleeping with the prince?"

"What makes you fit to be our queen?"

I was shocked by some of the questions. *These reporters really don't hold back, do they?* I turned to look for Vince but couldn't see him through the camera flashes.

I turned back and continued to walk straight down the red carpet. It was like a map, guiding me to where I needed to go. I could see the large opening of the palace doors just ahead. To my surprise, I spotted Knox just inside. My breath caught in my throat. His broad frame looked delectable in his crisp black tuxedo. It was a vast difference from the flannel shirt and glasses he had been wearing in New York. The Clark Kent vibe was undeniably sexy.

The relentless questions and snap of cameras brought me back to reality. "Is this your first time in Wexstone?" one reporter repeated as she shoved a tiny microphone in my face.

I smiled. "Yes, it is."

"How have you liked it so far?"

"It's been wonderful. The country is beautiful." These questions weren't so bad. It felt like talking to someone in line at the coffee shop.

"Where in America are you from?" another reporter shouted.

"I live in New York City." I felt a bit of pride rise in my chest.

"Is it true that when you first arrived, you were stopped at customs?"

Oh fuck. "Um, yes, that's true." I felt my smile start to falter but pasted it back into place. Maybe they wouldn't push any further on this.

"Why, Ms. Hamilton?"

"They uh...they thought they spotted something in my bag." *Shit.* I shouldn't have said that. This was definitely a "no comment" line of questioning. I started to laugh nervously, my default for awkward situations.

"What exactly did they find?" *Shit, shit, fuck, shit. I can't answer that! This is humiliating. But if I say "no comment" now, that will be even more suspicious.*

A large, warm hand wrapped tightly around my elbow and pulled me toward the door.

"No comment," Knox's deep voice sternly told the reporter, who immediately backed off, looking for someone else to interrogate.

I looked up and was met with those bright blue eyes and the scent of pine and mint.

Once we had passed the throng of reporters, Knox rested my arm in the crook of his elbow and led me the rest of the way up the red carpet. As we climbed the marble steps, I couldn't help but notice the way the tuxedo jacked hugged his biceps and the way the pants grazed his toned thighs. I caught a glimpse of his tattoos peeking out from the cuff of his shirt as he shook hands with the man taking coats and shawls inside the door. I tried not to think of his boxer-briefed ass in my tiny New York kitchen.

I handed off my shawl to the man and thanked him. I held onto my small clutch with all my might, as if the scraps of fabric could keep me from floating away.

"Thank you for saving me back there."

"Don't mention it," Knox growled. "They're vultures."

"With all of the prepping we did today on how to handle a

herd of hungry paparazzi, that question wasn't exactly on the list," I muttered.

I caught a slight smile roll across Knox's face. I wondered if he knew why I had been pulled aside by customs, though the smile suggested that he must. I hoped I wasn't blushing too much.

The foyer of the palace had smooth white limestone floors with the same stone forming the walls. The ceiling was a large glass dome, through which you could see the stars.

"What did you think of the red carpet?" Vince asked as he passed off his coat and made his way toward Knox and me.

I cleared my throat. "It was something, that's for sure," I replied.

Bronson joined us. "And just why did Mr. Henderson have to come and escort you inside?" he inquired stuffily as he swiped his hands over his tuxedo jacket, checking for lint.

I paused. "It seemed prudent to keep everyone moving along, Lord Alexander," Knox cut in before I could spill out the reporter's line of questioning.

Thank you, I mouthed to him. I didn't know if Vince had told Bronson about my customs fiasco, though I had a feeling I would have already gotten an earful about it if he had. Now did not seem like the time or place to give him a heart attack about it. That was for another day.

"Let's proceed to the dining hall, shall we?" Vince offered his elbow for me to loop my arm through.

As Vince escorted me down the hall, I was taken aback by the paintings that lined the wall. Four years studying art history in undergrad and a master's degree in curatorial studies—never mind that I had yet to use said degree since graduating three years prior—had given me a sharp eye for fine art, and I could have sworn I spotted a Rembrandt. I shook my head. *Can that be right? An original Rembrandt? I guess we are in a royal palace, so anything is possible.*

I made a mental note to come back and look later. This wasn't the time to marvel. *Although I would give my left tit to skip this gala and look at the art instead.*

At the end of the hallway, we turned right into the spacious dining hall. The room was absolutely sumptuous with high vaulted ceilings, chandeliers dripping in crystals, and walls covered in champagne damask. It would take me days to recover from *fabric* on the *walls.*

A string quartet sat against the farthest wall, playing a classical rendition of "Bad Guy" by Billie Eilish. *Goddamn, what is this, Bridgerton?* Round tables draped in white linen and topped with gold plates surrounded a shining dance floor. No one sat in the navy-blue chairs pushed into the tables.

Along the wall opposite the musicians, a long, polished wood table sat on a platform raised a foot above the floor. Behind the table were six exquisite mahogany chairs, upholstered in navy velvet and accented with jewels of deep emerald and sapphire.

Vince gave my arm a gentle squeeze. "I'll go get us drinks." He casually wove his way through the attendees. Bronson had already been pulled aside by two older gentlemen.

As the room filled, my outsider status became harder to ignore. It seemed like everyone had *someone* to talk to. I knew I should mingle, but my nerves were really getting the best of me. I often felt out of place growing up, but somehow this was different. I was a ballgown-clad fish out of water.

I scanned the room, hoping to catch sight of Chauncey or Tej. I spotted Bronson in a corner, deep in conversation with the two men. He seemed to have relaxed a bit. He was comfortable in the royal court and knew his place. *Lucky him.*

Vince, meanwhile, had been waylaid by a group of middle-aged women and was clearly in his own element. His body language indicated that he was telling a lively story, and the women were enthralled, laughing along with him as he spoke.

A few feet away, a group of men in their mid-to-late fifties were deep in conversation. Nearby, a cluster of women around my age made polite small talk. I wondered who they might be and if they were my fellow contestants. I wished Vince had shown me pictures of tonight's guests during our earlier rundown to better prepare me. Proper etiquette and knowing how to curtsy would only get me so far.

"It's all a little bit overwhelming at first, isn't it?" I nearly jumped out of my skin at the voice just beside me.

"Jesus Christ, Knox! You scared me. I didn't even see you come up." I placed my hand over my rapidly beating heart.

"Sorry," he replied wryly. "Next time, I'll have Richmond, our Herald of Arms, announce my arrival."

I rolled my eyes, hoping Bronson wouldn't spot me doing so. "A simple clearing of the throat would suffice." I turned toward him. "So, what was it like growing up here in Wexstone?"

Knox's jaw tightened as he mulled the question over. "It was fine. Definitely different from America. But not bad."

"I don't imagine it would be. It's beautiful from what I've seen so far." I paused. "You wouldn't happen to know of any secret hiding places or escape routes I could use if I decided to run away, would you?"

He let out a soft, deep chuckle, relaxing. "Yeah, I know a few."

My stomach flipped at the sound of his laugh. I took a good look at him, admittedly the first time I had really studied him since our rendezvous in the closet. His haircut was fresh and precise. His beard was trimmed to a neat, clean stubble, showcasing a square jaw that probably made women leave snail trails behind them when they walked by.

Get it together, Birdie, you're not here to swoon over Broody Knox! Your make-out was just a game. You're here to fall in love with a prince and live happily ever after and all that fairytale shit.

I cleared my throat, trying to clear my head along with it. "So...when does this shindig start?" I asked, mostly to distract myself from thinking about the way Knox had picked me up in the closet.

Knox looked at his watch. "The royal family should be arriving in about five minutes. Do you want to get a drink?"

"Yes, that would be great. Vince was getting me one, but he seems to have gotten intercepted." I nodded to where he was still holding court halfway across the room.

Knox chuckled as he raised his hand, and a server hurried over with a tray of champagne.

"Thank you, Jefferson," Knox said as he handed me a glass and took another for himself.

"Wow. Do you know the names of all of the staff?" I asked, taking a sip and luxuriating in the feel of the bubbles as they danced on my tongue.

"Yes. I like to—"

"Well, I see they continue to let anyone come to these parties," said a shrill voice from behind us.

I turned to see a woman with fiery red hair wearing a forest-green evening gown approaching us, a glass of champagne in hand. She took a bite out of a strawberry that had been perched on the rim of her glass and tossed the stem onto a passing server's tray.

"Renata." Knox nodded curtly. So *this* was Renata Raines.

"Always a polite gentleman," she said with a dramatic eye roll. "Oh, I see you've brought a date with you this time."

"She's not my date. This is Bernadette Hamilton. She's a suitor for Prince Oliver."

Renata's eyes narrowed in on me like a heat-seeking missile. "*You're* the American?" she asked, sounding as if her mouth was suddenly full of bile.

"Hi, it's nice to meet you," I said as sweetly as I could muster. I started to offer my hand but quickly thought twice about it. No handshaking tonight.

"You have to be kidding me. I knew it had to be some sort of joke when I heard they were bringing in an American suitor, but I didn't think she'd look so plain."

CHAPTER 8
BIRDIE

It took everything in me not to make a face at Renata. Instead, I plastered on a smile and gave myself a pep talk. *You're not plain, you're just not royal-court fancy. You're proud to be an American, damnit. USA! USA! USA!* When I told this story to my future grandchildren, this woman was clearly going to be the villain.

"I guess it only makes sense that the two of you would be buddy-buddy, then," Renata said, looking down her nose at Knox and me as she took a sip of her champagne. She lowered her voice, leaning toward me. "Look, Bernadette. I don't know what you thought would happen coming here, but what I do know is that I am the next queen and I will do anything to make it happen. Do you understand?"

I mimicked her movement, whispering conspiratorially, "You have a bit of strawberry stuck in your teeth."

Renata's face turned about ten shades of red as she huffed back and almost ran out of the ballroom.

Suppressing a laugh, I turned back to Knox. "Please tell me the other suitors aren't as bad as her."

Knox stared at me, dumbfounded. "That was the best thing I've ever seen."

"What? Really?"

"No one ever stands up to her. They're all too afraid." He smiled broadly, one of the first true smiles I had seen from him. My stomach gave a small flip. "I think you're going to do well here."

"Oh, that was nothing," I said, waving my hand. "She's just a mean girl."

"That she is. She's been a pain in my ass ever since I can remember."

"Has her family always been a part of the court?"

"For centuries. They were pretty much a breeding house for royal suitors, which is why she thinks she's a shoo-in. Little does she realize, Oliver can't stand her. He's nice to her because he has to be, but he has always seen right through her fake smile and pleasantries."

His words made a small part of me relax a bit. I had gotten the impression in New York that Prince Oliver was more than just a pretty face, but the confirmation that he seemed to be a good judge of character as well was reassuring.

"Any chance you could give me the inside scoop on the family before I meet them?" I asked. "Vince went over a bit of their history with me, but I bet you can tell me more than that since you know them so well."

Knox observed me as he sipped his drink. I wondered if he was trying to decide how much he could or should divulge; he was protective of his family, I knew that much already.

He cleared his throat. "Well. You've met Oliver. He was second in line behind his brother, Xavier. When he abdicated,

Oliver became the Crown Prince. So, you know, here we are." He gestured around us. "Then there's Rosalind. She's eleven and hates these types of events. People tend to either overlook her since she's so young, or they baby talk to her and ask asinine questions."

"And Xavier abdicated because he didn't want to settle down?" I asked, clarifying.

Knox had such a stoic look on his face at all times. There were times when emotion would flash across it, but you had to watch because it was always quick to disappear. This was one of those moments. I saw a flash of anger, maybe annoyance, cross his eyes, there and gone within a second.

"Yeah, something like that."

"Hmm." I took a drink of champagne. "Can you tell me anything about his parents? Typically when I've dated someone, I have a little more background about their family and it's not as formal. I feel like I'm in over my head here." I didn't want to sound desperate, but that was exactly how I was beginning to feel.

"The Courtwrights have sat on the throne for hundreds of years. They take being sovereign very seriously and want someone for Oliver who will take it just as seriously. They love their country and the people they rule and want to make sure Oliver is set up for success."

"No pressure."

Knox let a smile roll across his face. "No pressure. They are nice people who care. If you also care and show interest in their country and their son, I think you'll do just fine."

"Sounds easy enough." I hoped that was true.

As the words left my mouth, the string quartet stopped playing. I looked around, searching for the reason why.

Knox leaned down. "Here we go," he whispered in my ear

as he left my side, disappearing across the room. Guests gathered toward the center of the space, leaving a wide path on either side of the ornately carved golden doors. Vince walked into my line of sight and nodded his head for me to follow him. I made my way to where everyone was gathered and took my place between Vince and Bronson.

The quartet began softly playing a song I hadn't heard before. As I looked around, I saw a few of the guests, including Vince, mouthing words I couldn't hear. I could only assume this must be their national anthem.

The doors opened, ushering in the royal family of Wexstone. The king and queen entered first, their hands clasped.

King Leroy was a handsome man; I could see where Prince Oliver got his chiseled jaw and light eyes. His salt-and-pepper hair was more salt than pepper these days, but he pulled it off well. He was tall and barrel chested, still in great shape for a man in his sixties. His ramrod-straight spine and precise movements indicated that he had been a military man; he carried himself well and with authority.

Queen Isobel had clearly been a knockout in her youth—hell, she was still a knockout. Her hair was twisted into an intricate updo upon which sat a glimmering crown. The sapphires and emeralds glittered against her rich, red hair as her white gown flowed behind her on a phantom wind. I suddenly understood why people were infatuated with royalty; there truly was an air of something special about them.

The king and queen continued their procession into the room. As they passed, men bowed, and women curtsied. I made a mental note to thank Vince and Bronson (*well, maybe just Vince—I wouldn't want Bronson to let it go to his head*) for making me practice my curtsy earlier.

Prince Oliver followed just behind his parents. He looked so prestigious in his tuxedo and royal blue sash hung with at least a dozen different medals. I wondered if they weighed heavily on his shoulders.

There was a man walking beside Prince Oliver who I assumed must be his older brother, Xavier. I could certainly understand why this man had women and men falling over themselves. He had a full head of copper hair like his mother's and a beard that covered the same strong jaw that I saw on his father. The sash across his chest held more medals than Prince Oliver's and was a deep green.

But what took me aback were the tattoos covering his hands and neck. Prince Oliver was the only royal I had seen in person before now, but I didn't think most would find it acceptable for a prince to have so many visible tattoos. Xavier carried himself with an air of defiance. The papers were right: he did look like a rebel.

The royal family moved closer to our end of the line. My nerves set in as I mentally walked through my curtsy. My legs started to tingle. Was this normal or was I about to keel over? *It's just nerves. It's just nerves. You're fine, this is fine. Just bend at the knee. The lower you go, the more respect you're showing. Get it together, Birdie, you spent years ice skating competitively. This is simple. You've got this.*

The procession was now in front of us and Bronson bent at the waist. Forget stuffy and stiff—the man looked like he did yoga five days a week with his swift, flexible bow.

I reached for the sides of my gown, pulling them out so I wouldn't step or fall on them. I dipped my head, curtsying as low as I could. I needed the royal family and the people of Wexstone to see how much I respected them.

As they passed by, I made eye contact with Prince Oliver and swore that I saw his cheek raise in a slight smile. Dang, was he really that happy that I was here?

Princess Rosalind and Queen Mother Evelyn walked side

by side just behind the princes. Princess Rosalind looked beautiful in champagne tulle and silk. She held herself so well for her age; you could she had been doing this for her entire life. The smile pasted on her face didn't quite reach her eyes, though.

A *tap, tap, tap* caught my attention, and I raised my eyes a bit to see Queen Mother Evelyn walking by with her cane, on top of which sat a large onyx stone. It caught the light, contrasting with her silver dress.

Just as my curtsy was starting to wane, the guests in the receiving line stood to their full height like a wave at a stadium game. I followed the rest of the guests' gazes to see that the royal family had taken their places at the head table.

As they sat, the guests transitioned to their own seats. I followed suit, walking close behind Vince and Bronson as they led us to a table. I tried not to feel overwhelmed by the fine china and the amount of cutlery laid before me as Vince pulled out my chair. I thought of the scene in *Titanic* where Kathy Bates's character tells Leo DiCaprio's Jack to "start from the outside and work your way in" with the cutlery and said a quick prayer of thanks for my childhood obsession with that movie.

"Bernadette, may I introduce you to Lord Collins and Lady Laurel of House Lewellen," Vince motioned to the couple sitting to his right. "They are very involved in the lumber production and conservation here in Wexstone."

"It is a pleasure to meet you both," I smiled, inclining my head toward them.

"And you. How are you liking Wexstone so far?" Lord Collins asked.

"It's absolutely beautiful. I am so happy to be here."

"This must be a culture shock compared to New York," Lady Laurel said kindly.

"That's an understatement," I laughed. "This is definitely a once-in-a-lifetime experience."

————

After finishing the five-course meal, I wasn't sure if I could stand, let alone dance along with the rest of the young guests now relocating to the center of the room. As I was trying to determine my next move, I felt a tap on my shoulder.

"May I sit down?"

I knew that voice. I looked up to find Prince Oliver standing with his hand on the back of my chair.

"Do you really need permission, Your Royal Highness?" I asked, winking.

"I always ask for permission," he winked back.

I nodded my head to Bronson's now-empty seat on my left. "How is your night going?" I inquired as he sat.

"Quite well, aside from suffocating in this tux."

Suffocating, suffocatingly handsome, same thing.

"I get that. After that meal, I'm not sure I could even walk right now."

"That's a pity. I actually came over here to ask if you'd like to dance." Prince Oliver smiled, laughter in his eyes.

"Well, who am I to deny the Crown Prince of Wexstone a dance?"

He stood, holding out his hand to help me up, then leading me to the dance floor. As we walked, he nodded and made brief pleasantries with the people we passed.

As we joined the other dancing couples, the quartet transitioned into a cover of "Kids" by MGMT. The prince set his right hand on the small of my back and took my own hand in his left. As we moved, I felt eyes on me. Not just one set, but the entire room. *Do. Not. Trip. Don't embarrass yourself right now.*

"How was your flight from New York? Did you have any problems getting here?" the prince asked.

Oh, you mean other than getting stopped by customs for my vibrator?

"Nope. No problems at all."

"And the Alexanders have been treating you well?"

"Absolutely. Their house is beautiful, and they've been very generous."

"Good. I had no doubt about Vince, but Bronson can be a bit..." He trailed off.

"Direct? Abrasive?"

"Yes. Quite." He laughed heartily.

I didn't miss the few female heads that shot our way at his deep laugh. God, was this how it was going to be the entire time? Every little sign of happiness or the slightest indication that he was making a connection with someone, and the vultures would be there watching, waiting to jump in and see what made the prince happy? It was so vastly different from our weekend in New York.

Prince Oliver twirled me around the dance floor, both of us enjoying the movements and laughing as he spun me to and from his body. A crescendo marked the end of the song.

"I think you have a line forming for the next dance," I said as I peeked around his large frame to spot the gaggle of women forming a border at the edge of the floor. Their eyes glistened with hope and lust.

"Geez," Prince Oliver huffed under his breath. "I need a drink after that dancing though. I suppose they'll have to wait." He smiled conspiratorially as we meandered to the back wall. A server passed by with yet another tray of champagne. Prince Oliver took two flutes, handing me one.

"Thank you," I said as I took the glass. "So, growing up here in the palace must have been incredible. I can only imagine what this place must look like all decked out for the holidays."

"You won't have to imagine for much longer. The staff and my mother will start decorating soon. She loves when it all goes up. My father tries to hold her off until the end of November, but he gets less successful with each passing year."

I laughed even as my heart ached. "My mom was the same way. She would have kept the tree up all year round if my dad would have let her."

"Would have?" His forehead scrunched inquisitively at my use of the past tense.

"Ollie! Oh, there you are," a shrill voice whined.

The prince turned stiffly. "Renata," he said, all the warmth leaving his voice.

"I've been looking for you since dinner. You owe me a dance. You know how I *love* to waltz." Renata clutched his arm like she was clinging to a life raft.

"Of course. I'm just in the middle of a conversation with Bernadette at the moment. I will come find you in a bit." Oliver motioned toward me.

"Oh, I'm so sorry, I didn't see you standing there," Renata said, sugary sweetness in her voice and the fakest smile I had ever seen plastered to her face. "The girl from America, right? It's so exciting to have you here. If you need anything, please let me know. I would love to help you while you're here."

It took everything in me not to roll my eyes at her. This bitch was as fake as her lip injections.

"Ok, well, I'll let you two finish your little chat. Ollie, do come find me when you're done."

As Renata crossed in front of Prince Oliver and me, I caught an evil grin sliding over her face just as she twisted her wrist and emptied her glass of red wine down my front. She threw herself into Prince Oliver, grabbing his arm again as if to steady herself.

"Good heavens!" exclaimed the prince.

"Ack!" I startled.

"Oopsie! I'm such a klutz. So accident prone!" Renata feigned embarrassment.

That trifling little bitch. Accident, my ass, I thought.

A staff member rushed over, a swath of cloth napkins in her hands. I wiped the wine from my chest but really needed to find a bathroom to clean up what had seeped down my cleavage and was now threatening the longevity of the tape holding my boobs in place. I tried to dab the wine from the bodice of my dress but made zero progress. I looked up at Prince Oliver.

"I'm so sorry. If you'll excuse me, I need to find the ladies' room and see if I can get this out."

"Of course. It's the first door on the right in the corridor," the prince answered, looking apologetic.

I excused myself and located the washroom, which held two stalls with thick wooden doors, across from which sat a large marble vanity. I turned on the sink and grabbed a hand towel from the neighboring basket, trying to remember if hot or cold water was better for removing stains. After wiping up the pool of wine from my cleavage, I started to rub at the large purple spot on the front of my gown.

"You really should dab at the stain. Rubbing it like that will just push it further into the fabric. Club soda can also help," a soft voice said from behind me.

I jumped, knocking over a bottle of hand soap on the counter. On a velvet settee next to the door sat a beautiful girl with soft, cornsilk hair. Her dress was a stunning lavender that fell loosely around her shoulders. I had been so flustered that I completely missed her when I came in.

"I'm so sorry, I didn't mean to scare you," she said, crossing the room.

"No, you're fine. I just didn't realize anyone else was in here. Thank you. I'll dab it and try to track down some club soda."

"Rough night?" she asked, handing me a fresh towel.

"It wasn't going too bad until that red-headed mean girl decided to dump her wine on me 'accidentally,'" I answered, placing air quotes around the word "accidentally."

"Ah, you must be talking about Renata." Her eyes flickered knowingly.

"Yep. That's the one." I rolled my eyes so hard I saw my brain.

"Here, let me help you." She took one of the towels and started dabbing at my dress. "I'm Adelaide, by the way." Another fellow suitor, though thankfully this one seemed far kinder than Renata.

"Hi Adelaide, I'm Bernadette. But please, call me Birdie."

"Oh, you're the American, right?" Her green eyes lit with excitement. "I mean, of course you are, with your accent. But, well, you know."

I knew exactly what she meant. "Yeah, that's me."

"What a way to welcome you to Wexstone and into this ridiculous 'competition.'" She rolled her eyes and grinned at me. "As if these things weren't awful enough to begin with, you add Renata and her puppets, Ginny and Gemma, into the mix. They're the absolute worst."

"Yeah, I'm starting to see that," I said with a sigh.

"They've always been atrocious human beings."

"I take it you've been around the royal court for a while?"

"Oh, no," she said, straightening up. "I'm not from a royal house, but yeah, I'm a part of all of...this." She waved her hand around, gesturing vaguely. "But I went to school with them when we were in primary. They were just as awful then. And part of the reason why I'm hiding out in the bathroom instead of mingling and talking to everyone out there." She sighed.

There was a knock at the door. Adelaide and I looked at each other like we had been caught doing something wrong. A second passed and we both started giggling. Adelaide walked to the door and opened it. It was Knox, holding a crystal glass filled with fizzy liquid.

"Ms. Hamilton? The prince sent me here with this, he thought it might help with the stain." He handed over the glass of club soda. "Ms. Levy." He nodded to Adelaide.

"Oh," I stammered as Adelaide took the cup, setting it on the countertop next to the sink. "Please tell him I said thank you so much." It truly was so thoughtful of him. Through all the chaos of the evening, he had thought to have Knox bring me this.

"You good?" he asked, nodding to my dress.

"Yeah, I'll be fine. It's just a little spill. Accidents happen, right?" I smiled, thinking of trying to get the tahini sauce out of his flannel shirt.

"Okay. If you need anything else, just let me know."

"Thank you." I waved as he turned to go.

Adelaide closed the door. "Wow, I wasn't aware the prince could think of someone else's needs once they were out of sight," she whispered in a smug tone.

"Ouch," I said. "Not a fan of Prince Oliver?"

"I'm sorry, I shouldn't have said that. He's not a bad guy. We just...have a history."

"Mmmm, yeah. I've been there before." I sensed there was more to the story, but didn't want to pry.

Adelaide helped me as we finished cleaning my dress. We got out as much of the wine as we could. The stain, at least, had changed from dark purple to navy blue.

"I think this is as good as it's going to get," Adelaide said, tilting her head as she took in our work. "I'm sorry."

"Girl, maybe this just gives me an excuse to leave. Honestly, my feet are killing me and as beautiful as it is, I'm ready to get out of this dress." I rolled my shoulders, feeling my back crack satisfyingly.

"Me too. I'm ready to take my bra off and get into my sweatpants." Adelaide giggled.

"That sounds like paradise right about now." I wiped up a few stray water droplets and threw the used towels into a basket below the vanity. "Thank you for your help, Adelaide. I really appreciate it. It was so nice to meet someone else here."

"I feel the same way. Maybe we can join forces and make it through this unscathed together." She winked.

I stepped out of the bathroom and spotted Vince leaning against the wall across the hallway, scrolling on his phone.

"Hey. Knox told me what happened. Are you okay?" he asked, pocketing his phone.

"I'm fine. Although I can't say the same thing about my dress. Clarence is going to have a cow."

Vince looked me up and down. A small smile crept across his face. "I can't take you anywhere, huh?" He smirked.

"It was nice to meet you, Birdie. I'll see you at the next event," Adelaide said as she moved toward to the ballroom.

"Vince, let's go home. I think I've had enough fun for one night."

"We'll need to go say goodbye to Oliver first." Vince winced. "Let's go find him."

"No need." Prince Oliver's voice carried from down the hall as he walked toward us. "I didn't see you return so I thought I'd check and see if you were all right."

"I'm fine. Although given the state of my dress, I may call it a night. That is, if it's okay with you?"

"Of course. I'm so sorry that happened, Birdie." Prince Oliver grimaced.

"It's not your fault; you have no need to apologize. Thank you for the wonderful night."

Vince said his goodbyes to Prince Oliver, and we made our way outside to the waiting car.

"What a night," I sighed as I leaned my head back on the headrest.

"And this was just the beginning." Vince laughed.

CHAPTER 9
KNOX

Nights like this one were exhausting. The walk from the palace to my cottage at the back of the grounds wasn't long, but my feet ached. I hated wearing dress shoes; I would rather be in hiking boots or trainers. I couldn't wait to get inside, strip off this stupid tie, shower, and climb into bed.

Snow had begun to fall, and I had forgotten my coat in Oliver's suite after getting ready. I rubbed my hands together, breathing on them to warm them up. Just a few more steps up the cobblestone walkway to my house and I'd be good.

I entered the code on the lock and waited for the soft *click*. The warm air hit my face as I opened the black-painted door, and my body instantly began to thaw. I knew better than to be outside at that time of night without a jacket, but for some reason, I was off my game. I couldn't put my finger on why. Maybe it was the whole competition surrounding Oliver that made me feel unsettled, or maybe it was just the pomp and circumstance of the gala. I hated being around large groups of people in general, but especially for formal events. I despised small talk with all of the ass kissers that surrounded the family. If it wasn't one person trying to push their agenda onto Leroy and Oliver, it was someone baby-talking Rosie. Infuriating.

I still couldn't believe that we were doing this. My not being blood may have spared me from being at the center of the circus, but Oliver was my family, and I wasn't going to leave him to the wolves. When I felt like I had lost everything, Oliver and his family were the ones who helped me sort out the pieces and figure out what I should carry into the future and what to leave behind.

Thundering paws trotted down the hallway as my beautiful boy, Eugene, barreled around the corner to greet me. As trained, he promptly sat, though he couldn't resist a whine as he waited for me to bend down to pet him.

Evelyn had gifted me the copper Vizsla puppy two Christmases prior, somehow knowing he was exactly what I needed: the most loyal companion. Although I always advised new visitors not to be fooled by his wide amber eyes: he was a spoiled fart machine.

"Hey, boy, what did you do tonight?"

Eugene answered me with a bark and a look toward the back door.

"Yeah, let's get you outside, because I'm ready for bed."

I walked over to unlock his dog door, Eugene running past me in a sprint. He dove outside, jumped off the porch, and pranced to his favorite peeing spot against one of the tall pine trees behind the house. After doing his business, the little stink ran in circles in the yard, trying his damnedest to eat the snowflakes as they fell from the sky.

I let him run off some of his energy before I opened the door, whistling and calling for him to come inside. As much as I loved this country, the winter months could be rough. My family moved here from Pennsylvania when I was ten, when my dad got a job teaching at the Royal College of Wexstone, and winters here were quite a bit colder than I remembered them being in the States. Right now, it had to be below zero—not the kind of weather Eugene needed to be gallivanting around in.

After locking the cover on the dog door, I wiped Eugene's paws, slid my shoes off, and undid that insufferable bow tie. I walked to the bedroom just off the kitchen and chucked my tux into the chair in the corner of the room. I'd hang it up later—I just didn't have the energy right then.

After pulling on my favorite gray sweats, I headed to the kitchen and grabbed a glass from the cupboard. The gala had been a lot. I thought I had prepared myself for Birdie being in Wexstone and courting Oliver, but the sight of her in that blue dress had nearly brought me to my knees. And the way her eyes were glued to Oliver's as they laughed and spun their way around the dance floor had flooded me with a level of envy I had never felt before.

I was going to need a lot of whiskey to get me through this.

Pouring a finger of the amber liquid, I downed it in one swig, relishing the burn as it slid down my throat. I gazed at the bottle, thinking of how it was the same whiskey that had gotten us into this whole mess in the first place.

———

A fire blazed in the fireplace as we sat in Oliver's study. Chauncey handed each of us a glass of Wexstone Original Whiskey before sitting next to me on the soft leather sofa that mirrored the one where Oliver, Tej, and Vince sat.

"I can't believe he abdicated," Vince mumbled as he stared into the fire.

Xavier had dropped the announcement that morning during a family meeting, before boarding a plane to God-knew-where and leaving the rest of us to deal with the aftermath.

"I can," Oliver responded bitterly. "He hates this place. And most days I'm pretty sure he hates this family."

"He doesn't hate our family," I said.

"He must if he's chosen to do this." Oliver downed the whiskey, grabbed the bottle from the coffee table, and poured another two fingers.

"He doesn't hate this family," I affirmed. While Xavier had fucked over everyone by choosing to abdicate, I knew for a fact he didn't hate his family. In truth, I suspected that he had done it out of love for his family and his country. He likely thought he was doing everyone a favor.

"What does this mean for you, Oliver?" Tej asked.

"I'll be crowned king and will have six months from my coronation to get married, or the seat goes to Rosalind. If that were to happen, my parents or I would have to serve as regent until she turns eighteen. And once she comes of age, she will be in the same spot as I am, looking for someone to marry—except at eighteen instead of thirty. I refuse to let that happen to her. I could never do that to her." He shook his head despondently.

"Wow. Fuck these old-school laws, right?" Vince spat.

"Honestly, fuck everything." Oliver took another drink of whiskey. "How do I even go about finding a wife? Nearly every woman I've ever been with has been more interested in the fact that I'm a prince than in me as a human being."

"Maybe you should get on one of those dating apps and see if there are any eligible women." Chauncey laughed. His eyes were glazed and his words slurred slightly.

"Absolutely not." I cut him off before they could take that idiotic idea and run with it. "This family—this country—has gotten enough awful press for the time being thanks to Xavier's fucking

antics. We don't need it to get out that Prince Oliver is on some trashy swipe-right app. God, the media would eat that up."

Oliver gave me a nod of thanks, and we all sat in the quiet for a moment with nothing but the fire crackling and the ice knocking against the glasses as we drank. Suddenly, Vince shot to his feet like something bit him.

"I've got it!" The rest of us shared puzzled glances. "You know I've been seeing that girl, Lauren? She's been making me watch this stupid American show when I go over to her house on Tuesdays," he explained breathlessly. "There is one guy and like, two dozen girls. They go on dates as a group and sometimes one on one. At the end of each episode, he hands out these roses and then at the end of the season there are like, a few girls left, and he chooses which one he wants to propose to."

"The Bachelor?" I asked incredulously.

"Yeah, he's a bachelor, obviously. And most of the girls are single, but I guess sometimes one of the girls will have a boyfriend at home."

"No, you idiot, the show is called The Bachelor.*" My mom and her friends used to have watch parties where they would crowd onto the couch, eating snacks and yelling at the TV like it was a sporting event, while my dad and I hid upstairs and watched hockey.*

"Oh. Yeah, that's the name!" He snapped his fingers and pointed at me. "We do that. We get a bunch of ladies from around the country, bring them here, they date Ollie, he finds a wife, and I've saved the Kingdom of Wexstone." He collapsed back in his chair as he raised his arms in a victory pose befitting Rocky Balboa.

"It's actually not a bad idea," Tej considered as he tipped his glass to Vince.

I turned to Oliver, who looked like he was actually contemplating it. Holy shit, he looks like he's actually contemplating this. *I rubbed my temples. This was exactly the kind of foolishness that happened when you mixed whiskey and desperate men.*

"Oliver?" I beseeched. He was deep in thought and didn't even hear me. "Hey!"

He finally turned to me, giving me the look we had perfected over the years that said, "Open your mind's door and get ready for some telepathy." I could hear exactly what he was saying: He really thought this was a good idea.

I shook my head no, only for him to answer with a half smile. It was the first semblance of a smile I'd seen on his face since that morning.

"I like the idea. But I think I would make some changes to it. Vince, grab a pen and some paper off my desk over there and write this down," Oliver said.

"On it!"

"Hear me out," Oliver started. "It shouldn't be just anyone, you know? The media has already been after Xavier and the abdication is just going to set off more of a shitstorm; we really don't need random people hanging around right now. We could ask the Council for some suggestions, or perhaps my parents would know a few women who they think may be a good fit?"

"You know that they will just suggest the daughters of those in the inner circle. The noble families. Do you even like any of them?" I reminded. Oliver had been surrounded by the daughters of the nobility since birth, but none of them were fit to be our future queen. Sure, there were some perfectly nice ones, but as Oliver had said before, most of them seemed more interested in status than in who Oliver truly was.

I continued. "What if you tried to find someone who isn't necessarily already 'in'? Include women who have a pulse on the everyday Wexstonian and what they need. Just think about the team you would make with a woman like that by your side. It would be the best of both worlds: A wife who knows the people, and you, who knows the political inner workings of the Council."

Oliver rubbed his jaw, his eyes narrowing as he mused. "You're right. That's actually really good. People might be kinder to the family and receive this idea a little better if they know there are 'normal' people in the running, too." He paused, continuing to map out his thoughts. "But I'm not going to give out roses or have a big ceremony where I send someone home each week. That's awful, and I can't imagine the press being even remotely agreeable to that notion. No, the women need to know that they can leave at any time, but I will dedicate the holiday season to courting each of them."

Somehow, it wasn't a completely shit idea. I still wasn't fully on board, but I had to admit that a couple of months was usually enough to know if you wanted to move forward with dating someone. I just didn't know if it would be enough time for Oliver to know if he wanted to marry someone.

"Brilliant," Vince said as he scribbled down his notes. I knew we'd be lucky if we could even read what he'd written. His handwriting was awful on a good day, but throw in three glasses of whiskey and counting...

I set the empty glass in the sink. It was funny how we didn't want any "random" women that we didn't know in this makeshift contest and yet: There was Birdie. A random girl from New York City, who I bumped into at a coffee shop, only to discover that she worked at the bar the barista had suggested we go to? It was all too weird.

I was never one to believe in coincidences, nor did I really believe in fate or destiny. I'd seen how women "just so happened" to stumble into Oliver at every given opportunity, trying to set up their perfect fairytale scenario with him. Renata was a prime example.

I couldn't stand that woman. She was awful, and I didn't

know why Oliver even let her be there. She liked to think that we didn't see through her act, but we'd known and heard what she had told everyone since we were in year eight: that she and the Crown Prince would get married, since it was her "birthright" by being a Raines.

The royal family and the Raines family had a long-standing history. Way back in the day, the Raines men served as royal advisers. Every other generation or so, they would arrange a marriage between their children and one of the royals, interweaving the families throughout the years as they accumulated more wealth and land in the process.

In recent decades the Raineses had fallen out of favor as advisers to the crown, though Lord Anthony Raines—Renata's father—still enjoyed his titled status and monthly poker nights with his fellow lords. Rumor had it that he had tied up a chunk of their money in some risky investments and was eager to have Renata become queen, in hopes that they could return to the old days of vast prosperity and power.

But Birdie. Maybe she was what Oliver needed. She was carefree and kind and confident and unbelievably sexy. I still hadn't stopped thinking about the sounds she made when I kissed her neck in the closet.

But how could she just drop everything in her life to come here? Especially during the holidays. What type of family would be okay with their daughter missing the holidays for a man she barely knew? I couldn't shake the questions in my mind. Was it because there was something to be worried about, or was it the mystery of not knowing much about her?

The palace's head of security, Sheffield, had run a background check on each suitor before their arrival. I wondered if I should reach out to him to read through Birdie's file. Surely that would answer some of my questions, right?

I had to let this go. My skeptical nature was getting the

best of me, but it was hard to quiet the nudge in the pit of my stomach to find out more about her.

After pulling the comforter back and letting Eugene hop up onto the bed and burrow into his preferred place at the foot, I set my alarm, settling under the covers and thinking about the next day's events. We'd be with the ladies during a press conference and then again as they visited the artisan workshops in the afternoon.

The workshops were one of my favorite places in the city. When I was a teenager, I would spend hours there in silence with the owner, chopping wood to be used for whatever project was up next. It was a safe place to work through my torrent of adolescent emotions.

There was a knock on my door. I wasn't expecting anyone that late at night. I checked the security camera app on my phone and was shocked to see Birdie. Her cobalt-blue dress shone in the light of my front porch.

I unlocked the door and opened it. As the cold air hit me, I noticed she didn't have a coat on. Just that insanely beautiful dress.

"Hey. Come in," I said, opening my door.

"I'm sorry to show up unannounced." She stepped inside and stood in the small foyer that opened up into my open-plan living room. I had done all of the renovations on the cottage myself. It had been a form of therapy for me, making this place my own, redoing everything from scratch. It was like making my own little mark on this palace.

"How did you know where I lived?"

"Vince." She smiled.

My brows knit together in a mix of confusion and concern. "Is everything okay?"

She looked around, taking in the small cottage. She walked over to the built-ins on the opposite wall. They held my dad's old books along with my own and a few pictures that I cherished. A photo of my parents on vacation in Mykonos for their twentieth anniversary. A snapshot of my dad and me at a Steelers game when I was ten. And the last photo of all of us together.

"Is this your family?"

I nodded, still perplexed about why she was there.

She ran her hand along the smooth pine shelf and took a deep breath. "Okay. I know you're probably wondering why I'm here and what's up…" She turned toward me, hesitancy in her eyes. "I can't do this. I can't move forward with all of this."

"Okay. What happened?" I was frozen where I stood, my hands in my pockets.

"I can't stop thinking about the weekend we met. We bumped into each other that morning and then you showed up at my job. You walking me home. Making out with you in that closet. And then you saved me from those reporters tonight. It just got me thinking." She looked down at her hands, twisting her fingers together. "This all feels like I was supposed to meet you, not Oliver."

The air left my lungs. I didn't know what to say. Was she serious? This never happened. From the time we were teenagers, girls always flocked to Ollie and Xavier over me. Never once had someone chosen me over them.

"So, what now?" I asked, my voice barely above a whisper.

She walked toward me, her dress making a light *woosh* as her hips swayed. I couldn't take my eyes off her. The heart-shaped neckline accentuated her breasts in all the best ways as the silk hugged her waist, giving her the perfect hourglass frame. She looked absolutely stunning.

She stopped just in front of me and ran her hands up my chest, lacing her fingers together behind the nape of my neck.

Our bodies were so close that I could feel her breasts as they rose and fell against my own chest.

"Kiss me," she whispered.

I heeded her request by leaning my head down and running my nose along the bridge of hers. I took in the smell of lavender and vanilla—Birdie's signature scent. I placed my hands on her waist and gave her a light squeeze as she looked up at me with those eyes. Those fucking eyes. I could get lost in the way they shifted from golden honey to burnt sienna in the changing light.

A few tendrils of her coffee-colored hair had fallen out of her updo and brushed against my nose as I nuzzled into her neck, placing a few light kisses along her throat. She let out one of those soft moans that turned me inside out.

"You can't make noises like that," I whispered against her lips. My voice was gravelly as I struggled to hold myself together. I slid my tongue along her bottom lip, teasing her. She pressed into me, wanting more. I enveloped her mouth with mine as she welcomed my kiss.

"You don't like my noises?" she pulled back and asked as she ran her hands up the back of my neck and fingered my hair.

"I *love* those noises, but I don't have much self-control. It's been a while since I've been with anyone." I kissed her again, this time with less patience. There was a hunger in her return as she slid her tongue into my mouth, searching for I didn't know what. After a few minutes, she slowed and sank into a slow, languid speed, like a well-rehearsed dance. Like we'd done this many times, not just once before.

"Maybe we should remedy that, yeah?" She pulled back and gave me a devious smile.

My gaze followed her hand as it slid under the waistband of my gray sweatpants. She cupped my heavy balls and a moan slipped from my own lips.

"Fuck, that feels good."

She slid to her knees and pulled my pants down, my hard cock springing free. She wrapped her hand around it and gave it a few pumps, then looked up at me.

"Is this okay?" she asked.

I'd lost all ability to speak. I just nodded and prayed to whatever God was listening that I could last long enough, because I was aching and just the thought of her rubbing me any harder had pre-cum slipping from the tip of my dick.

Before I could reach down to wipe it away, Birdie's warm mouth was on my tip, running her tongue over it and swallowing me down. She took me deeper into her mouth and hummed as she went deeper and deeper and deeper. As she slid it out of her mouth, she ran her tongue along the bottom and flicked the tip. She did this one more time until she pulled me all the way out.

"Holy shit, Birdie," I huffed as I threw my head back. "I'm not going to last long if you keep doing that with your tongue."

She let out a small laugh as she put me back into her mouth, cradling my balls and running her finger along the seam between them at the same time. That's when I lost all control. I lifted her up and carried her bridal style to my bedroom. Thank God I knew my way around the cottage, because I couldn't see a damn thing as I ravaged her mouth with mine. The taste of me and her mingling was heavenly.

I set her down in front of my bed and turned her around, looking for a way to get her out of that gown.

"Are you attached to this dress?"

"No. Why?"

I ripped the few buttons at the top, and they flew across the room, rolling under the dresser against the wall. I yanked the zipper down and tore her out of it. As soon as the silky fabric hit the floor, I turned her around to face me. I lightly grabbed her throat and brought her mouth to mine, sucking her tongue between my teeth. I ran my hands down her spine, grabbing handfuls of her firm ass. I couldn't take it anymore. I grabbed the back of her knees, lifting her and throwing her onto the bed. Her laughter filled the room.

Her soft, warm skin and white lace underwear contrasted against the black of my comforter. There was a slight sheen to her skin—she was ready, and I could tell.

I climbed onto the bed and spread her legs wide. I could feel the heat coming from her center. Just the thought of her taste made my cock twitch. A small wet spot was starting to grow on the white lace.

"Mmm. You're ready, huh?" I smirked as I leaned over her to suck on one of her pert nipples. Her breathing picked up faster. I ran my hand up her body and grabbed her other breast, circling one nipple with my tongue and giving the other a light squeeze. As much as I wanted to stay here and focus on her gorgeous tits, I kissed down her torso slowly, sucking and licking every few inches.

"I think it's time for me to return the favor." I slipped my fingers under the light fabric at her waist and pulled it down.

"So ready and willing," I said as I threw the scrap of fabric to the floor.

"I can't help it. Every time I see you, I'm instantly wet."

God, I loved hearing that. I leaned down and continued my kisses down her body, landing on her inner thighs. I kissed and gave light, little bites.

She moaned. It was music to my ears. "Please."

That word meant I was doing something right. I couldn't help but smile.

I slid my middle finger into her center, and she started to move in time as I pumped it in and out.

"Knox, I need more. Please," she whimpered.

I pulled my finger out and she grabbed the sheets in frustration, then gasped as I licked the small nub at the apex of her thighs. Her breathing quickened as I continued to lick and then added in one finger, then two.

"Knox. I'm so close."

"Not until I say you can. Be a good girl and listen. It'll be worth it."

"Fuck me," she ground out in frustration.

"Not yet," I smiled. I wanted to edge her right to the brink and then take her all of the way. She'd asked for this, and I was going to give her everything I had.

She was so goddamn wet and tasted delicious. The perfect combination of sweet and salty. God, I was going to think about this for days.

As I continued to flick her clit with my tongue, I reached down to rub my free hand along my cock. It was rock hard; just a few brushes of my hand and I was ready to blow. I had to get inside her.

I pulled my fingers out of her, and she mewled.

"What do you want?" I smirked.

"I want you..." she breathed. "Inside of me. Now."

Getting off the bed, I walked over to my nightstand and fumbled around for the foil package I was looking for. Of course, when I needed it, I couldn't find it. The box was in the back of the drawer. I grabbed one of the condoms, opened it, and rolled it onto my stiff cock.

I crawled back onto the bed where Birdie was splayed out. She looked like a dream. Covered in a light sheet of sweat, her breasts were perky and perfect, heaving with excitement and want.

"Are you sure you want to do this?" I asked.

"Absolutely." She smiled and pulled me down so we were

face to face. She grabbed the back of my head and kissed me with so much force. "I just want you...please."

I lined up my cock with her entrance and made a slow circle before sliding into her. She was so tight and warm. Birdie let a small moan slip from her lips right into my ear as I laid my forehead onto her shoulder. We stayed like this for a few seconds, adjusting to each other and soaking in the feeling.

I made a few slow thrusts into her as she started to move under me, giving me the sign that she wanted it faster. As I picked up speed, I palmed one breast and sucked on the other one. God, this was amazing. She leaned up and I pulled out.

"What's wrong?" I questioned.

"Nothing. Lay back."

She didn't have to tell me twice. I settled back against the wooden headboard, and she climbed onto my lap, grabbing my still-hard dick and sliding it into her. She wrapped her hands around the back of my neck and bounced a little.

"Fuck, Birdie. You feel amazing." I laid my head back and watched as her tits bounced up and down with each thrust. "I'm not going to last much longer if you keep this up, baby."

"Good. Because I'm about to come."

"Let it go, baby, I want to feel you fall apart on my dick."

She pulled me closer to her, and I buried my head into her neck, wrapping my arms tight around her. Her walls started to contract around my cock, inching me closer and closer to release.

"I'm there, Knox. Please let me come."

"Let me hear it, baby. I want to hear how good it feels."

She fell apart around me, her moans louder and louder as she screamed my name. I gripped her hips and guided her up as I thrust harder and harder until I felt that heavy pull at the base of my spine. One more thrust and I was there with her.

I emptied everything I had into her as she leaned against

my chest and made soft noises of satisfaction. I caught my breath and then rolled her over onto the bed so I could toss the condom in the trash.

When I turned back, Birdie was gone, and there was a ringing in the room. I looked around and couldn't find where it was coming from...

The sun shone through the slit in the blackout curtains that hung against the window of my room. My phone alarm was ringing.

CHAPTER 10
KNOX

I reached over to silence my alarm as the realization hit me.

...It had been a dream.

Holy shit, that was far too real. So much so that my dick was rock hard and felt like it was about to rip a hole in my boxer briefs. *Fuck.*

I flipped back the covers and was met with two very judgmental eyes.

"Don't look at me like that. You don't even have balls, so you don't get to judge."

Eugene let out a snarky bark.

I got up and made my way to the bathroom—a difficult task given my raging hard-on. I flipped the switch, turned on the heated floor, and stepped inside the shower to get the hot water and steam going as I discarded my pants.

I wish it had *been real.*

The thought flitted through my mind before I could stop it. I knew that Birdie was here to court Oliver, and I shouldn't be having these thoughts about her. I had tried so hard to put her out of my mind from the moment she agreed to join the competition, but last night had clearly demonstrated my failure in that regard.

Maybe it was just lust or the fact that I hadn't been laid in a while. Yes, that must be it.

Water flowed from the rainwater shower head in the ceiling of the shower, and the built-in jets along the black slate walls shot right into my shoulder blades. The tight knots started to melt away. I stood there for a good five minutes just letting the water do its work before I grabbed my shampoo and started to massage and lather it through my hair.

The hot water did nothing for the rage going on down below. I knew there was only one way to get it to go away and I started to rub myself. I couldn't stop thinking about my dream and how corporeal Birdie had felt.

Birdie. The girl my best friend was supposed to be courting. Guilt washed over me along with the water. I tried pushing her from my mind as I grabbed my aching cock, starting from the base and running my hand along the length. But as I pumped my hand, flashes of Birdie's face, the way she moaned my name in the dream, and the way her ass had felt in my hands back in New York danced through my mind.

Jesus, I was the worst. This girl was there for my best friend, not me. And I was going to have to see her today. I tightened my grip and thick, white ropes of cum flew across the shower and washed down the drain. I hit my hand against the stone wall.

"Fuck!" This couldn't be happening. I could never think of this again. I couldn't fuck this up for Oliver.

———

As I took a seat on the antique damask sofa in the queen's office, a staff member hurried over and set a small teacup and saucer in front of me, pouring the hot liquid into the cup.

"Thank you," I said, a tinge of guilt running through me because I didn't know her name, something I made a point to learn for every new palace employee. As head of the grounds team, I knew the hard work that each staff member put in and wanted them to know that they were seen and appreciated. Making sure that everyone was recognized and thanked was important to me.

"Would you like any sugar, sir?" she asked, barely above a whisper.

"No, thank you," I replied with a smile. "Are you new here?"

"Yes, sir. This is my first week."

"What a week to start." I picked up the dainty white cup painted with pine boughs. "What's your name?"

"May, sir."

"It's nice to meet you, May. I'm Knox. I apologize for not making your acquaintance sooner; the grounds team and I have been a bit busy lately getting ready for everything. Thank you for the tea."

May dipped her head, gratitude on her face as she turned pour a cup for Queen Isobel's assistant, Mirabel, before leaving the room.

"Is everyone here?" Isobel asked Mirabel as the office door clicked shut.

"Yes, ma'am. The press are enjoying their refreshments in the Godric State Room. The women are in the Nickles room, waiting."

"Thank you, Mirabel." She scanned the room, taking count of everyone in attendance. "Oliver, where is your brother?"

"Probably drunk and passed out somewhere," Oliver said. I gave him a wary glance, and he shrugged his shoulders.

I didn't doubt Oliver's love for Xavier, but his resentment toward him was clear. Not that I could blame him, but I had never heard him be so vocal about it. I wasn't surprised that Xavier hadn't shown up for the family meeting before the day's press conference, but I was still disappointed in him. The least he could do was show up for a short period.

"Oliver," King Leroy reprimanded, his voice authoritative. He turned to Isobel and his voice softened. "Everything will be fine, sweetheart." He wrapped his arm around his wife, giving her a light squeeze. She closed her eyes and took a deep breath before releasing the tension in her shoulders.

I tried not to let envy wash over me. I was happy for Leroy and Isobel—lord knew how rare it was for a royal marriage to be so full of genuine love and affection—but they had the very thing that I craved. The ability to comfort someone, to relax them with just a look or a touch, was a connection my parents had shared as well. I had always hoped to find that for myself, but it didn't seem to be in the cards for me.

"You ready for this?" I asked Oliver.

"Sure," he answered unconvincingly. Something was clearly wrong.

I pulled him aside and looked him in the eyes. "Hey." *Talk to me.*

"I'm good," he said quietly. He ran a hand down his face. "I'm annoyed that Xavier isn't here is all. And..." He looked at his parents and then back to me. "When we came up with this, I didn't realize it would stress Mum out so much."

"Dude, let's be honest, your mom would stress out over you getting engaged no matter how it happened and no matter who was involved. You know how she is."

Oliver let a small smile roll over his face that said, *You're right.*

"All right," Isobel said from behind her desk as she straightened a stack of papers. Behind her, a window flanked by sheer cream curtains overlooked the bubbling fountain in front of the palace, the built-in heaters keeping the water running even in the winter temperatures. Looking at the peaceful visage, with the additional vehicles and valet staff just out of view, it was almost possible to pretend that this was any other November morning. "Boys, it's time. Oliver, do you have your notes with the names of the attending press and who they are representing today?"

"Yes, Mum. It's right here." He picked up a piece of paper from the coffee table.

"Knox, darling. You're going to sit in the front row next to Gram and Rosie, all right?"

"Yes, ma'am." Although I would much rather have been in the very back row, out of any pictures or attention whatsoever, I knew better than to argue with Isobel, especially when she was in planning mode. While Leroy and Isobel had initially shared my reservations when presented with the idea of the competition, Oliver had quickly assuaged their concerns, and the queen had taken on overseeing preparations in her typical organized, efficient manner.

We left Isobel's office and made our way to the Godric State Room. The formal space had plush navy carpet with the Wexstone coat of arms—a golden shield bordered by pine boughs and featuring two blue lions standing on their hind legs, facing away from each other—inlaid at the center of the room. The high, champagne-colored walls were topped by a gold-filigree barrel vault ceiling.

Today, instead of formal dining tables or even the long table that usually sat at the far end of the room for press conferences, about twenty chairs were arranged in rows in the center of the room. Facing them were nine velvet wingback chairs, each with a small table and a glass of water beside it. Journalists mingled as they waited for the event to begin, nibbling on pastries and sipping drinks from the tea and coffee stations set up around the periphery.

Isobel and her staff had taken the idea of giving press access to the inner workings of the courting season and run with it. Her idea had been to make the morning cozy and welcoming, rather than stuffy like a typical press conference. In that vein, she had suggested that Oliver serve as moderator, with the goal that it would make the attendees feel like they were having tea with him and the participating women. Isobel was a genius when it came to publicity and how to turn it in her favor, and we all hoped that this would mark a change from the negative press the family had received lately. What had started out as cynical rumblings around Xavier and the abdication had spiraled into piece after piece critiquing the royal family on every small thing they did or didn't do. It was critical to bring the media back to our side leading up to Oliver's coronation.

Oliver and Isobel greeted the attendees, making small talk and letting everyone know that we would begin soon. As the journalists settled into their seats and fired up their laptops, tablets, phones, and the occasional analog notebook, I stood back waiting with Leroy, Rosalind, and Evelyn.

"As much as I hate having these people in my home, this wasn't a bad idea. Good job, son," Leroy said to me under his breath.

"What?" I replied, shocked. "This wasn't my idea at all."

"You may not have come up with it, but if it were a bad idea and going to be a disaster, you wouldn't have let him go through with it. He trusts you and your opinion."

I was taken aback. Oliver and I were close, yes. But to have Leroy acknowledge my influence on his son was more meaningful than he could know. Leroy was a man of few words. Instead of sucking up all the air in a room with a loud, boisterous personality, he was quiet and reserved, observing even the smallest details that many didn't notice. He was not effusive with his praise, rather doling out compliments only when they were most earned. It was a trait that he and my dad had shared.

"Well, time to put on my king hat and make some small talk." He patted me on the back and stalked over to where the press sat.

"I think he'll pull out of all this within two weeks," Rosalind piped up beside me, her eyes following Oliver as he moved around the room.

"No, he won't." I looked down at her. She was a very bright young girl, but she still didn't understand Oliver's love for his family and the sacrifice he was making to save her from this very predicament.

"I'll bet you fifty euros he chooses that golden-haired one, the teacher." Evelyn stuck out her hand to shake Rosalind's. I blinked at them. Those two were always into something together.

"Double or nothing, he chooses the American," Rosalind retorted. *Where did she even learn to talk like that?*

Something twisted in my gut. It must have been the residual guilt from the dream and what happened in my shower.

"You both are awful, you know that, right?" I tried to plaster on my sternest face.

"Want in?" Evelyn asked.

"Gram, he can't bet with us!" Rosie exclaimed. "He has insider info and has too much sway. It wouldn't be fair."

"Oh, Rosie," I laughed, grabbing the bottom of the braid hanging over her shoulder. "I would think you'd know better by now. That old bird," I pointed to Evelyn, "is the hustler of all hustlers. You never bet against her."

"Hey," Evelyn narrowed her eyes at me and rapped her cane on the floor. "Mind your own business, Knox. I have to school the next generation somehow."

I laughed loudly and moved to the front row to take my seat.

———

"Ms. Thorne. John Astor, *Wexstone Daily*. If chosen to be our queen, do you think you could put aside your personal bias for your family to make sure the other businesses of the kingdom get your full attention and you don't unfairly favor the forestry department?"

Sabine Thorne, well-known environmentalist and daughter of one of the country's largest flower producers, cocked a well-shaped eyebrow. "Well, John, I think my family has made a name for themselves on their own two feet for over three hundred years. We will do fine with or without the extra money from the forestry department. Can you say the same thing about your own column funded by the palace?"

I chuckled. I always loved when that dick John Astor got his ass handed to him.

"Ms. Levy, Sasha Cabot from *The Independent*. What makes you think that you are qualified to run our country?"

"I don't know that I am, Ms. Cabot." Adelaide let a saccharine smile roll across her face as she tucked her hair behind her ear. "I think someone else would be much better. I think His Highness would be better off choosing someone who knows the ins and outs of the court." I heard Evelyn huff as the loud click of fingers against keyboards filled the room.

"I couldn't agree more," Renata chimed in, pursing her lips. Today they were painted in a garish shade of pink that clashed with her red hair. "As someone who has been around the court her entire life, I fully believe that I have the knowledge to run this kingdom well."

Mr. Astor stood quickly to cut off Renata. Anger flashed in her eyes before turning back to her fake, sweet facade. She and her cronies, Gemma Rousseau-Wu and Ginny Wu-Murphy, first cousins who had attended prep school with us, were clearly annoyed that most of the questions this morning had been directed toward the suitors who were not already a part of the royal court.

I had tried to keep my eyes on Oliver as he moderated the press conference. But I couldn't help when my gaze trailed to Birdie, just two seats to Oliver's left. Every time I looked at her, a wave of guilt crashed over me. She looked like sunshine sitting on the stage in a bright yellow high-necked day dress. The belt at her middle accentuated her hourglass figure, and my fingers flexed at the thought of how Dream Knox had dug his fingers into that waist as she rode him.

Ugh. I had to stop this. Birdie was here to court Oliver. I just needed to buy myself some time to let the memory of the previous night's dream wear away.

Astor turned to Mellie Schneider, a writer for *Kingdom Magazine* who looked distinctly uncomfortable in her charcoal pencil skirt and heels. "Ms. Schneider. Should you be chosen to be the prince's bride, do you plan to leave your career in favor of raising his children?"

Mellie stiffened, her face paling. I wanted to punch Astor; he had a long-standing rivalry with *Kingdom Magazine* and certainly had only asked that in hopes that their best writer *would* leave.

Birdie glanced at Mellie in the chair beside her. As Mellie opened her mouth, searching for a response, Birdie jumped in.

"Excuse me. Mr. Astor, was it? Might I ask, do you have any children?"

Astor blanched. "I don't see how that is at all—"

"Answer the question please, John," Oliver said.

"We have three children, yes," Astor answered, cowed by the authority ringing in Oliver's voice.

"And did you leave your job to care for them?" Birdie asked calmly, though fire flashed in her eyes. The room was silent.

"Well...no," Astor stammered.

"Then I don't see why you should ask such a question of Ms. Schneider. In this day and age, I would hope an accomplished journalist such as yourself would see that it is more than possible for a woman to be a mother and a wife *and* have her own career."

Astor sank back into his chair, his face flushed. Mellie looked to Birdie, gratitude on her face.

"Ms. Hamilton," another voice spoke up. "Alistair Davies, *Pine Times.* Your mother passed when you were a teenager, and your father could not be reached for comment. Do you think your rocky family life would hinder your ability to help run the country?"

My stomach sank as my head whipped around to spot the lanky, pimple-faced man who had asked the question. She had also lost her mom as a teenager? Of all the things for us to have in common, being in the Dead Parent Club together was not what I would have wanted.

"Um..." Birdie cleared her throat, a mixture of surprise and panic on her face. "I, um..." she stammered, fingers toying nervously with her bracelet.

I briefly considered going back there to give Alistair Davies a piece of my mind. How dare he bring up something that was clearly so traumatic in this way? Before I could react, Oliver stepped in. "I think that's enough questions for now." A flurry of protest came from the reporters. "You can thank Mr. Astor and Mr. Davies for ending this press conference with their inappropriate inquiries. We will not be moving forward with any further questions." He stood, then paused.

"One last thing you should all note," he said slowly, looking around the room to each reporter. "This country could use a fresh perspective. We could all use a shake up from the old traditions. So, whether my future partner is an American," he gestured to Birdie, "or a schoolteacher," he nodded to Adelaide, "or a baker," he motioned toward the round-faced blonde on his right, "or one of the other beautiful women here who have spent their whole lives around the court, there *will* be changes. I suggest you prepare accordingly."

I wanted to give him a standing ovation. *There's my best friend.* This was the next king the country needed, not some palatable kiss-ass. I looked at Evelyn to find pride radiating from her every pore.

"That's my boy," she whispered.

"That will be all. You are dismissed," Oliver said, striding from the room.

CHAPTER 11
BIRDIE

I followed Adelaide through the doors of the glassblowing studio back out into the center of the artisans' square. The large courtyard was bordered by buildings housing workshops for many of Wexstone's artists and makers. Each shop sported a picture window that held an array of finished art pieces, giving passersby a glimpse into the artists' minds and spaces. Twinkle lights were strung between the copper signs above each door, and lampposts decorated with holly and pine cones led to a fountain in the center of the square.

The afternoon had been spent with Prince Oliver and the rest of the suitors, visiting a potter specializing in delicate porcelains followed by the country's first all-female-run glassblowing studio. At each workshop, Prince Oliver had introduced the artists, giving them an opportunity to share their work with us.

I was in heaven, although I tried to behave myself and not ask too many questions; I didn't think that hogging the artists' attention would make a great impression on anyone.

I had been in a daze as we filed out of the press conference and proceeded to a line of sleek black sedans. That last question from the gangly man from *Pine Times*—what was his name, Davies?—had likely been intended to throw me off my game and had struck its mark.

They know about Mom. And they tried reaching out to Dad? Fuck. I wasn't even sure where my dad was living—definitely the last thing I needed anyone to know.

I was lost in thought, mulling over Prince Oliver's defense of me back at the press conference, when Adelaide grabbed my elbow and pulled me into the backseat of one of the cars.

"Best to be in this together," she whispered as we settled into the spacious bench seat.

The morning's press conference and the afternoon outing had been an interesting chance to observe and feel out my fellow contestants. As we walked to our final stop, the wood-carving workshop, I lagged behind, watching the rest of the women.

Adelaide, golden hair gleaming in the sunlight, chatted with Mellie, a short, lithe woman who wore her black hair in a pixie cut that accentuated her exquisite cheekbones and pale skin. She had approached me at the potter's studio to thank me for speaking up for her at the press conference.

"Truthfully, I would have assumed that the rest of you would be glad to let me flounder there," she admitted. "You know, with this being a competition and all."

"We may be courting the same guy," I answered, giving her a conspiratorial smile, "but that doesn't mean I'm going to let some dickhole reporter get away with asking wildly inappropriate shit."

Adelaide piped up from my other side. "Mellie, I've known this girl for less than twenty-four hours, but I can already tell she's someone you want on your side." She elbowed me play-fully in the ribs.

"I can see that, and I'm glad to have some allies here. And please, call me Mel."

"Allies indeed, Mel," I had said, putting my arm around her shoulder. "Maybe we can all survive this circus unscathed together."

Now, as my two new friends walked the pebbled pathway to the woodcarving shop, a blonde woman wearing a high-necked blouse and an ill-fitting skirt that fell past her knees bobbed along behind them. She had introduced herself as Cora and was one of the bakers at the café and patisserie in town. In the few minutes I had chatted with her, she seemed kind, if perhaps a bit starry-eyed. I was afraid this competition would chew her up and spit her out.

In front of them strode Sabine, who Adelaide had told me was one of the country's greatest environmental activists. Apparently, she was also one of the country's most talented floral designers and consulted on sustainable floristry around Europe. The way she carried herself in her pencil dress, blazer, and mustard-yellow wedges, head of tight black curls held high, told me that she was used to navigating uncomfortable spaces. I wasn't sure if she was someone I would find an ally in, but I certainly knew I preferred to stay on her good side.

Renata strutted at the front of the group, flanked by her cronies Gemma and Ginny. According to Adelaide, they were cousins but acted more like twins.

"Renata fancies herself a businesswoman. She founded a makeup company, although it's really one of those multi-level-marketing schemes. She did it all with her daddy's money, of course," Adelaide had explained in the car, rolling her eyes. I snorted. "Gemma and Ginny are a part of it. They're at the top of the pyramid, just under Renata, and do pretty much anything she tells them to. I've always wondered who they'd have become if they hadn't been caught in her thrall when we were children."

I caught back up with Adelaide and Mel as we approached the woodcarving shop. The building appeared humble at first glance, but closer inspection revealed intricate carvings of vines decorating the porch posts and railings. The sign, which read "Lewellen Woodworkers," was adorned with hand-carved berries and pine cones, while the front door featured windows edged in reliefs of pine trees and woodland creatures.

We filed through the front door into a room filled with spacious tables. The walls were lined with shelves overflowing with paints of every color, every size of paintbrush imaginable, aprons, palettes, palette knives, and drying racks with art of every kind. Opposite where we stood, a large door led to the back of the building.

We gathered in a semicircle around Prince Oliver, who now stood next to a gray-haired man in his sixties. Knox, Vince, Cordell—the palace's press secretary——and a single black-clad security guard lingered near the door. The rest of the security team was stationed outside, remaining somehow both present and inconspicuous.

"Ladies, allow me to introduce you to Darren Lewellen, owner of Lewellen Woodcarvers." We applauded as Mr. Lewellen nodded to Prince Oliver and stepped forward.

"Thank you, Your Highness." He turned to us. "My family has been involved in Wexstone's lumber production for close to a hundred years. My brother, Lord Collins Lewellen, continues that legacy while supporting conservation efforts." He inclined his head toward Sabine, who smiled and nodded back to him.

As he spoke, I remembered meeting Lord Lewellen and his wife, Lady Laurel, the night before. I would never have guessed that this man before me, so casually dressed in a worn flannel shirt and brown work boots, was the brother of the tuxedoed Lord Collins.

Mr. Lewellen continued, "As a boy, I learned the art of woodworking from my grandfather. My wife and I opened this space soon after we married, with the goal of training other woodworkers and nurturing artists of all types. From this building," he gestured to the room around us and toward the back of the building, "we were eventually able to build out the rest of the artisans' square. This room still serves as an open space for aspiring artists to work while also providing our own woodcarvers a place to finish their pieces. The back of the building houses our woodworking shop, where we produce everything from furniture to serving ware to decorative pieces."

Prince Oliver picked up where Mr. Lewellen left off. "Each year, the palace hires one of Wexstone's artisans to create a set of ornaments for our main Christmas tree. This year, we have asked Mr. Lewellen and his carvers to do the honors. At the end of the holiday season, the queen chooses her favorite orna-ment to add to our family's personal collection, while the rest are sold to benefit a charity of the artist's choosing."

Mr. Lewellen moved to a table near the edge of the room, picking up a large box and carrying it over. "Our team has been working on our ornament collection for months, designing pieces that portray the natural beauty of our country." He lifted out several ornaments, passing them around our group. One was a relief carving of the night sky. Another was shaped into a miniature pine tree, lacquered until it gleamed in the sunlight. A third featured delicately painted holly berries. While each one was wildly different, they were all stunning and would make for a beautiful Christmas tree.

Mr. Lewellen continued as we admired the ornaments,

"We thought it would be fun to have all of you take part in this tradition." His eyes glittered as he pulled a stack of small pine rounds out of the box. "We fashioned some of our scraps into blank slates for each of you to paint and decorate as you like; the finished pieces will join our collection on the palace tree. As you can see, we have a large stock of supplies here for you to work with. I invite you to take an ornament, get creative, and have some fun. Remember, there are no rules and you're limited only by your imagination."

I glanced at the women around me. Cora had an eager look on her face. Sabine's expression remained unchanged, although I spotted a gleam of pleasure in her eyes. Renata and the cousins looked like they would rather be anywhere else but here.

We each took an ornament from Mr. Lewellen and made our way to the tables. I took my time perusing the paints, trying to decide what I would paint on my ornament. I was an artist at heart, and this felt familiar, like home. By the time I gathered my supplies, there was only one spot left at the end of one of the worktables.

I set to work, sketching out an outline and mixing colors together.

"May I join you?"

I started. Prince Oliver was standing in front of me, looking slightly sheepish, an ornament in one hand, a few paintbrushes in the other. I could feel eyes boring into the back of my head.

"Of course," I said. *Twice now, he has asked to join you. That must mean something, right?* I couldn't deny that it was, at least, flattering. But why wasn't I more excited by it?

The prince took the seat to my right. "I must confess," he said, voice low as he leaned in close, "I am terrible at this kind of thing. I fear that any illusions you had of me being good at anything will be dashed when you witness my lack of artistic skill."

I laughed as I took a brush to my sketch, filling in the background. "Trust me, I've witnessed plenty of my brother's terrible drawings. Nothing can surprise me at this point. I'm sure you're much better than you think."

"I assure you, I am not. But in the spirit of the occasion, I shall at least try." He peered over at my ornament. "And of course it would happen that you actually are an artist," he said, putting his hand to his forehead in feigned shame.

I looked down at my work: A tiny rendering of the New York skyline at night, lights glittering. "I think 'artist' is a generous term, but thank you." I glanced over to his ornament, which was currently a mess of blue paints. "Yours is...um..."

"A wreck?"

Heat rose to my cheeks. "Well...yes."

Prince Oliver threw his head back, laughing earnestly. From two tables away, Renata's head spun around like she was in *The Exorcist*, her eyes narrowing.

"What are you going for there?" I asked.

"I have no idea. I was just hoping if I put enough paint on it, something would magically appear." It was his turn to blush.

"Okay, we can fix this," I said, reaching across him and selecting a deep purple paint and grabbing the white that was in front of me. "Swirl in some of this purple with the blues. Then you can take some of this white and add some stars. Ta-da, it'll be a night sky."

Prince Oliver looked at me as if I had hung the real stars. "You are a genius," he said, a smile filling his face. He added some of the purple paint to a tray, dipping his brush in. "So have you always been into art?" he asked, brows furrowed as he concentrated on his work.

I turned back to my ornament, filling in details with a liner brush. "Yes and no. I loved drawing and painting as a kid but was way more focused on ice skating than anything. We couldn't afford for me to be a part of the skating academy, so my mom—she owned a dance studio, and my dad was a mechanic—gave ballet lessons to all their top skaters in exchange for my lessons and ice time. When my mom passed away, skating lessons weren't really an option anymore, so I kind of channeled that energy into art instead." I took a deep breath. "My real love is art history, though, which is why I got my master's degree in curatorial studies. Except you probably already know a lot of this, I guess, since it's got to be in the file they put together on me before I came here."

Prince Oliver paused, paintbrush in hand. "Actually, I made a point not to read any of your files," he admitted. "I know that Sheffield compiled detailed information on everyone for security purposes, but I didn't want to come into this experience with any preconceived notions. I'd rather you tell me your story when you're ready and comfortable."

I caught his gaze. "So, you probably didn't know about my mom until this morning when that journalist—"

"No. No, I didn't. And I'm sorry he did that to you. That wasn't okay." His eyes blazed. I was seeing that behind the calm, even-keeled exterior was a man who would fight like hell for the people he loved.

"Thank you for speaking up for me. I wasn't prepared to talk about her to the press yet."

"You're welcome. It was the least I could do. Some of those reporters are nothing but vultures dressed as human beings." He reached over, taking my hand in his. "Please know that you don't have to tell me anything you're not ready to share." He squeezed my fingers gently, then turned back to his ornament.

My heart warmed at his kindness. I resumed painting, working alongside him in companionable silence.

"It was cancer," I said softly after a few moments. I kept my eyes glued to my work but felt him pause beside me. "Lymphoma. She died when I was fourteen." My heart pounded. I so rarely talked about Mom that sharing even these small details felt monumental.

Prince Oliver took my hand once more. I liked the feeling of my hand in his, his palm smooth and his fingers strong. He looked into my eyes as he spoke. "Thank you for sharing that with me. It means so much that you trust me with that."

This time, I squeezed his hand. Suddenly aware of the many sets of eyes around us, I pulled away, pointing at his ornament. "Look, you were really on a roll, but your stars are looking more like amoebas, Your Highness."

The prince threw his brush down, laughing so hard his shoulders shook. "Okay, I give up."

I knew that we were always being watched, and I could feel the heavy heat of someone else staring at Prince Oliver and me. I turned my head to find Knox watching us. I locked eyes with him and gave a small smile. As if it took a moment to register, he nodded a hello and then walked out of the room. His vibe felt entirely off, far different from anything I'd felt from him thus far.

I pushed those thoughts to the back of my head when I heard Renata's shrill voice asking someone to wait while she touched up her lipstick, followed by the snapping of cameras. I turned to see that Cordell was taking pictures of Renata and the cousins.

She really did know how to turn it on for the camera. The way her face went from absolute boredom to fun and friendly was honestly appalling. I had met my fair share of mean girls living in New York and just by being a woman, but Renata would give any of the Real Housewives a run for their money.

"Ollie! Hey, Ollie!" She waved to Prince Oliver, trying to get his attention.

He looked over to her and let out a long sigh.

"Cordell is taking pictures for social media. Come over here," she said sashayed over to our side of the table. She looked down at his ornament and then back to him. "Oh my gosh, that is amazing!"

Liar, I thought.

Prince Oliver made eye contact with me, and we both laughed. I was glad to see that he also knew she was full of shit.

Renata's eyes shot to us. "What?" I wasn't sure how it was possible, but her voice managed to climb another decibel.

"Nothing." He cleared his throat. "Birdie, grab your ornament and come take a picture with us. We'll all get in it."

"Oh, um, Cordell only wanted you," Renata said sweetly.

"Well, good thing I'm the prince and can decide what goes on the official palace social media accounts." Though his expression was kind, his tone brooked no arguments.

She plastered on the fakest of fake smiles, pivoted, and moved back to her side of the table.

"Ready?" he asked.

We walked to the other side of the room and the entire group gathered around with their ornaments. As Cordell arranged us, I peeked at everyone else's pieces. As I had suspected from their reactions earlier, Sabine and Cora's ornaments demonstrated their comfort with art and painting: Sabine's featured tiny snowdrop blooms, while Cora's depicted a train car laden with presents. Adelaide and Mel may not have had the same artistic talent as Cora and Sabine, but they had approached the activity with enthusiasm, adorning their wood rounds with a stack of books and a wreath, respectively.

Ginny, it appeared, had a good eye, but her string of lights was only half finished. I was unsure what Renata or Gemma's ornaments were meant to be, but they made Prince Oliver look like Monet. *If you don't have anything nice to say, don't say anything at all,* I reminded myself, biting my tongue.

The camera lights flashed and by the time we were done taking pictures my face was hurting. Before we were able to disperse, Cora gasped, and I heard what sounded like one of the ornaments hit the floor. I craned my neck and spotted Cora's empty hands, a wooden round face-down on the ground in front of her. Her eyes welled with tears as she picked it up, the still-drying paint now smudged, the image smeared.

"Oh my God, Cora! So sorry, didn't see you there," Gemma said, her voice lacking in sincerity. "Did you ruin your painting? What a shame." Beside her, Renata shook her head and *tsked* in fake sympathy.

Cora's face was the shade of an heirloom tomato on a hot summer day. *This poor girl.* Gemma had been standing right next to her; there was no way she "hadn't seen her" and had clearly sabotaged her beautiful piece out of jealousy.

I walked jauntily over to Cora and looped my arm through hers, pulling her over to the other side of the room.

"What are you doing?" she asked, tears in her eyes.

"Come over here and sit with me, Cora." I led her to where Prince Oliver and I had just been working.

"Is Prince Oliver staring at me? This is so embarrassing. Everyone is staring at me and whispering."

"When I was in middle school, I think it was seventh grade, I was invited to my first boy-girl birthday party. I was so excited because my crush, Jake Goodwin, was going to be there and rumor had it that we were going to play spin the bottle." I sat down at my station, taking Cora's ruined ornament and grabbing a fresh paintbrush. "Here. You can sit here, I think Prince Oliver is preoccupied with talking to Adelaide." I pulled the chair out for Cora and continued my story as I worked. "Sophie Gonzales's mom was a huge health nut. So, for Sophie's birthday, her mom made this healthy cake and used bananas instead of butter or oil or something." I rolled my eyes. "Problem is, I'm extremely allergic to bananas and I didn't even think to ask, because honestly, who puts bananas in a birthday cake? Well, we sang 'Happy Birthday' and then ate the cake. I started to feel funny, but thought it was just my nerves because we were gathering around to start the game. Next thing I know, I was throwing up and pooping my pants at the same time, right in front of Jake! It was so embarrassing."

"Oh my gosh!" Cora gasped.

"Yeah. It's hard to come back from that. Especially in middle school. Just as it seemed as though everyone was about to move on to some other junior-high scandal, this other girl—Lulu Matheson—caught wind that Jake was going to ask me to the winter formal instead of her and started telling the story again, exaggerating it and making it worse with every retelling."

I inspected my work, mixing a bright shade of green to match one Cora had used. "Ginny was clearly jealous that your ornament was so beautiful. And apparently, she and good ol' Lulu have something in common: Not knowing how to attract a guy without tearing down another girl in the process." I handed the fixed ornament back to Cora.

Cora's eyes again welled with tears, this time from gratitude. "Thank you, Birdie." She shook her head. "Why would they come after me, though? I've done nothing to them."

Sabine chimed in from down the table. "They're mean girls, Cora. Haven't you seen that movie? They live sad lives and want to make those around them miserable because they aren't happy with themselves."

"They seemed so nice when I first met them at the gala. When I was talking to Prince Oliver, they made it a point to tell him all about the bakery I work at and how nice it was that he invited me even though I'm from a lower house."

"Oh, sweet little dove," Mel said, patting Cora's hand. "Welcome to the dog-eat-dog world that is inner court politics."

"Dogs aren't cannibals, are they? I thought they ate dog food?"

"Oh, honey." Sabine pressed her fingertips into her forehead.

"Cora, what she means is that they weren't being nice, they were trying to shame you for working at the bakery. And they were trying to imply they pity you. Which there is nothing to pity. You're a beautiful woman. And clearly a talented one, too." I smiled at her, putting my arm around her in a side hug.

Well, I thought, *there's the drawback to being here.* Catty women with their catty politics and mean-girl antics. People who made others feel little or less-than made my blood boil. I wouldn't let them get away with that shit was while I was around.

CHAPTER 12
KNOX

As much as I tried not to watch Birdie and Oliver talking together, I couldn't help from sneaking glances toward the table where they worked, heads close together. Right then they were roaring with laughter, but just moments ago had been staring into each other's eyes with such tenderness that I felt as though someone had punched me in the gut.

It had to be residual feelings from that stupid dream, or thinking of how Birdie had studied my face during our seven minutes in heaven. There was no reason for me to feel like this just because they were having tender moments and making each other laugh. For God's sake, that was the whole point of this contest—for Oliver to be happy.

Get your head right, Knox. You're not allowed to have feelings for this woman.

Thankfully, I was at my home away from home. I made my way to the back of the room and through the heavy wooden door that led to the workshop.

My dad used to bring me there as a teenager; he wanted me

to find a productive way to blow off steam after getting into a fight at school. What started as chopping wood for Mr. Lewellen evolved into a summer job shadowing the Lewellen family, taking care of whatever small tasks needed to be done around the shop. After losing my parents, it became my place of solace. Whether it was taking out my grief by swinging an axe against an innocent Scotch pine or sweeping the woodshop in silence as I sifted through my thoughts, this was where I came whenever I needed to think.

I heard the door open as I settled at my workbench, grabbing one of the animal figurines I was carving as a Christmas gift for Rosie. I turned around to see Mr. Lewellen walking in.

"Knox, I didn't see you sneak back here."

It didn't matter what time of year or how formal the occasion, I wasn't sure I had ever seen Mr. Lewellen in anything besides a flannel shirt and worn jeans—perhaps his way of rebelling in his adulthood against the formality of growing up in a manor house as a lord's son. Over the years, his belly had become more pronounced, and his gray hair had started to disappear. Seeing him age often made me wonder what my own dad would have looked like with the passage of time.

"Yeah, sorry. I needed to get out of the art room and come find some peace and quiet."

"It's a whole show in there, isn't it? I don't know how Prince Oliver does it, all the conversation and such. You know me, I much prefer the quiet of the woods and my shop."

"I feel the same way. But I'm sure you're going to love the media coverage of the place—-it should be great for business."

Mr. Lewellen chuckled. "Oh, Celeste is already worked up about the influx of customers and orders we're going to get. But we'll handle it."

"If you need any extra hands, just let me know and I'll make sure you have the help," I assured him.

"We'll manage. It'll be good to stay busy right before Christmas, and it'll give us a little extra money to put into Lyla's wedding this spring."

I huffed a laugh through my nose. "That should make her happy."

The Lewellens's youngest daughter Lyla and I had dated for a few months about four years prior. She was an amazing woman—intelligent, beautiful, witty. We tried to make our relationship work when she moved to France for school but ultimately concluded that it was best we break things off while we were still on good terms. I had been afraid that Mr. Lewellen would be angry and think I broke his daughter's heart, but the next day he had walked into the shop and let me know, man to man, that he understood and just wanted us both to be happy.

She met her fiancé, Laurent, at London Fashion Week two years ago. I had met him a few times and he seemed like a very kind man. He was the polar opposite of Darren Lewellen, working in a high-rise, financing one of Paris's largest fashion brands, but that's one of the reasons why Lyla loved him. I think we both knew long ago that she wouldn't end up in Wexstone, and she was looking for something different for her life.

"What are you working on there?" Mr. Lewellen pointed to the horse I was carving.

"Oh, this? It's a horse for Rosie. Every year for Christmas, I give her a few new animals to add to her collection. She used to play with them alongside her dollhouse, but now she keeps them displayed in a glass case."

"That's real nice of you. If she ever lets it slip that you made them, the country's little ones and their parents are going to be knocking down your door to make and sell them."

"I guess I'd better swear her to secrecy then," I chuckled. I had no desire to make this into a business. Carving was something to keep my hands busy while I sorted through my thoughts.

"So, Prince Oliver is looking for a bride. Do you have your eyes on anyone these days?"

Before I could answer, the door to the shop swung open and Birdie walked in, looking around in confusion.

"Oh crap," she huffed. "I thought the bathroom was through here."

"It's inside the gift shop, two buildings down," I told her.

"Gift shop building. Got it." She paused as she turned back toward the door, taking in the woodshop. "Wow, this place is amazing!" She moved toward my workbench, and I felt my muscles instinctively tense.

"Well, I'm going to head back out there, make sure everyone is settled," Darren said, patting me once on my shoulder.

"All right." I didn't want him to leave; I didn't want to be left alone with Birdie. Not after that dream, and not after seeing her with Oliver.

I scooted back from my workbench, putting as much space between us as I could without getting up and walking away. I reminded myself that she had no idea that she was the reason I had even snuck away to find some solace.

"Wow, Knox. Did you make this?" She held up the horse I had just been working on.

"Yeah."

"This is amazing. I had no idea you were so good at this stuff." She set the horse back on the table. "I mean, I figured you chopped wood since, you know, that's your whole vibe." She waved her hand toward me, referencing my clothes. "But I didn't know you were also an artist. That's so cool." She smiled brightly.

No one had ever called me an artist. Typically, they just called me an ass, or moody, or a recluse. Artist wasn't a description that had ever been used before.

"If you say so," I mumbled, suddenly embarrassed.

"Is this where you work?" She gestured vaguely around the workshop.

"No, I'm head of the grounds crew at the palace. This is where..." I stopped, wondering just how much I wanted to divulge to her about why I came here. I cleared my throat. "This is just a hobby." Short answers seemed better. Less chance of a prolonged conversation.

"Well, it's such a neat place. I can see why you'd want to come here. I really enjoyed the tour and meeting everyone today."

Her joy was evident—she had been nothing but smiles the entire afternoon, asking so many questions and being the first to volunteer at each workshop. I could tell that she was really trying to get to know Wextone's people and culture. It made me like her even more, especially when contrasted with the other women, who thus far seemed to either think they were too good for this place or were too shy to speak up much. Oliver needed someone outgoing who could at least feign interest in his country.

"What's this called?" Birdie asked, pulling me out of my thoughts. She held up one of my carving knives.

"That's a flat chisel knife."

She placed it back in my knife roll and picked up another. "And this one?"

"That's a pen knife."

She set it down. "Amazing. I didn't know there were so many different knives to carve with."

"Yeah."

"Could you show me how to carve something?"

I started, taken aback. "Uh, sure?"

"My granddad had a woodshop in his backyard. He made my mom shelves, benches for her garden, and all these little birdhouses. She loved them. He died when I was little, though," she said, the words rushing out.

I picked up a long, flat-head knife and a random chunk of wood from the scrap pile next to my bench. I handed her the wood and the knife and stood beside her.

"Okay, so take the knife and just start scraping down the wood with it. Make sure you're always working *away* from your body," I instructed.

She started working, making large divots that hurt my soul. I placed my hand on her wrist, stopping her.

"All right, you see how you're making those divots? That means you're pushing down too hard when you rake down. Hold the wood tight but move the knife a little faster, and don't push down so hard."

"Okay..." she said as she swiped down again, this time sending the knife flying across the worktable. "Shit!"

I held back a laugh. "It's okay. I don't think your grip was tight enough on that one. And that's a good example of why we always work away from our bodies." I reached for the knife and handed it back to her.

"Can you show me? I'm more of a kinetic learner."

I moved to stand behind her, placing my hands over hers. Standing behind her brought back flashes of grabbing her ass in the closet and ripping off her dress in the previous night's dream. This was torture. "I'll try," I said, attempting to keep my breath calm and steady. "Although you're a leftie, so it'll be a bit trickier." I wrapped her fingers around the knife and guided her hand down, trying not to think of how those same fingers had felt in my hair. "Like this. Firm, yet gentle."

I could feel her breath catch. *Oh God, can she feel my dick poking into her back?* A quick self-check confirmed that it wasn't. Why did her breath catch, then?

"Firm yet gentle." She cleared her throat. "Got it," she whispered.

"Try again."

This time I let her take the reins and glide our hands along the wood. Her right hand shook a bit, causing the knife to get stuck.

"Damnit," she said, flustered.

"It's okay. You just weren't holding on tight enough. Adjust your grip." She flexed her fingers, grazing mine as I held the wood. "It's all in the wrist. Hold the wood firmly and just guide the knife down. You want to clear out all of the blemishes and make it as smooth as you can."

"All right. Keep it all in my wrist."

I guided her hand again, making a flawless, clean stroke.

"That was perfect!" I told her.

"Well, I have a good instructor," she laughed, pleased with herself.

The door to the shop opened and I leaped back. *Way to play it cool, Knox.*

Vince's face appeared around the door. "Um," he paused, looking between Birdie and me. "Mr. Lewellen said he saw Birdie in here looking for the bathroom."

"Yeah," she laughed, setting down the piece of wood and my knife. "I got lost trying to find the bathroom and found Knox's man cave here instead. He was showing me how to carve."

"Well, everyone is getting ready to leave. I thought you might want to say goodbye to Oliver."

"Yes, definitely." She smiled, turning to me. "Thanks for showing me around the shop, Knox." She waved and followed Vince back into the art room.

Shit. I sat down, suddenly shaky and glad it had only been Vince who walked through that door.

————

After the day we'd had, I was happy to crack open a beer and toss the red squeaky ball across the living room, watching Eugene gleefully run to catch it.

I still needed to get a few things done around the grounds, though most of them would have to wait until morning. Everything was covered in snow, as was typical this time of year, but we liked to make sure the many statues were cleared off so they didn't break under the weight of the ice. The walkways from the terrace to the gardens needed to be salted and cleared, and the heater for the front fountain was on the fritz.

I enjoyed working with my hands and appreciated that leading the grounds crew made it possible for me to live on the property. I knew in my heart that Isobel and Leroy would have let me live here regardless, but I hated taking handouts. Besides, I was able to do work I loved. It all worked out.

I headed into the kitchen to make myself a sandwich and feed Eugene. If I didn't have his dinner out by six in the evening, he became insufferable with the whining and begging. There had even been a few times when the little shit stole my meal off the counter.

As I was digging in the fridge for some sliced ham and my favorite aged cheddar, I heard my phone chime from where it was charging in the living room. I walked over to grab it, pushing down the anxiety I felt nearly every time my phone went off. I knew from years of therapy that it was a lingering trauma response to losing my parents, though that knowledge didn't erase the worry I felt about the people I loved, especially Oliver and the family.

I opened my phone to a text from Vince.

VINCE

So about this afternoon…

What about it? Everything seemed fine.

I'm talking about when I walked in on you
and B

I should have known something was up the moment he looked at me earlier.

Nothing happened, man. I was just showing
her how to whittle.

A few moments passed, Vince's typing bubble appearing and disappearing.

VINCE

Look, I know she's hot and you guys probably
made out in the closet in NYC and I don't
blame you, but you told Ollie there wasn't
anything between you two. Think about what
the press would say if they caught wind of you
hooking up with one of the women

There isn't anything going on.

I rolled my eyes, aggressively slathering mustard on a piece of bread. Like I needed a reminder that Birdie was here for Oliver and not me. I was annoyed that Vince would even think I would do anything to cause a stir in the press or hurt Oliver. My phone chimed again.

VINCE

OK. Just make sure nothing else happens. It's
not just you guys that would get the shit end
of the deal. My family would too, you know?

My temper flared. This entire conversation was bullshit. I knew exactly what it would cost everyone if I had feelings for Birdie. I had spent the entire day thinking about what it would cost everyone.

> I KNOW!

I threw the dirty knife into the sink, and it landed with a loud *bang*, causing Eugene's head to jolt up from his bowl, cocking worriedly to the side. He wasn't used to this kind of anger from me, but Vince's words had really struck a chord. I had to get out of the house and work this energy out.

I grabbed my coat and slid on my work boots. Eugene loped up, eyes pleading to tag along.

"Of course you can come."

He answered me with a bark as his tail thudded happily against the kitchen island.

———

The steps leading to the service entrance at the back of the palace were a bit icy. As soon as I got through the door, I checked the list of tasks, mentally adding salting the steps to the top of the it. Having someone slip down those was the last thing I wanted.

I grabbed the large bag of de-icing salt and took care of the steps. Once that was done, I flipped through the clipboard with the work orders, looking for a smaller project that could be completed tonight. Spotting an order that had come in earlier this afternoon for Rosalind's room, I fetched my toolbox and headed upstairs.

The palace was quiet. I figured that everyone was probably finishing up dinner or already in their suites for the evening, given the busy day. If it weren't for my agitation and need to fix something, I would probably have been in bed watching a movie.

Eugene padded behind me up the back stairwell. No one minded if I used the ornate staircase by the palace entry, but I tried to avoid it when both Eugene and I were tracking in snow and salt. No need to give anyone extra work cleaning up our footprints in the morning.

At the top of the stairs, we entered a corridor filled with doors to everyone's offices. Isobel had begged and pleaded with me to take one of them, but I refused every time she mentioned it. There was no reason for me to take a royal office when I had a perfectly good desk downstairs in the basement.

The door to Leroy's office was cracked open and I spotted a head of copper hair. Eugene and I approached to find Xavier examining the bookcase, running his fingers along the spines of the books.

I was surprised to see him in the palace at all after his absence today, much less in his father's office. Leroy typically didn't like anyone to be in there alone.

"Hey," I said, trying not to startle him.

"Oh—hey, Knox." He turned and gave me a nod. "I'm just looking for something. What are you doing here?"

I held up the pink slip with the work order on it. "Headed to Rosie's room."

Xavier nodded approvingly, then shoved his hands in his pockets, his shoulders bowing inward. "I was just looking for something. Father said I could come look through his books to find any answers."

I made it a rule to stay out of other people's business, but I couldn't help but examine Xavier closely as he spoke. He had been acting strangely since his abdication. Even now, there were dark circles under his eyes, and his worried posture was a change from his normal ramrod-straight back.

"Okay. Well, I need to go finish this work order." I turned to leave.

"And I think I found what I needed. See you later."

I paused, knowing I was about to overstep but deciding I didn't care. "Hey, Xavier, where were you today?"

Xavier's eyes shot to me, guilt plastered on his face. "I had some unexpected business to take care of. Took quite a bit longer than I thought."

"You couldn't have texted to let anyone know?" I asked, accusation creeping into my voice.

His eyes narrowed. "You sound like Mother."

I gentled my tone. "Oliver was upset."

Xavier let out a breath and ran his hands through his hair. "Look, I know Oliver is pissed that I abdicated. I figured he wouldn't care whether I was here or not."

"You're still his brother. Even if he's mad, he wants your support. He's doing this for everyone, not just himself."

"I'll make sure I'm there for the next event." A few seconds passed. "Thanks for watching out for him, Knox. You're a better brother than I am."

"That's not true."

"Yes. It is."

I didn't know what to say. I had grown up with Xavier—shit, I had idolized him when we were kids. I knew how much he loved his family, but these last few months had shown a different side of him. He was emotionally and physically absent in a way he'd never been before.

"Well, I should be going. I'll see you around," Xavier said, stepping past me to exit the office, stopping to give Eugene a scratch behind the ear as he closed the door.

"See you later, man," I said.

Eugene and I continued our way down the hall and up one more flight of stairs to the royal suites. We approached Rosalind's room, the farthest door on the left, and I knocked three times.

"Come in," she answered softly.

I opened the door, and Eugene barreled past me, nearly knocking me over. Rosie was sitting in an overstuffed armchair with her back to the door, a book in hand. Eugene wasted no time jumping up onto the chair and licking her hands.

"Hi, Eugene!" Rosie exclaimed gleefully. She had adored Eugene from the time he was a puppy. "What are you doing here?" she asked, looking over her shoulder at me.

"Hey, squirt. I got a work order for your room. Mind if I fix it now?"

"I don't mind. The drawer to my desk is stuck and my toilet is making a funny noise."

"Did you clog it up with your big ol' dookies again?"

"Knox!" she squealed. "You *know* it was Princess Catherine who clogged my toilet when she visited!"

I roared with laughter. I knew it hadn't been Rosie, but Oliver and I were forever teasing her about it. Princess Catherine had clogged the toilet so badly that it flooded the entire bathroom and ruined the ceiling of the floor below. Catherine was so embarrassed that Rosie took the blame, but after endless amounts of teasing from Oliver and me, Rosie finally confessed that it was Catherine. It was one of the realities of living with royals that no one wanted to talk about: Everybody shits.

"Sure it was," I winked.

"Ugh, I should never have taken the blame for her. Brothers are the worst," Rosie muttered under her breath.

I chuckled, my heart warming that she included me when she talked about her brothers. She had a sweet and generous spirit that made everyone adore her, and it was an honor to be one of her big brothers.

"What are you reading?" I asked as I strode to her writing desk.

"*Treasure Island.*" She held the book up to show me the cover. "Father said I should read the 'classics' and that there is some good stuff to learn from this, but I'm not getting it."

I jiggled the drawer. It didn't budge. "You're telling me that you don't like a story filled with pirates and treasure and adventure?"

Rosalind, in all her preteen wonder, rolled her eyes and slammed the book shut. She walked over to watch me work.

Moving to the floor, I looked underneath the desk to investigate and spotted something sticking out from the back of the drawer. There was just enough space to use my finger to push it back, releasing the drawer.

"I see the problem," I said, holding up the wooden dolphin I had carved for Rosie about five years before.

"Oh no! Is it broken or anything?" She took the dolphin from my hand, giving it a careful once-over.

"No, I think it's okay. Its nose got caught at the back of the drawer," I answered. "Why is it in the drawer and not in the curio cabinet?"

"Well..." She blushed, looking at me and then at the wooden dolphin in her hand. "I know you made it for my collection, but when I heard that Oliver was getting married, I decided to give it to my new sister since dolphins represent friendship and loyalty. Sort of like a welcome-to-the-family gift. I put it in the drawer so nothing would happen to it." She wrapped her fingers around the small figurine.

My heart squeezed at her words. Rosalind had always wanted a sister. From the time she was a tiny girl, she would take turns asking Oliver and me when one of us was going to get married, because she wanted a sister and to have more girls around.

"That's really sweet, Rosie. I think your future sister-in-law will love it." I smiled.

"As long as it's not that bitch Renata, I'll be happy."

"Rosie!" I exclaimed, surprised. I had never heard her swear before.

"What?! She is, and you know it."

All I could do was laugh. She wasn't wrong, although I was surprised she had picked up on just how bad Renata was. I wondered how much this little girl, with one foot in childhood and the other in adolescence, really observed when the rest of us thought she wasn't watching.

After fixing her toilet, which turned out to be a loose valve, I checked my watch. Time to head home.

"All right, squirt. I think I fixed everything. Don't clog any more toilets for a few more weeks, okay?"

A low huff came from the overstuffed chair.

"Let's go home, Eugene," I called from the door.

"He told me he wants to stay here tonight," Rosie answered from under the dog.

"Oh, he did, huh?"

She burrowed her head into his neck and scratched his ears. Eugene let out a loud, satisfied sigh. They were insufferably cute.

"Fine. Steal my dog for the night. I'll get him at breakfast."

CHAPTER 13
BIRDIE

"Birdie! I miss you!" Sam's face filled the phone screen, her smile wide.

"I miss you, too! What's new at home?" I rolled onto my side, snuggling into my pillow and relishing the warmth of the down covers. It was early and I still had at least half an hour before Sonya would be in to officially wake me up to get ready for my private palace tour with Prince Oliver.

"Literally nothing. Dating is dumb, people are off their rocker, work is boring. I'd much rather hear about your life, thanks very much. Tell me *everything*," Sam gushed. She had always been an extreme night owl, often doing her best work after midnight. It was baffling, but I was certainly glad for it now with the time difference.

I filled her in on the whirlwind of the last few days, including as many details as I could remember.

"We had yesterday free and, to be honest, I spent most of the day catching up on sleep. I'm headed to the palace later this morning for a private tour with the prince, though."

"Is Prince Oliver as nice as he seemed when we hung out with him here?"

"Oh, for sure," I said. "He is genuinely kind and caring, maybe even a little bit shy at times. Although I think he does have his limits; he was really pissed when that reporter asked about my mom. He handled it well, but I could tell how mad he was."

"Sounds like he's protective of the people he cares about," Sam said thoughtfully.

"I mean, I dunno if he knows me well enough yet to care about me," I hedged.

Sam gave me a skeptical look. "Okay, sure. Keep telling yourself that, Birdie," she laughed. "So...what about Knox?"

"What about him?"

"Like, has he been around? Have you seen him much?"

"Oh yeah, he's been at all the events so far. I actually ran into him at the woodshop the other day while I was looking for the bathroom. He has a workspace there, showed me some of his carvings, and then he showed me how to work with the wood."

"Work with the wood or *work with the wood*?" She wiggled her eyebrows.

"What the hell is that supposed to mean?"

I knew exactly what she meant but didn't want to admit to spending the rest of that night trying to tell myself that I in fact did *not* like the way his hands felt on mine. I had questioned why carving a piece of wood was so erotic before realizing it was because any time Knox put his hands on me, my body came alive and buzzed with anticipation of how he would touch me next. The moment I felt myself get hot and wet below, I had to remind myself that I was here for the prince, not his best friend.

Sam plastered an innocent look on her face. "Girl, you

know exactly what I mean. I remember your shit-eating grin when you came out of that closet."

I shook my head. "As fun as that was, Knox knows I'm here to date Prince Oliver. And besides, the man is so standoffish. He didn't even seem like he wanted to talk to me at the wood-shop; he was giving the most perfunctory answers to my questions." I thought about the way he had tensed when he touched me and had held his body as far from mine as possible. The exact opposite of the man who gripped my ass and made me give him an "enthusiastic yes" before he sucked my soul out of my body. "There's definitely nothing going on there." I felt a knot at the pit of my stomach. "I am fully in this moment, here for Prince Oliver, and giving this my all." Maybe if I told myself that enough, it would be true.

With a soft knock, Sonya peeked into the room. "Good morning, Ms. Hamilton."

"Good morning, Sonya," I greeted. I looked back at my phone, trying to ignore the irritatingly bemused look on Sam's face. "I've gotta go. Talk later this week?"

"Absolutely. Have fun, make good choices, love you," she said, blowing a kiss.

I blew a kiss in return. "Make good choices, love you."

I climbed out of bed, stretching as I turned to Sonya, who was setting a much-welcomed tray of coffee on the desk. "How are you this morning?"

Sonya turned. She wore a hesitant look on her face. "I'm well, miss. How are you?"

"I'm fine. I was just chatting with my best friend." I took in Sonya's unusually tight posture. "Sonya, is everything all right?"

She paused, wringing her hands. "I don't suppose you've had a look at the news, have you?"

Several articles had come out the day before detailing the

contest, the welcome gala, and the prince's suitors. While the details varied, all the articles were fairly benign, more focused on what we were wearing than anything else.

"I saw yesterday's articles, but I haven't looked online yet this morning. Did something else come out?"

Sonya nodded. "Yes, miss."

I held my phone out to her. "Show me."

She took the phone, opening the web browser and typing for a moment before handing the phone back to me. "I'll let you have a few moments while I draw you a bath." She headed into the bathroom, closing the door behind her to give me some privacy. I heard the tub faucet start to run as I sat on the end of the bed and looked at the article Sonya had pulled up on *Pine Times:*

PRINCE OLIVER'S SUITORS: ARE THEY EVEN SUITABLE?

BY: ALISTAIR DAVIES

AS OUR CROWN PRINCE SEEKS A WIFE TO FULFILL HIS ROYAL DUTIES, IT IS UP TO THE PEOPLE OF WEXSTONE TO ASK: ARE THE WOMEN VYING TO BE QUEEN PREPARED FOR THE CHALLENGE OF LEADING OUR GREAT COUNTRY?

OF THE EIGHT CONTENDERS FOR THE PRINCE'S HEART, IT SEEMS CLEAR TO THIS REPORTER THAT VERY FEW MAY TRULY BE SUITED TO ROYAL LIFE.

LET'S BEGIN WITH CORA MAXIMO. WHILE IT CANNOT BE DENIED THAT HER CRANBERRY SCONES ARE THE BEST IN THE CAPITAL, HOW MUCH CAN A BAKER POSSIBLY UNDERSTAND ABOUT THE DEMANDS OF RUNNING A COUNTRY? AND WE MUST TAKE INTO ACCOUNT MS. MAXIMO'S FRUMPY ATTIRE AND APPEARANCE. CAN A WOMAN WHO CANNOT EVEN DRESS HERSELF APPROPRIATELY BE TRUSTED WITH PRESENTING WEXSTONE FLATTERINGLY TO OUR ALLIES?

NEXT: SABINE THORNE. WHILE SHE MAY BE THE PRINCESS OF HER FATHER'S FLORAL EMPIRE, HER WORK IN ENVIRONMENTAL SUSTAINABILITY BRINGS INTO QUESTION WHETHER SHE WOULD HAVE THE TIME TO BE OUR QUEEN. WHAT'S MORE, MS. THORNE IS SURE TO PULL THE ROYAL PURSE-STRINGS IN HER FAMILY'S

FAVOR, LEAVING THE REST OF THE COUNTRY'S INDUSTRIES FLOUNDERING FOR FUNDS.

I'LL ADMIT THAT ADELAIDE LEVY HAD ME FOOLED AT FIRST. SURELY ONE OF THE CITY'S MOST BELOVED PRIMARY TEACHERS, WHO IS OFTEN FOUND VOLUNTEERING HER TIME WITH THE LESS FORTUNATE, WOULD MAKE A REASONABLE RULER, OR AT LEAST SERVE AS A GOOD MOTHER TO OUR KING'S CHILDREN? YET MS. LEVY SEEMS AS UNINTERESTED IN BEING A PART OF THE PALACE'S CONTEST AS MY CAT, UNDOUBTEDLY REVEALING HER TRUE NATURE.

MELLIE SCHNEIDER IS THE SUITOR I HAVE PERSONALLY KNOWN THE LONGEST, GIVEN HER CAREER AS A FELLOW JOURNALIST. I CAN SAY WITH CONFIDENCE THAT MS. SCHNEIDER HAS HER FULL FOCUS ON HER CAREER AND THAT SHE HAS NEVER EXHIBITED A SINGLE MATERNAL INSTINCT IN ALL THE TIME I HAVE KNOWN HER. IS THAT WHO WE WANT RAISING THE NEXT GENERATION OF PRINCES AND PRINCESSES?

AND FINALLY, WE COME TO THE AMERICAN: BERNADETTE HAMILTON. MS. HAMILTON MAKES THE PREVIOUS FOUR WOMEN SEEM LIKE IDEAL CANDIDATES FOR THE PRINCE'S HAND. TO USE AN AMERICAN PHRASE, TO SAY THAT MS. HAMILTON IS "ROUGH AROUND THE EDGES" IS A VAST UNDERSTATEMENT. SHE IS UNFAMILIAR WITH OUR CUSTOMS, EXHIBITS AN APPALLING LACK OF REFINEMENT, AND—AS I LEARNED FROM AN UNNAMED SOURCE—WAS SEEN WAVING A MONSTROUS SEX TOY AROUND THE AIRPORT, SCREAMING THAT THEY "COULDN'T TAKE HER FAVORITE PASTIME FROM HER," UPON HER ARRIVAL IN WEXSTONE. THE FACT THAT SHE WAS ALLOWED TO BE A PART OF THIS CONTEST FOR PRINCE OLIVER'S HEART IS CONCERNING AT BEST.

YES, IT WOULD SEEM THAT RENATA RAINES, GEMMA ROUSSEAU-WU, AND GINNY WU-MURPHY ARE, IN FACT, THE ONLY PARTICIPANTS WHO HAVE SPENT TIME IN THE ROYAL COURT AND THUS ARE THE ONLY WOMEN HERE WITH A TRUE UNDERSTANDING OF WHAT IT TAKES TO BE ROYAL. LET US HOPE, FOR THE SAKE OF OUR COUNTRY, THAT OUR BELOVED PRINCE SETS HIS SIGHTS ON ONE OF THESE FINE WOMEN.

I dropped my phone into my lap, my jaw slack with shock. *Is this asshole for fucking real right now?* And where had he gotten the idea that I had waved the vibrator around or screamed about it being my favorite pastime?

As quickly as the shock set in, panic followed. What would the prince say? Surely this would mean the end of my time here in Wexstone. And what about Vince? I had clearly failed him; Bronson would be furious, and it would be all Vince's fault for bringing me here in the first place.

The sound of the faucet turning off floated to me, and a few moments later, Sonya quietly opened the bathroom door. She walked over to me, setting her hand gently on my shoulder.

"Are you okay, miss?"

Face flushed with embarrassment, I looked up at her kind face and the concern in her eyes. "Not really, no." I took a deep breath, swallowing back tears.

Sonya knelt to look me in the eyes. "Listen, love. Alistair Davies is a miscreant. John Astor at *Wexstone Daily* is more prominently known as a bastard, but Davies has long flown under the radar while writing absolute filth. The prince is a level-headed man; he surely won't pay this garbage much mind so neither should you."

I gave her a wobbly smile. "Thanks, Sonya. Let's hope so. Do you mind bringing my breakfast up here? I don't think I'm quite ready to face Bronson. I'd rather avoid him until after I see the prince."

Sonya gave me a knowing look and patted my hand. "Of course, dear. You take a nice long bath—it'll make you feel right as rain. Your breakfast will be here waiting for you when you're done. If Lord Alexander asks, I'll make your excuses for you."

———

I took a shaky breath as the car stopped in front of the palace. I felt more jittery than I had in days, thanks to that article. I had successfully avoided Bronson before leaving the manor, although Vince had caught me on my way out the door. He had tried to be reassuring, repeating much of what Sonya had said, but his lack of eye contact told me that he was a bit shaken, too.

"Don't worry, Birdie. We'll figure it out," he had said, squeezing my upper arm in a brotherly way.

I turned now to see Prince Oliver waiting at the bottom of the marble steps, hands in the pockets of his charcoal-gray peacoat. He was wearing dark wash jeans paired with a light gray sweater, looking more comfortable and casual than I had seen him since New York.

Carter opened the door for me, a custom I still wasn't quite used to. I stepped out of the car and was surprised to see the prince smiling broadly at me.

"Good morning, Birdie," he said warmly, closing the distance between us and kissing me on the cheek.

"Good morning, Your Highness," I replied.

"Please, call me Oliver," he said quietly. "I know Bronson probably gave you a lesson on proper titles, but it feels strange for you to call me 'prince' or 'Your Highness'—I'd much rather just be 'Oliver' to you."

"Well then: Good morning, Oliver." I gave him a nervous smile as I bit my bottom lip and fiddled with the buttons on my white wool coat.

Concern filled his eyes. "Are you all right?"

I cleared my throat. "Um...not really. Did you see the article?"

A look of understanding crossed his face. "Oh, of course. I should have known you would have seen it by now. Here, come inside and we'll talk." He ushered me up the steps and into the palace, his hand at the small of my back.

Once inside, Oliver helped me remove my coat, handing it to a short, stocky man who appeared from around a corner. "Thank you, Preston. We'll come find you to retrieve that before Ms. Hamilton leaves." He turned back to me. "There's a sitting room just down the corridor where we can talk."

I followed as he led me down the hall into a spacious, yet cozy, room filled with plush couches and bookshelves. A grand piano sat in the corner, sheet music spread across the music desk. Sunlight poured in through a set of windows into which was set a window seat. I wanted to curl up like a cat in one of the sunbeams and nap the day away.

"Please, have a seat," the prince said, motioning to one of the couches.

Oliver was handsome, there was no denying that, but he also carried himself with poise and presence. Behind the kind blue eyes, he held the power of a king; he was not someone you wanted to disappoint or disgrace, though I was afraid that I already had.

I sat, turning to face him as he lowered himself into the adjacent armchair. "Oliver, I'm so sorry. You have every right to be upset, and I understand if you and your family want me to leave—"

"Leave? What? No! Birdie, I am upset, but not at you," he interjected, running his hands through his hair.

"You're not?"

"Of course not. None of this is your fault. And I certainly don't want you to leave—unless you want to go." He reached over, resting his hand gently on top of mine. "I would never want you to stay if you didn't want to."

"I don't want to leave."

Oliver grinned sheepishly, squeezing my hand gently

before removing his. "Well, I'm glad for that. The only one I'm upset with here is Alistair Davies. He had no right to write those things about you or any of the other women. And I spoke with Vince first thing this morning. He explained what happened to you at customs." He blushed furiously. I felt my cheeks redden as well. "Either Davies or his supposed source purposefully mischaracterized the situation to slander you."

"I appreciate your understanding," I said, my nerves finally lessening. "But what about your parents?"

The corner of Oliver's mouth quirked upward. "My parents know well what it is like to be under the press's microscope. I can assure you there have been plenty of unflattering pieces written about them in the past thirty years. They know better than to judge someone based on a single news article. I have already spoken with them about dealing with Davies, and they have given me their full support in however I choose to deal with him. I'll be making sure the rest of the women who were maligned in his article know this as well."

I sighed, taking my first full, deep breath since Sonya had shown me the article. "Thank you."

"It is my pleasure. Now," he said, bracing his hands on his knees as he stood, "you're here for me to give you a tour of the palace and grounds. Where would you like to start?"

The morning was spent in pleasant conversation as Oliver showed me the sprawling palace. He was easy to talk to and demonstrated a level of thoughtfulness I hadn't expected, anticipating my desire to see as much of the palace's art as possible and planning his tour accordingly.

"I just can't imagine growing up surrounded by so much beautiful artwork," I said, pausing in front of a Vermeer in the larger of the palace's two galleries. "Look at his use of light, isn't it incredible?"

Oliver stood beside me, his hands clasped loosely behind him as he admired the painting. "I must admit, I don't think I appreciated these paintings all that much as a child. I spent so much of my time in the nursery with my brother and our nanny or outside on the grounds. I considered the ballrooms and galleries and staterooms to be stuffy and boring—you know, for the adults and their endless dinners and galas. It's only now, as an adult myself, that I am starting to truly appreciate the history housed within these walls." He bowed his head. "I suppose that must sound terribly out of touch."

I cocked my head to the right as I moved on to admire a mountain landscape that the description said was of an area in the north of Wexstone. "I don't think so," I replied. "I mean, I get how someone might think that, but I don't. Like, I think I took growing up around a dance studio for granted—it was what was normal for me, so I didn't really think a lot about it until it was gone."

We were both quiet for a moment. "Thank you," Oliver said softly.

"For what?"

"For seeing my humanity."

I swallowed. Had so few people seen the human being inside the royal exterior? *You were guilty of the same until recently,* I reminded myself. I vowed not to make that mistake again.

"Okay, Your Highness," I said, knocking my shoulder playfully into his upper arm, "tell me a secret. What's something no one knows?"

Oliver eyed me as we continued through the gallery. "I'll tell you," he said apprehensively, "but you have to promise to share one, too."

"All right. And your secret is safe with me. Pinky promise." I held out my right hand, pinky finger extended.

Oliver laughed, hooking his pinky around mine. "Pinky promise." He turned to face me, placing his palms together just in front of his chin and took a deep inhale. "I love eighties hair bands." He exhaled.

I took in his chiseled features, his clean haircut, his preppy clothes. "Hair bands...like Mötley Crüe and Guns N' Roses?" I asked incredulously.

"*Not* like Guns N' Roses. But yes, like Mötley Crüe. And Poison, and Whitesnake, and Twisted Sister. Mum made each of us kids pick a musical instrument to play. I chose guitar so I could play hair metal in secret. I also have an extensive collection of hair metal T-shirts that I wear when I'm alone."

I shook my head. "Well, I certainly would not have guessed that one," I said, laughing.

"Rosie knows about it, and of course Knox does as well. My security team has caught on—just doing their jobs, really—but I've managed to keep it from Xavier. He would never let me live it down. In another life, I might have been a rock musician." He shrugged. "But instead, I'm about to be king, so I suppose I'll have to stick to rocking out when I'm alone."

"Can I ask you something?"

"Of course."

"Do you want to be king?"

"You didn't hold back with that one, did you?" He chuckled as he ran his hand over his jaw. "Honestly, I never thought much about it. It was always assumed it would be Xavier. When he abdicated, it shocked everyone—no one more so than me. But to answer your question: I don't know. I don't think it's about what I want anymore, to be honest."

"But you don't *have* to become king, do you?"

"Rosie is so young, I couldn't do that to her. By law, she'd have to find a husband once she turned eighteen—I can't imagine asking that of her." He sat on a bench in front of a portrait of the royal family in 1832. I took a seat beside him, our thighs grazing. "It's my responsibility now."

I didn't know what to say. I admired the sacrifice he was willing to make for his sister but wondered what it was costing him.

"By my calculation," Oliver said, his tone brightening, "you still owe me a secret."

"You're right. Hmm...well. When I was in undergrad, I waited tables at this local restaurant. The manager was awful—he was mean to the back-of-house staff and super inappropriate with the servers, all of whom were pretty girls. If anyone tried to push back, he would lie and get them fired and blast their name all over town so they would struggle to get another restaurant job. The owner was a nice guy, but he wasn't in often, and the manager would put on a total good-guy act when he was. After about six months of working there, I found one of my coworkers crying in the walk-in; apparently, he had grabbed her ass and told her that if she didn't start wearing tighter shirts, he'd be skimming her tips. She was afraid to report him because she was a single mom who really needed the job.

"Well, I'd had enough. I created a burner email account and tipped off the owner anonymously. I didn't know if it would work or not, but it turns out that it did. He did a bit of an 'undercover boss' move and sent his sister in as a new server. Within a few hours, the manager had groped her, and she caught him spitting into an appetizer. He was fired that night. They never figured out who sent the email, and I never told anyone."

"Wow, don't mess with Birdie. Got it."

"You only have to worry if you make my friends cry," I said with a wink.

"Duly noted." Oliver stood, holding out his hand to help me up. "Shall we make our way out to the grounds?"

"Sure," I said, stretching as I stood. "Who manages the art here?" I asked as we exited the gallery, turning left down a long hall. "I'd love to meet them and talk to them about the collection."

"Our palace curator retired recently, actually," Oliver answered, collecting our coats from Preston before leading me down a short staircase and out a set of glass doors onto the sprawling grounds. "We have yet to hire his replacement. We're struggling to find someone with the necessary background who is more interested in caring for the art than being near royalty."

We walked in companionable silence across the grounds, Oliver occasionally pointing out a sculpture or tree along the way, while I considered how hard it must be for the royal family to surround themselves with trustworthy people. Our lives were so different, yet at the end of the day, it seemed all Oliver wanted was to know that the people around him were there because of who he was and not what he could do for them. And wasn't that really what we all wanted—to be loved for who we were? My heart ached that Oliver had to fight so hard for something so human.

After a few minutes of walking, passing several sprawling gardens and more fountains than I could count, we turned a corner, and a small cottage came into view. I heard a sharp whistle accompanied by the sound of something running toward me before I was knocked off my feet by a brownish-red blur.

A loud *oof* escaped me as I fell onto my back, only to be

silenced by two large paws on my chest and a very wet tongue lapping at my face.

"Eugene! Off! Come!" I heard a familiar voice shout. The weight lifted from my chest; I lifted my head to see a lanky, floppy-eared dog slink to Knox, tail between his legs. Oliver, meanwhile, was doubled over, struggling to catch his breath between peals of laughter.

"I'm so sorry," Knox apologized, reaching out his hand as he approached and helping me to my feet. I thought I felt a surge of electricity as we touched, his calloused fingers clasping my hand tightly. My stomach dipped. "He usually has much better manners than that," he added, shooting a vexed glance over at the dog, who was now sitting on his haunches, gazing at us angelically as though to say, "Who, me?"

"Are you hurt?" Knox asked.

I did a quick body scan as I steadied myself, looking up into his deep blue eyes laced with worry. "I'm okay."

Knox furrowed his brows. "Again, I am so sorry." He pushed a stray piece of my hair behind my ear, sending another shiver of electricity down my spine.

I straightened my collar and brushed the snow off my coat. "You said his name is Eugene?" Crouching, I held out my hand to the dog, who glanced at me before looking to Knox.

Knox nodded to the dog. "Go ahead," he said, taking a step back. "Yes, this is Eugene."

Eugene trotted to me, sitting before nosing my hand in a request for ear scratches.

Oliver had, by now, collected himself and moved to where Knox, Eugene, and I now stood. "Eugene is the favorite member of the family," Oliver said, giving the dog an affectionate pat on the head.

"Well, when his competition is Xavier..." Knox said quietly.

Oliver coughed into his fist, choking back laughter.

I wasn't sure what to make of the joke, although I had heard enough about Xavier to think that Knox was probably right. "What breed is he?" I asked as Eugene flopped down in the snow, belly in the air. I happily responded by rubbing my hand across his chest. He snorted with joy.

Knox rolled his eyes. "He's supposed to be a Vizsla, but right now all he's being is a big flirt." He stuffed his hands in his pockets.

I laughed. "Well, I like you too, Eugene."

"We should actually get back to work," Knox said, motioning vaguely behind him. "Sorry to have interrupted your...date." He coughed awkwardly. "Enjoy the rest of your tour." He nodded to Oliver and me, then snapped his fingers. Eugene sprang to his feet and followed as Knox turned and strode back across the grounds, past the cottage and toward a greenhouse.

"That's where Knox lives," Oliver said, inclining his head toward the cottage as we went in the opposite direction.

I glanced back at the house. "He does? I thought he lived in the palace? Or..." My voice trailed off. I guessed that was just an assumption I had made; I hadn't really wondered where Knox lived before. The image of Knox lifting me and wrapping my legs around his waist back in the closet flashed across my mind. I shoved the thought aside. "How long has he lived there?"

"Since I left for university," Oliver answered. "Knox is one of the smartest people you'll ever meet and reads more than anyone I know, but he didn't want to go to university. He said he didn't want to accidentally become one of those miserable old men who spend forty years working in an office only to realize after retiring that they'd missed out on life. Instead, he decided to stay here and work on the grounds crew and asked Mum and Dad if he could move into the old groundskeeper's cottage if he fixed the place up. He needn't have worried; my parents would have gladly let him live anywhere he asked and would have happily paid for as many degrees as he wanted if he had decided to stay in school. But Knox has always tried to repay my parents for taking him in after his parents passed away. I don't think he realizes how unnecessary that is and how much our family loves him. Mum and Dad won't even let him dip into his inheritance, always finding ways to pay for anything he needs and insisting that he save it for his future family."

"Oh wow," I said, feeling a bit speechless. Oliver placed his hand gently on my lower back as he led me back toward the palace. I realized with a start that I had touched Oliver several times now over the course of the day, and none of them had elicited the same kind of reaction in me as Knox touching my hand or tucking my hair behind my ear. Not even one of Oliver's touches was seared into my brain the way the kiss I had shared with Knox was. I was certainly becoming fond of Oliver, but my heart only raced when Knox was in the room.

Oh fuck. I was in for it.

CHAPTER 14
BIRDIE

"Hello, everyone. May I have your attention?" Adelaide's smooth voice sounded through a small speaker at the back of the school library. The room of about a hundred volunteers quieted as we turned toward her, gathering closer.

It was a chilly Monday morning, and my fellow contestants and I were participating in the annual donation drive at the primary school where Adelaide taught. It was the first time I was interacting directly with the citizens of Wexstone, and I was looking forward to seeing more of the people who made this country special. I ran my hands down the thighs of my high-waisted brown dress pants, partially to wipe off the nervous perspiration that had soaked my palms and partially to remove any fuzz from the thick cream sweater I wore.

Adelaide showed no nerves as she held the microphone, speaking to the small crowd effortlessly. It was clear she was used to speaking in front of people on a regular basis.

"Thank you all for being here for our community outreach day. As you all know, the Garland Neighborhood is one of the lowest-income areas of Altborn, and many of the families whose children attend school here struggle to afford new coats, school supplies, and sometimes food. This donation drive is one of our most treasured annual events—so much so that we give our students the day off. We are so grateful for the donations we have received, and we are especially thankful that the royal family is here this year to help shine a light on this event." She gestured toward Queen Isobel, who nodded in return.

Adelaide continued, "I'm sure you noticed the increased security screenings when entering today. Thank you for your patience and your attentiveness to the added safety protocols as we keep our royals safe."

The air around me shifted, causing the hairs on the back of my neck to rise. I glanced to the right and caught Knox watching me from where he stood by Oliver, Tej, and Chauncey about ten feet away. Our eyes locked for a split second before he turned back to the front, his face a mask of nonchalance. Every single time we had touched flashed through my head in quick succession, just as it did while lying alone in bed at night. The way his lips had felt kissing my neck, the way his hands had felt around my own as he guided them across the wood in the workshop—it was hot. *He* was hot. I kept reminding myself that I was there to court Oliver, not Knox, but Knox was the intrusive thought that would not quit.

Adelaide's voice drew my attention once again. "You will notice that there are a few volunteers wearing green vests—these are some of our amazing teachers who will oversee our stations today. Clothing donations and the food pantry lines will be set up in the gymnasium; Coach Littlefield"—a man in his forties wearing an emerald-green vest raised his warm to wave—"can show you where to go if you're not familiar with the building.

"There will be signs in the corridors leading you to the school supply donation room, an activity area for the children while their parents get the food and other supplies they need, and a break room where Joleta from Jolly Java has donated some refreshments for our volunteers. Are there any questions?"

After a beat of silence, Adelaide dismissed everyone, and the crowd dispersed. Vince had informed me over breakfast that he had signed me up for the activity room with the kids after hearing me gush about playing with my niece, so I found him, and we walked to a classroom where we were met by a woman in her sixties with snow-white hair. It was cut close to her head, and she wore an embroidered sweater that read "Oh what fun it is to teach" next to a dancing snowman. She was adorable.

"Hello, I'm Mrs. Sallow. Are you here to help with the kids today?"

"Hi," I said, grasping the warm hand she held out to me. "I'm Bernadette, and this is Vince. Yes, we're here to help you with whatever you need."

"I love to hear that. I'm just getting the arts and crafts table ready now. I took home the pillows and blankets from our reading corner and washed them last night. Vince, you look like you have some muscles, could you bring that big laundry basket over here and set them out?"

I giggled as she pointed him to the desk at the back of the classroom.

Vince placed his hand over his heart, pretending to be hurt. "I'm more than just my muscles."

"I'm sure you are, dear. But now is not the time to let your mind be wounded. We have things to do before the kids get here," Mrs. Sallow quipped back. I liked her.

As we finished setting up, four families walked in, each

with two kids ranging from about four to ten years old. The kids sprinted to their favorite activities and settled down to play.

Suddenly, the chatter in the room stopped and everyone stood up, bowing or curtsying. I looked to the door as Queen Isobel, Oliver, and Knox walked in, shadowed by a security guard who stayed by the door. They nodded in greeting and the activity in the room resumed. I noticed that Knox seemed to be going out of his way to avoid looking toward my corner of the room.

"Your Majesty." Mrs. Sallow approached the queen and curtsied again. "It's a pleasure to have you here in my classroom."

"The pleasure is all mine," Queen Isobel replied, grasping Mrs. Sallow's hand kindly. "I thought Prince Oliver might like to spend some time here with the children if that's all right?"

"I'm sure the children would love that. Prince Oliver, it's a pleasure to meet you." She bobbed again in his direction.

"It's nice to meet you as well. How long have you been teaching here?" he asked.

"This will be my fortieth year."

"Amazing. That is dedication. Thank you for your service to the children of Wexstone."

"It's my passion, Your Highness. I don't take lightly the responsibility of molding and shaping young minds. I started out teaching third years and then they needed a kindergarten teacher. I lasted one year. Those kinder teachers are a special breed," she laughed, shaking her head. "Well, you would know. Ms. Levy, one of our kindergarten teachers, is one of your suitors, correct?"

"She is," Oliver replied, his tone soft and reflective.

"She is a good one, that girl. She's very determined. Smart, too. But I'm talking too much. I apologize, Your Highness."

"Don't," Queen Isobel chuckled. "We love to hear what you have to say."

"May I show you around, ma'am?"

Mrs. Sallow escorted the queen around the classroom, sharing with her about the projects her fifth-year students were working on before the upcoming holiday break. Oliver approached the table where I was sitting and coloring with a little boy.

"How am I not surprised you're at the art table?" he laughed.

"Very funny," I said. "Here." I slid a white piece of paper with an outline of a Christmas tree on it and a box of crayons toward him. "I think this might be more your speed, Your Highness. Just make sure to stay in the lines." I winked.

He let out a loud laugh, causing several of the volunteers to turn to look at us.

"How is your day so far?" he asked.

"It's been good. I'm really enjoying being here. I'm impressed—this building is quite nice for being a low-income school."

"Just because the children who attend here have families who struggle financially doesn't mean that they deserve to receive an inequitable education."

I sighed. "America could take some notes."

As Oliver and I colored with a small group of children, we heard a loud voice echo through the room. "KNOX!"

I turned toward the door, spotting a little boy of about ten sprint to where Knox was reading to two little girls. The boy leaped onto Knox, knocking him over into the nest of pillows.

"Who is that?" I asked Oliver.

Oliver's smile reached his ears. "That's Archer."

"Is he related to Knox?"

Oliver chuckled. "That depends on who you ask," he

answered. "A few years ago, Knox and I were visiting the pediatric wing at the local hospital. Archer had just had surgery to have his tonsils removed. Apparently, chocolate pudding was the only thing that Archer would eat while recovering, but the staff had just given out the last one. Knox tracked down another one for him and achieved hero status in Archer's eyes.

"Long story short, Knox went back to visit the next day and got to know his family a bit. Archer and his siblings live with their aunt and uncle; their parents haven't been in the picture since Archer was about five.

"Something about it hit Knox hard. He started by just sending chocolate pudding to Archer and his siblings. Then Knox happened to volunteer at a summer rugby camp Archer was attending. Since then, Archer's been like a little brother to him. He always makes sure the family has what they need, and at the beginning of the school year he helps them with their school supplies and new clothes."

"Wow. That's amazing." My eyes returned to Knox, who now had five kids, including Archer, around him. They were all captivated by the book he was reading.

"Yeah, he's a great guy." Oliver smiled, clearly proud of his friend.

"Who would have known that the porcupine would have a gummy bear center," I mused quietly.

———

After a few hours, Oliver left to assist with the food drive and hand out boxes of food to families. I was sitting on the floor building a tower of blocks with a little boy named Hunter, when a girl with tight black curls came to stand next to me, watching us play. She couldn't have been any older than six.

"Hi, do you want to play with us?" I asked.

She nodded.

"You can sit here. I'll get us another box of blocks." I stood and grabbed another tub and settled back down on the floor between her and Hunter. As I pulled the blocks out, Archer ran over to our group.

"Hi!" he greeted, his head of disheveled black hair going in every direction. "Can I play with you guys?"

"Of course. This is Hunter, and this is…I'm sorry, sweetie, I haven't asked your name."

"Her name is Belle. She's my neighbor," Archer answered.

"Oh. Well, cool. I'm Birdie." I waved to Archer and Belle.

"Birdie. I love birds. Did you know that ninety percent of birds are monogamous but only three to five percent of mammals are monogamous and mate for life?"

"I had no idea." I grinned at him, surprised to hear words like "monogamous" coming out of the mouth of a ten-year-old.

"Archer, are you bombarding your friends with random information again?" Knox had approached and was now standing over us, his hands in his pockets.

"I'm not bombarding, her name is Birdie, and it reminded me of a cool bird fact."

"Hey, I would rather be given some cool facts than be debated with." I winked at Archer. Knox's face remained stony.

"Knox, sit down. We can build a cool racetrack!" Archer looked up at Knox as he sat down with us. "Did you know the first purpose-built motor racing track was built in Australia in 1905?"

"You know a lot of really fun things, Archer," I said.

"I like to read and know stuff. Knox always brings me books when he comes over to my house."

"That's really kind of him." I smiled at Knox, trying to make eye contact with him. The way he was still avoiding my gaze reminded me of how tense his body had been when he showed me how to carve at the woodshop. *Does he not want me here?*

Hunter leaped up, running to his mom as she arrived to pick him up.

I turned to Archer and Belle. "Are you kids excited for Christmas?"

"Not really. I get sad at Christmas," Archer answered, stacking another block around the makeshift racetrack he and Knox were working on.

"What makes Christmas sad?"

"I just really miss my mom and wish she could be with me at Christmas."

My heart cracked open. "I feel the exact same way," I said softly. I thought about all the Christmases I had spent without my mom and how much harder it must be for Archer, knowing his mom was out there and he just couldn't be with her.

"My dad won't be home for Christmas, and it makes me sad, too," said a quiet voice beside me.

I looked at Belle, shocked that the girl who had yet to say a word had shared this small piece of information.

"At least your dad is doing something really cool," Archer said. Belle's face fell.

"Archer," Knox cautioned sternly. "That was rude."

"I didn't mean to be rude! I just meant her dad has a neat job in the Royal Army."

"You may think that, but it's not cool that Belle doesn't have her dad home for Christmas," Knox reminded Archer firmly, but kindly.

Archer looked down at a red block as he turned it over and over in his hand. "I'm sorry, Belle. I didn't mean to hurt your feelings. I'm sorry your dad won't be home for Christmas."

"It's okay, Archer," Belle said, offering another block for the racetrack.

My heart melted watching Knox stand up for Belle and validate her feelings. "You know what I do to feel closer to my mom at Christmas?" I asked the kids, sneaking a glance toward Knox. I supposed he felt the same way as the kids and me since losing his own parents. "I make my mom's favorite foods."

"Oh!" Archer exclaimed. "My aunt said that my mom ate pickles on everything when she was pregnant with me. One night she found her in the kitchen eating them dipped in ice cream." He scrunched up his face in disgust.

"Ewww," Belle giggled, covering her mouth with her hands.

"I know! I don't think I could eat that," Archer laughed, shaking his head vigorously.

"Well, maybe you could make something with pickles and ice cream separately," I suggested, suppressing a laugh.

"Your aunt makes a really good toffee ice cream, right?" Knox put his hand on Archer's shoulder.

"Oh, yeah! It's my favorite!"

"She brought us a container of it when my dad left," Belle smiled. "It was so good."

"I can bring over some pickles and we can make a meat and cheese tray. And for dessert we can have some of your aunt's toffee ice cream. How's that sound?" Knox asked, squeezing Archer's shoulder.

"That sounds great! What were your parents' favorite foods, Knox?"

I looked to Knox, wondering if Archer's question had thrown him off. But all I saw on his face was quiet contemplation, like he was really trying to think.

"My dad loved bratwursts and sauerkraut, and my mom loved anything lemon. My parents grew to be good friends with King Leroy and Queen Isobel after Oliver and I became best mates, and the queen would make Mom these little lemon cakes every year on her birthday." He smiled softly to himself, lost in his memory.

"You should bring those over, too! Do you think Queen Isobel would make them for us?"

Knox smiled ear to ear. "Yeah, I think she would."

"Wow! Homemade treats from the queen," Belle murmured, doe-eyed.

I loved the adoration and magic in her eyes. It made me wonder if the wife Oliver chose would have this effect on the country's children. To spread that kind of magic was something special.

"Birdie," Knox said, finally acknowledging me directly, "what food do you eat for your mom?"

He held my gaze, making my heart flutter and my palms sweat. I wasn't sure if it was the look in his eyes or the unknowingly intimate question he had asked, but I was surprised to find myself so willing to answer.

"White-chocolate-covered Oreos," I replied, holding his gaze. "She would buy a dozen boxes and hide them from us."

The children's laughter broke Knox's and my gaze, but it didn't stop the butterflies that were taking flight in my stomach. I had to get this under control. The lust I felt for this man was starting to get out of hand.

"Hey, Belle." A girl in her teens walked up to our group.

"Sadie!" Belle jumped up and hugged her.

"Hi, Archer," Sadie greeted.

"Hi, Sadie!" Archer smiled and went back to work building his block racetrack.

"Belle, Mom wanted me to come get you. They're packing more food pantry boxes, and she said you wanted to help with that."

"I do!" Belle smiled.

Realizing that the room was now nearly empty, I turned to

Sadie. "Could I come with you? I'd love to help pack some boxes and see more of the school."

"Of course! We could use all the help we can get," Sadie replied enthusiastically.

"Knox, do you mind letting Vince and Mrs. Sallow know where I went?"

"No problem. Have fun," he said, smiling at me for the first time in days.

The two girls and I walked through the hallways to a large gymnasium. There were a few dozen volunteers, including Tej and Chauncey, carrying bags and baskets of clothes to tables set up along one wall. A few other volunteers sat next to a table covered in canned goods and boxes of nonperishables with bags in hand for the shoppers.

It warmed my heart to see so many people serving the community. And better yet, everyone had a smile on their face, and the chatter was loud throughout the room as people talked and laughed together.

Sadie and Belle walked over to a woman filling a cardboard box with food.

"Hi, Mummy!" Belle said, wrapping her arms tightly around the woman's waist.

"Hey, Bells. Want to help me finish packing this box?" She looked up and saw me standing behind the girls.

"Hi. I'm Birdie. I was hoping to help you guys."

"Freya." She offered her hand and shook mine. "Are you one of the royal suitors here helping with the event?"

"I am. How did you know?"

She looked me up and down and a small quirk of a smile hit her lips.

I sighed. "I told Vince I was overdressed for this. But Lord Bronson insisted I dress to impress."

"Honey, I would dress the same way if I were vying for the

prince's attention. I don't blame you at all. The accent also gave you away, though," she added with a wink.

I let out a self-conscious laugh. Sometimes I still forgot that here, Knox and I were considered the ones with the accents, rather than the other way around.

As we filled box after box with canned goods and nonperishable items, I let my thoughts drift to Oliver, trying to piece together what was missing in my feelings for him.

On paper, he was perfect: Handsome with his square jaw, clean-cut look, and top-notch fashion. Loving and protective toward his family—certainly not the type to check out at the first sign of trouble. Passionate about his country and how he could better serve his people. Genuinely kind, thoughtful, and a great conversationalist.

So why wasn't I more attracted to him? It was the question I couldn't stop asking myself. Why did Knox make my heart race and my body shiver, but Oliver didn't?

"Birdie, I'm so glad to see you helping the Carmichaels."

Queen Isobel had approached the opposite side of the table. Her bright red hair was knotted on top of her head. She wore a chunky black turtleneck sweater paired with fitted black pants and caramel leather knee-high boots. She exuded elegance even in casual clothes.

"Your Majesty." I bent into a curtsy.

"Oh, none of that here," she said kindly, motioning me up. "Freya, how are you, darling?" Queen Isobel leaned forward to kiss Freya's cheek. "Freya and I met at a function supporting military spouses a few years ago; I just adore her and her family," the queen noted to me.

Freya's face lit with gratitude. "Queen Isobel. It's wonderful to see you here. We're doing great."

"Freya." The queen gave her a knowing look. "How are you really?"

Freya looked down at her hands, her fingers twined together anxiously. She took a deep breath and let it out slowly, lowering her voice as she answered, "Honestly, my stomach is in constant knots. I haven't heard from Dante in a few weeks and that always makes me worry. These special missions are always the worst because they're essentially no contact. I'm not even sure when he's going to be back, but it isn't likely to be before Christmas. It's even harder on the girls because they always have questions and I don't have answers. And now with the holiday coming up and knowing he's not going to be home..." She cut off her sentence and looked at her girls, who were busy packing bags of toiletries at the far end of the table. Her eyes misted over as she held back her tears.

Queen Isobel stepped around the table, wrapping Freya in a hug. She whispered something I couldn't hear. Freya nodded as she withdrew from the hug.

"I know it doesn't make up for the fact that Dante won't be here, but I would love to have you to the palace for Christmas Eve dinner."

"Oh, Your Majesty," Freya said as a few tears slid down her face. "We can't intrude, especially on the holiday."

"You are not an intrusion. You will be a guest. Dante has done so much for this country and my husband. I want to take care of his family in return. Please, come."

"Mum! You can't say no to the queen!" Belle's voice piped up, intruding on their conversation.

"My point exactly." Queen Isobel winked at her.

"Okay then." Freya nodded to the queen, gratitude pouring from her face.

"I'll have my assistant get in contact with you to set up a time and find out what types of foods the girls like."

"We have to have salted sunflower seeds!" Belle interjected.

"What? Why?" Freya questioned, her cheeks reddening at her daughter's odd request.

"That's Daddy's favorite thing to eat! He eats them all the time when he's home. And Birdie said when she misses her mom at Christmas, she eats her mom's favorite food to remember her. So, we have to have sunflower seeds!"

I looked up from the box I was packing. The queen glanced over to me, her eyes full of emotion. It was clear she was grateful that I had tried to help Belle with her dad being gone, but I knew the look of pity just behind the gratitude. It was the look that people gave you when they found out you had lost a parent far too young. I hated it.

"Belle, the only reason Dad eats sunflower seeds when he's home is because it helps his anxiety to crack them open and not think about the stuff he does. It's a distraction for him to keep his mind busy." Sadie rolled her eyes at her little sister.

"Sadie." Freya's tone was sharp and reprimanding.

"What? It's true."

"We've talked about this."

"Sorry." Sadie rolled her eyes again. *Ah, to be a teenager again.*

Queen Isobel stooped down to meet Belle's eyes. "Belle, I will make sure that we have a bowl of salted sunflower seeds so we can all enjoy them and think of your dad."

Belle smiled from ear to ear. I could only imagine Queen Isobel or Queen Mother Evelyn cracking open sunflower seeds in their formal attire at the palace's large dining table. It took everything in me not to chuckle at the thought.

CHAPTER 15
BIRDIE

ADELAIDE

SOS, I don't know what to wear for the Thorne Ball. Who schedules a garden party in the dead of winter?!

MEL

You know how much Sabine loves her garden

ADELAIDE

Dead. Of. Winter.

LOL I'm cold just thinking about it. Do you want to go shopping this Saturday? I could ask Vince to help us arrange something?

ADELAIDE

YES! M, should we take her to The Snowdrop, too?

MEL

I'll literally never say no to one of Cora's cranberry scones

It's a date!

———

Growing up in Michigan and then living in New York for the last six years, I had seen my fair share of snow. Yet somehow Wexstone eclipsed what I was used to. In just over two weeks here, I was sure I had seen more snow than I had in an entire winter back home.

I awoke Saturday morning to find that it had snowed nearly two feet overnight. The storm did little to deter the Wexstonians, though; Council staff had made quick work of clearing the roads as the citizens of Altborn started their day.

Thankfully, unlike at home where I would have been left to navigate public transportation or pay through the nose for a cab, Vince had arranged a car to take me into the city for my day with Adelaide and Mel. He had also organized for a body-guard to shadow us for the day, given the media attention around the competition.

Adelaide and Mel, accompanied by a tall man dressed in black and sporting an earpiece, were just about to open the door to the small dress shop as I stepped out of the car.

"Good morning, ladies," I said, waving as I bounced toward them.

"Good morning!" they greeted in unison.

"This is Jacob," Mel added, indicating the bodyguard. "He said he will stay out of our way, but close enough to step in should we need him." He nodded at me as he spoke quietly into his earpiece.

"I don't know if I'll ever get used to how beautiful this place is," I mused as we entered the shop, the golden antique bell above the door jingling. The street outside was lined with tall Tudor buildings covered in snow-frosted garland and ever-green wreaths. Shutters of every color of the rainbow stood out against the black and brown buildings. Glistening icicles hung from the eaves above the cobblestone sidewalks, as carolers sang of decking the halls.

"I've lived here all of my life and every time I drive around the turn of the mountain going to the palace, it takes my breath away," Mel said.

"I feel the same way every year when the first snow hits in September," Adelaide added.

"I'm sorry, first snow in September?" I squealed, earning a quiet chuckle from Jacob. "I hate it if it snows before Thanksgiving at home!"

"Better start loving the snow, sweetness, it snows from September to April," Mellie informed me as my body did a full shiver.

A petite woman clad in a white sheath dress and nude heels appeared from the back of the store and rounded a large alabaster counter to greet us.

"Bonjour! Welcome to Fleur de Laroche," the woman spoke a heavy French accent. "My name is Ambre. What brings you beauties into the store today?" A quick flash of realization washed across her face. "Ah, you must be my eleven o'clock appointment, here to find dresses for an elegant garden party, no?" She brought her clasped hands to her chest.

"We are indeed," I confirmed.

"*S'il vous plaît*, right this way."

Jacob posted up by the entrance as we followed her down a narrow, whitewashed brick hallway to the back of the store. She led us through a door into a large room lined with dresses, pantsuits, and clothing racks full of undergarments. In the corner was a built-in shelf that housed shoes of every color. It was like Barbie's dream closet come to life.

"Okay, who wants to try on first?" Adelaide asked, taking in the dozens of options before us.

"Not it," I said, touching my finger to my nose.

"Not me!" Mellie said at the same time.

"Wow. Thanks, guys." Adelaide rolled her eyes. "I don't even know where to start," she complained as I sifted through a rack of couture gowns.

"Ooo," I said. "I have an idea!"

They both looked at me with raised brows.

"When Sam and I go shopping for special occasions, we each pick out outfits we think the other should try on, on top of whatever we find for ourselves. Nine times out of ten, we end up picking what the other person chose. Let's pull some options for each other."

"I love that idea," Adelaide said.

"Honestly, that sounds great because I hate choosing for myself," Mel sighed, clearly relieved.

Perusing the racks of formal dresses and pantsuits, my eyes landed on a beautiful black fur-lined blazer with a full train that flowed down to the ground. I knew that it fit Mellie's style to a tee. I pulled it and handed it to Ambre, who set it to the side for Mel. As I continued to search, a stunning high-neck, long-sleeved dress in sparkling forest green jumped out at me. I couldn't decide if I liked it for myself or Adelaide. I picked it off the rack and held it up.

"Mel!" She looked over to where I stood. "Adelaide or me?"

"I'm only saying Adelaide because she already found the perfect dress for you." She winked.

I was having so much fun, I knew the only thing that could have made the day better would be to have Sam there, too. My fashion-forward friend would love this. I briefly wondered whether I could convince Sam to move to Wexstone if I married Oliver, before reminding myself that I still wasn't sure I could imagine marrying Oliver.

I walked the dress to the changing room and tapped on the door.

"Adelaide, try this dress on, too." She opened the door, and I handed her the dress.

"Speaking of your Thanksgiving," Mel said, continuing our earlier conversation while we waited for Adelaide to change, "isn't that this Thursday? Are you missing a big family celebration?"

I nodded as I perched on a pink settee. "It is. I probably would have flown out West to visit my brother and his family, but it would have just been the four of us. We're going to celebrate over a video call, though."

"For some reason, my mom always uses American Thanksgiving as her marker for when she can start playing Christmas music," Mel said, laughing.

I chuckled wryly. "She's not alone, that's pretty common back home."

I had a love-hate relationship with Christmas music. Every year on November 1, my mom would bust out her old vinyl records, and each evening while she cooked dinner, Bing Crosby would serenade us with songs about winter wonderlands and chestnuts roasting over an open fire. The more I thought about it, the more I knew that Mom would have loved it here. It was probably what her version of heaven looked like: Carolers on the street corners, wreaths on every door, snow-capped mountains, and delicious peppermint tea. That all-too-familiar knot of grief formed in my stomach at the thought that my mom would never see this place.

After a few minutes, Adelaide stepped out to the small dais in front of three floor-to-ceiling mirrors. She looked devastatingly beautiful in the green gown. It made her blonde hair shine and her emerald eyes pop.

"Holy shit!" I yelled.

"Girl! You look stunning!"

"Oh my gosh, stop." Adelaide blushed.

"No seriously, this is the dress," I urged.

"I don't know." Her hips swayed left to right, and the dress followed. Ambre appeared again through the doorway and let out audible gasp.

"Mademoiselle. You look absolutely beautiful." She set her hands on her chest like she was catching her breath. "For a moment, I thought I was looking at the picture of Queen Evelyn from the state dinner in 1959. *Quelle chance!* I have the perfect gloves and hat for this outfit in the front; I must go fetch them for you."

Mel snapped her fingers. "I was trying to figure out what you reminded me of! That's it."

"Pull it up on your phone, I want to see!" I said, hurrying to peek over Mel's shoulder as she brought up the search engine on her phone.

I looked to Adelaide as she stood on the dais, looking herself over. I could tell she liked the dress, but something was bothering her. Adelaide wore her heart on her sleeve; her emotions were easy to guess.

"Found it." Mellie passed me her phone. "This was the 1959 state dinner. It was the year that she and King Leroy's father, King Francis, got engaged. Their marriage was also arranged because of the marriage decree."

Adelaide's head snapped up, and her eyes met ours in the mirror. "I had forgotten about that..." She slid her hands down the front of the dress, the fur-lined cuffs framing her wrists. "I really like this one," she whispered.

"You look amazing in it," I agreed.

"And it is Oliver's favorite color," she said quietly. She cleared her throat. "Which means I should definitely choose another dress," she announced more loudly as she moved to step off the dais.

"Hold on." I held my hands up to halt her. "If it's his favorite color, shouldn't that be a plus?"

"Yeah, I'm confused," Mel agreed.

"I just...it's just that...he...ugh!" Adelaide couldn't get her words straight. She let out a huff of frustration. "Oliver and I slept together," she blurted out. She immediately turned red from her chest up.

"What!" I exclaimed as Mellie gasped, "When?!"

Adelaide bit her lip. "The last time was right before they announced that Prince Xavier was abdicating."

"The *last* time? Meaning there have been multiple times?" Mellie's tone was excited, like she was interviewing someone for a juicy story.

"Well...yeah," Adelaide said, looking between both of us as though trying to get a read on how we were handling this news.

I had been so eager to hear the rest of my friend's story that I had briefly forgotten that I should have felt instantly jealous.

"Oh, do go on!" Mellie, completely unfazed, egged Adelaide on.

"There was a fundraiser at the school a few months ago, and he and I—"

"Here you go!" Ambre said excitedly as she strode through the door straight to Adelaide. "Put these on so we can see everything together." She handed Adelaide the gloves and set to bobby pinning the small hat onto Adelaide's head.

"Yes! That's the outfit," Mel said. I chuckled to myself; for someone who declared how much she hated doing this type of stuff, Mel sure did love telling Adelaide how great she looked.

"Birdie, what do you think?" Adelaide asked, her eyes wide.

"I think he's going to forget his name when he sees you."

She gave me a half smile and turned back to Ambre. "Well, I guess this is the one."

———

After scheduling the delivery of our dresses with Ambre, we made our way down the street to The Snowdrop for lunch. As we walked in, the smell of cinnamon and spices filled my nose, and my mouth instantly began to water. I felt as though I had been transported to a fairy garden; ivy vines and twinkling lights hung from the ceiling, giving the feeling of standing under a willow tree. Vibrant potted plants were scattered throughout the shop, contrasting with the dark countertops. It would have been easy to forget that it was nearing Christmas were it not for the holiday insert in the menu.

After ordering at the counter—a feat I hadn't expected to be so difficult thanks to the variety of delicious options—we settled in at one of the tables to wait for our food, Jacob taking a two-top within earshot. I couldn't wait to dig into the soup I had ordered, hoping it would warm me up from the short walk.

About ten minutes later, Cora carried a tray with our food out of the kitchen.

"Hey, Cora!" I greeted, giving her a warm smile. "How's your day going?"

"Hi," she answered, looking around the busy café and patisserie. "It's going well. Busy. But I spotted you come in and wanted to bring your order out."

"Are you looking forward to the garden party?" Mel asked her.

"I was…" Cora's voice trailed off as she fiddled with the edge of the tray that was still in her hands.

"What changed your mind?" I asked.

"I'm just nervous. After the stuff that happened at the artisans' square, I'm so nervous to be around Prince Oliver. I managed to avoid pretty much everyone at the school drive this week. But seeing Renata today just brought all those feelings back." She tucked the tray under her arm and wiped her hands on her soft pink apron.

"You saw Renata today? Was she nice to you?" Adelaide asked, alarmed.

"Yeah. She wanted to use the private party room upstairs. She was with that reporter from the press conference. The one who wrote the *Pine Times* article."

Alistair Fucking Davies.

"She was probably doing her own interview so she can paint herself in a good light and they don't write some sham article about her, too. Buttering up the press," Adelaide said, rolling her eyes. "No offense, Mel."

"None taken," Mel laughed. "But I don't think that's the case. Alistair got fired."

Adelaide, Cora, and I all gasped, our mouths wide.

"Yeah," Mel continued, taking a bite of her sandwich. "I can't believe I forgot to mention it earlier. Turns out, he was accepting bribes to write articles with false claims about the success of various businesses. He's in a world of trouble right now."

"That's insane. I wonder why he and Renata need to have a private meeting," I mused, not at all liking the idea of the two of them being up to something together.

"Do you think she's a part of the bribe stuff?" Adelaide asked.

"I don't know," Mellie answered. "I mean, her father does have money tied up in a lot of investments, but I don't see her being a part of that. She's an influencer at best; I don't think she has the business acumen to use the press to her advantage in that kind of way."

"They didn't seem like they were up to anything malicious when I showed them upstairs. They were laughing and huddled over his computer when I took some pastries up to them a little bit ago," Cora said. "They could just be friends." She shrugged.

Adelaide, Mellie, and I shared a glance and smiled. *Bless her sweet, naive heart.* Cora said her goodbyes and went back to work.

"I think that girl would believe you if you said the sky was orange," I mused.

We finished our meals, the girls regaling me with stories of growing up in Wexstone while we ate. As I savored the last few bites of my cranberry scone, I glanced at the time. "My car is on the way; I'm going to go wait outside. I've had so much fun today. I really needed this," I said to the girls as I gathered my things.

"I'll walk out with you, I need to go stop by my office," Mel said. She and Adelaide stood and shrugged into their coats.

As we walked toward the door, a long, bony hand grasped my arm. I looked down to find that the hand belonged to an elderly woman sitting with three of her friends at a table covered in yarn and books. Jacob stepped forward, ready to intervene, but I held up my free hand, indicating for him to wait for a moment.

"You're the American girl who is here for Prince Oliver, right?" the woman asked, still grasping my arm.

"I am. I'm Birdie, and this is Adelaide and Mellie," I smiled at the woman and her friends.

"I'm Hilda. This is Polly." She released my arm as she gestured to the white-haired woman next to her who was busy casting green yarn onto her knitting needles.

The red-haired woman across the table waved. "I'm Mildred and this is my partner, Ida."

"I really loved that purple dress you wore on the first night," Ida said, pointing to Adelaide.

Adelaide smiled. "Thank you!"

"So, you gals are in the inner circle now that you're courting the prince. Why do you think Prince Xavier abdicated?" Hilda asked.

Adelaide, Mellie and I looked at each other, not knowing what to say. I definitely wasn't in the "inner circle"—I barely knew Oliver, let alone Xavier.

Polly swatted at Hilda's arm. "Hilda, you know they wouldn't tell you even if they did know. They probably signed so many contracts and agreements going into this. Don't pester those girls with your nosy questions!"

"Fine. I'm just saying, my niece's neighbor works at the palace, and *she* said she heard from one of the butlers that he abdicated because he's gay and didn't think he would be able to produce heirs."

"I call bullshit on that," Polly yelled. "You know well enough that these days that's not a reason to abdicate. There are plenty of ways to make a family." Mildred reached over to pat the top of Polly's hand. "That's just nasty gossip."

"I didn't say I agreed! I'm just telling you what she told me. Calm your britches," Hilda retorted, waving her off.

I could see Mel stiffen as the conversation continued, clearly uncomfortable.

"I think that he did something illegal and that if he takes the throne, it will all be uncovered and the royal family will no longer be able to exist and the entire country will collapse," Ida said.

Mildred rolled her eyes and let out a huff. "Dear, you're reading too many mystery books again."

Ida looked at her with a playful grin. "You're the one that said you wanted to read something other than smut in our book club."

I saw the corner of Jacob's mouth quirk upward and took

the opportunity to change the topic of conversation. As much as I believed what Oliver had told me—that Xavier abdicated because he wasn't ready to give up his partying lifestyle—I also wasn't sure Xavier owed the public a reason. Wexstone was thriving and would continue to do so. It didn't seem to be their business what his personal reasons were.

"Is that what you ladies are doing here? Book club?" I motioned to the books peeking out from underneath the yarn.

"It is! We come here for a book club and stay for lunch and to knit," Mildred answered, digging out a book from under the pile of yarn.

"Oh, I love reading," Adelaide gushed. "My book club only likes to read thrillers and I had to stop going because I was too on edge. I live alone and one time I was in the shower when my dad stopped by unexpectedly to drop off some supplies for my classroom. I was so freaked out that I came out of the bedroom and hit him in the face with my paddle brush." She laughed. "I decided then that it was time I found a new club that reads romance or fantasy or self-help."

Polly looked over the rim of her cat-eye glasses at Adelaide. "You look like you'd be a good fighter. You'll need that when you become queen."

Adelaide's face flushed red as she smiled politely at the sweet, white-haired woman.

Hilda leaned over, muttering loudly to Polly, "Don't let that red-haired bitch hear you say that."

I clapped my hand over my mouth as a laugh escaped. We all knew exactly who she was talking about, though I was surprised that Renata's less-than-sparkling personality was known by even this gaggle of women.

"I don't know how Prince Oliver stands to even entertain the notion that she could be queen," Ida said.

"Me neither," Mel agreed, shaking her head. "When we

were in primary school, she would make everyone call her Queen Renata. She was so sure that she would marry Xavier and become queen someday."

"And now she's moving on to Oliver." Adelaide sighed deeply.

"And if Knox had been legally adopted by the royal family and taken the throne instead of Oliver, she'd be going after him, too." Mel nodded.

Something like jealousy stirred in my stomach. *Whoa, rein it in, Birdie. He's not yours. Calm down.*

My mind flashed to a few hours ago when I had felt indifferent about Adelaide's announcement that she had slept with Oliver. But the thought of Renata pursuing Knox filled me with rage and jealousy.

"Birdie, did you hear me?" Adelaide asked, pulling me out of my thoughts.

"I'm sorry, I didn't. What did you say?"

"It looks like your car just pulled up."

"Oh! Great. Okay, well, that's my ride. Ladies, it was a pleasure meeting you. I'm sure we'll see you again." I waved.

I thanked Jacob and said goodbye to Adelaide and Mel, promising to text them later with what shoes and jewelry I was going to wear on Wednesday. As I stepped outside onto the cobblestone walkway, I spotted Renata and Alistair Davies coming out of the bakery's side door. They crossed the street and stepped into the doorway of one of the apartment buildings that overlooked the street, oblivious to those around them. Renata leaned in like she was about to kiss Alistair, but instead handed him a small pink USB drive.

Those two are definitely up to something.

The driver opened the door to the black SUV, blocking my view. I got in, pondering what Renata and Alistair Davies could be plotting as we drove back to Lexington Manor.

CHAPTER 16
KNOX

"I'll take this and make those final alterations this afternoon, Your Highness."

"Thank you, Ahmet," Oliver said as he slid his arms out of a charcoal plaid suit jacket and the tailor returned it to its hanger.

"We will also have your coronation wardrobe ready for the first fitting next week, sir. Queen Isobel said that would be best with your schedule."

Oliver's mouth quirked in a wry smile. "She likely knows my calendar better than I do. That will be fine."

The pear-shaped man bowed before rolling the rack of suits out of the suite. Oliver looked over to me, exhaustion washing over his face.

"A whole wardrobe just for my coronation." He rubbed his hands over his face as the door closed. "Do you think we can just fast-forward to after the new year when it's all over?" he asked, turning to King Leroy.

Leroy chuckled warmly. "You're doing great, son. I know this isn't what you thought you'd be doing with your life, but if it's any consolation, you're a natural at it. I couldn't be prouder of how you've handled the bombshells dropped on you these past few months."

"Thank you," Oliver said with a small smile. He pulled his phone out of his pocket, looked at it, and slid it back in his front pocket.

"Got somewhere else to be?" I asked from where I lounged in a nearby armchair.

"Nope. Just trying to figure out if I have enough time to go catch a quick nap before the garden party tonight," he laughed.

"Speaking of the garden party," Leroy started, clearing his throat, "are there any leading ladies in this race? I'd like to make sure that I'm spending my time prioritizing the right ones tonight."

Oliver let out a breath as I held my own, hoping Birdie's name wouldn't leave his lips.

"There are a few I'm seriously considering," Oliver said as he took a seat in the chair next to mine. "Adelaide Levy, Sabine Thorne, and..." He looked at me and then down at his hand, which was now tapping a rhythm on his thigh. "Bernadette Hamilton."

"The American, huh?" Leroy raised his eyebrows. "That would definitely cause a shakeup. Maybe not a bad one, but certainly a shakeup." He ran his fingers along his jaw. "Who would have thought you would fall for an American?"

My body went stiff, and I felt my shoulders rise toward my ears from the tension. I knew that they had hit it off, but it was still hard to think that he could have her and I couldn't. I always wanted the best for Oliver and Birdie was just that: the best. I immediately itched to get out of this room and remove myself from this conversation before there was any more talk of the women vying for Oliver's heart and the throne.

"But I think she's more than that. Right, Knox?" Oliver said.

"If you say so. You know her better than I do." That was a lie. I knew how it felt to have her lips on mine and how her ass tightened when I squeezed it and the soft moan she let out when I ran my tongue along her lip. Did he? *God, I hope not.* And if he did, I didn't want to know. But I also knew that her mom's favorite treat had been white-chocolate-covered Oreos and that Birdie preferred runny eggs and loved bagel breakfast sandwiches.

"Sabine Thorne is very intelligent, and she is beautiful," Leroy continued. "You two would make a great pair when it comes to economic plans and how to further our nation in trades and allies. And since her family has been around the court for generations, I think it would be a smooth transition."

Oliver nodded like he was mulling over what his dad was saying.

"But then again, I've known Nixon Levy since I was in primary school, and we've been friends for decades. They're a down-to-earth family and it might take a little work on both of your ends to figure out how to adjust, but I think you could do it."

"It's a lot to ask someone to marry me and take on all this responsibility. But if you're going to corner anyone tonight, I suppose that's who to go for." Oliver laughed nervously, shaking his head as he stood up. "I'm going to try to take a nap since it will be a late night. You should go take one too, Knox." He patted me on the shoulder.

"I can't. I have too much stuff to get done around the grounds."

"That will change, I assume, when Oliver takes over, correct?" Leroy inquired.

I glanced at Oliver, who was shaking his head warningly at his father. I tilted my head inquiringly.

"I haven't had a chance to speak with him about it," Oliver answered, clearing his throat.

"Well, you have my attention now, so go on," I pushed.

Oliver sighed and sat back in the chair he had just vacated. "When I take over, I'm going to need a Chief Counselor. Someone to help me make decisions and stand in for me when I can't make it to events. Just until Rosie is older or I have an heir who can do those types of things."

I couldn't believe my ears. I knew that Oliver trusted me as a friend and brother—but to be trusted as his stand-in? I was deeply honored, but was it something I would want? When I pictured my future, I always thought about being outside, walking the grounds with Eugene, chopping wood for the workshop, fixing leaky fountains, and salting pathways. I had never imagined myself giving speeches to foreign ambassadors or hosting fancy dinners in Oliver's place. It seemed like an alternate life.

"Wow." I cleared my throat, buying myself another moment to think, and ran my hand over the back of my head. "When do you need a decision?"

Oliver looked to Leroy.

"We'll need to know before the coronation," Leroy answered.

I nodded. A little over a month—that was doable. I needed some time to mull this over and decide if it was what I wanted for my life. "Let me think about it. It's an honor and I don't take it lightly. It deserves the respect of some contemplation."

"I know you don't take it lightly. That's why we both think you'd be the perfect person for the job." Oliver inclined his head to Leroy, his smile hitched up one side of his face. "Now, on to more important things." He stood again, this time stretching his arms over his head. "I have an appointment with a pillow and blanket."

———

We stepped out of the royal convoy of cars and straight into what could only be described as a winter wonderland. The Thornes' manor was one of the oldest in the country, but you wouldn't know that by how well cared-for it was. The lime-washed stone shone under lit sconces that hung above each of the dozens of windows lining the home. Winter ivy trailed the side of the manor and circled up and around a tower over-looking the back of the property where the garden party was to take place.

Leroy and Isobel led the family procession up the steep stone staircase into Kanter Manor. The train of Isobel's maroon dress flowed down at least three steps behind her, leaving Oliver and Xavier to follow several paces behind their parents. We entered through the frosted-glass doors into the foyer, where we were greeted by Lord and Lady Thorne.

I was glad that I had Evelyn and Rosie by my side as we made our way to the party. I hated the formality of walking with the family. It brought with it far more attention than I was comfortable with, with all eyes on us any time we entered a room. Evelyn had her arm looped through mine and she gave my bicep a small squeeze, surely feeling the tension that ran through my body.

"Gram, I'll bet you ten euros that by the end of the night, one of the girls is crying and making a scene," Rosie whispered across me to Evelyn.

"I'll bet you fifteen that someone pretends to faint in front of Ollie," Evelyn countered with a sly smile.

I rolled my eyes. These two and their wagers. After the

wedding was finally over, I was going to have to check their bank accounts and make sure they hadn't bankrupted each other.

"Should we tell Knox about the bet we made about him?" Rosie asked Evelyn.

"Absolutely not. If he knows, he'll screw it up for everyone."

"You both are out of your minds. *Especially* you, you old bird," I winked at Evelyn.

We processed through the manor and out to the back terrace. I didn't often find myself speechless, but my breath was taken away by the garden. A sprawl of winter jasmine was edged with pots of blooming camellias ranging in shades from shell pink to cherry red. The sea of color in contrast with the white snow was stunning. Mixed in with the natural aroma of pine that suffused all of Wexstone, there was a faint smell of witch-hazels.

Tables and heaters were arranged along the stone terrace, with forest-green faux-fur blankets laid across the back of each chair. Below, on the middle terrace, couches circled two large, brick-lined fire pits. On the lowest level before the expansive gardens sat a string quartet playing Christmas music.

"Oh, there's Mazie! I'll see you later," Rosie said as she practically sprinted to her friend.

There were times that I really felt for Rosie. It had to be hard being the youngest member of the royal family and having to attend these events. She often brought books and would sneak away with her security detail to find a nook or library to read in. But lately her parents had been making sure that she had friends at the events so she wouldn't be by herself. I admired that, even with everything else going on, they were still able to see what their daughter needed and gave her people her own age to socialize with during the chaos.

Evelyn and I started to make our way down to where guests were mingling around the fire pits for warmth when I saw *her*. The long, white dress glimmered against the firelight. The faux fur that lined her white gloves was accented with gold thread, which caught the light as she tucked a small strand of hair behind her ear, giving the illusion of a halo above her head.

The neckline of the gown stopped right below her breastbone, and I had to give myself a quick talk to make sure my cock didn't stand ramrod straight. I was instantly taken back to the closet of the hotel suite—except the white dress she wore that night had barely covered that supple ass.

As if she could sense my presence, Birdie turned her gaze to where I stood at the top of the staircase and gave me a small wave. I responded with a nod and counted to ten, hoping that would help soften the current problem in my pants. Evelyn started down the stairs, and I had no choice but to hold tight to her arm and help her.

Oliver, standing at Birdie's side, looked up to where she had waved and motioned for us to join them. I took a deep breath and hoped that my black pants would hide any indication of what I was feeling below. I started running through the script I kept from when this happened as a teenager:

Grandpas in Speedos. Political economics. Chili beans. Stoichiometry.

Thankfully, I could feel my cock start to deflate as we approached. Birdie glanced from her conversation with Oliver and locked eyes with me. The pure white wool of her coat brought out the specks of copper and chocolate in her hazel eyes. I couldn't help but stare into them; they were captivating. My gaze traveled down to her red-painted lips as I remembered what they had felt like against mine.

Birdie dipped into a quick curtsy when she realized who

was at my arm. I wondered if I had the same effect on her as she did on me.

"Your Highness," she greeted Evelyn as she came up from her curtsy.

"Hello, Bernadette. You look stunning, my dear. Doesn't she, boys?" Evelyn looked at Oliver and me.

"She does," Oliver smiled, looking at me.

"Yeah," was all I could get out. My mouth had gone dry from being near her. I knew I needed to push these thoughts and feelings down.

"Birdie was telling me that she and a couple of the other women met the Golden Gals in town on Saturday," Oliver said.

"Oh lord, I can only imagine how that went." Evelyn threw back her head in laughter. "Those ladies have been a menace to the crown for years."

"Says the woman who used to run around with them before she became queen," Oliver laughed, rolling his eyes. Evelyn had the biggest smile on her face.

"You did?" Birdie exclaimed.

"Yes. Polly and I have been best friends since we were in nappies."

"That's so sweet. It must be nice to have such a long friendship."

"There were a few years that were rough right after I got engaged to Francis. I felt like their protests, sit-ins, and utter disregard for the crown were personal attacks on me. But after a few years and one big mediation session, things fell back to normal. Or at least, normal for those old bats," Evelyn said with a wink.

"Oh, I definitely need to hear more about this," Birdie said, looking between Evelyn and Oliver.

"Where should I start?" Oliver scratched behind his ear. "Well, one of my favorite stories is in the nineties, the Council had a few different bills they were contemplating. But one that didn't get passed would have removed sales tax on feminine products. The Golden Gals were very upset, so they covered themselves in red paint, came to the state building, and marched outside for hours while chanting, 'Pussy power,' and wielding signs that read 'Fight like a girl' and 'Grow a pair' next to a drawing of a uterus. The Council asked them to stop and told them that they would hold a special meeting if they would just go home. The Golden Gals weren't having it and said they wanted to be a part of the meeting. They ended up getting the bill passed the next day."

"Well, it's official. I love them!" Birdie grinned.

"And that's just one of the many protests they've organized over many years," I added.

"One time they…" Oliver's voice trailed off as his gaze zeroed in on a beautiful blonde in a forest-green dress. We all looked to Adelaide as she walked up the steps from the garden.

"Hi," she smiled as she joined our circle, giving Evelyn a curtsy.

"Adelaide, darling, you look magnificent," Evelyn smiled, grabbing Adelaide's gloved hands and looking her over.

"Thank you, Your Highness." Adelaide's cheeks glowed a faint pink.

"When we were dress shopping, the shop owner said that Adelaide looked like you from the 1959 state dinner in that dress," Birdie said, smiling proudly at her friend.

"I was just thinking about that exact night." Evelyn smiled wistfully. "That was a night I will remember for the rest of my life. Francis and I also had to get married because of the marriage decree. And, speaking of the Golden Gals, they were there that night as well."

"Gram, please don't tell that story. I don't need my suitors getting any ideas," Oliver groaned.

"Well, I must hear it now," Adelaide said, a sparkle in her eye.

"Let's sit down and I will tell you everything. I need to get under a blanket," Evelyn said, rubbing her hands together to warm them.

Linking my arm with hers, I led Evelyn to one of the couches and held out my hand as she lowered herself into the cushions.

"Here you go," I said as I grabbed a blanket from the back of the couch and laid it across her lap.

She swatted me away and adjusted the blanket. "I may be an old bird, but I can cover myself up. Your chivalry is too much sometimes, Knox."

All I could do was smile. I was a gentleman, but caring for Evelyn was more about love than chivalry.

"All right. Now that I'm settled, let me tell you about the night of that state dinner. Francis was about to become king and needed a wife, just like our Oliver here. My father ran one of the country's largest law firms, and they decided that merging the royal family and my own would benefit everyone.

"I had zero desire to get married. I loved the life that I lived, out of high society. My mother had badgered me for years about attending dinners and dances, but I preferred staying home to read or riding horses with my friends. My father gave me no choice, and I was very resentful about his decision."

She adjusted the blanket on her lap. "What's funny is that, looking back on it now, I wouldn't have changed anything other than taking the opportunity to meet Francis sooner." She smiled, briefly lost in her memories.

Around the fire pit, Adelaide and Birdie watched Evelyn with doe eyes, entranced by her story. You could practically see the wheels turning in their heads, planning out their own love stories.

"Francis and I had been engaged for two weeks by the time the state dinner rolled around. It was our first royal event since announcing the engagement. I had sat in my room for three days at that point, refusing to do anything with him. I hated life and didn't want to be queen. I would stay up late at night, reading through my father's law books and trying to find a loophole to get out of the marriage arrangement. Then I moved on to trying to figure out how I could run away and live in some mountain cabin and survive by myself, even though I had zero experience being on my own.

"But Francis was a kind man, and he knew I was having a hard time. He offered the olive branch of inviting my friends to the dinner so I had someone with whom I could talk and mingle."

Birdie and Adelaide looked at each other. Birdie gently bumped Adelaide with her shoulder as they shared a smile.

"The night of the dinner arrived, and I hadn't seen Francis in a week. He had no idea I had concocted a plan to get the hell out of dodge and fly to Switzerland. I wasn't sure what I was going to do when I got there, but I would figure it out."

"Why Switzerland?" Birdie asked. She was leaning forward with her elbows on her knees, her gloved fingers laced together, completely entranced in the story.

"I had found in Papa's books that Switzerland had made a treaty to house any refugees from Wexstone when the war broke out in previous years. They refused to deport anyone who came there to find solace." Evelyn smiled ruefully. "I thought I had it all figured out at eighteen years old."

"Oh gosh. I can't imagine what I would do at eighteen, knowing the things I know now and the things I didn't know at that age," laughed Adelaide.

"Exactly," Evelyn replied. "The night of the state dinner, I pulled Polly and Hilda aside and told them my plan. Polly had just gotten her pilot's license, and she said she could get us a plane. We just had to find a way to sneak out of there."

"I still don't know how you slipped security," Oliver laughed.

"And I will never tell any of you because I love you and want you to always be safe." She patted Oliver on the cheek.

"So did you end up getting to Switzerland?" Birdie asked.

"Yeah, what happened with the plane?" I smiled at Evelyn, knowing exactly what had happened.

Evelyn let out a laugh.

"We were able to give security the slip and Hilda found a chauffeur who drove us to the small airfield in the back of the palace grounds. I still don't know how she got the keys, but Polly unlocked this little puddle jumper and we all quickly climbed in, skipped the safety check, and got going so no one could stop us. Well, Polly kept feeling resistance, and I looked back and there was a banner trailing the plane that read, 'Congratulations, Prince Francis and Evelyn.' As we flew over the palace, everyone outside started cheering and celebrating, and that's when they noticed I was gone.

"A few minutes later, Francis came over the radio and let Polly know that if she didn't return me and the plane, she would be an enemy of the state and that the poor chap she took the keys from would lose his job. She was all for still flying me to Switzerland, but I couldn't do that to my friend and the man who worked at the airfield."

"Oh my gosh!" Adelaide exclaimed.

"Those are some great friends!" Birdie laughed.

"After that incident, the Golden Gals weren't invited to any more events and we grew apart for a few years. When I had Leroy, I had the baby blues very badly; we didn't understand it very well back then, and Francis tried everything to help. He called the girls to the palace, and they helped as much as they could. They weren't the answer, but they really did help. Having them back in my life healed a little part of me."

I watched as Adelaide grabbed Birdie's hand and they gave each other a smile. I had seen how close Birdie and her friend Sam were. I could understand how it must be for her to be away from her best friend—I had felt that when Oliver went away to university. I was happy that Birdie was making a friend here, especially someone who understood what she was going through.

"But just because I was queen does not mean they stopped causing a ruckus," Evelyn chuckled.

"Another of my favorite stories when I was a kid was when my father announced some new farming plan. They showed up and started throwing bruised and battered fruit at him. I had never seen security move so fast in my life. I remember that a strawberry hit him straight in the chest and he thought he had been shot," Oliver laughed.

Evelyn grinned. "I remember that. They were mad about all of the fruit for export being so heavily monitored and so much of it going to waste."

"I mean, they had a good point," I interjected. My mom had used those bruised and battered fruits to make the best jams and jellies.

"They did," Evelyn agreed. "And that's when Isobel suggested that the Council move some money around and invest in jam production. It gave us another export and cut down the waste from the orchards."

"Wow. That's so smart of Queen Isobel," Birdie breathed.

"She is brilliant, that daughter-in-law of mine. That's why, even though many chastise the marriage law, it's so crucial to have two heads instead of one. Where one is weak, the other is strong. Where one lacks, the other is sufficient. It's so important to have two people who can balance each other out." She looked at Adelaide and Birdie.

What did Evelyn see when she looked at them? She had a sense about people, and I wanted to get inside her brain and pick apart what she was thinking when she surveyed the women.

Who did she think would best complement Oliver?

Deep down, I hoped it wasn't Birdie.

CHAPTER 17
KNOX

A voice came over a set of speakers hidden at the edge of the terrace, asking us to please proceed to the solarium.

We stood and meandered up the steps and into the bright, warm room. Lord Thorne stood by a table that held seven clipboards. *Why are there seven clipboards?* I looked at Oliver with alarm.

"Why are there seven clipboards and not six?" I had a sickening feeling in my gut.

"Because whether you want to admit it or not, you are a part of the royal family and you will be treated as such." He smiled ear to ear.

"No one is going to bid on me. The women here couldn't care less about what I have to say."

"And they're idiots if they truly believe that. You're a part of this family, my best friend, and my right hand, whether you make it official or not. If they don't see your value, then they don't deserve to be queen."

I closed my eyes and took a deep breath. *This night just*

keeps getting better. Not only did I have to watch Birdie walk around looking like an absolute goddess, but now I would have to endure the humiliation of not getting a single bid.

"Ladies and gentlemen, if I may have your attention," Lord Thorne spoke from the front of the room. "Thank you all for attending our garden party this evening. This fundraiser is a great tradition that the Thorne family holds close to our hearts. All the proceeds will directly support our community gardens.

"This year, our silent auction will allow each of Prince Oliver's suitors to bid for a two-hour time slot tomorrow evening with their chosen member of the royal family." He cleared his throat of the emotion that seemed to briefly clog it. "We are so very grateful for the royal family's generosity. It means so much to us that they would donate their valuable time, especially during this holiday season. So, thank you, Your Majesties."

"All right, let the bidding begin," Lady Thorne cheered from beside him.

I noticed that Renata and Ginny made a beeline for the tables to start their bidding. No doubt they were bidding on Oliver.

"That's weird," Birdie said to Adelaide, who was standing to my right.

"What is?" Adelaide asked.

"I haven't seen Gemma tonight. I thought those three only traveled together."

"I guess we'll find out soon," Adelaide responded as Renata and Ginny walked over to where we all stood in the middle of the room.

"Ollie!" Renata screeched. Her high-pitched voice was like nails on a chalkboard.

"Good evening," he greeted flatly.

"I made sure that I put a substantial amount down for you, so you don't have to worry about being with someone you don't like." She winked at him and ran her hand down his lapel.

"Great." He side-eyed her, and it took everything in me not to burst out laughing.

"Knox, I was so surprised to see you had your own clip-board," Renata said snidely.

"Why is that surprising?" Oliver asked, his tone stone cold.

Shock flashed across Renata's face. "I just thought this was supposed to be royal family only," she said, her voice suddenly sugary sweet.

"Knox is family," Oliver said sharply. "And you'd do well to remember that, Renata."

"I didn't mean to offend anyone." She laughed nervously. "It was just a joke, Ollie."

"You know that Knox has been a part of this family for decades. And the future queen will treat him as such. Regard-less of whether he shares my last name, he's a royal family member and will not be treated as anything less."

"Okay." Her voice was softer, like a child who has just been reprimanded.

A few moments of silence passed, and the tension started to dissipate.

"Ginny. Where is Gemma tonight? I haven't seen her," Birdie asked.

"She wasn't feeling well so she stayed home." Ginny smiled nervously.

"I'm so sorry to hear that."

"Oh my God, Ginny. Tell them what really happened," Renata laughed maniacally. Ginny gave her a sharp look.

Renata rolled her eyes and continued laughing. "Gemma got a new type of lip filler yesterday, but she had a reaction and her lips puffed up like a blowfish. She can't even talk! She looks like a Dr. Seuss character," she cackled.

"That's awful! I hope she's okay," Adelaide said, her eyes wide with concern.

"She'll be fine," Renata waved. "That's why you should stay all natural." Renata ran her hand down her body.

Oliver and I gave each other one of our telepathic looks that said, *She's kidding right?*

"Well…" Oliver started but was interrupted when Lord Thorne walked up.

"Your Highness." Lord Thorne bowed. "Mr. Henderson." He nodded at me. "I'm so happy you are both here tonight."

"Thank you," we said in unison.

"Mr. Henderson, may I introduce you to my new head of landscaping, Charles, tonight? The grounds always look impeccable at the palace, and I would love for you to talk to him and give him some advice. As the head of the forestry industry, it looks bad when my own gardens are barely thriving," he chuckled.

"I would hardly say they are struggling. I was floored when I walked onto the terrace tonight and saw the camellias and could smell the witch-hazels. That is an amazing feat to have in the dead of winter. Whatever he is doing is great."

Lord Thorne laughed. "Well, actually, those are thriving because of Sabine, not Charles."

"Oh. Well, then," I cleared my throat. "I guess I should go speak to him." I loved talking about the outdoors and anything that had to do with it. *Maybe I should push for Oliver to marry Sabine so I can have someone around to help me with the grounds.*

I excused myself from the group and followed Lord Thorne to the side of the room, where he introduced me to Charles. We talked for about thirty minutes before I suggested he give me a tour of the gardens. We finished the tour with a walk along a beautiful maze of holly bushes that led to four greenhouses. The greenhouses lined the back of the gardens and were lit with twinkle lights.

"That's about it," Charles said.

"I can draw up a plan for you and send it over in a few days."

"I would really appreciate that, Mr. Henderson. I'm a little over my head here."

"It's not a problem at all. I enjoy doing it. And you'll get the hang of it. It's always hard starting off. Feel free to call me with any questions." I extended my hand.

"Thank you so much," Charles said, shaking my hand. "Well, we better get back to the party."

We walked a few yards back to the manor when something caught my attention from the corner of my eye. At first, I thought it might have been a deer, but upon second glance, I saw Birdie opening the door to the farthest greenhouse and walking in. My curiosity piqued. Why was she all the way out here? And why was she going into the greenhouse?

"Hey Charles, I think I'm going to walk around a little bit more if that's okay? Can I check out the greenhouses?"

"Of course," he said. "I'll see you back inside."

I approached the greenhouse and opened the door. The warmth hit my face and thawed my fingers that had grown numb from walking the grounds.

She stood on the other side of the small building, running one hand along the leaves of a beautiful blooming bush lily. The other arm held her white wool coat. I couldn't help but stand in silence and watch her. She always took my breath away.

Her white gown stood in stark contrast against the greenery of the greenhouse. She was like a lighthouse, and I was a ship lost at sea, looking for a way home. How was it that no matter how hard I tried to push these feelings away, each time I thought about her, they came back tenfold?

I found my feet walking closer to her. She was clearly caught up in her own thoughts and I knew I should probably announce myself, but I was mesmerized by the way she fingered the leaf through her gloved hands. I watched the way her breasts slowly rose with each breath and her eyes danced back and forth to each petal of the flower. I lived for the moments that I caught her lost in thought. Her features tended to soften, allowing the full range of her emotions to show, not just the smiling face she put on for everyone.

Caught up in watching Birdie, my shoe scratched the pavement and startled her. She dropped her coat to the ground and let out a high-pitched squeal.

"Holy shit, Knox!" she yelled.

"I'm sorry." I put my hands up in surrender. "I saw you walk in here and I was just seeing if you were all right."

"I mean, I'm having a heart attack at the moment, so no, I'm not all right."

"I'm sorry. I should have said something when I walked inside."

"You think?"

"Here." I bent down to pick up her coat and dust it off. "What are you doing all the way back here?"

"I took a walk to clear my head. Then I got lost and I was really freaking cold. When I saw the greenhouse, I thought this would be a good place to warm up before I started to try and find my way back."

"Fair enough."

"What are you doing here?" she asked, her tone clipped.

"Charles, the Thornes' landscaper, was showing me around. When I saw you come in here, I wanted to check on you."

"Well, I don't need to be checked up on, okay? I don't need some knight in shining armor to come save me and make all my choices for me. I can take care of myself and make my own decisions, okay?"

I held up my hands, taking a step back. "Whoa."

She let out a huff and then started pacing back and forth in front of me.

"I'm sorry," she said.

"What's up? Clearly, something is bothering you if you needed to take a walk and then...whatever that was." I waved my hand in her direction.

"This is all starting to just become too much. When Queen Mother Evelyn told that story tonight, all I could think was that this woman is a badass. And then she talked about how Queen Isobel is this great counterpart to King Leroy and helps him. I can't be that, I can't do that." Her voice rose. "Then Oliver and I were talking, and he was telling me about the country tour that he would take after the wedding and all of the coronation events. It's just a lot!"

My heart cracked witnessing anxiety take over her usually convivial demeanor. *How much else is she hiding from the world?* "Just take a breath. I think you're thinking too far into the future right now."

"And you're not thinking far enough into the future! I have weeks—*weeks,* Knox—to decide whether I can move forward with all of this, okay? You don't understand what kind of pressure that puts me under."

I did understand the pressure, more than she knew. Oliver wanted me to dedicate the rest of my life to serving at his side, to being his stand-in when he couldn't be there. It was different but also the same.

"You're right. I'm sorry. I don't know the exact stress you're under. It's a big decision that you have to make. You would have to leave your country, your family, your friends to move here and marry Oliver."

"Yeah!"

"But is he worth it? Is he worth all of this? Is this what you want?" I waved my hand around and then looked at her, really observing her. A slight sheen of sweat was forming along her hairline. "Only you can answer that question."

She stopped pacing and looked at me like she was dissecting every word I had just said. She cleared her throat and plastered a tense smile on her face. "I think we should probably get back. They're going to be announcing the winning bids soon."

"Yeah." I looked down at her coat in my hands. I was hoping she would tell me what she was thinking. If I heard from her lips that she was fully in this, and that Oliver was it for her, I could put these thoughts and wants to rest once and for all. I needed to hear her say it. But the way she had just masked her emotions told me I wouldn't be getting my wish tonight.

"Here. Let me help you put your coat on and I'll walk you back up." I moved closer and held open the white wool coat.

"Thank you. For everything." She gave me a soft smile that didn't reach her eyes. The closer she walked to me, the more her signature scent of lavender and vanilla filled my nose. As she turned her back to me, flashes of the dream I'd had flitted across my mind. I tried not to think of how little strength it would take to pop the buttons off the back of her white dress.

I cleared my throat. "What are friends for, right?"

"Yeah. Friends." She looked up at me over her shoulder. Her hair fell over her other shoulder, giving me a clear and unobstructed look at her throat. I wanted to taste her skin and make a slow trail of kisses up her neck.

I moved my gaze from her throat to her hazel eyes. Did

she want me to kiss her as badly as I wanted to? The way that her eyes bore into me made me think yes. Her eyes roamed from my lips to my eyes. She turned to face me and set her hand on my chest and fingered the thin black tie around my neck. She slid her other hand up my pec, stopping over my heart. I knew she could feel the way it beat hard and erratically because of her. Birdie brought her eyes back up to mine and when she did, she sucked in that full bottom lip and bit it.

God, I want that lip in my mouth.

I threaded my fingers through her hair at the nape of her neck. I bent down for our mouths to meet, her lips parting, waiting for mine.

A loud bang went off above us. We both jumped back.

"What the fuck was that?" Birdie exclaimed.

I looked up to see blue, green, and white sparks raining down over the glass roof of the greenhouse.

"Fireworks."

"Of course." She let out a soft laugh.

"We should get back up there," I said.

We exited the greenhouse and wended our way through the holly maze and up through the garden as the fireworks continued. I stopped right before the last arch of the red berries. Birdie turned around and looked at me quizzically.

I cleared my throat. "I think maybe you should head up the terrace first and I'll wait. I don't want anyone to question you."

Her brow arched. "What is this, the 1700s? Will my honor and virtue come into question?" She tried to play it off as a quip, but fire laced her tone.

"There is a lot of press here tonight, and we know that they aren't the best at reporting the truth. You don't need them publishing another shit article—and God knows what they would say about Oliver and you. I wouldn't want him to question your loyalty to the competition. Better you just walk the rest of the way by yourself."

She considered my words as she looked down at her hands and messed with the lining of her gloves.

"You're a good man, Knox." She looked up at me. "He's so lucky to have a friend like you."

I nodded. I so badly wanted to grab her hand and walk her those last few yards. I wanted more than anything to tell her not to continue with all of this. To move here for me instead. To be with me instead. But that's not who I was, and that wasn't my story. This was about Oliver's happily ever after, not mine.

————

"Ladies and gentlemen, if you would please make your way inside. The results of the auction will be read in just a few short minutes," the night's emcee spoke over the loudspeakers.

I grabbed a glass of champagne from a passing waiter and downed it in two gulps. I knew I was about to be thoroughly embarrassed when my name wasn't read, because who would even bid and want to spend time with me?

Absolutely no one.

"Where have you been? I've been looking for you," Oliver asked from behind me.

"The Thornes' landscaper was showing me the gardens. We were talking about potential plans for spring."

"Mhm," Oliver murmured, taking a sip from his glass of champagne.

Vince walked up to us. "Have you guys seen Birdie? Bronson was asking where she went but I can't find her."

Shit. Play it cool. I know she's here; I watched her walk back into the party.

"I talked to her about an hour ago, but haven't seen her since, now that you mention it," Oliver answered.

"What about you?" Vince asked.

"Nope. Haven't seen her," I lied.

Oliver looked at me quizzically in my peripheral vision. Did he know that I was lying? Had he seen us in the greenhouse somehow? *Fuck.*

"Damn. I hope everything is okay. Maybe Adelaide has seen her." Vince looked around the room, scanning each cluster of guests.

"Hey, guys." I heard her beautiful soprano voice.

"There you are!" Vince said. "I was getting worried; I couldn't find you."

"Sorry. I got lost in the garden and just found my way back." She laughed. "I am not great with directions."

I could feel Oliver's eyes drilling into me. I knew he wanted me to look at him so we could have one of our mind talks, but I wasn't going to do it. I sucked at lying to him and I didn't want him to figure out that I had been in the garden with one of his suitors. This morning, he'd said that she was a frontrunner. Yet, just minutes ago, I had made the shitty decision to almost kiss her. I was a bad friend, and I knew it.

A few minutes passed while I gave him the cold shoulder, before he finally gave up and engaged with Birdie as she told a story about how she once got lost driving home from high school.

"Ladies and gentlemen, if I may have your attention," the emcee spoke from the small stage against the far wall.

"The Thornes would like to thank everyone for attending tonight, with a special thanks to the royal family. Thank you for your generous donations to the Wexstone Community Garden Foundation. Now, without further ado, we will announce what I'm sure you have all been anticipating: the winning bids of the silent auction."

"God, I pray that I didn't get stuck with Renata," Oliver muttered under his breath.

Vince snorted quietly as I coughed into my fist to suppress a laugh. I had a feeling that it didn't matter what he wanted; that was exactly who he was going to be spending the following evening with.

As he read down the list, I was taken aback by how much these women had spent to get alone time with the royal family. Sabine, or her family, had spent over one hundred thousand euros on Leroy. I was shocked. Surely that had to be the largest bid tonight.

I was so sure in my assumption as they read off the rest of the list. I was a little surprised when I heard that Adelaide won with her bid of twenty-five thousand euros for Evelyn. I figured that she would have surely bid on Oliver, but when I heard his name called and how much the winning bid was, I knew that there was no way that Adelaide could have won even if she did bid.

"And with a winning bid of two hundred and fifty thousand euros for Prince Oliver: Renata Raines."

"Holy shit," I whispered.

"You're kidding me," Oliver groaned quietly.

Vince clapped him on the back. "Smile, mate. They're all looking at you."

Applause filled the room. I couldn't believe that the Raines family had spent that much money on alone time with Oliver. On second thought, I could believe it, because I knew that the Raineses would do anything to make sure that Renata became queen.

"And that brings us to our final royal family member of the

night, Knox Henderson. With a winning bid of one hundred thousand euros, Bernadette Hamilton."

Birdie let out a small gasp from my right. Her eyes were wide with curiosity as she turned to Vince.

"You spent that much money so I could hang out with Knox?" she questioned.

"No, I most definitely didn't." He looked from her to me, studiously ignoring Bronson's vexed gaze from across the room. "Did you put her name down?" he questioned me.

"No. Why would I do that?" I answered.

Vince puffed his chest slightly. "I don't know, mate. You tell me."

My eyes narrowed. "I can't because I didn't. How do you think that would look if I put her name down for myself?"

"My thoughts exactly." He turned back to Birdie. "Honestly, you didn't put your name down?"

"Look, I love the fact that you think I have that much money, but I don't. And if I did, I wouldn't be so worried about being homeless because I could buy a place in Jersey or something."

"Oi. It's fine," Oliver interrupted, placing a hand on Vince's shoulder. "It doesn't matter who did it. That's a lot of money for the fundraiser. Think of how many people that's going to help. This is amazing."

"Yeah." Birdie gave a small smile that didn't fully reach her eyes.

"You guys are friends and will have fun." Oliver patted me on the back.

"Yeah. We're friends," I said, pushing down the twisting guilt in my gut.

CHAPTER 18
BIRDIE

The gold stiletto hit the floor-to-ceiling cabinet in the closet as I kicked it off, sighing in relief to have feeling back in my toes. My feet ached and I was ready to strip this dress off and get into loose clothing. Sonya knocked on the door.

"Miss, do you need help getting out of your dress?"

"I do! You can come in."

Sonya walked into the closet, and I held my hair up off my back so she could unzip the zipper hidden underneath the row of faux buttons. If I had any reservations about her seeing me in my undergarments, those had been tossed out the window by the third time she helped me get dressed and undressed. She took the gown and put it back in the garment bag that hung on the rack.

"I appreciate you staying late tonight to help me. I don't think I could have reached that zipper on my own," I said.

"It's my pleasure, miss. I have been there a time or two myself," she replied with a wink. "I'll take this downstairs and get it dry cleaned." She smiled. "How did tonight go? Did you have any alone time with the prince?"

I returned her smile. "Yeah, we did. We sat and had a lovely conversation."

I couldn't let her know that the conversation about the future and what it would look like had sent me into a tiny spiral and led to me getting lost in the garden and in a greenhouse with Knox. I *definitely* couldn't let her know how close I came to kissing Knox again. That I couldn't stop thinking about his lips on mine. That if he had kissed me, it would have led to me getting on my knees in front of him, because I couldn't stop picturing the night he stood in my kitchen almost naked or the way he looked down at me with those hooded eyes and half smile. That I would have done anything to keep that smile on his face. I absolutely couldn't tell her any of that.

"That is wonderful. He seems like such a nice man."

"He really is." I smiled again, though it felt empty.

It wasn't a lie. He was a great man. And yet: *the spark.*

That was the one thing missing when it came to Oliver. Yeah, he was handsome but there wasn't that spark.

My body didn't light up when he touched me like it did with Knox.

I didn't forget my words when I was around Oliver, and I forgot my own name when I was with Knox.

I didn't get jealous when Adelaide looked at him with her little doe eyes when she thought no one was looking, but the thought of Renata even hypothetically going after Knox caused a strong sense of possession to take over my body.

I *wanted* to feel that spark with Oliver because I knew I should, and it would make the decision for my future so much easier.

After Sonya said her goodbyes and closed the door, I

washed my face and moisturized and then climbed into bed. It had been such a long night, and I needed to turn my mind off. If I didn't, there was zero chance of me falling asleep.

An hour ticked by and I still couldn't fall asleep. My mind just wouldn't quiet. Between the almost-kiss with Knox in the greenhouse, the conversation I had with Oliver about everything that was to come, and then trying to figure out who put my name down and spent that much money so I could spend time with Knox, I just couldn't slow my racing thoughts.

Then I remembered the Vegas bachelorette party and the weed gummies that had been in my suitcase. Even though I had panicked over them at the airport, I had never checked to see if they were still in my bag. If I did have them, they were exactly what I needed to calm my mind and get a good night's rest.

I jumped out of bed and went into the closet where my bags were stored. I flipped through a few pockets of the first suitcase, not remembering where I had put the little baggie. I moved onto the next bag. It had been stored upside down, so I pulled it out and started to unzip it when a black vibrator fell out onto my big toe and started vibrating across the floor.

"Oh shit!" I yelled. I picked it up, flipping it over and over trying to find the buttons. I finally found the power button and turned it off. I started to put it back into the bag but stopped.

I stood there for a minute just looking at the vibrator. It was black silicone, about six inches long, and had two little rabbit ears that sat at the base and vibrated like crazy when it was on. If I couldn't find my gummies, maybe this was the next best thing to calm me down and silence my mind.

Yeah, this would do the trick instead. And honestly maybe if I got off, I could put all those Knox thoughts to rest. Get him out of my system by proxy, right? I took the vibrator and climbed back into the big bed. I knew it wouldn't take much to get myself in the mood. All I had to think about was the way Knox ran his fingers through my hair earlier and pulled at the nape of my neck. That had made me soak through my panties right there in the greenhouse. Or I could think about the way he picked me up and put me against the wall in the closet at the hotel.

I turned the vibrator on the lowest setting, slid it down the front of my white lace underwear and rubbed it through my folds. Thinking about Knox was exactly the thing to get my core dripping wet.

I thought about the way his eyes roamed over my body last night. He was shit at keeping his thoughts off his face when he was turned on. And I knew that he was excited by the way that his considerable cock had bulged through his pants and pushed into my stomach when I was pressed against him in the greenhouse. I had almost told him how badly I wanted him to take that tie off and wrap it around my hands and have his way with me right there.

That thought led me to wondering what it would be like if he was in the bed with me. He would take that tie and bind my hands above my head, maybe even to the headboard so I wouldn't be able to move, as he kissed down my neck, to my chest and focused on my breasts.

I ran my free hand up under the baggy shirt I had put on to sleep in. As I palmed my breast and ran my thumb over my nipple, I had to hold back a small moan. Squeezing my nipple a little bit, I imagined Knox sucking and biting on it.

God, I want that so badly.

My core was growing slicker, and I needed more. I kicked the vibrator up another setting and rubbed it along my clit before setting the tip just inside of me. I imagined that it was Knox's large hands rubbing in and out of me. It felt amazing—

not as good as I knew Knox would be, but it was definitely doing the job. I was so close to coming.

The thought of Knox moving down my body, leaving trails of kisses and little nips on the inside of my thighs, was edging me closer and closer. I imagined the way it would feel when he got to my core, breathing his warm breath on my sensitive flesh and telling me how delicious I looked. I flipped the vibrator around and skimmed the little bunny ears over my clit, picturing Knox running his tongue over it. I wanted to feel him licking me so badly. I knew what it felt like to have his tongue in my mouth, skimming along my bottom lip, but I wanted to know what it felt like to have it inside of me. What was it like to have him suck and kiss me down there? What noises would he make if I came on his mouth?

Maxing out the speed of the vibrator, I started to edge the tip further inside of me. Remembering what the outline of Knox's dick looked like from the night in my apartment, I knew that if the day ever came, he would have to be slow and gentle to fully fit inside of me, and that made me even wetter. The thought of this man stretching and filling me up made my breath quicken. I pushed the vibrator all the way in and brought it out, gasping for air. The image of Knox shirtless, pushing in and out, his abs contracting and relaxing, flashed across my mind, and after two more thrusts of the vibrator, I was close to climax.

One more drive in and I was there. I saw stars as the room exploded around me. Knox's name came out of my mouth as I pulled the vibrator from between my legs. My breath was heavy, and I couldn't believe that I had just fantasized about the man I was most definitely not here for.

———

"Aunt Birbie, look at my turkey!" My three-year-old niece Eleanor smiled wide as she held up a handprint turkey covered in crayon scribbles, her blue eyes gleaming and strawberry-blonde curls framing her face in a messy halo.

"Oh my gosh, that's the best turkey I have ever seen!" I exclaimed, my heart melting.

"Can I see yours?" Eleanor asked, leaning toward Connor's iPad as if it would allow her to see the page I was coloring at my desk.

I held my paper up to the camera, letting her see the hand-print turkey I had traced. On its head sat a ski cap and goggles, and I had drawn skis on its feet, angled to look like it was sliding down a steep mountain slope bordered with pine trees.

"What do you think?" I asked.

"I love it, Aunt Birbie!" Ellie exclaimed, clapping her hands with delight.

I set my page back on the desk. Behind me, the coffee table was filled with more food than I could possibly eat: two Cornish game hens with cranberry sauce, whipped potatoes, and roasted brussels sprouts with cranberries and what looked to be a balsamic glaze. On a side table rested a tray with tea and a whole chocolate tart. The food smelled heavenly. I couldn't wait to dig in.

"Ok, let's see Mom and Dad's," I said, giving my brother a pointed look.

Connor sighed and rolled his eyes. "Not fair, Birdie. You know you got the artistic genes," he said as he held up his turkey. It looked like a seven-year-old had drawn it. I couldn't suppress the grin that took over my face.

"Hey, you're the one who wanted an activity we could all do together as part of our Thanksgiving tradition," I quipped back.

"Yeah, I'll get you back soon enough," he grumbled as he

added what I guessed was supposed to be a Santa hat to his drawing.

A knock sounded from my bedroom door.

"Hold on one sec," I said, hitting mute and turning off my camera as I got up.

I opened the door, expecting to have to remind Vince that I was celebrating American Thanksgiving with my family this evening. Instead, I found Knox.

CHAPTER 19
BIRDIE

Knox stood in the hall, his hands in the pockets of his jeans, wearing the same beanie and thick plaid flannel from the day I met him in New York. Eugene sat by his feet, tail wagging excitedly.

Shit! I had been so focused on talking to the kitchen staff about what I needed for Thanksgiving that I had forgotten all about our auction "date" that night.

"Knox! Oh my God. I totally lost track of time."

"Oh." Knox shifted uncomfortably on his feet. "I can come back later if you want," he muttered.

I glanced behind me to the iPad where my brother and his family were still drawing and laughing, and to the spread of food by the loveseat. "No, you know what? Come on in. I'm just FaceTiming my family for Thanksgiving and was going to eat in a minute, but the cooks made me way too much food. You should join me."

Knox peered around me, taking in the scene. A wash of

realization swept over his face. "Oh no, I couldn't impose like that."

"Don't be silly. My niece is going to have to go down for her nap soon and then it was just going to be me and a whole chocolate tart. You may as well save me from myself there."

"Okay, if you're sure," Knox said, stepping into the room, Eugene bounding along behind him.

I strode back toward the desk. "We just have one more family tradition to finish up. My brother and sister-in-law are for sure gonna make you participate, so you better be ready," I said, turning the camera and microphone back on.

"Hey guys, this is Knox," I said, gesturing to where he stood awkwardly behind me. "He's Oliver's best friend and stopped by for a contest thing. And that," I said, turning the camera toward the armchair where Eugene had immediately settled himself, "is Knox's dog, Eugene. Knox, this is my brother Connor, his wife Colleen, and my niece, Ellie. Say hi to everyone."

"Hi. It's nice to meet you," Knox said, stepping up to stand beside me.

Connor's eyebrow raised. Colleen cut in before he could say anything. "Knox, it's nice to meet you. Are you American?" she asked, noting his accent.

"I am; my family moved to Wexstone when I was ten. It's been years since I celebrated Thanksgiving, though."

"Well, we were just going to each share something we are thankful for before Ellie goes down for her nap. You have to join us!"

I glanced at Knox. *Told you*, my look said. The corner of his mouth tilted upward in a suppressed smile.

"It would be my pleasure," Knox replied.

"Ellie, do you want to go first or last?" Connor asked, putting his arm around the squirming toddler.

"First!" She exclaimed, jumping up and down.

Her mother chuckled. "What a shock," said Colleen, pinching Ellie's cheek.

"Okay then. Ellie, what are you thankful for?" Connor prompted.

"Ummmmmm..." Ellie put her finger to her chin, eyebrows scrunched, clearly thinking hard. Suddenly her eyes lit up and she leaped to her feet. "Elmo!!" She held her stuffed Elmo above her head proudly.

We all dissolved into laughter. I was surprised to see how heartily Knox laughed along.

"Okay, Connor, your turn," I said as Ellie settled back onto the couch between her parents.

"I'm thankful for my beautiful family and for special holiday traditions," Connor answered.

Colleen piped up, "That's my answer as well."

Typical, I thought. I loved them, but sometimes their *Leave it to Beaver* life made me roll my eyes.

"Birdie, how about you?" Colleen asked.

I paused, considering. "The opportunity to visit this beautiful country and make new friends."

Connor rolled his eyes. Colleen gave him a look that I knew meant *Be nice*.

"And last but not least. Knox, what's something that you're thankful for?" Colleen asked, turning back to the camera.

Knox paused. I was about to jump in to tell him he didn't have to answer when he spoke.

"Well, I guess tonight I'm thankful for the chance to celebrate Thanksgiving for the first time in fifteen years," he said, looking from my family to where I sat beside him. I caught his gaze and my heart caught in my throat at the gratitude in his eyes.

"Okay, well, uh, we should probably let you guys go," I

stammered, turning back toward the camera. "Our food is getting cold, and I know someone could probably use a nap before her grandma and grandpa get there." Right on cue, Ellie yawned, rubbing her eyes.

"No, I not tired!" she protested.

"Mmhmm, sure," my brother said, scooping her up. She nuzzled her curly head against his shoulder.

"Have a good rest of the evening," Colleen said. "Happy Thanksgiving! Lovely to meet you, Knox. We love you, Birdie!"

"Love you guys, too. Happy Thanksgiving," I said, reaching for my iPad.

"Happy Thanksgiving. Nice to meet you," Knox intoned as I hung up the call.

I turned to Knox. "Thanks for hanging in there through that. Time to eat!"

———

"So, how did you manage to get all of this food?" Knox asked, helping himself to a second slice of chocolate tart. "Chef Bruno isn't exactly known for being overly friendly."

"Chef Bruno just hadn't met me before," I winked at Knox, setting aside my empty plate. I knew I would probably end up eating another plate of dessert before I went to bed, but for now I needed to let the rest of the meal digest.

Knox eyed me, raising a brow as he chewed a bite of tart.

I laughed. "Look. I've been waiting tables for a while. I know how to charm and befriend grumpy line cooks. You never know when having them on your side will come in handy. When I got here, I just made sure I befriended the kitchen staff. Did you know that Bruno has a two-year-old grandson and a Weimaraner he adores in almost equal measure? Turns out, he was happy to make me as traditional of a Thanksgiving meal as he could when I asked. He was really upset that he couldn't get me an actual turkey. Although I'd say the game hens weren't a bad substitute."

Knox sat back against the loveseat and nodded. "Considering we picked them clean, I'd say they were more than satisfactory," he chuckled. Eugene whined from where he was now sprawled across my bed. "Oh, don't act like you didn't get a bite," Knox scolded, rolling his eyes at his dog. He turned back to me. "I have to say I'm impressed, though. It's not every day that you see people befriend the household staff."

"Says the man who knows the names of all of the staff at the palace," I said with a conspiratorial smile. "Wish I could say I was surprised, though," I sighed, thinking of Renata. "But I didn't grow up being waited on hand and foot. To be honest, I'm more comfortable doing things for myself, although it's been nice to have the staff to chat with on days when we don't have anything on the schedule."

"I understand that. Why do you think I chose to live in the old caretaker's cottage?" Knox poured himself a cup of tea. "Even after my family moved here, we never had any household staff, so it was a real shock to my system when I moved into the palace after my parents died. I never really got used to it, so when Oliver left for uni, I asked Leroy and Isobel if I could have the caretaker's old place and job since he had retired. They told me I could do anything that made me happy, although I still come home periodically to find all my linens freshly washed and folded, and my pantry and fridge never go empty, so I know Isobel still has some of the staff checking in on me if she doesn't do it herself."

My heart twisted, remembering what it was like to have a mother worrying about me. "You said you hadn't celebrated Thanksgiving in fifteen years. Is there a reason why?" I asked, reaching for the teapot and pouring myself a cup.

Knox took a sip from his mug. "My parents died in a car crash when I was fifteen. I assume Oliver told you that much?" I nodded. Knox ran a finger around the rim of his cup. "Even after we moved to Wexstone, my parents always made sure we celebrated Thanksgiving with a big, home-cooked meal. Oliver even joined us a couple of times. After they passed away, I wanted to continue celebrating. But it seemed like there was always something going on at the palace, and I was just a teenager, and..."

"And it was just too heavy," I finished quietly.

Knox met my gaze, a question in his eyes. "Yeah. It was. Isobel and Leroy offered to celebrate it with me, but...well. You said it. It was too heavy."

I set down my cup and turned toward him on the loveseat, pulling my feet up underneath me. I took a shaky breath.

"My mom's birthday was Christmas Day," I said. "To say that we went all out for Christmas is an understatement. The woman loved Christmas *and* she loved birthdays. So Christmas was always a huge fucking deal for us. Even the year she was sick, she still made sure that Connor and I had full stockings and tons of gifts under the tree, no matter how much she had to scrimp and save to do so." I picked at the sleeve of my sweater. "After she died, Christmas lost its magic. My dad checked out mentally and emotionally, so it was on me to make sure Con had gifts to open. I was only fourteen. I kept it up until I left for college, but it was too hard to be a mom and sister while taking a full load of classes and working..." My words trailed off. Knox reached over, grabbing my hand. A sea of sadness and understanding filled his eyes.

"Anyway," I continued, taking encouragement from the feeling of his warm hand over mine, "Christmas hasn't really been the same since she died. I enjoy the season but sometimes I kind of hide myself away from all the festivities."

"That's understandable," he said, squeezing my hand before pulling away. I felt suddenly cold without his warm fingers wrapped around my own. "Your dad, is he around much?"

I shook my head. "No. Honestly, I don't even know for sure where he's living these days. After Mom died, he stopped being able to hold down any job for longer than a year or so. We had always struggled to make ends meet, but it became almost impossible with him going from job to job like that. Connor and I were only able to pay for college thanks to money my grandparents had set aside in a trust specifically for our educations. When Connor left for school, Dad sold the house and moved to Alabama. Then to Montana. Then I kind of lost track. My college graduation was the first time he set foot on campus the entire time I was there. I was surprised he even showed up for that." I shrugged, taking a sip of my tea. I cleared my throat. "What were your folks like?" I asked quietly. Knox examined me, an unreadable expression on his face. "If you don't want to talk about them, that's okay, I get it," I added.

"No, that's not it," he said quickly. He took a deep breath. "It's just...no one has asked me about them in a long time. They probably think it's too painful to talk about, but I really like talking about them. It makes them feel alive again, even just for a moment." This time, I closed the distance between us to take his hand, weaving my fingers through his calloused ones. I squeezed, a silent encouragement.

"Well, I'd love to hear about them."

"Dad was a big guy, probably six-five or six-six—taller than me," he said, closing his eyes as he spoke. "He was a professor of literature at the university and wore these three-piece suits that made him look like a *Sherlock Holmes* character. He always had to custom order them because of his height.

"The only thing he loved as much as my mom and me was

books, although being outside came close behind that. I remember him reading to me every night as a kid."

I thought of Knox reading to the children at the school drive the week before. "What kinds of books did you read together?" I asked, leaning my shoulder against the back of the loveseat and tucking my feet underneath me, our hands still intertwined.

"Oh, everything. The first book I remember him reading to me was *The Fellowship of the Ring*. He loved Tolkien. I still look for unique copies of *Fellowship* whenever I'm in a bookstore, and sometimes Oliver will bring me back copies in other languages when he travels. But we read *Frankenstein* and *Little Women* and *Dracula* and all the original Grimms' fairytales—anything you can think of. He didn't really care what I read, he just wanted me to understand that books can be a safe place to land when the world around us is too much to handle." His voice trailed off.

I squeezed his hand again. "And your mom?"

Knox cleared his throat. "Oh, Mom was one of the kindest humans I have ever met. She came off quiet and shy at first, but she had a smile that could light up an entire room—not unlike yours." He blushed; I ducked my head to hide that I was blushing as well. "She and Dad met when she was working at the UPenn library and Dad was a PhD student there. She was a writer—mostly technical stuff. She freelanced so she could stay home with me. She gave the best hugs in the world."

"They sound like they were amazing people. Thank you for telling me about them."

Knox turned to meet my gaze. "Thank you for asking about them." His eyes were bright, and something like hope glimmered in their depths. He set his tea down on the coffee table, never breaking my gaze or releasing my fingers. With his now-free hand, he reached over, gently sweeping a small crumb from the tart off my lip. He then brought his hand to rest just below my jaw. My body lit up as he brushed his thumb lightly over my bottom lip as his gaze fell to my mouth.

Electricity crackled across my skin, following the path his fingers made as he trailed his thumb across my mouth, over my cheek, down the curve of my jaw, and back to my bottom lip. Heat filled my core as the room around us disappeared, my sight narrowing until all I saw was Knox. The only sound I could hear was the hammering of my own heart as he leaned his head forward, resting his forehead against mine, our noses lightly brushing and our breath mingling. I closed my eyes, savoring the pine and mint scent of him, imagining his strong hands slowly removing my russet sweater, then my jeans, before kissing his way across my torso and taking me into his mouth—

"Eugene! Drop it!"

My eyes flew open, the spell broken as I spotted what had caused Knox to shout: Eugene, sneaking out of the bathroom with a pair of white lace panties in his mouth. At least, they had previously been a pair of white lace panties. Now, the entire crotch was missing, chewed to bits by the dog.

Eugene dropped the tattered lace at Knox's feet, hanging his head in shame. "Bad dog! Sit. Stay," Knox scolded, reaching for what he didn't yet realize were my destroyed underwear. I leaped forward, snatching them up before he could get to them and sprinted to throw them in a desk drawer while Eugene sat as directed, his tail between his legs.

Knox cleared his throat, looking at his watch. "Well, I...uh... I should probably go. It's later than I realized, and I have work tomorrow." He stood, snapped his fingers, and strode toward the door, Eugene at his heels. I followed, making sure to keep a safe distance between us. I didn't think I could trust myself to get too close to him.

"All right. I guess I'll see you this weekend at the tree cutting?" I said, clasping my hands tightly behind my back as Knox opened the door and stepped into the hallway.

"See you then," he said gruffly. "And Birdie?" he added, his tone softening. "Happy Thanksgiving." I watched as he walked to the landing and down the stairs, Eugene by his side. I closed my bedroom door softly, leaning against it as I caught my breath. *You are so screwed.*

CHAPTER 20
KNOX

I shrugged on my favorite thick flannel shirt and rummaged around in my dresser, looking for my warmest pair of wool socks. As I laced up my winter work boots, I tried to quiet my nerves about the day.

December 1 marked one of the country's longest-standing traditions: The annual Christmas tree cutting. Each year, the palace was decorated with a dozen different trees, including the largest one in the grand foyer, which would be adorned this year with the ornaments from the Lewellens' workshop. All of these trees were cut today, along with several dozen extra paid for by the royal family and made available to any Wexstonians who struggled to afford a tree.

It was practically a national holiday. Many businesses closed for the day, with some residents joining in the festivities across the country's many tree farms and others waiting in their towns and villages for the trees to be brought in. Tonight, families across Wexstone would play their favorite Christmas records as they trimmed their trees.

Even though I never took a tree home to my own cottage, I still loved this day. While Isobel's office oversaw organizing the groups this year, I'd spent the last week of November assigning leaders to specific farms, and I always led the charge in cutting down the tree for the grand foyer and the royal family's private tree, around which we would all gather to open gifts on Christmas morning.

But this year, I couldn't shake the anxiety that had settled into the pit of my stomach knowing Birdie would be at the cutting. Hardly a moment had passed in the last few days without thinking about my near-kisses with her, first at the garden party and then in her bedroom on Thanksgiving. I couldn't believe I had let myself cross that line again, but the way she had held my hand and asked about my parents had ignited a spark in me I had thought was long dead.

She is here for Oliver, I reminded myself yet again as I zipped up my coat, making sure my gloves were in the pockets.

Yeah, but she didn't pull away from you either, the devil on my shoulder whispered. *Who knows where things would have gone if Eugene hadn't interrupted you...*

I couldn't deny that every time we were alone together there was a hum of electricity in the air, a pull to get close to her and have some part of my body touching hers. The more time I spent with her, the harder it was to fight those urges.

Eugene loped up to me and plopped down, tail wagging in excitement, next to the front door. He greeted me with a sassy bark.

"Sorry, buddy. You can't go with me today; there's gonna be too many people there and I won't be able to keep an eye on you. We can go on our own adventure soon," I promised him, scratching his favorite spot behind his ears. He huffed at me before trotting off to his bed.

At the front of the palace, Vince was waiting for me by a

black SUV. In typical guy fashion, we had long moved past our disagreement over his suspicions about my interactions with Birdie. He had apologized to me the morning of the school donation drive and I had gladly forgiven him. I pushed down the guilt that gnawed at me now as I tossed my work bag into the back of the vehicle; I wondered if he would ever forgive me if he knew how close Birdie and I had come to kissing this past week.

Isobel had arranged for Vince and me to ride together to set up at our assigned farm, The Green Grove. Given the country's increasing interest in the competition, additional security detail had been added, including riding as groups in palace-provided cars that had been swept and cleared by security.

None of us had truly anticipated how big of a deal the competition would be to the people of Wexstone; they tuned into every single news special about it, and a few of my land-scapers had told me there were even podcasts discussing each and every detail of the suitors and events. It was wild.

"Good morning," Vince greeted as I hopped into the passenger seat.

"Hey," I said, buckling my seatbelt and taking the cup of coffee he offered me. I suspected it was a peace offering. That didn't help my guilt.

"You ready for today?" he asked as we hit the road.

"I think so. I sent the farm assignments off to Mirabel on Friday morning, and the farms are supposed to have all the equipment we need on site. I just hope none of the women cut their fingers off or anything disastrous."

"Unless it's Renata or the cousins," Vince muttered.

I laughed. "You're not wrong. But can you imagine the legal shitshow that woman would rain down on us? You know it would be our fault no matter what."

"Good point. Although you can't deny that the Thornes'

party was ever so slightly more peaceful with only two of them there. Never thought I'd be so grateful for lip injections."

I huffed a laugh as my phone buzzed with an email notification. I opened the app to find a note from Mirabel:

Hi Knox,

So sorry for the last-minute email; we just finalized the groups for today. Queen Isobel wants all the women to take part, so she and King Leroy are choosing to observe rather than participate this year. We'll have three groups on site at The Green Grove, with yours selecting and cutting down the tree for the grand foyer and the royal family as per usual. Please find below the group assignments—see you shortly!

-M

Group leader: Oliver

Adelaide

Gemma

Ginny

Group leader: Xavier & Vince

Renata

Sabine

Rosalind

Group leader: Knox

Bernadette

Mellie

Cora

My mouth twisted into a wry smile as I saw Renata assigned to Vince's group after his comments a moment ago, followed immediately by my stomach dropping into my ass when I saw Birdie's name under my own.

Shit. Who made these assignments? I had been hoping she would be assigned to Oliver or Vince and Xavier, giving me a reprieve from the feelings that were becoming harder and harder to deny. But it seemed that today was not to be my lucky day.

———

"So we're in charge of picking out the two most important trees, right?" Cora asked as she bobbed along next to me.

I chuckled. "I suppose you could say that, yes."

"No pressure," I heard Mellie mumble under her breath behind me. I waited for one of Birdie's signature quips but was met with only silence.

Birdie didn't seem to be herself today. She looked amazing, bundled up in a belted white coat and pale pink mittens and hat that contrasted with her mahogany hair. But as I had walked the three ladies through a standard set of safety guidelines for the day, I had noticed that her smile lacked its usual sparkle, and she was uncharacteristically quiet, instead simply nodding along with the group. I wondered if she regretted Thanksgiving. The thought didn't help to ease my anxiety.

"Remind me what we're looking for again?" Cora asked.

I suppressed a sigh. We had gone over this several times. "For the grand foyer, we want an equally grand tree. Something tall, probably around three to four meters. For the family's tree, Queen Isobel loves a very full tree, usually around two meters tall." I pointed to a nearby tree. "About that height, but much fuller."

"I spotted a really beautiful one back near the barn that might work for the family's tree," Mellie said, motioning toward the farm's entrance.

"Great, let's go check it out," I said. "Lead the way, Mellie."

Mellie led us through the snow to stunning Scotch pine. It was about my height and easily four feet in diameter. The branches were full and pliable without any bare patches. I gave the tree a shake; only a small handful of needles floated down to the snow. Noah, the farm's manager, ambled over from the barn to admire the tree with us.

Cora gasped. "Mellie, it's perfect!"

"It sure is," I affirmed. "I think this is the one. Let's go ahead and cut it down, and they can start netting it up while we look for our second tree." I lowered my pack, pulling out two pairs of work gloves and safety glasses. "All right, who wants to hold the tree while I start cutting? I'll get it started and then you ladies can give it a go if you'd like."

Cora and Mellie looked at me, eyes wide. Birdie stared at the ground.

"Birdie?" She looked up, trepidation on her face. "Do you want to hold the tree for me?"

She cleared her throat, plastering on a nervous smile. "Sure." She stepped forward, sliding on the gloves and glasses I gave her.

Despite her obvious nerves, she moved as though she had done this before, reaching up to steady the top half of the tree without my instructing her further.

I pulled on my own gloves and glasses and picked up my handsaw. I looked at Birdie, catching her gaze. "You ready?" *Are you okay?* I asked with my eyes.

She hesitated, then nodded. *All right, then.*

Using the handsaw, I began cutting into the trunk of the

tree close to the ground. I had only been sawing for a few moments when my gut told me to stop. I paused, looking up to see what had triggered my senses, when my eyes landed on Birdie. Her face was pale, eyes wide, and beads of sweat rimmed her brow.

I dropped the saw, leaping to my feet. "Birdie." She stood as though frozen, her gaze unfocused. "Birdie," I said again, louder this time. I took a step toward her.

She started, her hands dropping from the tree. They were trembling. Her eyes darted to me, then over my shoulder. "I... I..." she stuttered, peeling off her gloves and throwing down her glasses before running past me, making a beeline toward the barn.

Silence fell as Mellie and Cora stopped the conversation they'd been having with Noah. They watched Birdie disappear into the barn.

"What happened? Is she okay?" Mellie asked, turning to me.

I ignored her, turning instead to Noah. "Can you finish this up?"

He nodded, taking the gloves and safety glasses I handed him. "Sure thing. Ms. Schneider, can you hold the tree?"

"I think I should go check on her," Mellie said as she turned toward the barn.

"No," I said, putting my hand in front of her. "I've got it." Picking up my pace to almost a full run, I rushed to the barn, vaguely aware of Noah and the two women moving into place to finish felling the tree behind me. My thoughts were on Birdie and on needing to make sure she was okay. *What happened back there?*

I entered the barn, blinking as my eyes adjusted to the dimness. Looking around, I couldn't find Birdie. I wondered if she had instead gotten into one of the cars, when I spotted the corner of a white coat peeking around the edge of a short wall midway down the building.

Grabbing a bottle of water from the refrigerator to the left of the barn's entrance, I all but sprinted in her direction, rounding the corner to find her huddled on the floor, knees pulled into her chest, back against the wall. Her breathing was fast and shallow, and her eyes were clenched shut. My heart plummeted as I realized what was happening.

I crouched down beside her. "Birdie," I said softly. "Birdie, I'm here next to you. Can you hear me?" She whimpered in acknowledgment. "Is it okay if I touch you?" She whimpered again, her head moving in the slightest nod.

Touching her lightly, I put my hand on her shoulder, then paused, waiting to see if she would react. After a moment I moved closer, circling my arms around her and drawing her into my chest. I held on tightly, whispering softly in her ear. "Shhh, it's okay."

After a few minutes I felt her body start to relax and her breathing became more even. I loosened my arms slightly but didn't let go. "Birdie, if you can, I want you to breathe with me, okay? We're going to breathe in for five seconds, hold it for five seconds, and then let it out for five seconds. Can you do that?" I felt her nod against my chest. "All right, let's breathe in together."

Inhale, hold, exhale. I counted softly as I guided her through the breath. With each second, more tension left her body. Without letting go of her, I reached behind me and grabbed the bottle of water, opening it as I handed it to her.

"Now I want you to name five things you can see, four things you can touch, three things you can hear, two things you can smell, and one thing you can taste. Can you do that?"

She took a sip of the water, nodding. She stayed pressed to my chest and I kept my arms around her.

"Five things I can see," she said, her voice shaky. "Um, I can see the wall of the barn. A bale of hay. A bench. My shoes. Your coat." She took a deep breath, steadying herself.

"Good. Now four things you can touch or feel."

She paused, thinking. "My hair on the back of my neck. This bottle of water. My legs against the ground. Your arms around me."

"Three things you can hear," I gently prompted.

"People laughing in the distance. Wind in the trees. Your heartbeat."

My stomach flipped. "Two things you can smell."

She inhaled. "Pine. Peppermint."

My soap and shampoo. "And lastly: one thing you can taste."

She paused again. "The water." She pulled her head back, chuckling as she took another sip.

I smoothed my hand over her hair. "Good girl. Better?"

She nodded. "Yeah. Thank you."

"You're welcome. Do you want to talk about it?"

Birdie looked down, the fingers of her left hand fiddling with the seam on the inside of her mitten. "You remember how I said my mom's birthday was on Christmas?" she asked.

"I sure do."

"Well, every year we would go out as a family the day after Thanksgiving to cut down our Christmas tree. The last time we went was the year Mom was sick. She was in the middle of chemo and was so, so sick. We had to bundle her up in two coats and multiple hats because she couldn't maintain her body heat and had lost her hair. We had to stop every few minutes to let her rest; toward the end, my dad had to carry her back to the car while Connor and I dragged our tree because she was so tired. But she didn't want to miss out on what she considered the official kick-off of the Christmas season. She hardly stopped smiling the entire time." Birdie blinked, and a tear trickled down her cheeks. "I didn't think today would be so hard," she said as the floodgates opened and tears started flowing down her face.

I opened my arms again, and she fell back into my chest, her shoulders shaking as she wept. "I miss her so much," she sobbed.

"I know," I breathed into her hair, running my thumb over her temple. "I know you do."

Time stood still as I held Birdie, letting her cry against my chest as I smoothed her hair away from her face. After what could have just as easily been a few minutes as a few hours, her crying quieted and she spoke quietly into my shirt. "It doesn't get easier, does it?"

I didn't have to ask what she meant. "No, sweetheart. Not really. It gets different—the sharp edges of the grief soften, and you learn to laugh and breathe and live your life again, but it doesn't get better. The grief is always there with you. The sweet moments are always a little bittersweet and the bitter moments are always that much harder. But it's not a reason not to live your life. She'd want you to live your biggest, fullest life, Birdie."

Birdie sat back, wiping her eyes. "How did you learn all of this?" I looked at her, my eyebrow raised in a question. "I mean, I know *how*," she corrected herself. "Obviously you've lived it. But the panic attack. Helping me through it...all of it. How did you know what to do?"

I huffed a breath through my nose and reached up to brush away one last tear from her cheek with the back of my hand. "My parents died in a car crash. It was snowing and they hit a patch of black ice. For a long time, I couldn't get into a car without having a panic attack. Leroy and Isobel eventually got me in to see the best therapist they could find. I saw her weekly for about eight years. She taught me how to manage my anxiety and bring myself down from a panic attack. It's been probably close to seven years since I had one, but I've never forgotten the grounding techniques she taught me." I ran my hand over the back of my neck, shrugging my shoulders. "I guessed that some of them would work for you, too."

Birdie stilled, surveying my face. "Knox, you contain multitudes," she whispered, her voice still hoarse from crying.

My heart tightened.

My phone buzzed in my pocket, bringing me back to Earth. I glanced at my watch. "We should probably get back to the group," I said, standing and brushing off my jeans. I reached down to help Birdie to her feet. "Are you okay to go back out there? I can make an excuse for you if it's too much."

Birdie shook her head, straightening her hat and coat and wiping her face one last time. "No, I can do it. If I need to, I'll just remember: five things I can see, four things I can touch, three things I can hear, two things I can smell, and one thing I can taste." She smiled at me.

I smiled back. "Atta girl," I said, gesturing for her to lead the way out of the barn.

She stopped as we neared the door, the water bottle still in her hand. "Do you need a sip before we go back out there?" she asked, offering me the bottle.

I grimaced. "No thanks, sparkling water is not my thing."

Birdie threw her head back, a laugh shaking her body. "Oh my God, of course you would fucking have opinions on *water*," she teased, shoving me lightly.

"What can I say?" I said, shrugging my shoulders with a sheepish grin. "It's the worst part of living in Europe: the popularity of sparkling water."

Birdie finished the rest of the water and tossed the bottle into the recycling bin by the door, shaking her head and chuckling to herself as she exited the barn. I followed her back to the group, steadying myself as my mind reeled from the flurry of emotions overtaking me. *Take a deep breath, Knox. You can do this. Five things you can see...*

CHAPTER 21
BIRDIE

"Ladies! I am so excited to have you here! Chef Alex has been gracious enough to lend us use of his kitchen today. We will be preparing a few of my favorite treats for the employees' Christmas baskets. Following that, we will go to the Godric State Room so you can meet the heads of staff and mingle with them," Queen Isobel said to the group as we walked into the palace's industrial kitchen. "I have laid out aprons for each of you on the counter there. And you can wash your hands at the sinks against the wall."

We approached the massive stone island that ran almost the entire length of the room, separating the kitchen into two areas, one for cooking and the other for prep. Copper pots and pans hung from brass hooks above the cooktops, and dozens of stainless steel and copper bowls lined the shelves on the opposite wall. I knew several chefs who would drool over this entire kitchen: only the best for the Courtwright family.

I turned the hot water on and started to scrub my hands with the velvet suds that smelled of honey and cherries.

"Do you have any experience with baking?" I asked Mel, who was washing her hands to my left.

"Absolutely none." She laughed. "I grew up in a manor in the country and we had at least two dozen staff."

"Oh, yeah. I totally get that," I sarcastically replied.

Mel jokingly rolled her eyes and asked, "What about you? Do you bake?"

"I grew up in a family where we were barely able to make ends meet. We ate canned foods and occasionally had fresh produce that didn't need to be thawed or microwaved. I know how to set the microwave timer or order a croissant from my favorite bakery in the city. The only thing I reliably know how to bake is brownies, thanks to my grandmother."

"I'm glad we're in this together, then."

We walked back to the group and located our aprons. I was glad I had been able to talk Bronson into letting me wear jeans. He was so insistent that I dress to the nines for every outing, but one mention that the very expensive clothes might get dirty from all the flour and butter and he gladly retreated and agreed that my own jeans were the ideal choice.

Sliding my apron over my neck and tying it behind my back, I got into the line forming against the counter in front of Queen Isobel.

"Okay, ladies." Isobel clapped her hands together. "We have a few different baking stations set up around the kitchen, and I've printed off some recipe cards that you will find at each." She waved her hand around the kitchen, indicating the stations. "This tradition is very near and dear to my heart. I love to bake but more importantly, I love my staff. They are a part of our family, helping us run this country. If I had to solely focus on the laundry, house chores, preparing meals for my children and such, I would be in over my head." She ran her hands down the front of her apron, a nervous tick that I had started to pick up on. "I know that is a very privileged thing to say, and it's truly a privilege to have a palace full of staff, which is why I try to show them some extra appreciation during the holidays."

She wiped a stray tear from her left eye and cleared the emotion from her throat. "Feel free to work together, and please do your best. We want to show the staff how much we love them and appreciate everything they do for us."

I quickly perused the baking stations, glancing over the different recipe cards. Cranberry walnut bread, Linzer cookies, almond crescent cookies, and gingerbread cake were all on the roster for the day. I spotted Adelaide and Mel by the back wall gathering bowls and measuring cups and made a beeline for them.

"Hi," I whispered, leaning in close. "What are y'all baking?"

Mellie inclined her head toward Adelaide. "Well, this one knows how to bake, so I think one of us needs to pair up with her and the other one should buddy up with Cora. You know she'll be in her element today."

I glanced over to where Cora was already measuring out flour and sugar for the Linzer cookies.

I nodded. "Excellent thinking. I'll pair up with Cora. Snag the station next to us and make the almond crescents."

Adelaide laughed. "You'd think we were about to step into the Hunger Games arena, the way you two are planning your survival here."

"You laugh, but you've never seen me burn toast three times in a row before," I quipped, making my way to Cora.

Mellie and Adelaide fell into giggles as they followed me to the neighboring station and we all settled in, measuring ingredients, creaming together butter and sugar, portioning out dough, and shaping our respective cookies.

Cora was in the best mood I had seen her in yet, clearly in

her element as she talked me through the recipe. She was a patient teacher, explaining the steps clearly and sharing why each was important. I was learning more about baking in one afternoon than I had learned in my entire life.

"You know, Cora," Adelaide spoke up as she shaped their dough into small crescents and placed them on a baking sheet, "you really should offer some baking classes at the café. You're a natural teacher!"

Cora blushed, ducking her head. "Do you think so?"

Mel nodded in agreement. "Absolutely. You could start with a class on your famous cranberry scones. God, I could go for one of those right about now."

I laughed. "They're right, Cora. This is what you love and you're so good at it!"

"Thank you. That's really nice. I'll think about it."

"If you do decide to teach some classes, I would love to host one here in our kitchens," Queen Isobel chimed in, approaching our table. "I couldn't help but overhear and I think it's a wonderful idea."

Cora stopped in her tracks, mouth agape and face beet red. "Th-thank you, Your Majesty," she stuttered.

"You're quite welcome, darling. Don't forget what you're good at and don't let anyone dull your shine," the queen said, giving Cora a wink as she continued to the next station. I noticed as she walked away that Cora's back was a bit straighter, her head held just a bit higher.

When all of the cookies, bread, and cake were out of the oven, we gathered back around the island for a quick taste test.

I was proud that Cora's and my Linzer cookies came out beautifully, raspberry jam shining in the center of each. Adelaide and Mellie's almond crescents were also perfect: buttery, a bit crumbly, and coated in powdered sugar.

Next up was the gingerbread cake. Queen Isobel passed

each of us a small slice on delicate white plates. I took a bite of the rich, dark cake.

"And who made this one?" Queen Isobel asked.

"I did," Renata quickly claimed.

"Hmm." Queen Isobel slowly chewed, brows slightly furrowed. "There is something different about this and I can't place my finger on it. What did you add to the recipe?"

My arms and torso started to itch as I swallowed the last bite of my piece. That's when it hit me that I knew exactly what was "different" about the cake.

"...banana," I whispered.

"What was that, Birdie?" Queen Isobel asked.

"It's banana," I said, fumbling to untie my apron.

"Oh my God, Birdie. Aren't you allergic to bananas?" Adelaide said from beside me.

My stomach rolled and I felt like I was going to be ill. My eyes darted around the room, looking for the nearest exit. I needed to find a bathroom immediately.

"Yeah. I'm sorry, but can you excuse me?" I ran out the nearest door and down the hall to find a bathroom, praying to every God I knew that I could find one before I got sick.

I found a small powder room a few doors down and was blessedly able to close the door behind me and make it to the toilet before the first wave of vomit hit.

I rested my head against the toilet, thankful for the cool porcelain doing wonders for my on-fire skin. My entire body felt like it was expanding, and my stomach felt like the bowels of hell had taken up residency inside of me.

Another wave of vomit came barreling out of me as I heard people talking outside the door.

God, in all of your mercy, please don't let anyone of importance be standing outside that door hearing me release everything I've eaten today.

"Birdie?" Oliver asked as he knocked on the door.

Damn it to hell.

"I'll be out in just a minute," I lied. "I'm fine, I promise." Another wave of vomit splashed into the toilet.

"You're not fine," Oliver said as he cracked open the door.

He's right, I am so not fine.

I felt like the little girl from Willy Wonka who turns into a blueberry: big and puffy and like my body could explode at any moment.

"Birdie. Oh my God. You are covered in hives. Look at your neck."

"Shit." I wretched another time into the toilet. "Do you think you could have someone bring me my bag? It's in the kitchen..." I grabbed a wad of toilet paper and wiped the corners of my mouth. "I keep a few doses of antihistamine in there."

Oliver gasped. "Birdie, I'm so sorry, I didn't know you were allergic to bananas."

I let out a small laugh. "Yeah, I think I accidentally ate some."

"Fuck. I'll be right back with your bag." I heard him tell someone in the hallway to stand watch and make sure I didn't pass out.

Wonderful, someone else listening to me evacuate my stomach.

A moment came where I felt like I could move without passing out. I needed to rinse my mouth out, but immediately regretted it the moment I started to stand. The room began spinning and I knew I was going down. But instead of hitting the floor or the vanity, two large, muscular arms wrapped around me and guided me to sit against the cool tile wall.

"I got you, sweetheart," Knox said as he gently set me down. "Can we get these meds in you?"

I leaned against the wall and nodded. But before either of

us could make another move, my stomach rolled again. I was barely able to lift the toilet seat up enough to get the contents into the bowl, splattering a good portion of it onto my shirt.

"Shit," I heard Knox say.

"Fuck," I croaked.

"You're okay," Knox soothed, helping me sit me up against the wall again. "We need to get this antihistamine in you, but you've got to be able to keep it down. If not, we'll need to call emergency services."

I shook my head as my stomach finally calmed. "I can take it now; I think that was it."

Knox placed two pills in my shaky hand before cracking open a bottle of water. I placed the fast-acting tablets on my tongue, allowing them to dissolve before taking the water from Knox and washing them down. I sighed, knowing I was about to have some relief from my symptoms.

I couldn't believe that I had accidentally ingested bananas, and at a palace function no less. It had been years since I'd had an accident. Not only was I embarrassed beyond belief, but I felt so stupid. I thought I had been thorough when reading through the recipe cards, but I must have been so wrapped up in the contest and talking to the girls and the queen that I missed something. I felt like such an idiot.

This is absolutely mortifying. Not only had I puked in front of Knox, but I had gotten it all over myself. I hated getting sick in front of people; I didn't even like throwing up in front of my own mom when I was a kid. I preferred being sick in private like a goddamn normal person. But then to have it happen in front of the guy that I finger-banged myself to? *Put me in the grave right now.*

"How are you feeling?" Knox asked. I could see the worry in his crystal blue eyes.

"You mean other than throwing up on myself, in front of

you, and being covered in hives? I've had better days," I half smiled.

"Glad you still have your sass about you," he said, sounding relieved.

"I hate having to miss out on the rest of the evening, but those meds make me super drowsy. I should probably go back to Lexington Manor with Vince."

There was a knock on the bathroom door. Knox stood to open it.

"Hey," he said to Oliver.

"Hey. How's our girl?" Oliver asked.

"She's going to need to sleep off the meds she just took. Can you grab Vince? I'll call for the car and he can get her home."

Oliver looked between Knox and me and ran a hand over his jaw.

"With so much press here today, I don't think we can get her out the front without being seen. I really don't want this becoming a story. You know how the press would spin this, and I don't want Birdie's name to be dragged through the tabloids. Can you take her out the back to your place instead?"

"Oh God, if they found out I was throwing up, they would spin it into some wild story about how I am pregnant or drunk or something. And I'm covered in my own puke! Do you think someone has an extra shirt I could wear? I will be even more mortified if I have to walk in front of the press covered in this." I waved my hand in front of my shirt.

"Exactly," Oliver said.

"Yeah, you're right." Knox looked at Oliver and then me, his eyebrows knitting together.

"Everyone is almost done cleaning up, and then they're going to the Godric State Room on the other side of the palace. Give me a few minutes to get everyone over there, then I'll text you and you can exit through the kitchen so no one spots you. Once you're out, I'll call the doctor to come check on her just to make sure she's in the clear."

"Okay. Sounds good." Knox nodded.

Oliver clapped Knox on the shoulder. "Thanks for taking care of her."

"No problem."

Knox shut the door and then turned around and kneeled in front of me. "You had me scared there for a minute."

"What? Knox Henderson doesn't get scared," I replied, only having the strength for a half smile.

"Lift your hands. Let's get that shirt off you."

"I can't walk out of here topless, that would be worse than walking out of here wearing a vomit shirt."

"As much as I wouldn't object to you being topless, I'm going to give you my flannel to wear."

I didn't even have the strength to dissect him saying he wanted me topless. I just lifted my arms as Knox rolled the hem of the shirt over the saturated part so it wouldn't get in my hair or on my face. After he pulled it over my head, he tossed it in the trash; I was sure that Bronson wouldn't miss it.

Knox wrapped the warm flannel around my back and I slid my arms into the sleeves. The shirt hung off me three sizes too big, but I didn't care. It smelled like Knox: pine and mint. The flannel was so soft and warm from being worn by him. He knelt in front of me to button up the shirt.

"It looks like your hives have stopped spreading." He ran his cool fingers along my collarbone and neck and my body shook from his touch.

"Good," I whispered.

The drowsiness took over my body and my eyelids felt like they weighed a ton. I probably looked like a milk-drunk baby trying to fight sleep.

"You look like you're about to fall over."

"Yeah, I'm starting to get super sleepy. Hopefully they get out of the kitchen soon, I'm ready to pass out." I laughed softly. "Figuratively, not literally."

"Come here."

Knox put his hands under my knees and along my back and lifted me off the floor.

"What are you doing?" I asked.

"Just close your eyes. I've got you."

As much as I didn't want to be treated like a baby or be pitied, the pressure of his arms around me calmed me almost as much as the medicine had. My eyes grew heavier and heavier, and I couldn't fight the urge to close them anymore.

"Knox?"

"Yeah?"

"Thank you."

"Anything for you, sweetheart."

I dozed off in his arms to the sound of his heart beating. I woke to the feeling of being laid down onto something extremely soft and then being wrapped up in something warm. I felt pressure on my back and warm air on my neck—something, no, someone—laying against me.

The last thing I heard was Knox saying, "Keep her safe tonight, boy," as a door closed.

CHAPTER 22
BIRDIE

Light shone through the small gap of the blackout curtains that hung on the wall, and it took me a second to get my bearings and realize where I was. The heavy black comforter wrapped around me and the copper dog next to me made me certain that I was in Knox's bed, with him nowhere in sight. Eugene stood up and nudged my shoulder with his wet nose.

"Good morning," I croaked as I scratched his head. My throat was still on fire from all the throwing up I did the night before. I needed water and to brush my teeth as soon as possible.

I got out of the bed and went through the door to the ensuite bathroom. Sitting on the counter was a new toothbrush, toothpaste, mouthwash, and a note:

I thought you might appreciate having this whenever you wake up. Flip the switch on the far left for the heated floors. I already put a towel in the warmer against the wall, just press the power button on the top. Use whatever you need in the shower. Brushes and combs are in the drawers of the vanity.

Oh, and you can grab whatever clothes you'd like out of my closet.

-K

I started the shower and let the water get warm as I brushed my teeth. I took off Knox's flannel, my jeans, underwear, and socks and folded them into a neat pile on the vanity. He wasn't kidding about the floor warmer; the tiles were so fucking cold I was afraid I was going to get frostbite. I flipped the switch, and the floor slowly started to heat up. I pressed the button on the towel warmer as I stepped into the massive stone shower.

Water rained down from the head in the center of the ceiling above me. I reached for the knob to increase the pressure and jets started hitting me from all angles. *Damnit, Knox, I don't know how to work this high-tech shower.* Jets hit my back and thighs, and...

Wow! Hello. That feels nice...

Birdie! Snap out of it. Focus.

Finally, I hit enough buttons and turned enough knobs that I got the temperature right and the jets off *things* so I could focus on washing my hair and body.

As I lathered the shampoo in my hair, I realized this was where Knox got part of his signature scent. The shampoo smelled of mint and made my scalp tingle. It was amazing. After I rinsed it out and ran the conditioner through my ends, I opened the soap, and the smell of pine filled my nose. As I soaped up my body with his loofah, I realized that I always figured that the pine smell was from Knox working outside with the trees, when really it was his body wash.

I closed my eyes and let the water run over my body as I recounted everything that had happened in the past twenty-four hours. It had been such a shitshow. I felt like I was transported back to middle school, getting sick in front of my crush. Instead, this time my crush cleaned me up, made sure I had a new toothbrush, and let me sleep in his bed with his dog.

I turned off the shower, grabbed the towel from the heater, and wrapped it around my body.

"Holy shit." I pulled the towel tighter around my body. "It's like a fluffy warm hug."

After I went into Knox's attached closet and snagged one of his many flannels and a pair of black boxers that had to be rolled up a few times to fit, I combed out my hair and ran the blow dryer over it.

I heard a little whine come from the bedroom as I walked out. Eugene sat next to the bedroom door and scratched gently at the frame.

"Oh my gosh! Eugene, I am so sorry. I should have let you out to potty before I got in the shower." I barely cracked the door open, and the lean copper dog jetted out through the living room and to the attached sunroom. He let out a bark, letting me know that this was where he wanted to be let out.

I unlocked the door and was hit with an icy blast of air and snow. I knew a blizzard when I saw one, and this was a monster. I shut the door for maybe a minute before Eugene was at the door scratching to come back in.

Knox was nowhere to be found in the main living area of the house, so I assumed he was still asleep in the second bedroom. I walked into the small kitchen and opened the refrigerator to see if there was anything to drink. On the shelves were sandwich fixings, fruits and vegetables, butter, condiments, beer, and a pitcher of water. I found a glass in a nearby cabinet and filled it with the water, downing half of it in one go.

I headed into the living room and to the built-ins that lined the far wall, the shelves filled with books upon books. All of the classics like *The Outsiders*, *The Great Gatsby*, *To Kill a Mocking-bird*, and *Pride and Prejudice* sat on the highest shelf. They looked worn and well-loved, my favorite type of books. The next shelf was lined with history books, and the bottom shelf held all of J.R.R. Tolkien's works, including about ten different copies of *The Fellowship of the Ring*. Mixed in among the volumes sat a few pictures.

In the top picture was an older gentleman with glasses who had Knox's dark hair and broad shoulders, and a woman with Knox's cerulean eyes, matching the water behind her. The couple looked at each other with such love, much like the love that I had seen in my own parents before my mom passed away. These had to be Knox's parents. In the picture on the middle shelf, a young Knox stood with his back to a football field, decked out in Steelers gear with his dad. I ran my finger over the frame that sat on the bottom shelf. A teenage Knox stood between his parents, their arms wrapped around his shoulders as they stood in front of the palace. Something in my gut told me this was probably one of the last pictures he had of his parents.

"That picture was actually taken the day before my parents' crash."

I jumped and knocked the picture over. Quickly standing it back up, I turned around to see Knox standing at the front door of the cottage with a canvas bag full to the brim.

"Jesus. You scared the shit out of me."

"Sorry. I thought you heard me come in."

He kicked off his snow-covered boots and made a beeline to the kitchen to set the overflowing bag on the countertop.

"How do you feel this morning?" he asked, giving me a once-over.

"Good. Thank you for the toiletries and clothes." I waved my hand over my outfit.

"No problem. I went up to the palace. While I was there, I ran into Oliver, and he said that they're declaring a state of emergency. The roads are closed. There isn't a way to get you back to Lexington Manor right now."

"Oh." It was all I could get out. My mind was racing through this scenario that I had gotten myself into.

"Yeah, this storm picked up speed pretty fast last night and has just gotten worse this morning."

"When I let Eugene out, I could see it was snowing pretty hard, but I guess I didn't realize it had been going on that long."

He chuckled. "Yeah, you were pretty out of it last night when I put you to bed. You woke up enough when the doctor stopped by to mumble at him—he said you'll be fine, by the way—and then immediately zonked back out."

I huffed a laugh. "I don't even remember that. And hey, thanks for letting me sleep in your bed. I would have been fine on the couch."

"I wasn't going to make you sleep on the couch."

I just nodded, trying to wrap my head around the fact that I was stuck in Knox's cottage. I didn't dislike the idea, and that's what made me feel guilty. I liked the thought of being stuck with him, just the two of us, with nothing to do but be together.

"What do you have there?" I pointed to the bag.

"Oh, I went to get some food for breakfast. Sorry it took so long and I wasn't here when you woke up."

"You walked through a blizzard to get food?"

"Yeah? It's not a big deal." He waved me off.

"I went through your refrigerator to find a drink and it looked like you had plenty of stuff to eat. What did you need from the palace that was worth walking through a blizzard to get?"

He turned his back to me to face the counter and avoid my gaze as he unpacked the bag.

"Knox?" I laughed. "What did you go and get?" I walked around the small kitchen island and stood by him, getting on my tiptoes to see what he was pulling out of the bag. There was already a pack of six eggs on the counter sitting next to bacon wrapped in parchment paper.

"What else is in there?" I hip-bumped him out of the way and pushed my way to the bag. There was a block of cheddar cheese, cream cheese, apples, grapes, a bag of chips, popcorn, pastries, sausage, and four bagels.

I looked at Knox. "Did you get stuff to make breakfast sandwiches?"

He shrugged his shoulders and gave a soft, "Yeah."

I was speechless that this gummy bear of a man had walked through a fucking snowstorm to get stuff to make me a breakfast sandwich, even though he hated them. I had never had a man do something like that for me before.

"Thank you." I give him another hip bump.

"Did you find everything you needed in the bathroom?" he asked, still not looking at me as he laid out the ingredients for the sandwich on the counter.

"I did." I smiled. "And can we talk about your bathroom? What the fuck!" I laughed. "Who would have guessed that Knox the lumberjack was so bougie?"

He looked over his shoulder and gave me that panty-melting half smile.

"I'm assuming you liked the towel warmer and heated floor?"

"Not to mention the high-tech shower with the jets that hit all the right places."

That made him turn his whole body to face me. He cocked his eyebrow. "What kind of places?"

"You know, my back and neck, and...Oh do you have coffee by chance?" I quickly changed the subject.

"I do." He looked me over again before turning his back to me and lighting the gas stovetop. "It's on the bar over there." He pointed the spatula behind his back.

I turned around and spotted a refurbished buffet that was set up as a bar and coffee station. The carafe already had hot coffee waiting in it. I grabbed a mug from the floating shelf above it and filled it to the brim.

"Can I help you with anything?" I asked.

Knox had done so much for me in the last twelve hours that I wanted to do something for him. I filled another mug with black coffee and took it to him at the stovetop.

"If you want to grab the toaster from under that cabinet there, you can slice the bagels and get them toasted."

"Heard, chef." I gave him a fake salute, and he rolled his eyes and continued to cook the bacon.

"Hey, Alexa, play The Lumineers," Knox said.

Music filled the cottage as I sliced bagels and put them in the toaster. I looked over to Eugene with his head propped on the arm of the couch, watching Knox and me in the kitchen, then back to Knox, and was hit by a moment of realization.

This was why Connor was so insistent on me finding someone and settling down. He knew that lazy-Saturday feeling of being in the kitchen making brunch with your partner, your heart feeling whole and full. This must be what he felt with Colleen.

Knox was focused on cracking eggs and frying them in the leftover bacon grease. His arms flexed as he moved the spatula around the edges of the eggs. I loved the way that his veins strained a little as he tightened his grip on the handle.

Could I have this someday? Am I missing out on this, right here, if I continue courting Oliver? I didn't know. But I did know that I wanted nothing more for the day: I wanted to enjoy that very moment. I wanted to soak in whatever the day had to bring and simply *be*.

"Here you go." Knox set a plate in front of me.

"This looks delicious, thank you."

He came around the island and sat down next to me.

"So..." He took a drink of his coffee. "Bananas, huh?"

"Fucking bananas."

"I'll make sure there is never a fruit salad at any state or formal dinner ever." He smiled.

I laughed. "Thank you." I took a bite of the sandwich, the egg bursting and dripping onto the plate.

Knox shuddered. "Fucking runny eggs on a bagel."

"It's amazing. Seriously, this is one of the best things I've ever had in my mouth."

Knox coughed and I set my sandwich down to pat him on the back.

"Hands up, big guy." I moved his arm over his head and patted him on the back again until the coughing spell subsided.

"There," I said. "We're even now. You saved my life, I've saved yours."

He smirked at me. "God. You and your fucking smart-ass mouth."

———

VINCE

Birdie, are you okay? What the fuck happened last night? One minute you're with the queen tasting pastries and then the next thing I know, Oliver told me Knox took you out the back because you had an allergic reaction?

Hi. I'm doing fine. I did have an allergic reaction and got sick. Oliver decided I should go to Knox's house so the press didn't see me and make up some wild story. But now I'm stuck here until this storm passes

This sucks. I'm the worst friend ever. I should have been there. I'm so sorry, B

Vince, stop! You're not a bad friend. It was an accident. Oliver and Knox were there for me and got me sorted out. It's all good.

I mean, you're at the palace, this could be good. You could walk up and stay with Oliver 😉

Oh God 😳

I set my phone next to me on the couch and pulled the fuzzy blanket around my shoulders, cuddling deep into the cushions. We had spent most of the day on the couch with drinks and junk food, watching holiday movies. The only time Knox had gotten up was to let Eugene out for about two seconds and to refill the popcorn bowl and our drinks.

Knox's phone chimed with a few text messages. He read them, letting out a huff and throwing his phone onto the coffee table.

"Everything okay?" I asked.

"Yeah." His tone was clipped and unconvincing.

"Try again." I nudged the side of his leg with my foot.

"Vince is blowing up my phone asking what we're doing."

"What did you say?"

"I told him we're watching movies and eating junk food."

"And that made you mad?"

"No. He asked if I would walk you up to the palace so you could stay with Oliver."

"Oh." I looked at him. *Really* looked at him.

He sat in the corner on the opposite side of the large couch, feet resting on the coffee table and Eugene's head on his lap. He wore gray sweatpants and a black T-shirt, his tattoos spilling out from the sleeve. His scruff had grown out a bit and was well on its way to being a beard if he didn't shave it soon. Those gold wire-rimmed glasses sat on his nose and his hair was messy. He was so hot. But he was also clearly bothered.

"Do you want me to go up to the palace and stay with Oliver?" I asked.

His head snapped to the side, eyes softening as they took me in.

"Do you want me to take you to Oliver?"

The fire crackled in the fireplace as the Christmas movie marathon we had started hours ago played on the television. I was happy. For the first time since I had been in Wexstone, I was truly comfortable and happy. I didn't have to worry about squeezing into a fancy dress and praying that my feet would callus over before I had to shove my fat toes into another pair of heels. I didn't have to listen to Bronson critique every little mannerism. I didn't have to put on a fake smile for people I couldn't care less about, and I didn't have to convince myself to feel something for someone I didn't love.

That day with Knox had been the perfect day.

"No. I don't."

"Then I won't," he said as he stared into my eyes for a few seconds longer. Then he grabbed my foot, pulled it onto his lap, and rubbed my sock-covered toes.

"What should we watch next?" Knox asked as the credits rolled along the screen.

"What are my options?"

"*Christmas Vacation* or *It's a Wonderful Life.*"

"*Christmas Vacation*," I answered, perhaps a bit too adamantly.

Knox gave me a questioning look.

"My mom's favorite Christmas movie was *It's a Wonderful Life*. We watched it every year on Christmas Day."

"Her birthday," he said knowingly.

"Her birthday," I answered.

"*Christmas Vacation* it is." He hit play and the music started. "This was my dad's favorite Christmas movie. Honestly, it was one of his favorite movies in general. He loved Chevy Chase."

"Knox," I said as I pulled my foot back and sat up. "We don't have to watch this. We don't have to watch movies anymore. We can play cards, put on a TV show, whatever."

"Birdie," he answered, grabbing my other foot and pulling it into his lap. "I want to watch this with you. I love this movie."

"Oh." I lay back against the arm of the couch and pulled the blanket up to my chin. "I want to be there."

"Where? Chicago?" Knox asked, pointing to the television that hung above his fireplace.

"No," I giggled. I paused, taking a breath. "There, where you are. That place where you can experience things your parents loved without being triggered into a panic attack or being flooded with memories that wreck you."

Knox picked up the remote from the coffee table and paused the movie. He turned so his whole body faced me, giving me his entire attention.

"This," he waved his hand over his body, "took nearly a decade of talk therapy and a few years on an antidepressant to get to. It wasn't easy, but I'm glad I did it. Have you ever done any therapy or anything?"

I ran my hands along the hem of the blanket.

"You don't have to answer that. I shouldn't have asked. It was intrusive, I'm sorry."

"No, it's fine. I think we're at the point in our friendship where you can ask me those things." I took another deep breath. "I went to the school counselor for a few months after my mom died because I wasn't doing great in school."

"But that was it?"

"Yeah. I don't like to talk about the hard stuff. Talking about it makes me feel...well, it makes me feel like I did last night. Sick to my stomach and like I'm on fire."

He just nodded in understanding.

"I know I probably should. Connor found a therapist when he went to college. It's probably why he has the perfect life with the perfect wife and daughter," I laughed wryly.

"You don't truly believe that, do you?"

I shrugged. "Yes and no. I know that he went through the same trauma. It's just hard to remember sometimes when he lives this *Leave it to Beaver* life."

"Have you talked to him about your mom and how you feel about everything?"

"Oh, hell no. It's like this unspoken thing in our family."

"Maybe you should talk to him about it. I bet he would be happy to talk to you since she was his mom, too."

"Yeah, maybe." I fiddled with the hem of the blanket and ran the material through my fingers. Knox rubbed my foot, giving it a squeeze.

"You'll get there one day. You're determined, and if you want something, you get it."

CHAPTER 23
BIRDIE

By midway through *Christmas Vacation*, my stomach muscles ached from laughing so hard. Between the shenanigans of the movie and listening to Knox quote every other line, I could hardly breathe between fits of laughter. I thought I was going to pee my pants when Knox exclaimed, "Grace? She died thirty years ago!" with Aunt Bethany.

Once the movie was over, Knox got up to make us more hot chocolate. Eugene trotted to the door, whining, so I got up to let him out. He shot out the door, peed in the nearest corner of the yard, and jetted back inside.

"That's how I know it's cold out there. That dog loves snow and being outside, so if he doesn't even want to be out there in it, that means it's bad," Knox said from the stovetop as he heated the milk.

"That's because he's a smart boy. Aren't you?" I squatted to wipe Eugene's paws off with a towel so he didn't track in any snow.

"He really is. It was weird not having him sleeping next to me last night."

"He was the best little cuddle buddy." I scratched behind Eugene's ear, and he gave me a lick on my cheek before darting back to the couch.

"I'm going to go to the bathroom and then I'll be ready," Knox said, exiting the kitchen.

I checked the milk and finished making the hot chocolate, adding a few marshmallows to each mug before taking them to the coffee table. I settled back into my corner of the couch, stretching out to rub Eugene's back with my foot.

Knox walked back in, surveying the couch and the distinct lack of room on it.

"Wow. So first you took my bed last night, and now you're claiming my couch, huh?" he jokingly griped, tickling me on my ribs.

"You put me in your bed, you big goon." I tried to tickle him back and accidentally jammed my fingers into his side.

"Ouch!" He rubbed his side. "You're going to pay for that," he laughed.

"Oh yeah?" I giggled, trying to reach up and tickle him while keeping one hand in front of my stomach so he couldn't retaliate.

"Yeah, you are. I'm much stronger than you." He kicked one leg over and straddled me, our faces only inches apart, and grabbed my arms and held them over my head with one hand. I didn't know whether to laugh or be turned on; having him confine me like this was sexy. My mind immediately flashed back to my fantasy about him tying my hands up. For some reason, this was so much better and had me wanting much more.

"Do you surrender?" he growled in his husky baritone voice.

My breath started to pick up and my pulse moved from my chest to between my legs. I couldn't think straight, let alone answer. All I could do was stare into his eyes that had gone navy in the firelight. I glanced from his eyes to his lips and back as I bit my bottom lip.

His gaze fell to my mouth, and I knew he wanted to kiss me as badly as I wanted him to. Throwing any lingering reservations aside, I closed the inch that kept us apart. His body stiffened, then relaxed into mine. The kiss was soft at first, his full lips melting against my own. I adjusted my body to get more comfortable and with that movement, I could feel his length along my thigh grow harder. I opened my mouth, hoping he would explore it. And he did. He ran his tongue along the inside of my lip and gave it a little bite. I let out a soft moan and rolled my body against his, needing a little friction.

Eugene let out a small bark and Knox pulled back slightly, as breathless as I was.

"Hey," he murmured, his lips tipped into a sideways grin as he leaned his forehead against mine.

"Hey," I whispered back.

Knox glanced at the TV. "Should we uh...should we turn on another movie?"

No. Keep kissing me. "Sure." I nodded, and he pulled the mess of blankets off the floor and lay down behind me, his cock still very hard against my ass.

"Is this okay with you?" Knox asked as he settled in and pulled the blankets over us.

"Yeah." I smiled as he wrapped his large hand around my waist and lay it against my stomach.

"What about you? Is this okay?" he asked Eugene. The dog raised his head from the other end of the couch and gave a small huff, then lay his head back down sleepily.

"Little fucker." Knox laughed.

Knox hit play on the next movie, though I barely made it through the opening credits before my eyes were heavy, a feeling of peace washing over me with Knox at my back and Eugene at my feet. The next thing I knew, Knox's strong arms were lifting me as he carried me to his room and tucked me into bed. He smoothed the covers over me and swept my hair away from my face. As he turned to leave, I grabbed his hand.

"Stay," I mumbled sleepily.

He stopped in his tracks. "What?" he whispered.

"Stay with me in here. Please." I pulled the covers down so he could crawl in.

A pause. Then, "Okay."

My eyes followed him as he walked to the opposite side of the bed, took his shirt off and climbed in beside me. I scooted to the middle of the king-size bed and rolled to my side, giving him my back so we could cuddle up again like we were on the couch. He moved up behind me and wrapped his arm around me again. This time, his hand rested on my thigh, rubbing slow circles. The repetition of it was entrancing.

I tried to calm my mind and fall back asleep, but being in the same bed with Knox had my heart racing. I could feel his own heartbeat against my shoulder, his breathing becoming more even as he settled in.

"Are you asleep?" I whispered after several minutes.

"No. What's wrong?"

I turned over to face him, laying my hand on his chest and rubbing the same circles he was tracing on my thigh with my pointer finger.

"Today was amazing," I whispered.

"Yeah, I had the best day."

"I don't want it to end."

"Me neither." He pushed a stray hair behind my ear and let

his finger run down my neck and arm until his hand circled my waist.

"I wish we could stay like this."

"I'd give anything to have you forever," he answered, his gaze piercing.

My will broke. I couldn't hold back anymore. His words were too much, too real.

I brought my mouth to his and kissed him with force and passion, trying to push down my feelings for him down and let desire take over. I grabbed the back of his head and pulled him closer to me, pushing my tongue into his mouth and exploring every inch. He cupped my ass with his hand, then ran it along the back of my thigh to behind my knee, lifting my leg over his hip and pulling me closer to him. I felt his hard cock straining against the confines of his sweatpants as it twitched against my center.

"Knox..." I moaned.

"God, I love hearing my name come out of your mouth."

He pushed his cock harder into my center and my core started to throb. I rolled my body against his, causing Knox to let out the sexiest growl I had ever heard. I needed more.

"Remember the night in the closet?" I asked in between kisses, pushing his back to the mattress. He looked up at me with inquisitive eyes.

"Of course. I replay that night in my head frequently."

I paused, making a mental note to come back to that admission later.

"Remember your rule?"

"It's my rule, so yes, I remember." He chuckled.

"Well..." I climbed on top of him, settling my hips over his. "I'm stealing it. I want an enthusiastic yes before we go any further."

"Baby..." he breathed as he unbuttoned my shirt. "Hell yes."

He slid the shirt off my shoulders and tossed it to the ground before tracing his hand up my torso, grabbing one of my breasts and lightly squeezing it.

"God, you're perfect."

He leaned up and put the other breast in his mouth, running his tongue over my hard nipple. I sucked in a breath. It felt exquisite. He kissed his way to the opposite breast, making sure the other wasn't left out by pinching and lightly pulling on the hard peak.

"Lie back," he murmured as he pushed me onto my back. Doing as I was told, he ran his fingers along the elastic of the borrowed boxers around my waist. My body was already on fire, and the way his touch danced across my skin had me panting. The anticipation was excruciating as he slid the boxers down my legs and discarded them onto the floor.

With a pussy-throbbing half smile, he pushed my knees apart and leaned down. "I'm so fucking glad I don't have any neighbors because I'm about to make you moan so loudly."

"We'll see about that," I sassed back.

"Sweetheart, is that a challenge?"

"Maybe." I smiled slyly.

"Game on." He wrapped my legs around his shoulders and slipped his tongue right through my folds and straight to my clit.

"Holy shit," I whimpered.

His tongue moved up and down my lips and dipped back into my center before he moved back to my clit, lightly biting it. He pulled back, running a finger through my arousal and slipping it inside of me. I tried my hardest not to give him what he wanted but I couldn't help but let out a cry of pleasure. It felt so fucking good—better than anything I could have imagined.

His huff of victorious laughter tickled my center. I squeezed my thighs together.

"That wasn't that loud. I can do better." He added another finger as he rolled his tongue over my clit again, sucking this time. I let out a louder moan of satisfaction.

"Bee, you taste amazing." He licked me again, letting out a small growl of pleasure.

"Yeah, well, what you're doing feels amazing."

He moved his fingers in and out of me in rhythm with his tongue on my center. I was so close to coming that my body started to tighten up. Knox bent his finger and started tapping on that special spot inside of me. He gave one more thrust of his fingers and gave a deep suck and I came undone, crying out expletives that didn't even make sense.

"This is so much better than I imagined," I panted.

"You've imagined this, huh?" I felt him smile into my thigh as he kissed the inside of my leg.

"The night of the garden party, when I got home," I said breathlessly, "I used my vibrator and imagined this exact scenario, but it was nothing compared to what just happened."

"God damn, Birdie." He smiled up at me.

"What? It's your fault. You're the one who almost kissed me and got me all worked up in the greenhouse."

"I've thought about this, too." He kissed up my stomach.

"Oh, really?"

"I had a dream the night of the welcome gala that you came to find me here and we did exactly this."

"Is that why you were so tense the next day in the wood-shop?" I ran my fingers through his hair as he kissed along my collarbone.

"Yeah."

"What else did you dream about?"

"I'd rather show you than tell you."

He stood and opened the drawer of his nightstand, pulling out a condom before sliding his sweatpants and boxer briefs down his massive thighs. My mouth instantly watered watching his thick cock spring free. I rose and sat on the edge of the bed, taking the condom out of his hand.

"Let me do it."

He nodded, and I grabbed his stiff dick and ran my hand along it. It was so thick that I could barely fit my fist around it. The tip glistened with pre-cum and I wanted to taste him so badly. I licked my lips and slid him into my mouth.

"Holy fuck, Bee," Knox groaned as I took him deeper, opening my throat to try and take him all the way in. I brought him in and out a few more times, moaning as he hit the back of my throat. That aroused him even more, making his dick twitch in my mouth. I smiled to myself, knowing I was making him feel as good as he made me feel.

After a few more pumps in and out, Knox grabbed my chin and pulled out of me. "I fucking love that, but if you keep it up, I'm not going to make it."

I nodded, letting him pull away. I would have done anything he wanted to make sure we could keep going. I wanted this to last forever.

The condom wrapper opening was the only sound for a few seconds. I pulled it out and rolled it from the tip of Knox's dick down to the base.

I looked up at him. His eyes were heavy with need as he picked me up and kissed me urgently, the converse of our soft kiss on the couch. For several minutes we simply explored each other's mouths, his hands tangled in my hair.

Knox was by far the best kisser I had ever been with; I didn't know how I would ever move on from him. With the way he knew exactly what spot to touch or suck or kiss, I felt certain I'd never find anyone else who instinctively knew my body like this man.

Knox backed us toward the bed, laying me against the pillows. He surveyed my body and smiled. "You're absolutely gorgeous, you know that?"

All I could do was smile back at him. He sure knew how to make a girl feel beautiful and confident. He leaned down and brushed his lips against mine as he hooked his hand under my knee and hitched my leg up to rest on his hip.

"Are you sure you want to do this?" he asked quietly.

"More than anything."

As he kissed up my neck to my ear and along my jaw, he ran his fingers through my soaking wet folds. I was beyond ready.

"God, you're drenched. I fucking love it." He grabbed his cock, gave it a few strokes, and then rubbed the tip up and down my center, wetting it before he gently pushed in. He was so fucking girthy that I whimpered, first in pain and then in the deepest pleasure, taking a second to adjust to his size. After a moment, I rocked my hips, asking him to push in further.

"Are you okay?"

I nodded before he pushed in a little more.

"Bee, you're so fucking tight. You feel amazing."

He pulled out and then slid back in, faster this time, and I let another moan slip out as I scratched down his back. It was incredible, like nothing I had ever felt before.

"I need more," I breathed.

"Anything you want, baby." He pushed in hard and picked up speed, bringing both of my knees up to his waist as we found our rhythm. He squeezed his hands down the back of my thighs and grabbed my ass.

"I've been thinking about this ass since that night in the

closet. The way it felt in my hands." He squeezed my ass cheeks hard, surely leaving a mark, but I couldn't care less because everything he was doing left me soaring. "How it looked in that tight white dress." He gave a strong thrust, making me sigh in pleasure. "How badly I wanted it to be mine."

"Yes! It's yours, you can have whatever you want, just don't stop."

He pulled back and out of me. I had just a moment to look at him in surprise before he grabbed my hips and flipped me over onto my stomach, lifting my ass up off the bed. Lining his rock-hard cock up with my opening, he gently slid in, hitting my G-spot.

"Knox!" I screamed into the pillow.

"God, yes. Scream it louder," he panted as he drove into me harder and faster than ever. My breath quickened and I could feel my orgasm building with each hit to my spot.

"Knox! Don't stop. Right there. Please don't stop," I cried.

He brought his hand around my waist and stroked my clit as he continued ravaging me from behind. I had never experienced multiple orgasms with a partner before and this was everything. I totally got the hype. I didn't want it to stop.

I barely got out, "I'm going to come," before the room exploded and I saw fireworks. "Knox!" I screamed louder than ever, eliciting a loud bark from the next room over.

The wave of pleasure took its time washing over me. I had never had an orgasm this strong. My legs shook, my arms gave out from holding me up, and I was on the verge of tears from the intensity.

"I'm right there, baby," Knox ground out, pushing deeper and faster into me. "Birdie!" he cried as he finished inside me from behind.

"Oh my God," I breathed.

"Yeah," he panted.

"That was amazing." I could barely catch my breath, my body still tingling from the orgasm.

"You were amazing." Knox pulled out of me, moving to lie on his side. He grabbed me, pulling me back to him. I rested my head on his chest and tried to calm my heart rate. After a few moments of silence, I felt Knox's chest move up and down as he tried to hold in his laughter.

"Go ahead and say it," I told him, rolling my eyes.

"Say what?"

"That you were right."

He just laughed as he stood up to dispose of the used condom in the bathroom. I followed him through the door and into the small toilet room to pee. When I came back into the bedroom, Knox had pulled out a shirt from his drawer for me to sleep in. I put it on and crawled back into bed as he let Eugene into the room.

"Come here, Eugene." I patted the bed, inviting him up next to me.

"I think that dog is more obsessed with you than I am," Knox said as he climbed into the bed and pulled me into him. I rested my head on his tattooed arm as he wrapped the other around me, Eugene laying against my feet.

"Today was incredible," I whispered.

"Yeah, it was the best," he murmured, his voice heavy with sleep.

As I lay facing the window, I thought about how badly I didn't want the next day to come. I wanted to stay here in this perfect little bubble. I liked it here, where everything was uncomplicated and I didn't have to worry about anything.

The snow had slowed down, the flakes falling softly to the ground. Through the small crystals, I could see the outline and lights of the palace glistening in the distance.

Seeing the palace, I wondered if I had just gotten myself

into a huge mess. Guilt washed over me, for the amazing night I had just shared with Knox and for the feelings for him that kept growing. I was supposed to one of Oliver's suitors, and I had just slept with his best friend—who had made it clear how much he liked me. What the fuck was I going to do now?

CHAPTER 24
BIRDIE

A cold, wet tongue licked my feet and jolted me awake. Eugene had burrowed himself to the foot of the bed, under the comforter and sheet, and had tickled me awake by licking my toes.

"Good morning," Knox's husky voice said in my ear as he sprinkled kisses down my jaw and onto my shoulder.

"Good morning," I murmured sleepily.

The night before had been amazing. Despite the guilt I had felt before drifting off, I had slept so deeply. I wasn't sure if it was because of Knox's arms around me all night or the absolutely mind-blowing sex that had left me exhausted.

"How did you sleep?" Knox asked, rolling me over to face him.

"Great. How about you?"

"Don't tell Eugene, but I prefer your snuggles and morning kisses to his."

I laughed as Eugene wriggled his way onto the floor, whining as he trotted to the door.

"That's my cue," Knox said, squeezing my waist.

As he slid out from under the covers, I couldn't stop myself from admiring the way his powerful thighs flexed as he stood from the bed. The morning sunlight lit up his right arm, making the colors of the dragon tattooed across his shoulder come alive.

While Knox let Eugene out, I got up, brushed my teeth, went to the bathroom, and then brushed through the tangles that had appeared in my hair.

The smell of coffee filled the cottage and called to me like a siren song. I filled us both a mug and took Knox's to where he stood by the back door.

"Here ya go." I handed him the mug.

"Thank you." He kissed the top of my head and I melted. For someone who made an austere first impression, he was a real softy when it was just the two of us. I looped my free arm through his, and we stood at the back door watching Eugene hop in and out of snow drifts.

"He really does love the snow, doesn't he?" I giggled.

"Yes. He won't come inside unless I make him."

"Well, the temperature must be better than yesterday because it doesn't seem to bother him at all."

"Breakfast?" Knox asked me, changing the subject.

"I would love that."

As he pulled cookware and food out of the cabinets, my phone chimed. I grabbed it from the counter and opened it to a picture of Sam standing in front of the welcome sign in the Wexstone airport.

SAM

Surprise! I'm here!

What?! You're here early? You weren't supposed to get here until next week!

GIRL. You didn't think I would let you get engaged without me, did you?? I have to help you prepare! I'd have gotten here yesterday but we got rerouted like a bajillion times because of the storm, but who cares because I'M HERE NOW!

My stomach dropped into my ass at the thought of getting engaged to Oliver after everything that had happened in the last twenty-four hours. The thought of being with anyone else after sleeping with Knox brought a fresh wave of nausea over my body. I didn't know if it was the guilt or my own feelings that had grown so much despite trying to push them down, but I couldn't ignore the bile that rose in my throat.

I had to get out of there. My time in the fantasy bubble with Knox had to end. I couldn't let things go on any further.

"Hey? Everything okay?" Knox brushed the hair away from my neck and leaned in to kiss behind my ear and down my neck.

"Yeah." I stepped out of his touch, drawing a concerned look onto his face.

"Birdie?" he questioned.

"Sorry," I said as I made my way to his bathroom to find my jeans. "Sam just texted me that she is here—in Wexstone—a week early." I smiled. "I've got to get back to Vince's place."

I could see the realization that our time here was done wash over Knox's face before disappointment replaced it. He went to the cooktop and turned off the burner.

"Okay. Let me get dressed and I'll drive you."

"Okay." We held each other's gaze for a moment, neither of us knowing what to say or having the courage to address the elephant in the room: *What does this mean?*

The drive to Lexington Manor was the longest car ride of my life; you could have cut the tension with a knife. The only reprieve was Eugene whining from the backseat because Knox wouldn't let him sit on my lap.

Knox kept his hand on the center console the entire drive, never moving it. Was he waiting for me to grab his hand and tell him everything was good between us? Because I couldn't do that. Everything was, in fact, not good between us.

I was there to court Oliver, and instead I had screwed Knox. I was supposed to be falling in love with a prince, and I was growing big, unnamable, terrifying feelings for his best friend. I was going back to Vince's house, who had brought me here to become his queen, and I had betrayed his trust.

I wanted to crawl into a hole and hide from them all.

Knox pulled through the wrought-iron gates and up the slope of the driveway. My heart sank deeper into my chest. This was it; after I got out of this car, things would go back to the way they were before, except I could no longer allow myself to imagine anything with Knox. There could be no more lingering stares, no more quiet conversations alone with him, no more being kissed in all the right places, nothing.

The truck came to a stop in front of the manor.

"Birdie," he whispered.

"Thank you for the ride back."

"Birdie," he said, looking at me with pleading eyes.

"I've got to get inside. Sam is waiting." I opened the door. "Bye, Knox."

I walked up the front steps, pushing down every emotion that was trying to claw its way up my throat and out through my eyes. I thought back to the thousands of times I had watched *Frozen* with Ellie and tried to channel Elsa: "Conceal, don't feel."

I opened the front door and shut it behind me, not allowing myself to look back at the truck.

I leaned my back against the thick wooden door, trying to

compose myself and fight the overwhelming emotions running through my veins.

"Birdie!" Sam bounded around the corner and into the foyer. She wrapped her arms around me, giving me the deepest embrace.

"Sammy!" I said, fully enveloping her in my arms. This was exactly what I needed. I needed my best friend there with me to sift through the hole that I had dug for myself.

"I seriously didn't think that I was going to make it here. I was stuck in Germany for a good while because of that snowstorm."

"I can't believe that you didn't tell me you were coming early!"

"Vince and I wanted it to be a surprise. So, surprise!"

I let a smile wash over my face. The last six weeks had been full of surprises, yet this was one of the best to date.

"Let's take your stuff up to my room and I can show you around. You're bunking with me tonight. We have so much to catch up on."

"Sounds great. I can't wait to hear all about the competition and your budding relationship with Prince Oliver," she said, wiggling her eyebrows suggestively.

Or I could tell you about how I had the best sex of my life last night with his best friend.

"This way." I started walking up the stairs.

"You had sex with Knox?!" Sam squealed.

"Lower your fucking voice, Samantha!" I ran to her and clamped my hand over her mouth. "If Vince hears you, he will flip a lid, and the staff around here gossip more than high school girls."

"Tell me everything," she said, her big brown eyes wide with excitement even though her words were muffled from my hand covering her lips.

I lowered my hand and sat on the end of the bed. After a moment, words started spilling out, sparing no detail of the past few weeks. As I finished, I sucked in a deep breath, holding it for a moment before I let it out.

"Wow. Knox is totally in love with you."

"No, he's not!" I protested. "He's just a nice guy."

"Birdie, I've slept with some really nice people and none of them have ever walked through a blizzard to make me breakfast. They've DoorDashed me coffee at best."

I snorted a laugh in spite of the hurricane of thoughts and emotions swirling through my head.

"So, what are you going to do?" she prodded gently.

"I'm going to pretend this never happened. I'm not supposed to be here for him. I'm here for Oliver. I can't betray him or Vince any more than I already have. I'm going to keep going with this competition. If Oliver chooses someone else, great; I'll go back home. If he chooses me, then I'll tell him, and we'll move on from there."

Sam gawked at me.

"You clearly have something to say," I sighed.

There was a knock on the door. I took the opportunity to avoid Sam's scrutinizing lawyer stare and got up to answer it.

"Surprise!" Adelaide and Mel shouted as I swung the door open.

"What are you doing here?" I yelled in excitement.

"I called them," Vince said from behind the girls. "Bronson thought it best to go check on our country manor after the storm and since Sam's here, I thought we should relive our fun times in New York. It's party time, ladies!" He winked at Sam and me.

I turned to where Sam sat grinning on my bed. "You know what they say: When in Wexstone, do what the Wexstonians want to do," she said brightly.

"The guys will be here later," Vince added.

Fuck my life. Just when I needed a quiet night, Vince was throwing a fucking party. I was going to have to avoid Knox at all costs. I couldn't let myself be alone with him.

"Cool," I replied nonchalantly. "Well, I'm going to change, then. Adelaide, Mel, come on in."

I shut the door on Vince after letting him know we'd be down in a little bit.

"Sam. These are my friends Mellie and Adelaide. They're a part of the competition, too."

"Melanie Schneider, the journalist for *Kingdom Magazine.* Grew up around the court, your dad is the finance director for the Department of Health, and you have kickass taste in clothing?" Sam rattled off.

"Um..." Mel stuttered, gazing at Sam like I had never seen her look at anyone, not even Oliver.

Well, well, well, Melanie. Things are making a lot more sense.

"How do you know all of that?" I asked.

"Do you think I haven't been keeping up with the countless podcasts that have been created around this competition?"

"Oh, God. I can only imagine what they're saying about us," Adelaide rolled her eyes.

"Well, Miss Levy," Sam continued, using her courtroom voice, "they have been quite generous to you since you're a school teacher who is—and I quote—'of the people and for the people.' They love that your dad is a veteran, and after the school drive, your ratings skyrocketed."

"Ratings? Are there approval ratings on us or something? That's disgusting." I chimed in.

"Yeah girl, you're right behind Adelaide."

"I need a drink," Adelaide grumbled.

"Me, too," Mel agreed.

"You guys head down. I'm going to jump in the shower real quick and then I'll be down."

I headed into the closet, stripping off Knox's shirt and putting it in a neat pile next to my suitcase. If I was going to be able to function, I needed to wash Knox's scent off me. It was triggering too many memories that I just couldn't handle right now.

I was washing my hair, trying not to think about how the shampoo smelled of jasmine instead of mint, when Sam cracked open the door.

"Hey, Bee?" Her tone was wary.

"What's up?" I answered, waving her into the bathroom.

"I just got a social media alert. There's been another article..." her voice trailed off as she leaned against the vanity.

"Fuck. What is it this time? The articles have been so benign lately, I thought the nasty stuff was over."

"It's a blog post by Alistair Davies. Do you want me to read it to you or give you the Cliff Notes version?"

Alistair Fucking Davies. I was not in the headspace to deal with his bullshit right now. This was the last thing I needed.

"Gimme the summary," I said, my jaw clenched as I worked conditioner through my hair.

"Well, it's pretty much only about you. There's a bunch of photos in here, but they all look like they were taken from a distance. There's one of you by yourself in a greenhouse. There's another of you looking panicked at the tree cutting. And there's one of you dashing into the bathroom at the palace with your hand clamped over your mouth. The gist of the article is that you're mentally unstable, unpredictable, and regularly drink in excess. I think these photos are supposed to be 'proof.' They're noted as being from an 'unnamed source close to the competition.' Oh, and it brings up the airport vibrator situation again. Apparently, you're also 'sex crazed.'"

I stood still for a moment, water and anger washing over me in equal measure. *Renata.* She had to be behind this.

"Bee, are you ok?" Sam asked quietly, breaking into my thoughts.

"I think I need a minute, Sam. Can you go ahead to the party? I'll meet you down there."

"Sure," she said, closing the bathroom door behind her as she left.

I took the rest of the shower to gather myself. *Well, at least you have something else to worry about besides Knox,* I thought wryly.

After putting on an oversized knit sweater and leggings, I doused myself in my perfume and followed the sound of music and voices downstairs to the billiards room.

Vince hadn't been kidding when he said he was throwing a party. I walked in to find far more people than I had expected, with each arrival being checked off a list and screened by security at the door. Along with the women that I knew, there were probably a dozen people I had never seen before, including a group of women in their early twenties dancing on the pool table in the middle of the room. A bar was set up in the corner of the room, filled with every kind of liquor imaginable and half a dozen varieties of beer.

I looked around the room for Sam, not spotting her anywhere. I felt eyes on me and turned to find Knox and Oliver by the floor-to-ceiling bookcase on the opposite wall. Knox held a bottle of beer in one hand and had the other propped against a shelf as he talked to Oliver. His eyes watched me intently. Oliver spotted me and waved.

Nope, nope, nope. Can't do this yet.

Since Sam was nowhere to be found, I made a split-second

decision and darted out the open doors to the terrace, where I found Adelaide and Tej chatting by the stone railing.

"Hey," I said in greeting, hoping I didn't look as flustered as I felt.

"Hey, Birdie," Tej smiled at me. "How are you feeling? I heard about your mishap in the palace kitchen."

"I'm much better. Thanks for asking," I said, my heart warming. Tej was one of my favorites of Oliver's friends. He was genuinely kind and never seemed to have an ulterior motive. He cared about the people around him regardless of social standings or clout.

I spotted Renata, Gemma, and Ginny through the doorway as they strolled arrogantly into the billiards room. "Ew, why are they here?"

"Chauncey invited Ginny and she brought the other two," Tej answered, rolling his eyes.

I turned to Adelaide. "Have you seen Sam?" I had to find her before I threw caution to the wind and punched Renata right in her smug face.

"I thought I heard her say that she and Mel were going to try and find a bathroom or food or something?"

Neither of them mentioned the article. I hoped no one else had seen it yet; I wasn't ready to be the laughingstock of the party.

I could feel blue eyes on me again and when I looked, Oliver and Knox were making their way through the billiards room to the terrace.

"I'm going to go look for Sam." I sidestepped the group as the men approached, pointing over my shoulder as I backed away.

"I'll help you," Knox offered.

"No!" I said far too quickly. "I'm good. I can find her myself."

Oliver looked between the two of us, clearly questioning the awkward exchange.

He knows. I know he knows. I'm a shit liar and it's probably all over my face. He's going to know and freak out and kick me out of his country for being a big fat jerk for sleeping with his best friend when I was supposed to be here courting him.

Wait, no. He'll kick me out for being a mentally unstable, sex-crazed drunk who slept with his best friend.

Fucking damnit.

I booked it inside and down the hall. I heard Knox calling my name, but I didn't turn around. Moving faster, I sprinted into the kitchen, figuring I could hide in the walk-in pantry for a few minutes until Knox gave up his search.

I opened the pantry door and jumped back in shock. I had found Sam: She was locked in an embrace with Mel, her hand up Mel's shirt as they made out, neither one noticing me.

"Birdie?" Knox's voice came from right outside the kitchen.

Fuck it. I stepped into the pantry and closed the door.

"Birdie!" Mel started. "Um, this isn't what it looks like."

Sam's eyes were wide. "I was just asking Mel if she knew about the article and then...uh..."

"Shh!" I hissed. "I don't care. I mean, I do care. This..." I waved my hand between the two of them. "...is amazing. Love this for you two. And I want all the details later, but right now I'm hiding from Knox, so just be quiet until he passes."

"Birdie, you have to talk to him," Sam whispered.

"No, I don't. Not right now, anyway."

I put my ear to the door and waited a few minutes, the breathing of my two friends the only sound I heard. Once I felt certain Knox was gone, I turned around to Sam and Mel.

"I think the coast is clear. I'll leave you two to get back to what you were doing." I winked at them both. "And seriously, this is the only good thing to happen so far today. I want details about this later. Especially from you." I pointed to Mellie. "I mean, if you're okay with talking about it. If not, that's totally cool."

I slipped out of the pantry with a wave. I turned into the hallway to head back to the billiards room and was met with a large frame leaning against the wall just outside the kitchen.

Shit.

"Are you ready to stop avoiding me and talk, or do you want to keep doing this whole cat and mouse thing all night?"

Well, I guess if he's offering?

Knox gave me a hard stare, not breaking eye contact, waiting for me to answer.

"I'm not avoiding you," I lied.

"Birdie, you literally ran out of the room after I offered to help you find Sam."

I grabbed the hem of my sweater and started fiddling with a loose thread on the bottom.

"Knox, I don't think we should be alone." I darted into a side sitting room, hoping to find an alternate route back to the party. Spotting only closed doors, I turned back to the doorway where Knox was now standing. He held up an arm to block the door frame.

"Birdie, we have to talk about last night."

"No, we don't. What happened, happened. We just got wrapped up in the moment. No need to talk about it further."

"Is that what you want to go with?"

"Am I wrong?"

Knox watched me for a moment. "You tell me. Last night meant nothing to you?"

"All of this was just supposed to be a fun adventure."

He took a step further into the room. "Did last night mean nothing to you?"

"I'm supposed to be courting your best friend, your

brother. I'm supposed to be deciding if I can accept a proposal from him in a week." My voice cracked.

"Answer the question, Birdie. Did last night mean something to you?"

"No!" I yelled.

"Bullshit," he spat, his tone unwavering. "That's bullshit and you know it. You're not only lying to me, but yourself."

"I'm not lying!"

"Yes, you are. You and I both know that last night wasn't just an 'in the moment' type of thing. It was way more than that. Did you think you could just play house with me yesterday and then go running back to Oliver today?"

"No. You're reading too much into it. It just happened..." I faltered.

"Don't fucking gaslight me, Birdie. You and I both know that there's been more between us since day one, but you're too busy running away from your feelings. Your dad felt his feelings so deeply that it destroyed him, so you've decided it's safer to just shut yours down completely. And clearly you don't want to deal with the repercussions of your actions."

My anger flared. "Oh, you want to talk about repercussions? Have you told Oliver that you have feelings for one of the women he's courting?" I gave him two seconds to answer and when he didn't, I continued, "No, you haven't. So don't stand there and chastise me for something you yourself haven't even done."

"Tell me how you truly feel, and I will walk into that party right now and tell everyone about us, to hell with the repercussions."

"What?" I gasped, my chest growing tight with shock that he would potentially throw his friendships down the drain for me.

"What do you feel, Birdie? Do you love me?"

I couldn't do this. Not in that place, not in that moment. It was all too much. My body was starting to tighten up and I couldn't think straight.

He closed the gap between us, mere inches separating us. "Look me in the eyes and tell me you don't love me, and I will walk away right now and leave you alone and let you move on with your life." His eyes pleaded with me.

I couldn't stand there and tell him I loved him when I hadn't loved anyone else in my life except my family and Sam. How could I acknowledge feelings I couldn't even name? I had spent years not allowing myself to feel anything besides grief, and even that I had stuffed deep down and pushed away.

Knox didn't deserve that. He deserved more.

A ball of emotion filled my throat, and I could barely get my answer out.

"I don't love you, Knox."

"Okay," he said. He turned and strode out of the room as my heart plummeted right through the floor and straight to the center of the Earth.

CHAPTER 25
KNOX

"I don't love you, Knox."

Her words hit me like a bucket of ice water, shocking me to my core and stealing the breath from my chest.

She didn't love me. Whether what she said was the truth or simply the only truth she was willing to accept, it didn't matter. If she wasn't going to let me in, I wasn't going to push her.

Instead, I turned on my heels and walked away from the woman who had stolen my heart but wasn't willing to fully give me hers.

I strode to a door across the small sitting room, hoping it would lead me back to the party. Even better if it just led me the fuck out of there entirely. An eerie calmness settled over me as I turned the handle, pulling the door closed behind me as I left the room.

Despite the many hours I had spent in Lexington Manor over the years, I had never committed the home's layout to memory, so I was annoyed to find myself in a dark hallway that led to the back stairwell—certainly not to the billiards room.

"Fuck," I muttered, pausing for a moment, turning back toward the sitting room. I would wait a few minutes for Birdie to return to the party and then sneak out the back by the kitchen.

As I realized that the door hadn't latched behind me and was cracked open—*fuck these old buildings*—I heard an all-too-familiar voice address Birdie on the other side.

"He's right, you know."

Oliver. *Shit.* My heart stopped just at the thought that he had overheard us.

I peered through the crack in the door to see Birdie whirl around. "Oliver! What do you mean?"

"You know exactly what I mean," he said, his tone tired and his eyes steely. "You're only fooling yourself if you think you don't have feelings for him."

Shit, shit, shit.

"Oliver, I don't know what you heard, but it's not what you think."

Oliver shook his head, a wry grin splitting his face. "Birdie, it's exactly what I think. For fuck's sake, who do you think has been coaxing the two of you together all these weeks?"

My jaw dropped as Birdie sank onto the edge of an armchair, ice in her voice. "What?"

"You remember the day I gave you that tour of the palace?" Oliver said, leaning his hip against the back of a couch.

"Of course," Birdie answered.

"I could see it then even if neither of you could. Your attraction to each other was clear to me, and that was the day I knew you and I would never be romantically involved."

"Then why didn't you send me home?"

"And break my best friend's heart? Birdie, Knox's loyalty to me is unparalleled. I knew he'd never admit to me how he felt about you, so I decided to see what happened with a few…nudges."

"Nudges," Birdie said, her tone flat.

"Who do you think put your name down for Knox at the silent auction?"

I rubbed my face with my hands. *That bastard.* He continued, "I also made sure that you were in his group for the tree cutting."

"I suppose you also slipped me bananas the other day." The tight line of her shoulders and the bite to her words told me *exactly* how she felt about this conversation.

"God, Birdie, no! I would never do that! But I won't lie and say that I didn't hope having Knox take you to his cottage might encourage something to happen."

Birdie stood, her hands clenched at her sides. "Oliver, you had no right to interfere like that." I wasn't sure I disagreed with her.

"Birdie, I'm sorry, but—"

Birdie's hand flew up, cutting him off. "No, Oliver. No 'buts.' I don't care if you're the prince or king or fucking emperor of the universe, you had no right! Maybe you should have spent your time advocating for yourself instead of going along with this stupid contest when you clearly don't even want to get married right now anyway!"

"Excuse me?" Oliver said, coming to his full height.

"Oh, don't take that 'I'm royalty' tone with me. I know you've convinced yourself you're protecting Rosie by martyring yourself, but I think we both know that's a load of bullshit. You're the fucking Crown Prince; if you don't like the law, work to change it! If you don't want to be king, step down like Xavier did! You have options, Oliver—far more options than forcing yourself to marry someone you barely know just because an old, dead relative said you had to. Buck the fuck up and stand up for yourself and future generations in all of this."

Oliver's eyes widened. "You don't know anything about Wexstone—"

Birdie cut him off again. "Yeah, well, right now I'm not sure I want to. I'm out. I'm getting on the next plane home. Have a nice life, Oliver."

"Birdie, wait—" Oliver started as she stormed past him and out the door. My stomach clenched and my head reeled. I sank to the floor, putting my head between my knees.

"See, I knew I did it for your own good," a sickeningly sweet voice said from beyond the door where I still hid. *Jesus H. Christ, would this night never end?*

Oliver's voice turned cold. "Renata. What are you talking about?"

Renata slithered toward Oliver, her phone outstretched. "I knew that girl was good for nothing. I just made sure the country knows it, too. Now that she's out of the picture, we can be together like we were always supposed to be."

Oliver's face paled as he took Renata's phone, his eyes widening as he read the screen. I quickly pulled my own phone from my pocket, brought up Google, and searched "Wexstone Bernadette Hamilton." Ice slid down my spine as I clicked on the top headline result: *Wexstone Palace Source Reveals Contestant's Instability.*

Fire now licked through my veins. The article was full of the most ludicrous lies I had ever read. A quick skim of the rest of the search results indicated that nearly every outlet in Wexstone had either written about the article or was posting about it on social media. I might have been angry with Birdie, but I would have never wished this kind of personal attack on her.

I looked up to see red-hot rage fill Oliver's face. "Renata, let me make sure I understand. You orchestrated this article?"

Renata preened around the room, somehow oblivious to Oliver's anger. "Of course. I knew she couldn't possibly be here for the right reasons. I just needed some time to get the proof I needed to show everyone else that she clearly was not cut out for the job of being your queen."

"Get out."

Renata stopped, spinning on her heels. "What?"

"Get. Out."

"But, Ollie—"

"Do not call me Ollie. In fact, you are never to speak to me again, is that clear?"

Renata's face paled and her hands shook. "I...but..."

Oliver placed Renata's phone back in her hands, grabbing his own and dialing a number. "I have spent years witnessing you talk down to everyone around you in an effort to elevate yourself. I have stood by as you drooled first over Xavier, then me, in hopes of becoming queen. I never should have allowed you to become a part of this competition in the first place, but I was foolishly hoping to keep the peace. No more. You are no longer welcome in this competition or in my presence." He turned to speak into his phone. "Hello, yes, I require an escort for Ms. Raines. She will meet you at the front entrance of Lexington Manor. Please ensure that the rest of the security team knows she is barred from all further competition events and the palace grounds for the foreseeable future."

Oliver hung up his phone, placed it back in his pocket, and gestured toward the hall. "After you, Ms. Raines. Let's make sure you make it out safely, shall we?"

Renata brushed her hands over her short dress, straightened her shoulders and put on her haughtiest face, her confidence not meeting her eyes as she stalked from the room with Oliver at her heels.

I leaned my head against the wall and let out a deep sigh. *What the fuck just happened here?*

———

My head was pounding, and when I turned over to the opposite side of my bed, waves of nausea came crashing over my body. It took a lot for me to be hungover, but after the night I'd had, I had given myself the greenlight to drink until I forgot everything.

If I was being honest with myself, I knew better, but I had to try to forget. I needed to forget what it felt like to have the woman I was in love with tell me she didn't love me back. I needed to forget that my sheets still smelled of her. I needed to forget what her lips tasted like, and I needed to forget that she left and I would never see her again.

Eugene whined from under the comforter. I knew that he needed to go outside but I wasn't sure that I could stand without throwing up. But he needed me.

Birdie may not have needed or wanted me, but my boy did.

I made it to the back door to let Eugene out when the nausea turned full force. I sprinted to the sink, barely making it there before the bottle of whiskey from the previous night made its way back up.

Once I let Eugene in, I grabbed a bottle of water out of the refrigerator and some bread from the pantry. I could have been a grown man and toasted it, but I was only eating it so I would have something on my stomach for the acetaminophen I was about to take.

I stepped back into my bedroom, but one sight of my bed triggered memories of Birdie that made me feel like I was going to be sick again. Instead, I settled for the couch, covering myself with a blanket as Eugene forewent his normal spot by my feet and curled up in front of me with his head on my arm.

Despite his pain-in-the-ass tendencies, Eugene was more adept at reading a room than some humans I knew, making him the first to recognize when my emotions were a wreck. I scratched that special spot behind his ear and he nestled deeper into my side, his breathing synchronizing with my heartbeat.

"Looks like it's just going to be you and me, boy." I put my arm around him. "I'm sorry. I tried to get her to stay, but I wasn't enough."

I closed my eyes, trying to push down the tears that threatened to fall. I drifted back to sleep, recounting the way that Birdie had felt in my arms in this exact spot and the fact that it would never be like that again.

I woke a few times throughout the day to feed Eugene, take more acetaminophen, and drink water. That night was Cora's birthday celebration and there was supposed to be a large dinner with Oliver's suitors, but there was zero chance of me attending. There was no way I could force myself to be anything other than miserable. Maybe Oliver would care that I was absent, but I would deal with that later. Guilt rose in my chest, but I pushed it away, numbing that part of me for the time being. I heard my therapist's voice in my head telling me that I needed to feel my emotions as they came, regardless of how much I wanted to ignore them.

I thought about how Birdie wouldn't acknowledge any of her feelings except the fun, lighthearted ones. I had recognized it from the first time she mentioned her mom and then quickly changed the subject. It was evident that she hadn't worked her way through her grief when I found her in the barn, not knowing where to start when the panic attack took hold.

It was clear to me because I had been there before. It had

taken me years to sift through my own shit when my parents died. Hell, it took twice weekly appointments with Dr. Sanchez over the course of a year just to manage the panic attacks.

But I couldn't hold onto my anger at Birdie for not dealing with her stuff and then turn around and do the exact same thing. I couldn't numb my feelings. I knew what I needed to do that day, and that was to sit with my feelings and feel them.

I would let all the tears come if they needed to. I would sit there in the dark and think about what it would have been like to have her choose me. I'd think about what it would have been like to have her stay and build a life with me. I'd think about how it would have been to have her be mine.

And once I had thought through all those things, I'd grieve what wasn't and could never be and then lay them to rest, setting them on a leaf in a river and letting them sail away down the stream.

———

The morning sun rose, and I woke up physically feeling a little better, aside from the giant hole that had taken up residence in my chest. It felt as if something was missing. Maybe it was my confidence, maybe it was the fact that the girl I loved had left without even saying goodbye. Maybe it was a bit of both.

I grabbed my gear and Eugene, and I headed over to the woodworking shop. I knew it would be one of the few places where I could sort through the shitstorm in my brain.

I pulled my truck up to the back of the shop, let Eugene out and unlocked the door. It was early and I was there even before Mr. Lewellen, though I knew he wouldn't mind me letting myself in.

I flipped on the lights and started the small space heater in the corner. After rearranging my tools on the table for a fourth time, I still couldn't get settled or decide what to work on. My mind wouldn't stop racing, and I knew that if I couldn't focus on this, I'd only waste perfectly good materials and my own time.

"Come on, Eugene, let's go out to the field." I put my coat back on and grabbed my pack with my axe, knives, and saw and threw it over my back. The sled we kept around to haul whatever wood we chopped was leaning by the back door. After dusting the snow off, I set it down on its rails so Eugene and I could start our mission of finding a way that we could both work out our pent-up energy.

My mind drifted to the last time I was at the workshop: it had been with Birdie. My chest constricted when I couldn't push aside the memory of what it had felt like to have my arms wrapped around her and the way that her breath had caught when I laid my hands over hers and showed her how to whittle.

Remembering moments like that, I knew in my heart that she felt more for me than she would admit, but the devil on my shoulder continued to insist that I wasn't enough.

I had never been enough. I had never been enough for the women around court who only wanted Xavier and Oliver. I never felt like I did enough for our family. I never felt like I did enough around the palace or for my staff. And I hadn't been enough to make Birdie stay.

My phone buzzed in my pocket, and I pulled it out, reading the text message.

VINCE

Birdie's gone.

I'm aware.

> What the fuck did you do to her, Knox? What
> is wrong with you?

Anger boiled in my chest. I turned my phone off and returned it to my pocket. *Fuck you, Vince. You don't even know the half of it.*

I spotted a bare tree that looked like it was about to fall over. Clearly something had gotten hold of it and torn it to shreds. Probably a moose or buck shedding their antlers, or possibly a bear had tried to climb it, not realizing it was too fragile. I pulled out my axe and went to work.

Whack, whack, whack.

I'd never been enough.

Whack, whack.

I should have fought harder for her.

Whack, whack, whack.

I betrayed my best friend.

Whack, whack.

I'll never be chosen for who I am and what I offer.

Whack, whack, whack.

I'll be alone forever, and this is my lot in life.

Whack, whack, whack.

The tree fell and a few branches detached as it hit the ground. This was Eugene's heaven. He scurried to grab one of the biggest branches and carried it over to me, setting it at my feet and giving an excited bark. I gave him a half smile and a pat behind his ear.

"Good job, buddy."

I cut the rest of the branches off and piled them on the sled. Eugene chose a branch that was about four times his own length as the one he would carry himself.

The weight of pulling the sled back to the shop and the energy it took to cut down the tree had given me a brief respite from my wandering mind. I opened the back door to the work-shop and was met with a large figure sitting at my worktable.

"We missed you at the rest of the party." Oliver's deep voice echoed through the room. "I was worried when I didn't find you in your office at the palace this morning."

"I'm fine," I said as I carried a load of lumber into the room.

"You don't look fine."

"Yeah, well, I just chopped a tree down. I wouldn't expect you to know what that looks like."

"What's that supposed to mean?"

"Nothing." I knew that I shouldn't take my anger out on Oliver, but the irritation took over as soon as I saw him.

"No. Go on. Tell me how you really feel."

"I'm good." I slammed down a pile of wood.

"Knox, don't keep things from me. You're my best friend; I'm here for you to talk to about all of this."

"Ha!" I let out a sarcastic laugh. "You have a lot of nerve talking about keeping things from each other."

"Whoa. Knox." He put his hands up in front of his chest. "Let's talk about this. I know a lot has happened."

"Talk to you? What do you want me to say? Do you want me to tell you how I'm pissed that you had Birdie come here for your competition, putting her off limits for me? How I'm pissed that she kept choosing you over and over again? Do you want to hear how I tried so hard not to fall in love with her and keep boundaries up because she was courting you, yet I still slept with her and the guilt ate away at me, all to find out that you were behind the scenes setting us up? How about we talk about how you wouldn't be upfront with me about having zero feelings for her, yet you kept on like you did, like she was a frontrunner. Is that what you want to hear?" I took a deep inhale, catching my breath, hoping my heart would slow down.

I threw one last log onto the pile, silence and tension filling the room.

"Yeah. Let's talk about all of that." Oliver took his coat off and hung it on a hook on the wall. "I came here to apologize to you."

"What?" I said, looking up from my worktable.

"I should have been upfront with what I was doing. I knew after the palace walk-around that there wasn't a spark with Birdie and me. And the day that we spent at the school, I saw the way you kept looking at her while she was playing with the kids, especially Archer."

He walked over to the miniature refrigerator in the corner, opened the door, and grabbed a soda. He walked back over to my worktable and took a seat on the extra stool, opening the bottle and taking a long swig.

"I finally knew that both of you were into each other the night of the auction. You should have seen the way her entire demeanor changed when you walked in with Gram. It's like she came alive—she couldn't stop smiling. She had completely checked out of the conversation that we had been having to watch you walk down those stairs, mate. But when Gram was telling the story about her and Granddad, she kept looking at you with guilt in her eyes. That's when I knew that you two needed some time together to sort your shit out. I had planned on making a donation to the community gardens anyway, so I used the opportunity to bid for you on Birdie's behalf."

My exasperation got the best of me, and I hit the worktable, shaking the tools that hung against the wall.

"Damn it, Oliver! You should have just been upfront about it all instead of trying to be some matchmaker behind the scenes."

"I know!" he yelled back. "I'm sorry. I'm sorry I wasn't, but you weren't either, Knox. You should have told me about your feelings for her. I would have stepped aside."

I knew he was right, but I had been trying to put him first. I always put him first. I always did what was best for everyone around me. If they could have made it right and worked it out, I would have stepped aside. I would have done that for him. "You're my best friend. I didn't want to do that to you. I didn't want to jeopardize the competition."

"Yeah, and I'm *your* best friend," he said, exasperated, "which is why you should have told me. There are plenty of other women who I could choose from. If you had feelings for her, you should have told me. It would have saved you a lot of guilt and heartache, mate."

"She didn't choose me. She chose you and being here for you over me. I wasn't enough." I wiped down the carving knife I had been cleaning and hung it up on the wall along with the other knives.

"What do you mean you're not enough? You don't believe that."

"Why wouldn't I believe that? It's the truth. For years I've watched as people have bypassed me to get to you and Xavier. I've watched as you've had your pick of dates and parties and women. I've always preferred to stay out of the spotlight, and it never bothered me until Birdie came along. But I wasn't enough. I wasn't enough for her to choose me over you. I wasn't enough to make her stay."

"Knox," Oliver said, his voice softening. "Look at me, mate."

I set the screwdriver I had been fiddling with down and looked at my brother. His gray eyes were full of emotion. I was unsure if it was hurt or pity.

"You're more than enough. And I'm sorry that you've ever felt like you aren't. I couldn't do life without you, Knox. You're the only person who has ever seen me as a person first and not just a prince. You've never treated me any differently, and I'm so sorry if I've ever made you feel less than. You've given everything you have to me and my family. You give your time, your loyalty, and your love to us, and I'm sorry if you have ever felt that wasn't returned."

"Look," I took a deep breath, shaking my head. "I'm the one who should be sorry. You and your family have been nothing but good to me. You're the family that I was given when I lost mine, and I don't want you to think I've taken that for granted or I'm ungrateful for you."

"I've never thought that for a moment."

"I'm sorry for going behind your back with Birdie and not being honest about my feelings."

"Maybe we should make a therapy appointment to work on our communication skills."

I couldn't help but laugh at that comment. When Oliver and I were fifteen years old and Xavier had just turned eighteen, Leroy and Isobel had called in Dr. Sanchez to talk to us about the importance of communication and consent when we were with women. It was essentially a huge sex talk that included how to communicate with your partner and voice your own needs. It's where I learned about the "enthusiastic yes" rule.

Oliver and I had laughed about it for years. We had never heard of anyone else having the "birds and bees" talk with a licensed therapist, complete with charts and graphs. Most of our peers would have been horrified to have to sit with two other guys and listen to your parents talk about sex, but Oliver and I just ran with it and made jokes about always having a clear line of communication open.

Yet he wasn't wrong when he said that we should make an appointment with Dr. Sanchez. I knew I could probably benefit from talking about everything going on right now. I had thought that I had sorted out my problems with my self-worth when my parents passed, but clearly I needed a refresher on that—and on voicing my needs.

"I do think you're right. I'll make an appointment. All of this has fucked me up more than I realized," I admitted. "I'm sorry for unloading on you. And I'm sorry for hiding everything from you. I thought I was protecting you."

Oliver walked over to me and put his arms around me, engulfing me in a huge bear hug.

"I love you, brother."

"I love you too, man."

VINCE

Birdie, what the hell happened?

I'm sorry. I should have talked to you in person before I left. I know I messed things up for you and Bronson and you both probably hate me now.

I just don't understand what happened?

I don't think I'm ready to talk about it.

Was it Knox?

Birdie??

———

ADELAIDE

B, are you ok?

Yeah.

No.

Fuck, I don't know.

I'm sorry I didn't get to say goodbye.

Girl, it's ok. Mel and I are just worried about you. Can we video call soon?

Of course. Miss you both. xo

xo

———

MEL

Sam told me what happened. I am so sorry.

Thx, I don't even really know what to do now. I'm staying at Sam's until I find a place.

I also want to apologize for not telling you about…well, being gay. I haven't really come out to anyone. I think my mom suspects and honestly, I think it's why she pushed for me to be a part of this stupid competition. Probably hoping that a prince is just what I need to suddenly be straight. I really wanted to tell you and Adelaide. I didn't want you to find out the way you did.

Mel, you don't owe me any explanation. That is your story to tell when you're ready. I just want you to be happy and if you and Sam make each other happy, then I'm happy for both of you.

I'm going to talk to Oliver tomorrow. I don't think I want to officially pull out of the competition, I think it would bring too much attention, but he deserves to know at least some of the truth.

If that's what you feel comfortable with, then I fully support you. I'm irritated as fuck with Oliver right now, but it doesn't change that he's a good guy at heart. I'm sure he'll understand.

I hope you're right.

Here for you, always.

This competition may be stupid, but I'm glad it brought us together.

HA! Couldn't agree more.

———

OLIVER

Birdie, I'm so sorry for how things ended.

B, please talk to me.

———

UNKNOWN NUMBER

Hi Birdie, it's Ginny. I got your number from Cora.

I just wanted to say I'm sorry to you. Renata told Gemma and me that she was going to sneak you banana at the baking thing but I didn't know you were, like, *that* allergic.

Wait, Renata gave me bananas on purpose??

Yeah, and she was behind all the mean articles about you and stuff. I told her I don't want to be friends with her anymore and stopped talking to her after Oliver kicked her out of the competition. Sorry that I didn't do anything to stop her sooner.

I set the phone down and leaned my head back against Sam's couch.

Jesus, some people's kids. I had known Renata was vile, but even I hadn't seen that one coming. Never seeing that woman again was the one good thing about leaving Wexstone.

Thinking of Wexstone—of what I had left behind—hurt too much, so I turned my attention back to the TV where *Queer Eye* was playing. Since returning to New York four days prior, I had been sleeping on Sam's couch and spending my days in a blurry cycle of Netflix, junk food, social media, repeat.

In fact, it was about time for another session of social media doomscrolling. I opened one of the apps to photos of an early Christmas celebration from one of my undergrad friends, followed by photos of an office holiday party from one of my high school classmates, and a video of my former skating instructor's dog dressed in a Santa hat.

"Geez, is anyone posting about anything other than Christmas today?" I mumbled. I looked at the date on my phone: December 21. *Oh. I guess that explains it.*

Somehow over the course of the last few weeks, I had found myself looking forward to Christmas for the first time in thirteen years. I thought I would be spending the holiday with my new friends, in a beautiful real-life snow globe.

Instead, I was sleeping on my best friend's couch, too embarrassed by everything that had happened to even call my brother and tell him I was back in the States.

My mind flitted to the book still tucked away in my suitcase: a leather-bound, illustrated guide to the world of Tolkien. I had found it hidden in a corner of a bookstore the weekend after Thanksgiving and had bought it as a Christmas gift for Knox. It had cost a fortune, but I hadn't minded—imagining the look on his face when he opened it made the price well worth it.

My heart ached knowing that I wouldn't get to give it to him now.

I stretched, catching a whiff of myself as I raised my arms. I tried to remember the last time I had taken a shower. Was it the day Sam and I got back? The day after? Time had started to meld together.

I heard Sam's keys in the door and glanced at the clock. Somehow it was already time for her to be home and I had just lain the day away on the couch, again.

"Hey," Sam said as she walked through the door, a shadow crossing her face as she glanced my way, no doubt taking note of the empty beer bottles that sat on the coffee table.

"How was your day?" I asked, not even lifting my head off the throw pillow I was lying on.

"Fine," she replied curtly. "What did you do today?" she asked as she took off her coat, then reached for a wine glass and a bottle of her favorite red.

"Nothing, really. Watched *Queer Eye*. That's about it."

"Mmm," she hummed, taking a sip of the wine.

"Is something wrong?" I asked, turning so my body faced her over the back of the couch. Sam liked her home spotless and in order, and I knew that me being here was throwing her off. Well, and the beer bottles and my dirty sweatshirt strung across the coffee table.

She paused, setting down the wine glass and anchoring her hands on the countertop. "Birdie, you know I love you."

"Yes. And?" I knew there was more coming.

"And I understand that your heart is hurting. I've been there." She looked down at her wine glass, fiddled with the stem, and took a breath in. "But girl, you need to figure your shit out."

I blanched. "Excuse me?"

She came around the counter, settling into the armchair adjacent to the couch. I watched her warily. "We've been friends for what...five years? I can count on one hand the number of times I've heard you talk about your mom, like *really* talk about her. I've heard you mention your dad even less. But fun stuff? That's never a problem for you. You're one of the most fun people to be with and I adore that about you, Bee, but Knox was right. I think you're so afraid of becoming your dad that you refuse to acknowledge your big feelings."

I crossed my arms and stared at her, my eyes narrowing.

"Yeah, I knew this was going to piss you off," she said with a sigh. "But I can't just sit here and watch you be miserable like this. I've enabled you enough by not pushing you to leave Americana."

"I like working at Americana."

"Oh, please. You said yourself it's a dead-end job. It's not even a decent job for anyone who *wants* to wait tables or tend bar, and you know it. You have a fucking master's degree—use it! Get a curator job! You know that's what you really want to do with your life."

I shook my head, trying to form the right retort.

She cut me off before any words had even escaped from my lips. "I know. I know it's scary," she said, her tone softening. "It's terrifying to send out your resume and put yourself out there and hope someone likes you enough to give you a chance, but you have to try, Birdie. You have to give yourself a chance."

I swallowed thickly, blinking back tears. I grabbed one of the couch's throw pillows and fiddled with the edge.

"And you need to tell Knox how you really feel."

My head shot up, tears starting to fall. "What?"

Sam stood up, coming to sit beside me. She put her arm around me. "Remember how I've known you for five years? I know you, bitch. I know you love him, even if you don't."

I sagged into her arms, finally letting out the torrent of tears and emotions that I had been holding back for days, weeks, years. I sobbed for my mom, for the years lost with her. I sobbed for my dad, who loved so hard that he couldn't pick himself back up when that love was lost. I sobbed for teenage Birdie, who had to cook dinners for her little brother and make sure he got to school on time.

But most of all, I sobbed for Knox, the only man I had ever truly loved and had lost as a result of my own inaction.

"He doesn't want to speak to me," I finally said through my tears, my voice muffled by the linen of Sam's favorite blouse.

"I don't think that's as true as you believe it to be," she said gently, rubbing my back as I continued to cry.

"I was awful to him. And then I was awful to his best friend in the whole world. And then I left without saying goodbye to anyone. I don't think I'm exactly his favorite person." I took a shaky breath, wiping my eyes. "Besides, he deserves so much more than a mess like me."

"Do you love him?" Sam asked.

"Yes."

"Well, look at that. That's progress, right? None of us are our best selves in the span of a day—that stuff takes a lifetime of work. But if you're willing to put in the work and be real and honest with him, I think you might just find that it changes everything." She kissed my head, gave me one last squeeze, then stood up. "I need to get changed; I have the firm's holiday party tonight and I probably shouldn't wear a shirt with your snot all over it," she said, picking up her wine from the kitchen as she made her way to her bedroom. "And take a shower, you reek."

————

After the longest and most satisfying shower of my life, I spent the evening making a plan for the rest of the week. I wasn't sure if I would ever have a chance to repair things with Knox, but I could at least start by repairing myself.

When I woke up the next morning, I texted several of my friends to ask for therapist recommendations. If I was going to start feeling my feelings, I knew I would need some help along the way. Knox had spoken so highly of his therapy experiences that it made me less afraid to take that leap for myself. Even if we never spoke again, I knew I could always thank him for that gift.

I spent the rest of the morning updating my resume and researching art curator jobs. By noon, I had bookmarked a handful of promising-sounding internships and entry-level positions to apply for after the holidays.

That afternoon was spent Googling the therapists' names I had gotten from my friends, trying to decide from their online profiles if any of them might be a good fit. A few of them seemed stuffy, but one of them—Lisa Andrews, LCSW— seemed promising and was in network with my self-pay insurance. Even better, she offered virtual sessions.

My hand shaking, I submitted an online form booking a consultation with her.

Step by step, Birdie. You can do this.

I woke up the morning of December 23 knowing what my next move had to be. I had to step away from my comfort zone if I was going to follow through on any of what I'd done so far.

"Hey, Chad," I said as I walked into the back office at Americana.

Chad looked up from his desk where he was working on payroll. "Birdie. What the hell are you doing here? Aren't you supposed to be off in London or something?"

I smiled wryly. Nice to see that some things never changed. "Wexstone, but yes. There was a change of plans, and I came home a bit early."

Chad grunted. "Mmph. Well, guess you probably want to get back on the schedule, huh? I might be able to get you on for Christmas Eve if you're looking to pick up a shift."

"Actually, I came here to give you this," I said, handing him a sheet of paper. He took it, glancing it over, his eyes widening.

"You're quitting?"

"That's my letter of resignation, yes. Normally I would give you two weeks' notice, but since I wasn't supposed to be back until after the new year anyway, let's consider this my final date of employment."

Chad's brows furrowed. "What are you going to do?"

I knew it would probably take a few months to get hired and onboarded for any of the curatorial positions I had bookmarked, so I had decided to apply as an instructor at one of those "wine and paint" places in the meantime. It would tide me over until I could get in at a museum and might even be pretty fun.

Not that I felt like I needed to share any of that with Chad.

"I have a plan and for the first time in a long time, I feel really good about it."

Chad grunted as I said my goodbyes and cleaned out my locker.

Back at Sam's, I was deep into the process of filling out job applications, early 2000s Matchbox Twenty playing on Spotify, when there was a knock at the door.

I paused the music, setting aside my laptop as I stood. I hadn't realized how long I had been sitting and working, and I stretched as I absentmindedly peered out the peephole.

My heart instantly started hammering in my chest as I recognized the chiseled jaw and blond hair of the man outside Sam's door: Oliver.

———

"Can I come in?"

I stood in the doorway to Sam's apartment, my jaw slack in disbelief. I was pretty sure a few minutes had passed since I had opened the door, but I still hadn't said a word.

I nodded, stepping back to let him in. I peeked into the hall as I closed the door, noting the black-clad bodyguard posted near the elevator. I could only assume there was at least one more in the lobby and possibly a third just outside the building.

Oliver shrugged off his coat and I motioned toward the hook by the door. He hung up his coat and followed me to the kitchen.

"Wine?" I asked. It was the first word I had spoken to him since our argument at Lexington Manor.

"You're offering?" he asked, his eyebrow raised.

I huffed a laugh. "I guess I am," I said as I grabbed a bottle of rosé from the fridge and poured us each a glass.

I handed him a glass and took a sip from my own, leaning against the fridge and silently appraising the prince now seated on the barstool in front of me.

"I'm sure you're wondering what I'm doing here," he said.

I raised my eyebrow in a *yeah, duh* gesture.

Oliver laughed. "Okay, sure. I deserved that." He took a breath and set his glass down on the counter. "Birdie, I'm here for a lot of reasons, but the first is to apologize to you. I know you were ignoring my texts, and rightfully so, but I hope you'll hear me out now that I'm here."

I nodded for him to continue.

"I was wrong. I meddled and I overstepped. I should have just talked to you and Knox instead of trying to set you both up behind your backs. It wasn't right and I can see now how much it hurt both of you—two people I care about so deeply. For that I am so very sorry. I hope you can forgive me someday."

I swallowed, taking in the man before me, remorse written on his face. I may not have fallen in love with Oliver, but I had certainly come to think of him as a friend, and seeing the shame he held in his body broke through my icy front.

I moved to the stool next to him, setting down my wine and taking his hands in my own.

"Oliver, you don't need to apologize. Well, maybe a little, but I know your heart was always in the right place. I've recently had something of a wake-up call and you're right: I did love Knox. *Do* love Knox; I was just too scared to admit it. I'm not sure I would have been able to admit it without your interference, so I should probably be thanking you." I laughed through my nose as I squeezed Oliver's hands. "But I should also apologize to you. I said some pretty hateful things to you that night, and I was way out of line. I don't know anything about being royal or in line for the throne, and the way you do or don't handle what life has thrown at you is none of my business. You're doing a great job. I hope you know that."

Oliver's mouth lifted into a half smile as he squeezed my hands in return. "You were right on most of it. And it really made me question if being king is what I want. I mean, I never had to think too much about it as a kid, since all the focus was on preparing Xavier for the throne. Him abdicating was the last thing any of us expected, so I really was thrust into all of this without any warning.

"But the more I considered it, the more I realized that I *do* want to be king—I'm not exactly sure what my reign will look like but I do know I need to, as you put it, 'buck the fuck up' for future royal generations and the people I love and serve. I know that I want to change things for the better, and while that may take a little time, I want my legacy to show that I helped those who came after me. I never want anyone else in this predicament. I may not be able to change things for myself, but I can make sure that my children—or Rosie, should the worst happen—are free to make their own choices about marriage."

I smiled at him, at the prince who had become a true king almost right before my eyes. "I'm proud of you."

"Thank you."

"I do feel pretty out of the loop on what's been going on in the last week. Wanna fill me in on who you're planning to propose to in"—I glanced at the date on my watch—"three days?"

Oliver sighed deeply.

I raised an eyebrow. "Oh, you're feeling that good about it, huh?"

"I know who I want to pick, but there are some big conversations that need to happen first. I owe it to her to approach her about it before I discuss it with anyone else."

I suppressed a grin, trying not to reveal I had a good guess who he meant. "You're a good man. She's a lucky woman."

Oliver leaned back and eyed me. "Now let's talk about your happiness, Birdie."

I blushed. "Oh, let's not," I sputtered.

"He misses you."

My eyes shot to Oliver's. "He does?"

He nodded. "He's miserable without you."

My stomach soared for a brief moment before falling back down into my ass. "I was terrible to him. I don't know if he could forgive me."

"I think you might be surprised, Birdie."

I looked down, playing absentmindedly with the cuffs of my NYU sweatshirt.

"I have one last thing I need to discuss with you, though."

I met his gaze. "Oh?" I said, taking a sip of wine.

"This part is official palace business, actually. I'm here to offer you a job."

I choked on my wine. "You—what?"

"I don't know if you recall from our tour of the palace grounds, but our palace curator retired earlier this year and we've been struggling to fill the position." I nodded, recalling the conversation. "Well," he continued, "I realized that I know the perfect candidate. Someone who has the necessary education and background, has a passion for art, and certainly doesn't care about being around royalty. In fact, she's unafraid to give the future king a piece of her mind." He laughed, winking at me.

A flush filled my face as my heart threatened to race out of my chest. "What? You want me to be your palace curator?"

Oliver nodded solemnly. "We absolutely do. My parents are fully on board, as is our head of HR. I believe she will have a formal offer letter for you, but I told her that I needed to make a verbal offer in person."

I shook my head, still in shock. "But I haven't actually worked as a curator before! I just have my degree, don't you want—"

"What we want, Birdie," he said, cutting me off as he took my hands again, "is someone just like you. I anticipate there will be a learning curve for you, but that's true of any job. Hell, I'm in for a real learning curve myself over these next few months. But we're confident in our choice. What do you say?"

I paused, my mind reeling. I took a deep breath in for five seconds, held it for five seconds, and let it out for five seconds.

"Yes, I accept. On one condition..."

CHAPTER 27
KNOX

Knock, knock.

My hands burned from the cold and the raps against the wood door of Archer's house. It had been a long week, and I hadn't had any desire to leave my house unless it was necessary. But having my annual Christmas Eve get-together with Archer's family was necessary. They had become an extension of my family and right now, I needed to be around people I loved.

Archer's aunt, Dahlia, answered the door, and Eugene wasted zero time dashing in and making himself at home. It always took me aback a little to see such a young woman taking care of three little children. But she and her partner Jordan—both in their mid-twenties—made it work, and they made it work well.

As promised, I brought several jars of pickles along with an assortment of cheese and charcuterie and a plate of lemon cakes. I unloaded the food in the kitchen first and then headed back out to my truck to grab my Christmas presents for the family. After three trips to the truck, I was finally able to sit down next to the fire and start to warm up. Archer's youngest sister, a lively six-year-old named River, had made her way into my lap and we watched their reserved eight-year-old middle sister, Riley, play tug of war with Eugene.

My mind wandered to what it would be like to have kids of my own one day and if I would ever have these moments—Christmas traditions and nights at home with the fire going and kids playing happily in the living room.

I had wanted that with Birdie. I had been doing pretty well the last couple of days with not letting my mind go to those thoughts, especially after a session with Dr. Sanchez, but with the Christmas classics playing on Jordan's vintage record player and River snuggled up in my lap with her wild curls tickling my nose, it was hard to push those intrusive thoughts away.

"Lunch is ready!" Dahlia called from the kitchen, and everyone bounded there and filled their plates in a buffet-style line.

After we were done eating and Eugene had made his rounds cleaning up the food the kids had "accidentally" dropped onto the floor, we went back into the living room, and I started handing out presents.

"I'm so excited to see what ornaments you made this year," Dahlia said as I handed her a gift bag.

"I'm excited to see what books he got me!" Archer said.

"Wow. Am I that predictable in my gift giving?" I gave a half laugh.

The presents were handed out and mayhem ensued with wrapping paper and bags being tossed left and right as the kids tore into their presents.

"Oh my gosh, these are beautiful," Dahlia whispered as she unwrapped the ornaments I had carved for her. I had spent two weeks in October in my woodshop carving Dahlia's family into ornaments, making sure I got every facial detail correct.

"Let me see," Jordan said, and Dahlia handed over the ornaments.

"Wow. Knox! These are amazing."

"Thank you." I smiled my first genuine smile in days.

"Auntie D, look!" Archer yelled, bringing Dahlia and Jordan out of their haze of joy. Archer held up two books from the World Book Encyclopedia set I had found and shipped back from New York a few months ago. "These are amazing!"

Dahlia looked over to me. Her eyes brimmed with tears, and one slid down her cheek. She set her hand over mine and gave a half smile.

"Thank you, Knox. You do so much for us, and I will never be able to thank you enough."

"And you don't need to. This is what family does."

After another hour of excitement and playing, the girls had fallen asleep for their afternoon nap as Archer laid under the tree next to Eugene, reading his new books. The alarm on my phone chimed, letting me know that it was time for me to leave so I could get back to the palace for Christmas Eve dinner.

Eugene and I returned to my little cottage and then started our trek through the snow-covered garden to the palace. Eugene trotted through drift after drift, covering himself in snow. *Isobel will love that*, I thought sarcastically.

I stopped a few yards outside the palace and looked up at it, taking in the huge exterior of the building. I had grown up there, with it being the heart of some of my earliest memories. It had always felt like home, a safe place. But right then, with pieces of me chipped away, it was hard to want to be there when it was also the center of so many memories with Birdie.

As badly as I wanted to take a vacation and get away from

everything for a little while, I knew that I couldn't. My family needed me. And even though Dr. Sanchez's words came to mind about doing things for myself and not just giving myself completely over to the family, I still couldn't just leave right then.

I also had to think about Oliver's offer to be his Chief Counselor. Was it what I wanted? I had given so much of myself to the country already, even if they didn't know it. Could I give more of myself and be happy? In truth, happiness was the furthest thing from my mind in that moment. I knew that I would be okay again one day, but that day seemed so far away.

My phone buzzed in my pocket, alerting me to a text message.

OLIVER

You on your way yet?

Yeah. Walking up right now.

Ok. Meet me in my office.

Eugene and I wound our way through the palace and up the stairs. When we hit the landing, Eugene took off in a sprint toward Oliver's office door. At first, I just thought he had the zoomies, but when he started sniffing the door and scratching at it, my hackles raised. Afraid something was wrong, I hurried to the door and didn't even knock.

"Oliver?" I said as I opened the door and stopped dead in my tracks. A beautiful chestnut-haired woman leaned against the desk and looked across the room at me with those big hazel eyes.

"Hi." She gave a soft, tentative smile.

I knew I should say something, anything. Ask her what she was doing here. Ask her why she'd left. Ask her what she was thinking. But while my brain was working overtime, my mouth wasn't working at all.

Eugene barked happily and ran to her, weaving through her legs like an oversized cat and rubbing himself against her. She leaned down and scratched his favorite spot behind his ears.

"Hi, Eugene. I missed you, too." She looked up at me after giving Eugene one more scratch. "Can we talk?" She had a mix of hope and fear in her eyes. Was she afraid that I would say no?

I nodded and walked fully into the room, closing the door behind me. I stood in front of her, giving her a little space. After all, the last time we had talked, space was what she had wanted.

"What are you doing here?" I asked.

She knotted her fingers together and threaded the bottom of her sweater through them.

"Oliver came to New York and asked me to come back."

My stomach fell to the floor. Oliver had flown back to get her? After our whole talk in the woodshop, and after everything he knew, he went to bring her back here? Was he still trying to pursue her? *No, he wouldn't do that.* Was he trying to meddle and play matchmaker again?

"Why?" was all I could muster up to ask. I don't even know if I truly wanted to know the answer.

"He offered me the art curator job at the palace."

Of course he did. "I think you'd be perfect for that job." And she would—they had been looking high and low for someone to fill the opening but hadn't found anyone who fit the bill. But the thought of having to see her day in and day out and not be able to be with her was going to kill me. And if I had to see her date someone else and live happily with someone that wasn't me, I didn't know what I would do. I would go crazy. But I also wanted her to be fulfilled in her life and if this did that for her, then I would just find other places to be.

She smiled a little and then nodded.

"I told him I'd only accept on one condition, though."

"Oh yeah? What's that?" I asked, my curiosity piqued.

She took a step toward me and looked me in my eyes.

"That you forgive me." She looked down at the thread she was fiddling with and then back up to me. "I know that it's a huge ask because I was really shitty, Knox. I said some nasty things to you, and I need to apologize." She took a deep breath. "I'm sorry. I'm sorry for what I said and for how I hurt you. You were right about everything. I do shut down my feelings. I have been terrified to open myself up. I'm working on that. In fact, I've made myself a virtual therapy appointment, thanks to you. But most of all, you were right— I do have feelings for you. I love you, Knox, and I know that I hurt you deeply, and you may not feel the same way anymore. I wouldn't ask you to. You just need to know that I'm so sorry for hurting you, and I hope that one day you can forgive me. I can't choose working for Oliver without knowing that you're okay with it and that you know how I feel."

She loves me.

"You love me?" I asked.

"That's what you're focusing on?" She let out a little laugh.

"Yeah."

"Yes, I love you. I shouldn't have run away from you or my feelings. You have helped me more in these past few months than anyone has in the last thirteen years since I lost my mom. You saw through all of my bullshit and still seemed to like me anyway. You make me want to do and be better, Knox."

"I love you, too." I smiled and took a step toward her.

"Do you think you can forgive me?"

"Done." I took another step toward her. "Just don't run away again. Promise you will stay, even if it gets hard."

"I promise." She took a step forward and we were chest to chest, our breaths syncing. I leaned my head down and set my forehead on hers.

"And don't think I missed that comment about going to therapy. I'm proud of you."

She smiled. "Thank you," she whispered.

"I missed you."

"I missed you, too," she replied as Eugene barked and tried to wiggle his way in between our legs. Birdie laughed. "I missed you too, Eugene."

I wound my hand up around the nape of her neck and tangled my fingers through her long hair, pulling her mouth to mine. What started as a slow and intimate kiss quickly stirred a hunger inside my chest. Her lips moved with mine at a quick pace and she ran her tongue along the entrance of my mouth, asking for entry. I walked her backward, stopping when I felt her ass hit the edge of the desk. I grabbed her hips and set her on top of the desk as she opened her legs so I could slide even closer to her.

As our kiss grew faster, I let my hand move up her torso and under her sweater. I gently grabbed her breast. I had missed the way that my body responded to hers. The way that, even though we hadn't known each other for very long, I knew her body and already had it memorized. I loved the fact that just the mere touch of my skin on hers had her panting and wanting more.

I pulled the lace cup of her bra down, freeing one of her perfect breasts, and rubbed the pad of my thumb back and forth across her perky nipple.

"Knox," she moaned.

"Mmm," I responded.

"I want you so badly," she said between kisses, "but I promised Oliver we wouldn't fuck in his office."

I pulled my head back quickly and looked her in her eyes, questioning if I had heard her correctly. "You what?" I smiled.

She let out a soft laugh, which made her free tit bounce in my hand. That did not help the situation in my pants.

"After he brought me up and told me that we could talk in here, he joked as he left that I had to promise we wouldn't have hot make-up sex in his office."

"So what you're saying is we could have hot 'I love you' sex in here?" I asked as I nipped the side of her neck.

She let out another one of those soft moans that I loved so much.

"Plus, your family is waiting downstairs to start Christmas Eve dinner."

I knew she was right, and I knew that we needed to get down there, but I didn't want to leave. I wanted to finish what we had started so badly.

"I promise that once we get back to your house tonight, I will more than make up for the lost time," she said, her hand on my chest.

"Let's get down there then and get Christmas started," I sighed. "I'm just going to need like five minutes before this goes down." I gestured to the dick that was making himself known by the bulge in my pants.

"Poor thing," Birdie laughed as she grabbed and rubbed at it.

"Baby, you are not helping," I moaned.

"Sorry." She gave me a salacious smile.

———

"Can you pass the bowl of sunflower seeds, please," Belle asked her mom, Freya.

Freya's cheeks turned red as she grabbed the small glass bowl that sat in front of her daughter and placed a little pile of the seeds on Belle's plate.

"Belle, I'm begging you to please not throw the kernels on the floor like we do outside in the summer," Freya whispered into her youngest daughter's ear.

Belle let out a high-pitched giggle and nodded. We were gathered around the long formal dining table in the grand dining hall for Christmas Eve dinner, Freya and her two girls joining us for the family dinner before the official party started.

I couldn't have imagined being there and being as happy as I was. When I woke up that morning, I was dreading every moment of dinner and the party later that night. But with Birdie beside me, and us working through all the logistics of everything that had taken place over the last few months, I didn't think that I could be any happier.

"Bernadette," Evelyn said from across the table, "Oliver told me that you are going to be the new art curator here at the palace?"

"That's the plan." Birdie grinned. "We agreed that after the holidays, I could start."

"Oh, that's wonderful. I'll make sure my secretary sets up a meeting with your secretary after you're all settled in. I have a few pieces that I would like to move from the country house to here, and then there are a few that I would like to sell."

"That sounds great." She smiled warmly at Evelyn and then leaned over to me and whispered, "Holy shit, I'm going to have a secretary. What kind of world is this?"

"Welcome to being a part of the palace staff. It's a fucking trip," I laughed into her ear.

"So, are things official with you two?" Rosie asked from beside me.

I looked from Rosie to Birdie and then grabbed Birdie's hand and placed it in my lap.

"Yes," Birdie answered before I could. "We're as official as Knox would like to make us, I think."

That wasn't true. At least not yet. I wanted Birdie to be in my future forever. I wanted her to not only work for the palace and the royal family, but I wanted her to be an official part of the royal family, at least as much as I was a part of the royal family. I wanted her to officially be mine in every way there was. And I planned on making that known soon.

"Ugh!" Rosie huffed, and I gave her an inquisitive look. Was she upset that Birdie and I had worked things out? This was going to be tough if the whole family wasn't on board.

"Rosalind," Evelyn chastised. "Don't be a sore loser."

"Sore loser?" I asked, looking between the two of them.

"Don't get me wrong," Rosie said to Birdie and me. "I'm super happy that you guys are together. I've wanted an older sister more than anything. I just needed you guys to hold out getting together until after Oliver's coronation."

"Well, they didn't, and that means you owe me, little lady." Evelyn winked.

"Oh my God. You two are the worst," I rolled my eyes, not meaning a word of it.

Birdie threw her head back with a hearty laugh. "Sorry, Rosie, the heart wants what it wants, when it wants. I'm sure you'll understand one day when you get older."

"Yeah, right. I'm never falling in love." Rosie made a face of disgust.

Preston appeared in the doorway, quietly approaching Isobel and leaning down to speak in her ear. A smile lit her face as she nodded. Preston straightened and disappeared again.

Isobel stood. "If I may have your attention," she began, and we all quieted. "I was hopeful that we would have another guest joining us this evening, and I have just been informed that he has arrived."

From down the table, I heard Freya gasp and Belle and Sadie collectively shout, "Daddy!" as a tall man with thick black hair wearing a military dress uniform entered the room.

The girls shot up from the table, running to their father, who leaned down to capture them in his arms. Freya stood, her shaking hand over her mouth, looking from her husband to Isobel with wonder and inquiry in her eyes. "How…"

Isobel crossed to Freya, taking her hand and guiding her toward Dante. "After I saw you at the donation drive, I put in some inquiries and discovered that Dante's mission was likely to wrap up this week. Leroy and I decided to do what we could to help their team get home in time to celebrate Christmas with their families."

Tears were now streaming down Freya's face, and at my side I could hear Birdie sniffling as well. I clasped her hand, swallowing back my own emotions as Freya now rushed into her husband's waiting arms, their family of four grasped in a group hug.

There was barely a dry eye in the room as Dante looked over his family's heads at Leroy and Isobel. "Thank you, Your Majesties. For myself, and on behalf of my men and women and our families; your kindness will not be forgotten."

After everyone settled back in—a place setting appearing for Dante between his wife and daughters—and finished dinner, Isobel ushered us into the ballroom and announced that there would be music, dessert, and drinks. I sent Eugene back to the cottage with one of the butlers, then sat with Birdie as we ate our servings of crème brûlée and watched Leroy and Isobel kick off the dancing to their favorite Christmas song,

"The Christmas Waltz." As I stirred a little sugar into my coffee, I felt the chair beside me pull out.

"May I sit here?" Vince asked.

"Of course," I answered.

"Vince! Hi!" Birdie said, her tone nervous.

I hadn't seen Vince since the night of the party at Lexington Manor, and I hadn't responded to any of his text messages. He had been very adamant that I was the reason Birdie had left and he wasn't short on his feelings about it. I wasn't sure how he would feel about Birdie and I being together, and I was worried that I might lose one of my closest friends.

"I owe you both an apology," he started.

"What? No. I need to apologize to you," Birdie said.

"No, you don't. I wasn't there for you, Bee. I was solely focused on myself and my family and not on what you truly wanted, and I'm sorry."

"Vince, I left without even talking to you and that was awful, especially after everything you and Bronson did for me. *I'm* sorry."

"Thank you. Can we put this behind us?" he asked her.

"Of course." She pulled him into a hug before he turned to me, worry lining his forehead.

"Knox, I'm so sorry for accusing you of doing something to Birdie and for questioning you. I know the kind of man you are. I should have known that you wouldn't have acted on any feelings toward Birdie unless they were the real deal. Again, I was too focused on myself to even consider that you were hurting or upset. I'm sorry, mate."

"It's okay. I get that you were upset and looking out for Oliver."

"So, we're good?"

"Yeah, man." I slapped him on the shoulder and gave it a light squeeze.

"So, this?" He gestured between the both of us.

"Yeah!" Birdie smiled from ear to ear.

"How are you going to make this work? Are you going to move to America?" he asked me.

I shook my head, unable to contain the pride in my voice as I said, "No. You're looking at the palace's new art curator. Birdie is moving here."

"No way! That's amazing. Birdie, I'm so happy for you. Congratulations. We should throw a party to celebrate the new job."

Birdie chuckled. "I think I'm good on attending any parties for a while," she said, eliciting a snort from me.

Vince let out a bark of laughter. "Fair enough."

The string quartet slowed down their upbeat melody to a soft version of "I'll Be Home for Christmas."

"Dance with me?" I asked.

"I would love to." Birdie's eyes were shining with joy.

I grabbed Birdie's hand and pulled her to her feet and to the dance floor. Wrapping my hands around her middle, I pulled her close to me, and we swayed to the strings playing in the corner. Birdie set her hand on my pec and lay her head against the center of my chest.

As we danced, I thought back to the night of the welcome gala. While Birdie was dancing with Oliver, I had wanted so badly to cut in and hold her close to me just like this. I pulled her in tighter and kissed the top of her head. I was so thankful that everything had led us to this, with her in my arms.

I was ready to get out of this party and take Birdie home and fully consummate this relationship. I couldn't wait to take her inside my cottage and show her how much I had missed her and all of the different ways that I loved her.

"Knox..." Birdie whispered.

"Hmm," I murmured, tightening my hands on her waist.

"What are you thinking about?" She pushed her stomach against my hardening cock.

I let out a shameful laugh.

"You. And how I can't wait to go home."

"Is that right?" She pulled back and looked at me with a heavy, amorous gaze. "I'm ready to leave whenever you are."

"Let's go," I said a little too eagerly.

CHAPTER 28
KNOX

With her hand in mine, I led Birdie to the side of the ballroom. A large, ornate tapestry hung against the wall. Birdie looked side to side, and I could tell that she was confused. I looked around the room to see if anyone was looking at us.

"I thought we were leaving?" Birdie asked.

"Do you remember the night of the gala and how you asked if I knew any escape routes?"

"I do." She grinned, catching onto my train of thought.

"Keep a lookout so I can open the door." I winked.

I pulled the corner of the tapestry aside and pushed against the top of the intricate chair rail until I felt a small click. A small passageway opened, and a cold breeze blew in.

"Okay, let's go." I took Birdie's hand as she bent down to crawl through the small door. I pulled my phone out of my back pocket and turned on the flashlight. We traveled down a stone-lined passageway, took a turn around one corner and then down a few stone steps.

"This is so cool," Birdie said as she ran her hand along the wall. "Do you know where we're going?"

I couldn't help but laugh. "I do. Oliver, Xavier, and I used to sneak around these tunnels to spy on our parents when we were younger."

"How very naughty of you."

"You have no idea, baby."

I stopped walking and pushed her back against the cool wall. Her breath caught as I laced my fingers through her hair and slid my lips along her neck. She let out a soft moan, which was now one of my favorite sounds in the world. As I moved my lips up her neck to her ear, I whispered to her, "Do you want to see what other naughty things I can do?"

"Yes, please." She grabbed the hem of my flannel and pulled me closer to her.

I fisted her wrists in one hand and lifted them above her head as I brought my other hand up her lean body and under her sweater. I ran my fingers across her stomach and up to her lace bralette. Pulling down the lip of the cup, I skimmed my thumb over her nipple and then gave it a light little pinch. I continued to kiss her throat, nipping and teasing her skin.

"Knox," she whispered.

"God, I love hearing my name come out of your mouth." Her breathy moans sent me over the edge of gentleness, and I took her mouth captive, biting and sucking her bottom lip. She was the perfect equal for me, sliding her tongue in my mouth in a beautiful dance we had cultivated together.

She rolled her body against my own, and I thrust my hips forward, giving her something to grind on. I could feel the heat coming from her center and I couldn't take it any longer. I unbuttoned her jeans and slid my hand down the front, her scorching wetness soaking through the lace panties she wore.

"Mmm, baby. You're drenched." I smiled.

"I want you so badly," she heaved.

I ran my fingers through her wet folds, lubricating my finger before I played with her swollen clit.

"Knox," she moaned, "that feels so good. Please don't stop."

"Anything for you, sweetheart."

I pushed one finger inside her and then two. Bringing them out slowly and then back in, I curved them forward on the upward thrust, searching for that special spot inside of her. I found it and pushed farther in as Birdie mewled. She fucking mewled, and it brought my dick to full attention. It grew and pushed against the zipper of my own pants, begging to be freed.

As my fingers pumped in and out of her tight pussy, I moved my thumb in little circles, giving her clit the attention it deserved and needed. I could feel how close she was by the way she rode my hand and how her breath picked up and faltered.

"I'm so close, Knox."

"Yeah, baby. I want to feel you come all down my fingers. Ride my hand and use it to get every ounce of pleasure you need."

As if she needed my permission to fall apart, her orgasm hit her and she rode it out on my fingers, screaming my name and a trail of expletives.

I let go of her wrists and held her up against the wall while she got her bearings and came down from her high.

"Please tell me you haven't done those types of naughty things here with anyone else," she panted as she caught her breath.

"Just you, sweetheart. Only you." I gently kissed her lips.

———

As we kicked our snow-covered boots off inside the door of my cottage, Eugene almost bowled Birdie over with his excitement. She didn't even bat an eye at my rude dog, going to sit on the floor and letting him lick her face with excitement. I couldn't blame him though; I was still just as excited to see her.

"Eugene, give her two seconds to get settled before you knock her down."

"Oh, he's fine. He's just excited that I'm home."

My breath caught and I thought my heart skipped a beat. She had just called my cottage her home. The woman who, two weeks prior, could barely voice her feelings and took pride in never having strings to hold her down. My shock was written clearly all over my face.

"What's wrong?" she asked.

"You just called this your home." I smiled broadly. "It made me really happy."

"Well...yeah." She scratched Eugene's ear and then looked back up to me. "You're my home now."

"Say more of that." I grabbed her hand and pulled her up from the floor.

"It's been a really long time since I've truly had a home, somewhere I was happy and comfortable and ready to put down roots. And I'm ready to do that, here, with you."

That's all I needed to hear. I leaned down and gave her a gentle and intimate kiss, a kiss that told her I wanted nothing more than to make her mine and build a life together. The slow gentleness washed away, and passion took its place.

I picked her up and she wrapped her legs around my waist, never missing a beat or breaking our kiss. I kicked the door to our room open, then gently laid her down on the bed. I wanted to show her how much she meant to me and what a life together would look like.

I pulled my shirt off and looked down at her body that was lying on the bed like my own personal Christmas present, just waiting to be opened.

"You are absolutely beautiful," I breathed.

"Knox?" she asked.

"Yeah?"

"I love you."

Hearing those words come out of her mouth was surreal; I didn't think I'd ever get enough of it. After stripping both of us of our clothes, I stood at the edge of the bed and grabbed her left ankle, bringing it to my mouth and trailing kisses up her calf.

"I love you," I said in between kisses. "Every single inch of you."

I grabbed her right ankle next and placed gentle kisses up the other side. "Everything about you."

I placed her leg back down on the bed so I could crawl up her body, kissing trails around her navel, her torso, and between her breasts. As I sucked one perky rose-colored nipple into my mouth, I squeezed the other one just the way I knew she liked.

"I think if you don't get inside of me soon, I'm going to combust," she panted.

"You need it that bad, huh?" I quipped back, my tongue still flicking her nipple.

"I want you, Knox Henderson," she said as she threaded her finger through my hair, lightly pulling on the strands to drive her point home.

The fact that she was choosing me, that she wanted me—that's all I needed to hear. I stroked the length of my hard cock and reached for the bedside table.

"Knox?"

I paused. "Yes, baby?"

"I have an IUD, and I got tested before I came to Wexstone..."

I grinned like a Cheshire cat. "I'm clear, too. Are you saying you don't want to use a condom?"

She nodded, want blazing in her eyes. She didn't have to tell me twice; I settled over her, giving my dick a few pumps before I lined myself up to her entrance. Rubbing my cock through her folds and wetting it down with her slickness, I pushed in just a few inches, letting her adjust until she was ready for my full weight.

"Mmm, yes," she moaned.

"Is this what you wanted?" I asked.

"Yes. More."

That was all I needed to hear. I grabbed her leg and lifted it up and onto my shoulder, giving myself deeper access to her tight, perfect pussy. She cried out as I pushed all the way to the hilt, sliding in as far as I could, claiming every inch of her. I needed to be as close to her as I could be. I wanted to be as much a part of her as she was of me.

"Bee, I love you and you're mine."

"I'm yours. Only yours," she breathed out.

I loved the way that I could tell when Birdie was close to coming. Her face grew tight and the walls inside her started to tremble. I reached up and ran my thumb over her swollen clit, and like the little button it was, it set her off.

"Knox! Yes!" she screamed as I continued to thrust in and out of her.

Hearing my name come out of her mouth, dripping in ecstasy, sent me over the edge. Two more pumps and I was unleashing everything I had inside her. I fell over, barely able to keep my weight on my forearms as I kissed her deeply.

"I love you," she whispered.

"I love you."

———

I awoke on Christmas morning, sunlight streaming through the window and warming my face, my eyes still closed. For a moment I was afraid to open my eyes, that it might reveal that yesterday had been yet another dream.

But there was the warmth of Birdie's body tucked into my side, the weight of her head resting on my arm, Eugene curled next to our tangled feet. I opened my eyes and soaked in the sight of her, her hair tousled from sex and sleep, her breathing deep and even as she slept.

Not a dream. She was here, all of her.

I gently disentangled myself, being careful not to wake her. Eugene opened one eye, surveying me. I put a finger to my lips and, as if he understood, he closed his eye again and burrowed in deeper next to Birdie.

I padded quietly out to the living room, opening a cabinet built into the bottom of the bookshelves to access a small safe. I pressed in the combination and the door popped open to reveal a small velvet box—the only thing precious enough in my life up to this moment to bother keeping in the safe. But now it deserved to be on the hand of my wild, wonderful girl.

I opened the box, revealing the delicate ring, the center sapphire encircled with diamonds. I removed the ring, tucking the box into the bookshelf as I returned to the bedroom and slid back under the covers.

Birdie was curled on her side, her left arm resting on top of the blankets and holding them by her face. I gently took her hand, sliding the ring onto her third finger. By some small miracle, it fit perfectly—not that I would have changed course if it hadn't. I needed Birdie to know that I was ready for our forever to begin now.

I surveyed the ring on her finger before placing her hand

back down on the covers and sliding into my space behind her, my arms encircling her torso. I nuzzled my face into her neck, taking in the scent of her.

She stirred, humming contentedly as she stretched slightly before turning over to face me.

"Good morning," she murmured, her eyelids still heavy as she blinked herself awake.

"Merry Christmas," I murmured back, kissing her forehead.

She smiled sleepily. "Merry Christmas."

"How do you feel this morning?" I asked, working hard to keep my voice casual.

Her smile widened. "Happier than I have ever been."

My own smile broke across my face, my heart soaring, as I pulled her in closer, kissing her deeply.

She moved against me, taking in my warmth and running her right hand across my chest. She propped herself up on her left elbow, pushing me back against the pillows as she swung her leg over my body and straddled me.

She leaned down, taking my face in both of her hands and kissing me fiercely, passionately. She pulled away slowly, about to sit up, when she stopped moving.

"Knox?" she said, a question in her voice as she pulled her left hand away from my face. Her eyes were wide as she looked from the ring on her hand to me and back again.

I took Birdie's hand in mine as I sat up, adjusting her to sit in my lap, her legs wrapped around my waist.

"This ring was my mother's. And now," I said, bringing her hand to my lips and kissing her fingers gently, "it belongs to you. Everything I am and everything I have belongs to you, Birdie. It would be the greatest honor of my life to be your husband. Will you marry me?" I asked, my eyes on her and only her. It had always been only her.

Tears flowed down her face as she nodded, choking

through her sobs. "Yes. Forever yes. The most enthusiastic yes!"

I smiled triumphantly, pulling her into a kiss, our souls entwining as she kissed me fervently. My hands roamed up her back to the base of her neck as I wound my fingers through her hair.

Birdie pulled back with a gasp. Eugene's head flew up, suddenly alert.

"What?" I asked, my eyes flying open. "Are you okay?"

"I just remembered that I have something for you, too!" she said, climbing off my lap. She put her hands on her naked hips. "Shit, I wonder where my suitcase is."

I laughed, pointing to the corner of the room. "I noticed it last night—looks like Oliver was thinking ahead of us."

She chuckled as she walked to the suitcase and unzipped it. "Remind me to thank him later. For a lot of things," she said, shooting a wink at me over her shoulder.

"We probably both owe him a few of those," I laughed again, throwing back the covers and pulling on a pair of sweatpants. "I'll be right back; I'm going to let Eugene out."

Eugene and I returned to the bed a few minutes later to find Birdie back under the covers, snuggled in one of my shirts, a package wrapped in shiny red paper and a white bow in her lap.

I scooted in beside her as she handed me the heavy gift. I carefully untied the bow and took off the paper to reveal a leather-bound book. A quick flip through the pages revealed hundreds of colorful illustrations and descriptions of Tolkien's creatures, countries, and so much more.

Birdie scooted closer to me so she could peer over my shoulder as I paged through the book. "I picked that up for you after our Thanksgiving dinner," she said into my shoulder. "I thought it might be a nice addition to your collection."

I blinked back my own tears at her thoughtfulness and the way she had remembered what I had told her about my dad. "Thank you, my love," I whispered, pulling her into my chest.

I was ready to show her my appreciation in the best way possible when I glanced at the clock.

"Baby," I said, pulling back from her, "I have about a hundred different ways I plan to worship this body of yours later today, but right now we will be toast if we don't make it up to the palace for Christmas breakfast."

Birdie threw back her head laughing. "All right, but don't think I'm letting you forget that plan," she said. She planted a kiss on my forehead and climbed out of bed.

"Never," I growled, telling my dick to calm down as I watched her pull clothes out of her suitcase. "I do have one more thing I need to discuss with you while we get dressed, though."

———

Thirty minutes later, we were on our way back to the palace, Birdie tucked under my arm. I gazed at the expansive building fully bedecked for Christmas and considered all the things this place had been to me over the years. First, my best friend's home. Later, my own home, though those memories were all colored through heartache. And finally, the place where I fell in love with the woman beside me—my fiancée.

While we dressed, I had told her about Oliver's job offer. I knew I owed him an answer, but also knew that I couldn't make this important decision alone. Not anymore.

I smiled as we walked, feeling peace with the decision Birdie and I had made together and excitement at giving Oliver my acceptance. As Birdie and I had talked, I realized that my reluctance to be a working royal had faded. I wasn't sure if I would want to keep the job forever, especially once we decided to grow our family, but for now, I would embrace the change and the adventures it would bring. After all, I reminded myself, being a part of the royal family had already brought me the best thing: a love to last a lifetime.

FIVE YEARS LATER

I awoke to a small kiss being placed on my cheek. Rolling over, I was met with Knox's crystal blue eyes, except they were smaller and bright with excitement.

"Mommy. Up, it Christmas."

Our beautiful little two-and-a-half-year-old Holland Noelle stood by my side of our bed, dressed in snowman footie pajamas, dancing in place with eagerness for Christmas morning and what awaited us in the family room downstairs. I couldn't blame her for her excitement; this was the first Christmas that she really understood what was going on. She had asked every single night for three weeks if Christmas was in the morning. It took Knox and me an extra hour last night after we got home from Archer's house to get her settled down and tucked into bed because she couldn't contain her excitement for what the morning brought.

"Good morning, Holly," I smiled as I brushed a wild strand of her dark hair out of her face.

She pushed my hand away and climbed up into our bed, lifting the comforter to look for Eugene, who was curled into a ball at my feet.

"Genie?" Her voice was muffled by the covers. I couldn't help but chuckle. Her nickname for Eugene melted my heart every time she said it. My happiness with my child quickly dissipated when she kicked me in my ribs and then rolled back and forth on the bed in a fit of laughter, her legs going wild and kicking anything they came in contact with.

"Daddy! Stop! No tickle!"

Knox's side of the bed bumped up and down with his laughter and Holly kicking and laughing. Eugene crawled up the length of my body and jumped off the bed, not wanting to be a part of the tussle. He loved snuggling Holly and was her fiercest guardian, but when it came time to wrestle and play, he was no longer about that in his old age.

A large, calloused hand wound around my middle and pulled me in for a family cuddle, one of my favorite things in this world.

"Merry Christmas, Henderson ladies," Knox's scruffy morning voice said as he rubbed a slow circle on top of my stomach.

"Merry Christmas, my love," I responded.

"Presents?!" Holly asked.

"Let's go see if your cousins and Grandpa are awake," Knox told her.

After going to the bathroom, brushing my teeth, and taming the wild mess of hair on top of my head, I descended the large staircase of our renovated manor.

Knox and I had flown to Mykonos, Greece, where his parents had vacationed often, and had a sweet, intimate wedding ceremony with our family. Neither of us had wanted a big expensive wedding. All we wanted was to be married and start our lives together.

King Leroy and Queen Isobel had generously gifted us this old manor as a wedding present. It had badly needed an overhaul, and although it took Knox three years to finish all of the renovations, he had worked day and night the final few months, making sure that it would be ready to bring home Holland and that we would have the perfect oasis for our family. I had offered many times to help him, having done odd jobs around my apartment in New York. But he refused to let me do any handiwork, reminding me of the first night we met. I stuck to painting and hanging the art.

I wouldn't have been upset if the manor hadn't been ready, though. Some days I missed the tiny cottage at the palace and all the memories it held. But this home was perfect. It was everything we both wanted. The perfect home for us.

I padded down the long hallway toward the back of the house that held the family room and kitchen. Christmas music and pots and pans clanging together let me know that the house was awake and Christmas morning was in full swing. My cheeks ached from the smile that graced my face.

"Holland, get away from those presents until your mom gets down here," Knox's baritone voice chided.

That daughter of ours was on a mission this morning.

"Daddy! Just one, I not tell."

"Oh, is that right?" I said, walking around the corner, smiling at my ornery little girl.

"She here!" Holland clapped. "John, Michael, time for presents!"

My nearly five-year-old twin nephews sat on the large sectional next to my dad, entranced in watching *The Grinch* on the flat-screen TV that hung above the fireplace.

"Merry Christmas, Birdie," Colleen greeted me from the kitchen that overlooked the family room. "I hope you don't mind that I started breakfast. Knox told me last night I was more than welcome to make breakfast this morning." Colleen truly was the perfect housewife. She had already made a pound of bacon, sausage patties, and biscuits, and she was scrambling eggs at the cooktop. Pitchers of orange, apple, and cranberry juice sat side by side along the kitchen island.

"Merry Christmas." I smiled. "Where are Connor and Ellie?" I looked around.

"They're still getting up. The jet lag hit them last night and they stayed up way too late watching movies together." She laughed.

"Here you go, love." Knox handed me a hot cup of peppermint tea and placed a kiss on my cheek. "I figured you wouldn't mind letting Colleen make breakfast this morning."

"Thank you." I inhaled the sweet scent of peppermint and herbs. It couldn't hold a candle to the way Knox smelled, but it was close. "Better her than me." I grinned.

"We've got breakfast going, and once Connor and Ellie come down, we'll get started opening the presents," he told Holly, who ran over to us and lifted her hands up so one of us would hold her.

I put her on my hip and walked to the sectional and sat down next to my dad. Connor and I had always spent the holidays together, especially after our mom passed. So having his family here wasn't unusual, but having my dad here, celebrating Christmas, felt unreal.

After I moved to Wexstone and started working for the palace, Dr. Sanchez, Knox's therapist, suggested that I see Dr. Ghana, her colleague. As hard as it was to dredge through all of the emotions and feelings I had suppressed over the years, I loved going each week to talk to her. The way she helped me view certain life events and reframe my way of thinking was freeing and so enlightening.

I was hesitant when she first brought up reconciling with my dad, but now I was thankful to her for giving me the tools to work through everything with him. We both wanted a relationship but just didn't know where to start or how to repair what had been damaged.

A year after I had moved here, he came with Conner and Colleen to visit. Dr. Ghana made time to see us together and even helped my dad find his own therapist in the States. It hadn't been rainbows and sunshine at first, and that first visit with him in Wexstone had been so awkward, but we both pushed through the tension and fought for the relationship we have now.

"Merry Christmas, Dad," I said as I sat next to him.

"Merry Christmas, honey." His eyes crinkled from the smile that took over his whole face. "This version is so different than the version I grew up with as a kid. The animation is great, and I love the music."

"I wike when Gwinch works out and put his booty in Max face!" Holly giggled from beside us.

I let out a belly deep laugh as Holly crawled into my dad's lap and laid her head back against his chest. I didn't miss the fact that my dad slowly closed his eyes as they filled with tears, clearly taking in the moment with his grandkids and daughter on Christmas morning and placing it in his core memory bank.

Everyone finally gathered into the family room, and the kids sat in a big circle on the floor as we divided up all of their presents. Holly could barely contain her excitement, her eyes roaming over all the presents, taking stock of which she would open first. She looked around the room, seeing that all the presents had been passed out to each recipient. She looked at me and asked, "Can I open?"

"Yes, baby. Open them!"

My girl had been waiting so patiently for this. At Knox's family Christmas, each person had to take a turn as everyone watched and gauged your excitement. In our house on Christmas morning, it was pure chaos. Wrapping paper and boxes and gift bags were tossed every which way. Squeals, laughter, and gasps echoed through the room.

Holly opened her last box and pulled out a pink shirt I had bought her at the last minute.

"Gwandpa. What say?" she asked my dad, who stood next to her with a trash bag in hand.

A huge smile overtook his face as he read the shirt out loud.

"It says 'Big Sister,'" he laughed, his eyes widening. "She's going to be a big sister?" He looked between Knox and me.

"She is." I smiled, rubbing little circles over my stomach, which already felt so much bigger in this second pregnancy than it had with Holly.

"Oh my gosh!" Colleen exclaimed. "This is so exciting."

"When are you due?" my dad asked.

"Late July."

"Congratulations, man." Connor gave Knox that pat on the shoulder that all men seem to do.

"Thank you." Knox smiled from ear to ear and leaned into Connor and whispered, "I blame the pumpkin ale and cat costume she wore at Halloween."

"Dude!" Connor exclaimed. "That's my sister, gross!"

Knox let out a boisterous laugh. He was always giving Connor shit, just like any older brother would. I gave him a playful slap across the knee and shook my head. He wasn't wrong; we had absolutely conceived our baby on Halloween night at the palace's party, but he definitely didn't need to let my brother know that.

After all the presents were unwrapped and the room was

cleared of the explosion of wrapping paper, the kids played together on the floor with their new toys and electronics while the adults sat on the sectional in a haze from the enormous breakfast.

"I'm going to head upstairs and shower and get ready for dinner at the palace," Knox said.

"Us too," Colleen announced, giving Connor *that look.*

As they cleared out of the room, my dad came and sat next to me, placing his arm along my shoulders and pulling me into his side in a sweet, fatherly embrace.

"I'm so happy for you, Bernadette," he said softly, pride in his voice. "Not just about the new baby, but for this entire life you have built for yourself."

"Thanks, Dad," I replied, tears filling my eyes. I blamed my hormones since they were all over the place lately. It definitely wasn't the fact that my dad was being so sweet.

"Your mom would be so proud of you." His own eyes started to fill up with unshed tears.

"Aw, Dad. I know she would be. She would love being here in this winter wonderland surrounded by her grandkids."

I never thought that I would be able to sit and talk about my mom, especially on Christmas of all days, with my dad. But here we were, making strides of progress and talking about the "could haves." Regardless of what the pregnancy hormones were doing to me, I knew that this moment was special and a huge win in the healing column for both of us.

"I have two boxes of white-chocolate-covered Oreos in the pantry. Want to go open one up? For Mom?" I smiled.

"I would love that," my dad smiled as he kissed the side of my head.

QUEEN ISOBEL'S FAVORITE HOLIDAY RECIPES

Bring a piece of Wexstone into your home by making some of Queen Isobel's favorite holiday treats. Enjoy them with a cup of tea, add them to your holiday dessert menu, or share them with friends—just don't try sneaking bananas into the gingerbread cake!

RASPBERRY LINZER COOKIES

Makes 24 sandwich cookies

Prep Time: 30 minutes | Bake Time: 12 minutes | Chilling & Cooling Time: 2 hours 20 minutes | Total Time: 3 hours 2 minutes

Ingredients

 1 cup (227 grams) unsalted butter, softened
 1 cup (200 grams) granulated sugar

1 large egg
1 teaspoon vanilla extract
1/4 teaspoon fine sea salt
1 cup (112 grams) almond meal or hazelnut meal
2 1/2 cups (313 grams) all-purpose flour
1/2 cup (170 grams) raspberry jam for filling
Powdered sugar for dusting

Instructions

1. In the bowl of a stand mixer fitted with the paddle attachment, beat together the butter and sugar on medium-high speed for 5 minutes, or until very smooth, fluffy, and light in color.
2. Scrape down the sides of the bowl and beat in the egg and vanilla until well combined.
3. Mix in the salt and the almond or hazelnut meal just until combined, scraping down the sides of the bowl as needed.
4. Slowly mix in the flour, beating until just combined. Turn the dough out onto plastic wrap, parchment or waxed paper and shape into a disk. Wrap and refrigerate for at least 1 hour.
5. Line two baking sheets with parchment paper. Set aside.
6. Roll out dough 1/4 at a time between two pieces of parchment or waxed paper until about 1/8 inch thick. Cut out cookies, making sure to cut windows in half of the cookies, and place on prepared baking sheets about 1/2 inch apart. Because tops and bottoms may bake at slightly different rates, place all tops on one sheet and all bottoms on another.

7. Chill cut-out cookies for 20 minutes. Preheat the oven to 375°F (190°C). Bake for 10-12 minutes, until cookies are set and barely starting to turn golden on the edges.

8. Allow cookies to cool for 5-10 minutes on baking sheets before moving to a cooling rack to cool completely.

9. When ready to serve, place a small spoonful of jam on each of the bottom cookies. Dust the top cookies with powdered sugar, then place the top cookies on top of the bottoms, creating sandwiches.

Notes

Cookies will soften if they are left filled overnight. If you prefer your cookies to be crisp, wait to fill them until just before serving.

GINGERBREAD CAKE

Makes 1 8x8-inch (20x20-cm) pan

Prep Time: 15 minutes | Bake Time: 30 minutes | Total Time: 45 minutes

Ingredients

1 cup (125 grams) plus 1 tablespoon (8 grams) all-purpose flour, divided use
1/2 cup (70 grams) finely chopped crystallized ginger
1/2 cup (100 grams) granulated sugar
1/4 cup (57 grams) unsalted butter, melted
1/4 cup (61 grams) unsweetened applesauce

1 large egg
1/3 cup (79 ml) molasses
1/2 cup (118 ml) buttermilk
1/4 teaspoon baking soda
1 1/2 teaspoon ground ginger
1 teaspoon ground cinnamon

Instructions

1. Preheat oven to 350°F (175°C). Grease an 8x8-inch (20x20-cm) baking pan, and line with parchment paper. Set aside.
2. In a small bowl, stir the crystallized ginger with 1 tablespoon (8 grams) of all-purpose flour. This will prevent the ginger pieces from sticking together and help keep them from all sinking to the bottom of the cake.
3. In a large bowl, stir together the melted butter, applesauce, sugar, and eggs until light and creamy. Add the molasses and buttermilk.
4. In a separate bowl, whisk together the flour, baking soda, ginger, and cinnamon. Add the dry ingredients to the wet, and stir until just combined. Fold in the ginger pieces.
5. Pour batter into the prepared pan. Baked for 25-35 minutes, until the center is set and a toothpick inserted into the middle comes out with only a few crumbs clinging to it.
6. Remove from oven and allow to cool in the pan. Using the parchment as a sling, remove the cake from the pan and cut into pieces. Serve dusted with powdered sugar or with lightly sweetened whipped cream.

CRANBERRY WALNUT BREAD

Makes 1 8x4-inch (20x10x6-cm) loaf

Prep Time: 15 minutes | Bake Time: 1 hour | Total Time: 1 hour 15 minutes

Ingredients

1 cup (100 grams) chopped fresh cranberries
1/2 cup (100 grams) granulated sugar, divided use
1/4 cup (55 grams) lightly packed brown sugar
2 1/4 cups (281 grams) all-purpose flour
3/4 teaspoon baking soda
1/4 teaspoon fine sea salt
1 large egg
3/4 cup (177 ml) buttermilk
1/4 cup (59 ml) vegetable oil
1 teaspoon vanilla extract
1/2 cup (55 grams) chopped walnuts

Instructions

1. Preheat oven to 400°F (200°C). Line an 8x4-inch (20x10x6 cm) loaf pan with parchment paper. Set aside.
2. In a bowl, combine chopped cranberries, ¼ cup (50 grams) granulated sugar and, all of the brown sugar. Set aside.
3. In a large bowl, combine flour, remaining ¼ cup (50 grams) granulated sugar, baking soda, and salt. In another bowl, whisk together the egg,

buttermilk, oil, and vanilla. Create a small well in the dry ingredients, pour in the wet ingredients, and stir just to combine. Fold in sugared cranberries and walnuts.

4. Spread batter into prepared loaf pan. Bake for 50-60 minutes or until top is golden and a toothpick inserted into the center comes out clean. Remove from pan and allow to cool on a wire rack.

Notes

Store well wrapped at room temperature for up to 3 days or in the refrigerator for up to 5 days.

ALMOND CRESCENT COOKIES

Makes 30 cookies

Prep Time: 1 hour | Bake Time: 14 minutes | Total Time: 1 hour 14 minutes

Ingredients

1 pound (454 grams) unsalted butter, melted and cooled
1 large egg yolk
3/4 cup (86 grams) powdered sugar, plus about 2 additional cups (230 grams) for dusting
1/2 teaspoon fine sea salt
5 to 6 cups (625 to 750 grams) all-purpose flour
3/4 cup (84 grams) almond flour or almond meal
1 teaspoon almond extract

Instructions

1. Preheat oven to 325°F (165°C). Line baking sheets with parchment paper or silicone baking mats. Set aside.
2. In the bowl of a stand mixer fitted with the paddle attachment, combine the melted butter, egg yolk, ¾ cup (86 grams) powdered sugar, and salt until well combined.
3. With the mixer on low speed, gradually add 5 cups (625 grams) all-purpose flour. Continue mixing on low speed for 15 minutes, scraping the sides of the bowl as needed.
4. Add the almond meal and almond extract. Return the mixer to low speed and mix for another 15 minutes.
5. In the last few minutes of mixing, if the dough is too soft to form into a ball, add the remaining all-purpose flour, half at a time, until the dough can be shaped.
6. Working with 1 1/2-tablespoon (#40 scoop) portions, shape the dough into crescents and place on the lined baking sheets.
7. Bake for 13-14 minutes, until the cookies are pale, the outsides are dry, and the bottoms are set.
8. Let rest on the baking sheet for 5 minutes. Place the remaining powdered sugar in a shallow bowl. Very carefully remove each cookie from the baking sheet and place in the powdered sugar, turning to coat all sides. Cookies are very delicate, so be very gentle.
9. Let the cookies finish cooling on a wire cooling rack. When completely cool, coat the cookies one more time in powdered sugar.

Notes

This dough needs to be mixed for 30 minutes to turn out right. You will need to use a stand mixer for this recipe.

The cookies are at their most fragile right out of the oven but are delicate even after cooling. You may have some break in the process of coating in the powdered sugar, but they will still taste great.

These are a delicate, buttery cookie with a crumbly texture; they are not soft or chewy.

Raspberry Linzer Cookies, Gingerbread Cake, and Cranberry Walnut Bread reprinted with permission from StephieCooks.com. Almond Crescent Cookies reprinted with permission from MyBakingAddiction.com.

THANK YOU

Thank you for reading *Royally Yours*!

Ratings and reviews help indie authors continue to do what they love: write and share stories for readers to enjoy. If you loved following Knox and Birdie's story, please consider leaving a rating or review.

Want more?

To find out what happens in Oliver's continued journey toward his happily ever after, check out *Hopelessly Yours*. For details on current and upcoming books in the Wexstone universe and beyond, visit www.JulesKyle.com or join our reader Facebook group.

ACKNOWLEDGMENTS

From both of us:

First and foremost, thank you to our editors, Katie Awdas of Spice Me Up Editing and Megan Myers, for being mean in the name of making this book what it is today. Katie, you saw the vision and helped us refine it, and for that we are endlessly grateful. Megan, your sharp eye is one of the many reasons we love you; thank you for putting it to use for us.

A most hearty thank-you to our beta and early readers: Amy, Caleb, Chelsey, Danielle, Haley, Jamison, Jazmine, Kaitlyn, Katie, Kayla, Lauren, Nick, Nicole, Olivia, Sabrina, Shay, Stefanie, Tasha, Tiffanie, and Whitney. Not only did your feedback and ideas help shape Knox and Birdie's story, but your encouragement kept us going and fueled our belief in this book.

To Jodi Quick of Spice Me Up Editing & Design: Thank you for taking formatting and layout off our proverbial plate and making this book look beautiful for our readers. We are so glad people like you exist in this community.

To our cover and character artist, Rebekah Hamersley: You are an angel with the ability to take our ramblings and turn them into something stunning every single time. We are so glad to have found you; please stay with us forever.

To our cover designer, Jess Clickener: Thank you for your friendship, creative eye, and pushing us to think outside the color box. It means so much to have someone we love design our covers.

To Bethany: Thank you for your library-minded insights, ideas, and—most of all—your friendship. We couldn't have done this without you and Jess; your support means the world to us. Shadow Daddies forever!

And, of course, we couldn't forget you, our wonderful readers. May you carry a piece of Wexstone with you always.

From Jules:

Khrystian, who would have thought that a Facebook post would have led us here? I am so glad you took a chance on me as a writing partner; it is a joy to build this world with you. Thank you for being the creative foil to my analytical brain, for listening to my hours of voice messages, and for your constant encouragement. I can't wait to see what else we create together.

To my husband, thank you for your steadfast love and support. Even when you don't understand what the fuck I'm yammering about, your unwavering belief that I can do anything I set my mind to keeps me going when my own doubt creeps in.

To my parents and Grandmommie, thank you for always believing I would one day be a writer and for reading every single story I ever wrote about our cats. Lord knows it was a damn lot.

Thank you to my first-grade teacher, Mrs. Hargan, for encouraging me to write and share my stories. Your Young Authors' Teas remain some of my most treasured elementary-school memories.

And last, but in no way least, thank you to my girlfriends: Ade, Andie, Amy, Beppie, Claire, Erin, Jenna, Kat, Megan,

Susannah, and Taylor. There was a time in my life when I couldn't have imagined having such a long list of girlfriends, and now I don't know how I could do life without each of you. You're my sounding boards, my meme dealers, and my stand-in moms in so many ways. This book exists in the wild because of the ways in which you love and believe in me.

From Kyle:

I want to first and foremost thank Stephie Predmore, aka Jules. I am so thankful that you messaged me back and agreed to do this with me. Without you, this wouldn't have been possible. Thank you for your editing, your countless voice memos, all the admin work you do, and keeping me in order! You will always be the black cat to my wild golden retriever side!

To my husband, thank you. Thank you for supporting (and funding) my dreams. Your words of encouragement mean the most, and I value them more than you know! Thank you for realizing when I need to focus and taking our little to the park. I will never have enough words to describe how much you mean to me. You're the best, BDD!

To my family, thanks for making me the person I am and supporting me.

To my mom Dawna, thank you for teaching me how to pursue what I deem worthy of my attention and focus. Without your guidance on how to be a boss babe, I wouldn't be here. Thank you for loving me and supporting me in my dream!

To my mom Joleta, thank you for always supporting me in whatever I do and never judging me on what I write and/or read. Thank you for loving me and supporting me and always being there when I need you.

To my grandma Christa, thank you for loving me so hard. For always calling me and checking on me—our phone calls are my favorite and always turn my day around for the better. Thank you for always showing up at whatever I do and cheering loudly for me. I am the woman I am today because of you.

Thank you to my best friends Adi, Justine, Kasey, Katie, Lauren, Mackenzie, Meg, and Melissa! You all are my rocks and without your encouragement and support I wouldn't be the human I am today. Thank you for always sending me book recommendations and listening to my crazy thoughts and ideas!

ABOUT THE AUTHOR

Jules Kyle is the combined pen name of two millennial women who became friends via the wild world of social media. Together they write the kinds of stories they love to read: spice-filled romances with plenty of heart.

Stephie (a.k.a. Jules) lives in Illinois with her husband, daughter, and menagerie of cats and dogs. When she's not writing or reading, she can most often be found in her sewing room like the thirty-something grandma she is.

Khrystian (a.k.a. Kyle) lives wherever the US Navy tells her to with her husband, daughter, cat, and dog. She can most often be found with a Diet Coke in her hand and a NSFW audiobook playing in her earbuds.